KU-508-502

ALRENE HUGHES

Martha's Girls

LIBRARIES NI
WITHDRAWN FROM STOCK

·THE·
BLACK
·STAFF·
PRESS

Many of the characters and events in this novel are
fictitious; but the Goulding family existed,
the Golden Sisters did sing and the
historical events are accurate.

First edition published in 2012 by Troubadour Publishing Ltd

This edition published in 2013 by Blackstaff Press
4D Weavers Court
Linfield Road
Belfast BT12 5GH

With the assistance of
The Arts Council of Northern Ireland

Supported by
The National Lottery®
through the Arts Council of Northern Ireland

arts
council
of Northern Ireland

© Alrene Hughes, 2012
All rights reserved

Alrene Hughes has asserted her right under the
Copyright, Designs and Patents Act 1988 to be
identified as the author of this work.

Typeset by CJWT Solutions, St Helens, England

Printed and bound by CPI Group UK (Ltd), Croydon CR0 4YY

A CIP catalogue for this book is available from the British Library

ISBN 978 0 85640 915 8

www.blackstaffpress.com
www.alrenehughes.com

For the Goulding sisters –
at last the story is told.

Chapter 1

It was difficult to know what Martha Goulding was thinking as she stood in the warm kitchen with her hands in the baking bowl rubbing flour and margarine together. Perhaps she worried about the small amount of meat compared to gravy in the pie, or the rush to get the girls' tea on the table for when they came home, so they could be washed, changed and out again for seven o'clock. She added water and, with a deft touch, worked the pastry into a pale yellow ball. Wiping her hands on her apron, she checked the range and stooped to shovel nutty slack into the fire.

Maybe she thought about the fact that she wouldn't be able to pay the coalman when he came for his money on Friday night. Robert hadn't been well and he'd missed three days at the shipyard. A carpenter didn't earn a great deal anyway and his pay this week wouldn't keep a family of six. The eldest girls, Irene, Pat and Peggy, earned poor wages, but they always handed over their pay packets unopened. Maybe when Sheila was old enough to work there would be no need to hide from a different tradesman every week.

Somewhere pushed to the back of her mind there was probably the thought that everyone had in the fading summer of 1939 about a man called Adolf Hitler and his armies and his plans, but she could do nothing about that. There were potatoes to peel, carrots to scrape, pies to be made and time was getting on.

Irene knew she'd been away too long, but there was no point in hurrying back. The foreman would tell her off for taking ten minutes to go to the lavatory, so she might as well take fifteen and make a detour. The weaving shed, where the huge cones of thread were woven into cloth, was noisy and lint clogged the air. She counted herself lucky she worked in the finishing room, where the linen goods were painted by hand. Better to be a brushie with paint on her hands than a stitcher sewing all day, or worse, a weaver going home with lint in her hair.

She found him leaning against a loom wiping oil from his hands.

'Hello, Sean.' His smile alone was worth the telling-off.

'Your Theresa wants to know if you're going straight home after work.'

'Oh aye, and why would she want to know that?' His eyes narrowed in mock suspicion, but the smile stayed the same. Irene felt the colour rising in her cheeks and lowered her eyes as though an answer lay on the dusty floor.

'You might be going down town or something and she could tell your Ma to keep your tea warm.'

'You can tell our Theresa I'm not goin' anywhere the night.' He returned to cleaning his hands.

The silence stretched between them until she said quietly, 'I'd better be getting back.'

'But Saturday night might be a different matter altogether.' His tone was friendly enough, but she suspected he was enjoying her embarrassment. His gaze moved from her face down to her paint-splattered overall. 'I'll probably get myself smartened up and down to John Dossor's; maybe have a few dances with a nice-looking girl.' He pushed himself off the side of the loom and winked. 'If I see one, that is.'

Irene watched him go, enjoyed the slight roll of his shoulders, too subtle to be called a swagger, and wondered if he might even dance with her, if she ever got the chance to go there.

'So ... the wanderer returns at last. Have we enjoyed our morning constitutional, Miss Goulding?' Alan Briggs was a squat little man, old beyond his years, with a look of Herr Hitler about him.

'Not feeling too well, Mr Briggs, you know how it is,' said Irene, holding her stomach.

'Aye, well, in that case you can work through your break this morning. Give your insides a rest.' And with that he went out into the yard, leaving Irene to click her heels and give the Nazi salute to the closed door.

'You didn't happen to see our Sean on your dander did you?' Theresa asked.

Irene picked up her brush. 'I might've seen him talking to someone in the yard.' Theresa looked suspiciously at her best friend, but said nothing. There were things she kept from Irene too and sometimes it was just easier to change the subject.

'What are you going to wear tonight then, Irene?' asked Theresa without looking up from the blue periwinkle petals she was painting. Irene raised her dark head and scanned the room to make sure the foreman hadn't returned.

'It's a lovely blouse, with puff sleeves.' Her hands shaped the outline on her shoulders. 'A bit gathered at the neck and a bow in the middle.'

'Is that so?' Pat Goulding caught her sister's eye.

'I can wear what I want.' Irene's defiant words were not matched by her quiet tone.

'Look, we all agreed that we have to be dressed the same when we sing tonight.'

'But those cardigans Mammy knitted make us look like schoolgirls. I want to look a bit more glamorous.'

'For goodness sake, Irene, it's a church and we're singing hymns. We're not in a dance band!' As far as Pat was concerned that was the end of the discussion. She dipped her brush in the jar and swished it, turning the turpentine bright yellow.

Irene mouthed, 'A dance band?' at Theresa and the two of them began to sway from side to side, then their toes tapped out a rhythm

3

and Irene sang under her breath: 'Come on and hear, come on and hear, Alexander's Ragtime Band.'

The swaying passed round the group, more voices joined in, the painting stopped and under the table their feet moved in dance steps. At the end of the second verse, Irene nodded at Pat who smiled in spite of herself and took up the difficult change of key. As the singing reached its climax the sound finally registered with Alan Briggs, foreman of the Ulster Linen Works, who hurriedly pulled up his trousers, flushed the privy and, with the *Belfast Telegraph* under his arm, ran back across the mill yard.

Margaret Doreen Goulding, known to everyone as Peggy, leaned on the counter of Goldstein's music shop and, not for the first time, congratulated herself on finding a job so well suited to her talents. She loved every part of it, even the dusting and there was plenty of that. For a start, there were the pianos, six uprights and a stunning baby grand, then the gramophones and radiograms, big as sideboards. Next the records, which all had to be flicked with her feather duster.

There were few customers in the shop in the morning, so she had time between the dusting to read the record labels. Even the titles were beautiful, like poetry – 'Pennies from Heaven', 'Paper Moon', 'Begin the Beguine'. Best of all, she could choose which records to listen to while she worked.

She straightened her skirt and checked the seams of her stockings, then stepped out of one shoe and bent her leg back to rub her aching foot. Shop work was hard on the legs, especially in high heels, but Mr Goldstein expected her to look smart – that's why he'd taken her on. That and the fact that when he interviewed her, he realised she knew far more about popular music than he did, what would sell and what would lie on the shelves because it wasn't catchy enough. Goldstein had been selling musical instruments since he arrived in Belfast in the early twenties; in the thirties he expanded into sheet music and then, when he acquired the lease on the shop in Royal Avenue, he added gramophones, records and, finally, an assistant. In doing so, Goldstein made it clear he was counting on Peggy to help him make a handsome profit this year. She was just lowering the needle onto the latest Ella Fitzgerald, when the shop bell rang and Goldstein hurried in.

'Peggy, fetch me a cup of tea, will you? Hot, strong and black, you know how I like it.' His accent was a curious mixture of tight Polish consonants, overlaid with the nasal Belfast vowels he had acquired since arriving in the city as a young man. He seemed agitated and his face was pale and clammy. In his hand was an envelope.

'Are you all right, Mr Goldstein? Has something happened?' Peggy lifted the needle off Ella.

'My sister in Warsaw has written that things do not look good.' He pulled an immaculate white handkerchief from his breast pocket and rubbed it over his face. Peggy wanted to ask where Warsaw was and what things didn't look good, but decided to make the tea first. When she returned he was re-reading the letter. 'Forgive me, Peggy.' He managed a half-hearted smile. 'My sister is convinced Hitler means to invade Poland and no one will stop him.'

So that was it – war talk. Peggy was sick of it. Every night her father would go on about the Hun and how they'd been beaten in the Great War and just let that upstart Hitler step out of line and he'd get what was coming to him. Now she was expected to listen to it at work!

'My father says the British government will stand up to Hitler.'

'Ah yes, the British government …' The half-smile again. 'Well, we shall see.' He seemed to shake himself, took a sip from his tea and went to check the cash register. 'Now, how has business been this morning?'

'I sold half a dozen records and a few pieces of sheet music.'

He nodded, satisfied.

'But that's not all. A customer enquired about the baby grand. Very well dressed he was. I asked him if he played. He said he didn't; he was thinking of buying it for his wife.' Peggy enjoyed the look of panic in Goldstein's eyes. The baby grand was the most expensive item in the shop and it had been sitting there, polished and elegant, for nearly six months. Peggy watched him wring his hands at the thought of the lost sale before adding, 'I played for him. He looked like a classical music lover, so I gave him a little Mozart, 'Eine Kleine Nachtmusik'. She watched the relief spread over Goldstein's face before adding, 'He said he'd be back in the morning to discuss the sale with you.'

The meat pie was in the oven and the potatoes peeled and waiting in a pan of cold water for a light under them. The scallions were chopped up small and soaking in milk. Martha had just finished washing the dishes when she caught sight of someone passing the kitchen window. She heard the latch and expected someone to call out. Silence. She wiped the soapsuds on her apron and opened the door to the back hallway. He was standing quite still, head lowered, shoulders slumped.

'Robert, what are you doing home?'

In reply he lifted his head and in that moment she took in his grey face, his rapid breathing.

'What's happened? Have you been hurt?' She helped him to the armchair.

'No, no.'

'What is it then?'

'I had a bit of a pain again this morning, like last week when I thought I had indigestion.' He went on, squeezing the words out between difficult breaths. 'We had to shift some big planks of hardwood, me and Jimmy. I thought I'd be all right …'

'Did you strain yourself?'

'No, it wasn't the carrying. I wasn't right before that. Sure I haven't been right for over a week.' His breathing was a little easier now, but the awful greyness was still in his face.

'I'll make you a cup of tea.'

She watched him closely as the kettle boiled. He didn't move, not a muscle. 'There you are, love.' She handed him the cup and noticed his lips were tinged blue. He drank a little, then let out a low groan and doubled over. The cup slid from his hand, landing with a crack on its handle, tea spreading in a pool at his feet. In a moment, Martha was on her knees, cradling him in her arms as he rocked back and forth in agony.

'I'm getting the doctor,' she whispered, but his hand tightened on her arm.

'No. I'll be all right. We'll not waste half a crown on a doctor.'

Martha reached out and pushed back the thick dark hair that had fallen over his sweating brow, and as she did so, she saw the blood-specked spittle at the corners of his mouth.

'No, Robert, I'll nip round to Mrs McKee and ask her to fetch him. She won't mind.'

He didn't argue.

Martha didn't think to take off her apron; she certainly didn't take a coat or a scarf for her head. The McKees lived two doors down and Martha ran straight to the back door. Locked. She looked through the kitchen window. Everything was tidy, no sign of anyone. For a moment Martha thought about Robert's face, his pain. How far was it to run – half a mile? He'd be all right on his own; she wouldn't be long. Anyway, she realised with relief, Sheila would be home from school any time now.

Joanmount Gardens was a street of grey pebble-dash semis with neat privet hedges just off the busy Oldpark Road, from where trolleybuses ran into the centre of Belfast.

Martha prayed that one would appear, but none did. There was nothing else for it but to run. I'll be back in less than twenty minutes, she thought, then realised, with a stab of shame, that she was still in her slippers.

About the time Martha lifted the brass knocker on Dr Patterson's door, Sheila lifted the latch at Joanmount Gardens, and by the time Martha heard the sound of her knock reverberate around the doctor's empty house, Sheila was at her father's side.

When Martha failed to find the doctor at home she wasn't sure what to do. Then she heard a sound coming from the back garden. It was the housekeeper, beating a rag rug hung over the washing line for all she was worth.

'Thank goodness you're here,' said Martha. The woman looked her up and down, taking in the slippers, the apron and the wisps of hair that had slipped from the clasp at the back of her head. The doctor, it seemed, had been called to a child with suspected mumps, but the housekeeper agreed to send him to Joanmount as soon as he returned and she was as good as her word, for he pulled up outside the house just as Martha reached her gate.

Sheila, her eyes wet with tears, stood up as they came in.

The doctor immediately crossed the room and raised Robert's bowed head. Martha looked into her husband's staring eyes and felt her knees give way.

She could still feel the smart of smelling salts in her nose an hour later when they came to remove Robert's body. It was a sudden death, the cause of which couldn't be determined by Dr Patterson, and there would have to be a post-mortem and an inquest. The ambulance in the street had attracted the neighbours and little Bernard Murray was there hopping up and down on one leg, chanting at the top of his voice: 'Touch my collar, touch my toes. Hope I never go in one of those!'

Martha knew they were wondering who was sick at the Gouldings' house. My God, she thought, they're going to get a shock when Robert is carried out wrapped in a sheet. The indignity of it made her shudder and she said another prayer for the girls on their way home from work. 'Please don't let them get here until Robert has gone.' But a part of her wanted them there to give her strength. She chided herself for being selfish; better they were spared these images that would surely stay with Sheila and her for ever. She turned as she heard the ambulance men coming through from the kitchen and at that moment Sheila shouted from upstairs.

'Mammy, Mammy! It's Irene, Pat and Peggy. They're home!'

'All right, missus, we'll be on our way now.' They carried the stretcher between them as though they were shifting a settee, manoeuvring it out through the front door.

Martha stood on tiptoe and watched her daughters come into view, Peggy chatting, Irene laughing, Pat looking ahead, frowning then breaking into a run. Her sisters stared after her, then they too ran.

'Wait!' Martha shouted as the stretcher disappeared through the door. She imagined the scene seconds before it happened.

On the path Pat and the man at the front of the stretcher stood face to face, neither moving.

'What's going on? Who's sick?' Pat fired out the words, the panic rising in her voice.

'Mammy, where are you?' Peggy ran round her sister, trampling the marigolds in the neat border and stopped short for a split second at the sight of the sheet. Then she reached out, her fingers like claws.

Martha grabbed them just in time. 'It's Daddy,' she said in a low voice. 'Daddy. He's gone.'

And at the gate Irene began to scream.

The Goulding family stood centre stage like characters in a music hall melodrama, their home a backdrop lit by the fading evening sun and by now half the street in the audience. It was Pat who moved first. Gently, she put her arms around Irene and shushed her screams into low sobs. Then, as she led her across the garden to the house, she nodded to the man she had confronted only moments before and he, anxious to retreat from all this public grief, quickly carried Robert Goulding away from his home and family.

Pat's eyes moved slowly around the table. There was nothing else to be told or known. Dr Patterson would return the following afternoon with the results of the post-mortem and he would also inform the undertaker. Sheila, still in her school uniform, had laid her head on her arms. Pat couldn't tell if she was still crying, but every now and again she would breathe in noisily. Irene stared straight ahead; she hadn't spoken since Pat brought her indoors and it was hard to tell if she had absorbed the meagre information Martha and Sheila had been able to pass on.

Martha was agitated, couldn't keep still. She made them all a cup of tea then put a plate of biscuits and some handkerchiefs on the table. Peggy was tugging at one now, a furious expression on her face.

'I don't understand it. He wasn't old. He wasn't sick. And where have they taken him? Why couldn't one of us go too?'

Pat tried to explain. 'We can't go with him, he's …'

But Peggy wasn't listening, her thoughts raced ahead. 'We've forgotten the concert! We're meant to be singing at church tonight!'

They looked at her in astonishment. Pat was the first to speak. 'Peggy, Daddy's just died. We can't sing at a concert.'

'But we have to. We promised and we've been rehearsing for ages.' She stood up. 'I'm going to get ready. We'll miss the beginning, but we're not on 'til after the interval.'

Martha spoke sharply. 'Peggy Goulding, you can put that notion right out of your head. What would people say, your father not dead five minutes and his girls out singing?'

'You might as well sit down,' said Pat, 'because Irene and I aren't going anywhere and you can't sing on your own.'

'But haven't you forgotten something? It's to raise money for the shipyard widows' – then, unbelievably, Peggy laughed – 'and that's just what you are now, Mammy, a shipyard widow!'

What little composure and dignity Martha had been clinging to since Robert died, dissolved in an instant. She covered her face and wept.

Pat blazed with anger. 'I can't believe what you've just said! What are you doing to Mammy, to all of us? This isn't the time for your selfish nonsense. For goodness sake, Daddy's dead. Don't you care?'

'He was my father too.' Peggy's voice was devoid of emotion. 'You might think, Miss Wonderful Voice, that you meant more to him than the rest of us, but it just isn't true. If he was here now you know what he'd say,' – and she did a passable impersonation of their father's voice – 'Now, Pat, let's not have the amateur dramatics.' Then in her own voice she shouted, 'And you know I'm right!'

Pat was near the limits of her self-control, and whether her sense of propriety, or the urge to reach across the table and grab Peggy by the hair would have prevailed she never discovered, because at that moment, Irene spoke at last. 'Daddy hated arguments. Do you remember he'd say, "If you can't say anything civil, say nothing at all."? He taught us respect and manners. "We mightn't have money, but we have self-respect," he said.'

They sat in silence a while, no sobs now, nor anger either.

The light was fading fast in the kitchen, but no one felt inclined to turn on the light. The clock high on the mantelpiece ticked on and Pat thought of the people at church singing hymns and, although she'd never admit it, she wished that she could sing right now, for it was the only thing she knew that could ease the pain she felt. The room was almost totally dark when Peggy broke the silence.

'Well, that's it. I've decided. If you won't sing, neither will I – ever! The trio of Goulding sisters is now a duo.' With that she left the room, switching on the light with a flourish.

Chapter 2

The grey clouds hung low over Belfast City Cemetery. The old saying 'If you can't see the Cave Hill it's raining and if you can it's going to rain,' was true enough today. The fine drizzle, which had begun in the early hours of the morning, seeped steadily through the coats of the mourners as Robert Goulding was lowered into his grave.

Martha and Robert had few relatives, but family friends and Robert's workmates from the shipyard swelled the numbers.

They were strong men used to hard and sometimes dangerous physical labour, men who clamped their emotions inside like a vice, and no doubt a few of them were strengthened this morning by a stiff drink to keep out more than the rain. They were in their working clothes, some with tin piece boxes under their arms, many carrying tool bags. After they had seen their friend laid to rest, they would return to their shift and not one of them would begrudge the two hours' wages they had lost.

Pat was aware that Jimmy McComb, her father's apprentice, was watching her closely, but she refused to meet his eye after his behaviour the previous evening. She'd been alone in the house; everyone had gone to the funeral parlour except her.

She'd pleaded a headache, but the truth was she couldn't bear to see her father lying in a coffin. Shortly after they left, Jimmy came to the front door, which suggested some formality in his purpose. Every other time he'd been to the house, he'd come round the back.

'I've come to bring you your father's tool bag. They had it in the office at the yard.' He held out the brown canvas bag with the outline of tools bulging its sides and the handle of a saw poking out of the top. Pat didn't take it. Instead she looked from the bag to his face and back.

'You'd better come in then. Mammy and the others have gone to the funeral parlour,' she explained. Then noticing how uncomfortable he was, she added, 'You can sit down for a while if you like.'

The windows were open and the sound of the children playing in the street floated in on the soft breeze that ruffled the curtains.

'I'm very sorry about Mr Goulding. The lads at the yard were shocked, so we had a wee bit of a collection.' He handed her a grease-stained paper bag. 'I know Mrs Goulding will get a pension, but we just wanted to show youse we were sorry.'

'Thank you, Jimmy. Please tell everyone we appreciate their kindness.' His face fell and Pat wondered if he had expected a less formal response.

'Would you like a cup of tea?' she offered.

'Ah … no.' He shifted awkwardly, but showed no intention of leaving. They sat in silence as the sound of a skipping rhyme filtered through the open window:

'Apple jelly, blackcurrant jam
Tell me the name of your young man.'

Pat smoothed her skirt over her knees. Jimmy stared at the hem where it met her firm legs and in a rush began to speak.

'The foreman offered me a permanent job at the yard when I finish my apprenticeship next month. I'll get a rise in pay.'

'That's great, Jimmy.'

He didn't detect her lack of interest. 'Aye, I'll have the money to be going out and enjoying meself. Mind you, I was thinking a wee bit a company would be good too, if you get me drift an' all.'

'Jimmy, how could you? Daddy's being buried tomorrow and you're round here trying to ask me out!' She stood up, hoping he'd realise she wanted him to go.

Instead, he stood to face her. 'But I've always liked you, Pat, ever since I first came round here with Mr Goulding. I think about that summer all the time, when I helped him fix the fence out the back garden and you talked to me about the roses. Do you remember?' He put his hand out to touch her face.

She moved her head back. 'No I don't. Why would I?'

'Look I'm only asking you to go out with me for a bit of company. I've told you, I'll have money to spend.'

How she wished she hadn't let him in. If only she'd taken the tool bag off him at the door. 'Jimmy McComb, are you suggesting I would go out with someone just because they had money to spend? Now you get this straight. I go out with someone because I like them and right now you don't come anywhere near that category.'

It was as though he'd been slapped in the face. He stepped back, all bravado gone. 'I just thought that …'

'I know exactly what you thought,' she snapped, 'but what you didn't think is that you've only got that job because my father is dead. You're so stupid, you didn't realise that it's Daddy's job you've taken and he's not even buried yet!' With that she pushed past him and ran into the kitchen. He could see himself out.

The curtains in the street were still drawn as a mark of respect when the funeral car deposited Martha and her daughters outside their home. The rest of the mourners arrived shortly after for a bite to eat and a cup of tea.

Martha and Irene had been up at six to start the baking: Victoria sponges, fairy cakes, seed cake and three different kinds of scones. Pat and Peggy had made the sandwiches and Sheila was given the job of washing all the china. Before they left for the funeral they had laid everything out, covered with tea towels to keep it fresh. As the first kettle came to the boil, Anna, Martha's younger sister, and her husband Thomas Wilson arrived in their new Rover motor car, gleaming red with plenty of chrome.

'Don't mind us,' said Anna adjusting the fox fur around her shoulders. 'We'll just sit in here and let you get on with things.'

She looked carefully at the armchair under the window, weighing up its worn beige brocade before, in one continuous movement, she smoothed the back of her skirt with both hands and sat down. Thomas didn't sit, but stood with his back to the unlit fire as though warming himself. His pinstripe suit was well cut, his shirt gleaming white and a gold watch and chain stretched across his waistcoat. The other mourners began to arrive and the front room steadily filled up.

'Bad business about Poland,' Thomas said to no one in particular.

'It was bound to happen,' said Kathleen, Robert's sister. 'I'm telling you, Hitler won't stop 'til he's got everything he wants. You can't reason with a man like that. You have to stand up to him. That's what Chamberlain's got to do now.'

'If he does, it'll be war for sure,' said Thomas, 'and we'll be hit hard in Belfast, I can tell you, living within spitting distance of one of the biggest dockyards in the country and as if that isn't bad enough, it's cheek by jowl with a huge aircraft factory. Oh aye, you mark my words, we'll get it in the neck all right.'

In the kitchen Anna, who'd slipped away at the first sign of war talk, was also getting into her stride. The fox fur had slipped a little, but she still wore her hat clamped firmly in place with a huge amber hatpin as sharp as the words she was directing at her sister.

'You've got to face up to it, Martha, now that Robert's gone you just can't afford it. This is a decent-sized family house in a good area. You've a garden front and back and an indoor toilet with a bath for goodness sake. I've no idea how much rent you're paying for this, but I'm certain you won't be able to afford it on a widow's pension.'

Martha struggled to defend herself. 'There's the girls' wages.'

'Sure that'll barely feed the five of you, let alone heat the house and put clothes on your backs.'

'I could get a job.'

'Get a grip, Martha! What could you do? Think about it, who'd take on a woman of your age with no skills to speak of?'

'In the name of all that's holy, Anna, my husband's dead. Will you not leave me be?'

'Oh I'll leave you be all right. You made your own bed when you married that man and if you've been left penniless and maybe even homeless, you've only yourself to blame.'

'How dare you speak to me like that, today of all days! I've put up with your slights all my life, but you've no business speaking about Robert like that.'

'It'll be my business, when you're on your way to the poor house and expect Thomas and me to bail you all out!'

It took less than half a second for Martha to grab the sneering fox and rip it from Anna's shoulders. Then Peggy was there, pulling her mother away and glaring at her aunt.

'I don't know what you've said, but it was a mistake. This is the worst day of our lives and you've probably made it worse! We don't want you here, so why don't you collect that pompous husband of yours, get in your big car and go home?'

Anna pulled down on the hem of her costume jacket and touched her hat. It hadn't moved. She didn't speak. Her brown handbag lay on the table, brown gloves on top. She picked them up, hung the bag on the crook of her elbow and began to pull on a glove. Very slowly and deliberately she dealt with each finger, pushing them into the tips. This would be no rushed exit, despite Martha's sobs and the anger blazing in Peggy's eyes.

'There's no need for hysterics, Martha,' said Anna. She refused to acknowledge Peggy. 'I was simply advising you to find yourself somewhere smaller and cheaper.' She smoothed out the wrinkles on the back of each glove. 'I'm going now because I don't like to leave Alice and Evelyn for too long. I'll drop you a letter in the week.'

Martha said nothing as her sister swept past her. A moment later she heard Anna in the front room interrupting Thomas mid-flow and sharply telling him it was time to get back to their daughters.

'She's got a nerve speaking to you like that!' Peggy was furious, but tried to keep her voice low. 'She's always bossing people around. Just because she's got a bit of money she thinks she can tell people how to live their lives. You shouldn't let her speak to you like that,

Mammy. You should have told her to go and not come back, never mind writing to you in the week. What's she going to write anyway, only more things to upset you? I'm telling you, if I see that letter I'll put it straight in the bin, so I will.'

Oldpark Presbyterian Church sat atop a slight incline, a little back from the main road, a sturdy red-brick building with a small steeple. The church, like its congregation, was not one for show.

'Pat, what's that wireless doing there?' whispered Sheila.

'It'll be for the broadcast.'

'What broadcast?'

'The Prime Minister is going to tell everyone whether there's to be a war. I never thought they'd allow a wireless in church, but if they didn't, I suppose people would be wondering what was being said and wanting to get home to find out.'

At eleven o'clock exactly the Reverend Lynas stepped up to the pulpit. 'Welcome everyone, on this momentous day. A day that could see our lives changed irrevocably. Mr Chamberlain will speak to the British nation this morning and I have taken the unprecedented step of setting up the wireless so that we can hear what he has to say. Before then we will sing hymn number ninety seven, "Come Down, Oh Love Divine".'

At eleven fifteen exactly, for the first time ever, the sound of an English accent reverberated around the church as Neville Chamberlain explained that the German government had not responded to the ultimatum to leave Poland and 'that consequently this country is at war with Germany'.

The broadcast ended … no one moved … no one spoke.

Poland, Germany and indeed England seemed so far away that some wondered how any of this could touch their lives. But those, like Martha, who had lived through the Great War, knew that the tentacles of war were long and would draw in those on the very fringes before it was done. Over twenty years before, the last conflict had hung over her youth like a black cloud, draining the pleasure from every day. Now she feared this war would do the same to her girls and for a moment she cursed men for bringing war on women. She might have cursed God too had she not been in church. Instead, she joined in the prayers being said to keep them safe and for a speedy resolution to the conflict.

Outside, people stood around talking about the announcement and Martha was listening to Betty and Jack Harper, her next-door neighbours, discussing the best way to put up blackout curtains when Ted Grimes joined them.

'Good day, Martha.' Even without his uniform Ted looked like a policeman: tall of course, but also upright, with shoulders back and an air of authority about him.

'What do you think, Mr Grimes?' asked Betty. 'Do you think there'll be bombing?'

Ted had a habit of looking into the distance when he was thinking, as though answers came to him from some unknown source. 'Ah well, Mrs Harper, I'm minded to think we're just a wee bit beyond the reach of Hitler and his Luftwaffe. He'd be lucky to get to Liverpool and back without running out of fuel, but across the Irish Sea as well? I doubt it meself.' Martha noticed how Betty and Jack hung on his every word as though it was he and not the British prime minister who had his finger on the pulse and knew the full implications of today's events.

'Mind you,' he lowered his voice, 'we mustn't forget the unknown factor in all of this.' He paused, while Betty and Jack considered what that might be, then looked over their heads to where the answer lay. 'The Republic,' he said simply. 'Which way will they line up? With the goose-stepping Germans or behind those of us they share this island with? Oh yes, if you're an Ulsterman, keep your eyes on the Irish, not the Germans.' Martha registered the look of shock on the faces of her elderly neighbours and caught the wink aimed at her.

With that, he raised his hat and wished them good morning.

Sheila, sitting alone on the church wall waiting for her family to stop socialising, also saw the wink and she didn't like it, not one little bit. Mr Grimes had called at the house a few times since her father had died. Mrs Grimes hadn't been with him. In fact she was rarely seen outside, she never came to church and, although she was a family friend, she never came to visit. Sheila knew she wasn't well; something to do with her heart. Lately, Mr Grimes had taken to dropping in when he was either going on or off shift. Last week, when she'd come in from school, his gun and peaked cap with the Irish harp badge were on the kitchen table. She'd gone through to the front room and there he was, bold as brass, drinking tea. He stood up to go when she came in. 'Now, don't you forget, Martha, I'm here if you need anything doing. Anything at all,' he said as he passed Sheila on his way to the kitchen, presumably to retrieve his cap and gun.

From where she sat, Sheila watched those who lingered chatting in the sunshine and was surprised to see Reverend Lynas deep in conversation with Irene. It wasn't like her to get drawn into a religious discussion, yet there she was listening attentively, giggling occasionally in the way she always did when she talked to a man, no matter what his age – and the minister was positively ancient. She was nodding, as though agreeing to something. She'd ask her about that when they got home.

'But it can't be right!' shouted Peggy. She had stopped sewing and pushed the heavy black curtain away from her. 'You must be entitled to more than that.'

Martha didn't look up, but continued making neat hemming stitches. 'Oh it's right, all right,' she said, passing the needle through a loop of thread and drawing it tight to finish off the hem. 'I told you, the manager explained it all to me. I'm to get ten shillings a week pension. It would have been different if he'd died in an accident, but a burst appendix is like an act of God, no one's fault.'

She drew the hem up to her mouth and bit off the thread. 'He said our family was grown up and earning, except for Sheila, and she'd be fourteen soon enough and able to bring home a wage.'

'I'm going to go and see that manager and I'll tell him it's wrong. He'll listen to me or he'll get what's coming to him,' said Peggy.

'I don't think you giving him a piece of your mind will get another farthing out of him, Peggy. Rules are rules and we'll just have to lump it,' said Pat.

'The McCrackens must have plenty of money,' suggested Irene. 'Maybe they'd lend us some.'

'I can't just ask them for money.' Martha was appalled at the suggestion.

'Why not? They're your cousins and they must have plenty of money if they own a shop.'

'Even if they lent us money for the rent this week, where would we get it for next week or the week after? Answer me that!' Martha looked round the table. No answer.

Pat fetched a jotter and pencil and began scribbling. After a few minutes she circled a figure. 'I've calculated all our income and outgoings and what we need is another wage like Irene's and mine. Now in three months they might let Sheila start work in the mill and we could just about manage.'

'In three months! We'll be out on the street in three weeks, if we can't pay the rent,' said Martha.

'And if we pay the rent, we'll starve within a month,' added Peggy.

'Don't exaggerate. We could live on bread and dripping,' said Irene, 'and we'll walk to work and back.'

'I think you're all forgetting something. I don't want to go to work yet; I'm staying at school.' Sheila turned to her mother. 'Mammy, that's right isn't it?'

'I don't know, love, we'll have to see.'

'I'm not going to work in a mill!'

'Maybe something'll turn up. It always does and there's time yet to decide,' said Martha.

'So, you'd better make the most of it,' Peggy chipped in.

'And you'd better mind your own business,' screamed Sheila.

'It's time you started pulling your weight around here,' Peggy said bluntly. 'You've always had it easy. We've had to help round the house since we were tall enough to set a table or reach the sink. But you ...'

This could go on all night, thought Irene – time to change the subject. She'd been saving her news to talk about at teatime, but it was just the diversion they needed.

'Let's worry about all that later. Do you want to hear some good news?' She secured her needle in the hem. 'The Reverend Lynas wants to know if we can sing at a concert he's organising. It's for the Red Cross to raise money for medical supplies and the best bit is …' She paused for effect. 'It's in the Grosvenor Hall!'

'The Grosvenor Hall!' gasped Pat. 'But that's one of the biggest halls in Belfast; nearly as big as the Opera House.'

'Sure it holds nearly two thousand people,' said Irene, her voice rising. 'Can you imagine singing on that stage?'

'When's this concert happening?' asked Martha, trying to suppress her excitement.

'A week on Saturday. We can sing three songs and I'm to let the Reverend Lynas know which ones by Wednesday night so they can be printed in the programme.'

'We don't have to sing hymns, do we?' asked Pat. 'I know the Grosvenor Hall is a kind of church, but if this is a concert where people are going to pay to get in, they won't want to listen to hymns all night, will they?' Pat's initial excitement was dwindling, but Irene quickly reassured her.

'No. No. We'll be able to sing something modern. Something with …' She searched for the word. 'Swing!' She moved her arms from side to side as though throwing something gently over her shoulders and at the same time clicking her fingers in rhythm.

'Nothing's impossible I have found,' she sang.

Pat sang the second line an octave higher and they turned to Peggy, expecting her to sing the next line. To their amazement she was still sewing, head bowed over the blackout curtain. The song stopped abruptly.

'What's the matter with you?' asked Pat.

Peggy looked up, her face expressionless. 'What do you mean?'

'You know perfectly well. Not joining in means you've got it on you about something.'

'Why should I join in? It's got nothing to do with me what you two sing.' She bent again to her stitching.

'Peggy, we're going to have to decide on our three songs, so we can start rehearsing right away. Sure it's not long 'til a week on Saturday.'

Peggy spoke as though she was explaining something to a five year old. 'It's got nothing to do with me, because I won't be at the Grosvenor Hall a week on Saturday.'

Her sisters looked at her in stunned incomprehension, but Martha had raised this child and recognised that ingrained tendency Peggy had, to cut off her nose to spite her face. Oh aye, thought Martha, I see what you're doing, my girl. 'Peggy, you're needed to play the accompaniment and if you don't go, Irene and Pat can't either.'

Chapter 3

Mrs McQuade arrived in her classroom at the Girls' Model School looking flushed and carrying two large bags.

'Now girls, there's going to be so many young men joining up to fight in this terrible war, it's up to us to do something for them in return and as young women we have the skills to give them something they will come to need desperately ...' She paused for effect, smiling broadly. Sheila could see Jeannie Cameron's ginger pigtails shaking two rows in front as she tried to suppress her giggles, but Mrs McQuade was too wrapped up in her master plan for defeating Hitler to notice. 'Scarves!' she announced. 'Each of us will send a scarf to a soldier.' She paused again as though surprised by her impromptu slogan and then emptied both bags over the work bench, covering it in a rainbow of coloured wool, to the sound of falling knitting needles.

Sheila had been taught to knit when she was five and by the time the bell rang for the end of school, she had six inches of scarf in moss stitch and a half-formed idea that would take her on a detour on the way home. Around the school were terraced streets of kitchen houses that ran like the weft in the fabric of north Belfast, between the main roads that led out of the city.

Sheila wove her way through them to the corner of Manor Street where John McCracken kept his grocers shop and lived a good Christian life with his sisters Aggie and Grace and their aunt Hannah.

On the pavement in front of the shop, wooden crates of vegetables were tilted against the wall below the window; the scales stood on an upturned crate and the large brass scoop, dulled by a thin covering of dust, lay on top of a sack of blue potatoes. Sheila hesitated. What had seemed like a good idea an hour before, when she cast on her stitches, now seemed like madness.

'Hello, Sheila!' Aggie McCracken swung her callipered leg out of the doorway and into the street and held tight to the doorpost as her good leg followed it. She wore a floral overall of blue and yellow and the late afternoon sun glinted on her wire-rimmed glasses. 'What brings you down here? Did your mammy forget something on Saturday?'

'No ...' Sheila hesitated. '... she just asked me to call round on my way home to see if you were all right. In case maybe you were worrying about anything. You know, with the announcement of the war and all ...' Her voice trailed off; it sounded pathetic, but Aggie looked pleased.

'Oh that's grand. Come on in and have a wee cup a tea. We can go in the back. Sure we'll listen out for the bell if there's a customer.'

'Is John not in?'

'No, he's had to go away down the town; didn't say what for. He'll be back soon but.'

They passed through a heavy chenille curtain and into the back room which served as both kitchen and sitting room. There was a small iron fireplace with tiled sides, and a low fire, more ash than flame, burned in the grate. The smell of baking filled the room and Sheila saw on the table the two matching halves of a sponge cake and beside them a jar of raspberry jam with a knife sticking out of the top. Aggie filled the kettle and put it on the gas stove, then brought out china cups, saucers and piece plates, white with gold rims. The McCrackens could afford to have such things for everyday use.

'It's a terrible thing, right enough, this war,' Aggie began. 'Never thought it would come to this.' She shook her head and began spreading the raspberry jam thickly on one of the sponge halves. 'Thought our prayers had been answered when Mr Chamberlain came back from Munich ...' She sandwiched the two halves together. 'Picture of him on the front of the *Belfast Telegraph* with that piece of paper. Useless it was.' She limped across to the larder and came back with a tall sweetie jar filled with caster sugar. She unscrewed the lid and, in one quick movement, dipped her hand inside and scattered a handful of sugar over the top of the sandwich. 'Peace in our time. Aye, well it wasn't to be, was it?' She sighed and cut two generous wedges of sponge, put each on a piece plate and handed one to Sheila.

'What do you think'll happen to us?' asked Sheila as she took a bite of the cake. 'Will we be bombed, do you think?'

'Well now, John seems worried. Sat there last night, read out a bit from the paper about air raid patrols they're getting up. Then Grace pipes up with the talk from Robb's, about how the manager says they're to have fire buckets in each department filled with water. In the end John got out the good book and read the story of David and Goliath to cheer us all up.' At that moment there was a loud banging from above. 'Bless us! She'll have the ceiling in, that one.'

'Is Aunt Hannah not so good today?'

'Oh she's up an' down. You wet the tea, there's a good girl,' said Aggie, 'and I'll see to her.'

Sheila had no sooner made the tea when the shop bell rang. She'd watched John many a time serve customers and over the next twenty minutes she sold bread, potatoes, sweets and cigarettes as if she'd been doing it all her life. By the time Aggie popped her head through the chenille curtain she was really beginning to enjoy herself. I could easily do this, she thought.

'Wee bit of a rush was there?' asked Aggie. 'That'll be the four o'clock shift from the mill. Good job you were here.'

It's now or never, thought Sheila. 'Aunt Aggie, do you think there's any chance ...' The shop bell rang behind her and moments later John McCracken, a tall man with a bony face and thinning hair, entered. He looks different, thought Sheila.

Then she realised it was because she was used to seeing him in the brown cotton coat he always wore when he worked in the shop and here he was in the suit he usually wore to church.

'Hello, Sheila. How's your mother keeping?' He had an odd way of smiling, so fleeting that Sheila wondered whether she had actually seen a smile, or simply a stretching of his lips that caused his teeth to show for a moment.

'Not too bad, Uncle John.'

'There's tea on,' said Aggie.

In the back kitchen, John took off his suit jacket and hung it carefully on a wooden hanger behind the back door. He put on the brown coat, deep in thought as he buttoned it up. Once or twice he looked about to speak, then seemed to think better of it. He settled himself in the wing-backed chair next to the fire and took a drink of his tea.

'I did a lot of thinking last night, thinking and praying.' He nodded to himself and went on. 'God is on our side in this war. He'll defeat the Nazis all right. But to my way o' thinking, he won't do it on his own. No, he'll do it through good Christian people, people who hear his call. So, I took myself down town to see about this here ARP work. There's an office in the City Hall where they tell you all about it, the fire-watching and checking folk are keeping to the blackout …' His voice trailed off. He took a long drink of his tea and stood to place the cup and saucer on the table. Then, as though addressing a public meeting, he straightened himself up, lifted his chin and spoke to the mirror over the fire. 'And the upshot of it is, I've signed up to be an ARP warden and I'm to report for training Saturday afternoon.'

Aggie didn't speak and Sheila felt obliged to fill the silence. 'That's great, Uncle John. Do you get a uniform and everything?' She thought of Ted Grimes in his smart bottle green, with the shiny badge on his cap.

'It's a bit soon for that, Sheila. I've many a Saturday training to do and we'll probably get an armband for the evening patrols.'

Suddenly, Aggie spoke up. 'What about the shop, John? Saturday's our busiest day. The men come home with their pay on a Friday night and this place is packed out from nine in the morning.'

'Aggie, God wants me to do this. He'll help us.'

Sheila could see Aggie's agitation, her hands clenched against her chest, shaking a little, as she struggled to find the words to get through to her brother. 'Well,' she said at last, 'it's to be hoped He has some experience with a bacon slicer then!'

John rounded on her. 'Now listen here, Agnes McCracken …' he began. Just then the shop bell rang and, as neither of them seemed to have heard it, Sheila gratefully slipped through the chenille to keep shop. The customer was a young woman who didn't look as though she had two ha'pennies to rub together. She carried a sleeping child wrapped in a shawl tied round her hip. She bought two eggs, a pan loaf and a quarter of Nambarrie tea. The child's head lolled backwards escaping the shawl as the mother counted out the coppers on the counter and when Sheila said the baby had lovely curls, the mother smiled with pride showing her rotten front teeth. By the time Sheila returned to the kitchen, John and Aggie were eating cake and smiling.

'Now then, young Sheila,' said John, dusting the crumbs from his hands. 'Aggie tells me you've a bit of a way with the customers, been helping out this afternoon while she tended Aunt Hannah.' Aggie winked at her and gave a smile of encouragement as John went on. 'How would you like a wee part-time job here at the shop?' Sheila's eyes widened and she opened her mouth to reply, but John carried on. 'Of course, you'd have to ask your mammy, see what she thinks. You could come here Fridays after school and on Saturday you'd have to be here at eight on the dot to help me open up and you'll work to six. We'd give you your tea both nights. Then when your mammy comes for her messages on Saturday night, you could go home with her. Now, how does that sound?'

Sheila beamed. It sounded great, better than great. It was just what she wanted. She hugged them both. It was true what they said in Sunday school, she thought, God did work in mysterious ways.

'Mammy, I love champ, but I'm fed up eating it,' complained Irene. 'Can we not have something else?'

Martha ignored her and called through to the sitting room.

'Pat, will you get this table set. The tea'll be ready in five minutes.' She drained the pan and mashed the potatoes vigorously, then tipped in the frothing pan of milk and green scallions. A big plate of champ would stick to their insides. Pat laid the table carefully, as always, then went to the foot of the stairs and called Peggy. Martha arranged the portions of champ in a circle on each plate with a hollow in the middle into which she slid a lump of butter, then carried each to the table as quickly as possible before it melted.

'I'll have to put Sheila's in the oven to keep warm. I've no idea where she's got to.'

'I'll have hers if she doesn't come in soon,' said Peggy.

'You will not!' snapped Martha, 'She'll have a proper meal like the rest of us. I'll not send a child of mine to bed with just bread and jam.'

'Sure I've been working all day and she's just been sitting in school doing next to nothing,' said Peggy.

Irene changed the subject. 'We'll need to decide tonight which songs we're going to sing at the Grosvenor Hall and I think we should have a practice every night. We've got to be on top form in front of all those paying customers.'

'Well, I think they've got to be classy songs,' said Pat. 'A piece of light opera would be nice. What about a bit of Gilbert and Sullivan, 'Three Little Maids from School' maybe?'

'Ach for goodness sake, Pat, people don't want that. We need something up to the minute,' said Irene. 'Peggy, what about that song you were playing last week? We could work out some good harmonies for that. What was it called again?' Peggy turned her head slowly and stared at Irene, who thought she hadn't made herself clear. 'You know the one with the great title. 'Paper Moon', that was it!'

Peggy ignored her and pushed her empty plate to one side. 'I'll leave you to it then. I'm off down the Oldpark to the pictures with Thelma.'

In unison Pat and Irene turned towards her. 'What?'

Martha caught Peggy's arm as she made to leave the table.

'Now, you listen to me, my girl. You're not going to let this family down. This concert is important; it's for the church and to raise money for a good cause. It doesn't feel like it yet, but make no mistake, there's a war on and if the last war taught me anything, it was that we have to help each other. Morale's important and the last thing needed is for us to fall out among ourselves.'

Peggy was calm. 'Mammy, I'm not letting anybody down, because I never agreed to be part of it. There's nothing more to be said.' And with that she got her coat and left.

Irene and Pat set about doing the dishes with heavy hearts.

'We've got to perform at this concert,' said Irene. 'It's too good an opportunity to miss.'

'But we need three of us for the harmonies to work.'

'Maybe we could get Sheila to sing too.'

'And have you forgotten?' said Pat. 'We're three sisters and a piano. We need to be accompanied.'

'We'll get Mammy to play. Sure she taught Peggy the piano. She could do it. I'll go and ask her.'

'Mammy's not got the same style as Peggy. It wouldn't suit us at all.'

'Ach it'll do rightly. It's the singing that counts. We'll just have to be brilliant to make sure nobody realises that Mammy's not familiar with boogie woogie!' The two of them began to laugh at the very thought of their mother playing in that style.

As usual, once Irene started she couldn't stop. She tried to wipe her eyes with her soapy hands and ended up with suds over her face. They were still wiping away tears when Sheila came in the back door and wanted to know what was so funny. They tried to tell her, but found it impossible to speak. It was just a moment to be completely silly and Sheila, without even knowing why the others were laughing, was soon in stitches.

'So, the plan is this,' explained Pat. 'You, Sheila, will become the third Goulding sister, and you, Mammy, will be the accompanist.'

She and Irene smiled expectantly.

'Lord, bless us!' Martha looked at them as if they were mad. 'I couldn't do that. Sure I've never been on a stage in my life, an oul woman like me, away on with you!'

'You could do it. Sure you're a great pianist.' Pat shot a sideways look at Irene who was struggling not to laugh.

'But I might not know the songs.'

'You know two of them well enough,' Pat reassured her. 'We've decided on 'The Mountains of Mourne' and 'Whispering Hope'. The third one's 'Zing Went the Strings of my Heart' and you could easily learn that.'

Martha chewed her lip. 'Right enough, it'd be a shame for you to miss out on an opportunity like this. I'll tell you what. I'll learn the songs and play for you to practise and, who knows, maybe Peggy'll come round before the concert.'

That'll do for now, thought Pat. 'Right, let's get practising.'

Sheila had followed all this without saying a word. There had been so much laughter and excitement since she arrived home and, with Irene and Pat chatting continuously about the concert, there hadn't been a chance to tell them her good news.

'There might be a bit of a problem on the Saturday night,' Sheila began.

Martha swung round on the piano stool. 'What kind of a problem?'

Sheila took a deep breath. 'I've got a part-time job. I'll be working on Saturday.' All the way home from Manor Street, Sheila had imagined the moment when she would tell her family the good news. She imagined them smiling with delight, praising her, saying how clever she'd been. Now all she could see was the surprise, followed by disappointment, spreading across their faces.

Irene was the first to speak. 'A job ... where?'

'What kind of job?' Martha raised an eyebrow.

It came tumbling out in a rush, although Sheila was careful to make it clear that it was John who asked her. She said nothing about why she'd gone to the shop in the first place.

'Well, well, well,' said Martha. 'So the McCrackens have come to our aid after all.'

'I'm to get three shillings a week and they'll give me my tea. But I'm likely to be there 'til half six at least on Saturday and I would need to get washed and changed and the concert starts at seven. So you see ...' Her voice trailed off and she hung her head and let the tears of disappointment fall.

Pat put her arm round Sheila's shoulder. 'Now, don't you worry, you've done well to find a job. We're really pleased for you. You know, it might still be possible for you to sing. If we could make sure we were on after the interval, you could get washed and changed before you leave the shop, then hop on a tram and be there in time.' She looked at Martha and Irene.

'What do you think?'

Peggy sat on the grass outside the City Hall, leaned back on her elbows and tilted her head to catch the warm September sun on her face. So what if things were a bit awkward at home, that wasn't her fault. Let them rehearse every night. Mammy might be a good pianist, but she didn't have any idea about modern music; how to use the keys to bring out the best in Pat's voice and add that syncopation to the beat that brought out the warmth of their harmonies. Sheila's voice was lovely, but she didn't use it to complement the other two and she had no stage presence at all.

The concert was two days away. Without her, their performance would be … she frowned slightly as she searched for the word … mediocre. That was it, neither good nor bad. Well, let them be mediocre, she didn't care.

She flipped open her compact and moved her head from side to side examining her makeup. The Bourjois rouge still gave her cheeks a glow, but her nose was shiny; she applied a touch of powder followed by a slick of lipstick and smiled at her reflection.

Suddenly self-conscious, she looked around her. A young man was sitting about ten yards away, his arms stretched across the back of the bench, looking straight at her, a slight smile on his lips. He had a look of Humphrey Bogart about him with his tie loose and his hat tipped back. Their eyes met, but he didn't look away. Peggy felt suddenly embarrassed. How long had he been watching her? All the time she'd been thinking about the concert? Her face had probably shown every expression to match her thoughts. She stood up and straightened her slim black skirt and her black and white polka dot blouse with its short peplum. She wondered if he was watching her walk away, but even if he wasn't, she knew she'd turn plenty of other heads as she strolled back up Donegall Place.

Goldstein was standing inside the shop window sticking up a large poster with the words 'GRAND CONCERT' picked out in red. Peggy scanned the rest: 'In aid of the Red Cross at the Grosvenor Hall'. Somehow it was worse to see it written down, made it seem much grander.

'Ah see, Peggy.' Goldstein gestured towards the poster as she crossed to the counter and began to put away some sheet music. 'A benefit concert; you mark my words, this will be the first of many in this city.'

'Oh, why's that?' Peggy tried to sound nonchalant.

'Many reasons. First, in times of hardship, and I understand these things, people want to be happy, to enjoy themselves if only for an evening. Second, money will be needed for a great many reasons in a war and the good people of Belfast will raise thousands of pounds because the authorities will have no cash to look after distressed citizens – and believe me, before this war is over we will see more distress than we can even imagine right now.'

Peggy stopped. She hadn't thought of that.

'And of course,' Goldstein went on, 'it will be good for business.' She gave him her full attention. 'People will want sheet music. Not just performers, everyone. And they'll all want records, wirelesses, gramophones, instruments. We might even sell a few more pianos. Oh yes, Peggy, you'll see, we are in just the right business.'

'And you think this concert could be the start?'

'I'm sure of it. That's why I have advertised the shop in the programme and made a donation. Now, Peggy, I need to get on with the invoices. Call me if it gets busy.'

She wanted to shout 'I'm going to be in the concert', but she couldn't because Mammy and Sheila had taken her place. How could this have happened? It was just so unfair!

'Excuse me.'

What's more, Mammy always said that Sheila was too young to go on the stage and now she was going to let her ...

'Excuse me, please.'

'Yes, yes, what is it?' she snapped. And there he was, Humphrey

Bogart from the City Hall, but even taller, broader and altogether more handsome than she remembered.

'I'm … ah …' He looked around the shop and smiled as he brought his eyes back to meet hers. 'I'm interested in buying a gramophone.'

Goldstein normally dealt with such important sales, but he was just disappearing into his office. Peggy touched her hair and found her best smile. 'Of course. I'll just demonstrate them and tell you a little about each one.'

He had straightened his tie and removed his hat. His hair was dark and brushed back. Her mother's words came unbidden into her head, 'Never trust a man who wears a hat indoors.' Well, he was off to a good start.

'We have three makes of gramophone: Bush, Ekco and Decca. Now the Bush is very simple to operate, but the Decca has a more stylish cabinet.' She was aware that he seemed to be looking at her much more than the gramophones.

'And what about the Ekco?'

'Aah, the Ekco …' She hadn't a clue about the Ekco. 'Look, the best way to decide which one to buy is to hear how they sound. What kind of music do you like?'

'What kind of music do you like?' That smile again.

'Oh, different types, depending on how I'm feeling.'

'And how are you feeling?'

She looked up at him, noticed the brown eyes and long dark eyelashes. 'Quite happy, I suppose.'

He pulled a serious face, as though considering his state of mind. 'Um, me too. So it looks like we need some quite happy music to test these gramophones. What would you suggest? Some Bing Crosby?'

'Too sentimental.'

He pretended to think hard. 'How about some Gracie Fields?'

Peggy pulled a face. 'Too silly!' She was beginning to enjoy herself.

'I know the very thing.' He nodded wisely. 'Ella Fitzgerald.'

Her eyes lit up. 'Yes, but which one?'

'There's only one quite happy Ella Fitzgerald worth its salt.'

'I Want to be Happy!' they shouted together.

Peggy lowered the needle carefully onto the record and waited with that frisson of anticipation she never failed to get as the needle settled into the groove followed by five seconds of soft static noise. Five seconds when without fail she held her breath and waited for the only thing that moved her. Music.

The distinctive opening bars began, her foot tapped. She felt an arm circle her waist, she swayed to the beat and Bogey took her hand. They swept around the shop. He was a good dancer, held her firmly and guided her confidently around the displays of instruments and grand piano as though they'd danced together for years. Peggy felt the roughness of his tweed sports coat as her hand rested on his back and felt her other hand disappear into his. She was aware of his smell, the blueness of his chin above her, and most of all the lightness in her heart. As they circled the piano for the third time, he stopped abruptly and it was a moment before Peggy remembered she was in the shop, selling a gramophone … and Mr Goldstein was standing in his office doorway looking at them in horror.

'Miss Goulding! What are you doing?' He looked outraged and moved swiftly to the gramophone to lift the needle.

'I'm sorry, Mr Goldstein. I was just demonstrating the quality of sound to this gentleman.' She had a sudden desire to laugh.

Meanwhile her dancing partner had crossed to the door.

'Well thank you, miss.' He smiled. 'I'll think about it.' And, with a wave of his hat, he was gone.

Chapter 4

The Grosvenor Hall was an imposing brick building with a grand portico at the lower end of the Grosvenor Road, just round the corner from the Opera House. Martha, Irene and Pat stood for a moment looking up at it, unable to believe that they were to perform there.

'It's huge,' said Pat. 'How many people did you say it seats?'

'Don't even think about that!' said Irene.

'Come on,' said Martha, 'let's get inside.'

The entrance hall was deserted, but a table had been set ready with admission tickets and programmes, and posters advertising the evening were on display. Their heels clicked on the marble floor as they crossed to the doors leading to the hall itself. Irene reached for the polished brass handle then hesitated.

'Go on,' urged Pat. 'We've come this far.'

Irene pulled open the heavy door and all three of them stepped into the hall. A sea of wooden chairs had been set out in neat rows disappearing into the distance, where the largest stage they had ever seen rose in a profusion of colourful flowers and foliage.

'Oh, my!' exclaimed Martha, her hand to her mouth.

They took a few steps further and stopped again, their eyes

drawn upwards towards the vast space above them. The ceiling was dusky pink, the colour of the tea roses in their garden, bordered by an elaborate white plaster cornice. Like interconnecting cogs the three of them, still gazing upwards, moved in a circle to take in the vastness of the auditorium.

'You know, girls. I'm not sure I ...' Martha was interrupted by a booming voice.

'Hello there!' They turned to the stage where a smartly dressed man stood with his hands on his hips smiling at them.

'You performers?' he asked.

Pat stepped forward. 'Yes. We're the Goulding sisters.' Then realising that wasn't quite accurate she added, 'Well, we're the sisters.' She indicated Irene and herself. 'And this is our mother.'

'Good show!' His voice echoed in the empty hall. 'I'm Derek, Stage Manager. Come on then, I'll show you to the dressing room.' With that, he took the steps at the side of the stage two at a time and signalled them to follow him.

Compared to the splendour of the hall, backstage was a disappointment. He led them down a passageway of green distempered walls, where buckets filled with sand or water had been placed at regular intervals. He stopped at a shabby door with the handwritten sign 'Ladies' Dressing Room' and pushed it open, making an expansive sweep of his arm to usher them in, whilst averting his eyes. 'See you later, ladies.' His voice boomed at the same volume it had in the hall.

Beyond the door was what looked like a school cloakroom with a continuous wooden bench running around the outside of the room, above which were brass coat hooks. A young woman dressed only in a slip had one foot on the bench and was leaning over fastening her tap shoe. Her blond hair had been rolled into little sausage shapes that framed her face. She looked up as they entered. 'Hello, there's plenty a room over here if youse want te get changed.' Her accent was broad Belfast. 'Are youse all doin' a turn?'

'Yes,' replied Irene. 'We're singing.'

'Ach, are ye? That's great. I'm dancing.' She gestured towards a group of girls at the back of the room. 'I'm with them uns. We're The Templemore Tappers, so it's not hard te guess we're from Templemore Avenue.'

Martha moved over to the bench and hung up their bags. Her heart sank as she looked around the various female performers preparing to go on stage. She was forty seven years old, for goodness sake! What was she thinking about, coming here? This was a place for youngsters, not oul women like her.

She took a handkerchief from her sleeve and wiped her clammy forehead. That was all she needed, a hot flush. Lord, what would she do if she got one on the stage in the middle of playing?

'Mammy.' Pat touched her arm. 'What's the matter? Are you all right?'

'No, I'm not,' she said bluntly, but could say no more. She couldn't think straight; couldn't put into words the notion of not being able to focus on anything, except the heat welling up deep inside her and the sweat beginning to seep through her pores. God, help me, she thought, I can't even remember the names of the songs I'm to play, let alone the notes.

Pat knelt down in front of her. 'What is it? Are you sick?'

'I can't do this, Pat. I thought I could. I wanted to do it to help you, but right now ...'

'Look, you just have to calm down. It might be a touch of stage fright that's all. It'll soon pass. Sure I get it all the time and Irene's worse than me, but it just goes when you get up there.'

Martha groaned and shook her head. Pat hurried on. 'We'll find the toilet and you can wash your face and hands. It'll make you feel better.'

Martha looked up into the face of her daughter so close to her own and saw the look of concern. It was a long time since she had been so physically close to Pat, to the rich auburn hair that framed her full face and those green eyes so like Robert's.

She tried to smile. 'All right, I'll go.' Pat glanced round for Irene and saw she was chatting away to the Templemore Tapper, like she'd known her all her life. That's Irene for you, she thought.

On Saturdays Goldstein kept his Sabbath and Peggy kept his shop. He had opened up early and stayed just long enough to give Peggy her instructions. 'Do not allow customers to handle the records; they might have dirty or greasy hands. Allow them only a brief look at the sheet music; they might try to memorise the words or notes. And don't allow anyone to play a piano unless they look like they can afford to buy it.' He would return just before closing time to put the day's takings in the safe and lock up.

Rain was beating off the streets when he left and Peggy hoped it might keep some shoppers at home. But around eleven the rain eased off and the late September sun quickly dried the pavements. Trade was brisk for the rest of the day, especially at lunchtime. She had expected to miss her usual wander around the shops to look at the style, but there hadn't even been time to have her dinner; it lay uneaten in her handbag under the counter.

The new Bing Crosby was selling well. Not really her taste, so she played some Billie Holiday, but nobody bought it. After lunch a stiff breeze cleared the sky of cloud, so she left the door open, something Goldstein didn't approve of, but it always brought the customers in.

'Do you have the sheet music for "The Londonderry Air"?'

The woman wore a black costume, with white piping around the collar. She rested her expensive leather handbag on the counter. Peggy noticed that one of her pencilled eyebrows was shorter than the other and smiled.

She was tempted to say, 'Of course we do, you stupid woman, we sell about fifty copies a week,' but instead she held her smile and asked, 'Would you like a copy with the words of "Danny Boy" to accompany the music?'

'Of course not!' The woman was clearly affronted, exactly as Peggy intended. 'It's for my son to play on his cello.' And not, Peggy mentally added, for a singsong round your house after a few port and lemons!

As Peggy turned to find the sheet music, someone shouted, 'What about the music for "I Want to be Happy"? I'd like it without the words too, so it doesn't put me off my dancing!'

There he was, leaning on the far end of the counter.

Peggy played along. 'Oh, do you find it difficult to concentrate on your steps?'

38

'Only when my partner is very attractive and whispers in my ear.'

'And what does she say … you're standing on my toes?'

'Ouch!'

She'd been trying to remember his smile and there it was.

He straightened up. Was he really that tall and maybe younger than she had thought too – twenty-two or three? She finished serving the woman and moved down the counter to face him. 'I thought you were interested in a gramophone, not sheet music?'

He rubbed his chin and pretended to consider. 'I haven't quite made up my mind. I'd need to hear the different models again, I think.' He looked at the small queue that had built up at the counter. 'But you're a bit busy, so perhaps I'll call in another time, when there are fewer customers to get in the way of the dancing!'

The afternoon dragged by. By five it had clouded over and the rain began to fall, slowly at first. Then as it turned darker she put the lights on and stood in the open doorway looking out.

Mammy, Pat and Irene would be at the Grosvenor Hall by now. They hadn't asked her again if she would play, hadn't even asked her if she was going to watch. It didn't matter, she would have said no to both. But right now she realised she wanted to be there, desperately. Well, either there or with Bogey! Where was he now? In a bar somewhere drinking with his friends, or at home relaxing, without his jacket and with his tie undone, as it had been that afternoon at the City Hall? Peggy crossed to the baby grand and began to pick out the opening bars of 'I Want to be Happy'.

'Miss Goulding! What are you doing?' Goldstein was in the doorway, taking down his umbrella and shaking it vigorously into the street. 'The door is open to the pouring-down rain, all the lights are ablaze and you …' He came inside and shut the door behind him. '… and you are playing the piano!' He raised his voice at the end as though it was a question and one look at his face showed he clearly expected an answer. Peggy was terrified he'd dismiss her on the spot.

'I'm sorry, Mr Goldstein. The last customer mustn't have closed the door properly and it's blown open in the wind.' That'll do for a start she thought, and the piano playing? '… and I needed to rehearse,' she said calmly.

'Rehearse?' That really was a question.

'Yes, rehearse. I'm playing in a concert.' She felt like her voice had a will of its own, picking words out of the air. 'You know … the benefit concert' – he raised a sceptical eyebrow – 'at the Grosvenor Hall.' She relaxed. That was it; say it again.

'I'm going to be performing with my sisters. We're the Goulding Sisters.' Goldstein looked puzzled. 'We sing,' she added.

'Peggy.' Dropping the 'Miss Goulding' was a good sign. 'Why did you not tell me this before?' He was clearly delighted. 'Let us lock up quickly and I will give you a lift to the Grosvenor Hall, yes?'

'No, it's all right. I couldn't take you out of your way. It's not far to walk.'

'It's not out of my way at all.' He smiled broadly. 'I too am going to the concert. The organisers have sent me a special invitation to thank me for my donation. You will be on the stage and I' – he paused for effect – 'will be in the front row!'

About the same time as Peggy was settling herself into the leather seat of Goldstein's Sunbeam Talbot, Sheila was climbing on board a tram at the end of Manor Street. She, too, had had a busy day. They'd brought Aunt Hannah downstairs after her breakfast to sit in the kitchen in front of the fire. The move proved to be a mistake. She was constantly calling through the curtain for Aggie. Could she get her a drink of tea; another cushion; the fire needed poked; needed more coal; she was too hot; too cold; thirsty; hungry. As if that wasn't distracting enough, every now and again she'd recognise a customer's voice and call out, 'Is that you, Mrs Jackson?' or whoever, followed by, 'Come on through and let's have a bit a craic.' Then it would be, 'Aggie, will you not give the woman a cup of tea in her hand?' Again and again, Sheila was left alone in the shop serving customers, while poor Aggie served Aunt Hannah and half the street in the back kitchen.

They'd locked the shop door at six o'clock, giving Sheila just enough time to have a good wash and change into her black skirt and mauve blouse. She tied the bow several times in front of the mirror in Aggie's bedroom, but she just couldn't get it to sit right. Never mind, Mammy would sort it when she got there, if there was enough time. She managed her hair much better. When she had taken out the rags that morning, her hair was in tight ringlets and she managed to resist the urge to put a comb through them all day. She would comb them out just before she left the McCrackens, when there would be enough bounce left in them to look natural by the time she got to the hall.

It was raining when she left the shop so she tied her scarf around her head and hoped it wouldn't flatten her hair too much. The tram was full and she had to stand up. When the conductor came for her fare she asked him to put her off close to the Opera House. As the tram lurched its way forward in fits and starts through the heavy rain, she began to feel a little sick as she tried to keep her balance. The smell of damp clothing and sweat wafted around her. Next to her a man sniffed constantly and she had to turn away each time he was wracked with coughing.

An elderly woman sitting further along the tram stood up and rang the bell for it to stop. Sheila moved to one side to let her pass and the woman looked up at her and frowned. 'Didn't you want the Opera House, dear?' Sheila nodded. 'Well, you've missed it, I'm afraid – it was the last stop.' Seeing the look of panic on Sheila's face she added, 'See these conductors, you couldn't trust them. Why don't you get off here with me and I'll show you where to go.'

In the growing dark and heavy rain, in a part of the city she didn't know, Sheila ran as fast as she could, back the way she had come, praying she would get there with enough time and breath to sing.

'And your woman over yonder, pacin' up an' down talking to herself, looks like a school teacher? That's because she is one. But on the programme she's down as an elocutionist, so she is. Do ye know what one a them is?'

Irene nodded. 'Poems and things?'

'Aye, she usually starts with "Up the Airy Mountain". Do ye know that one?' The Templemore Tapper, whose name was Myrtle, seemed to have the measure of most of the other performers.

'What about the wee girl,' asked Irene. 'What's she doing here?'

Myrtle rolled her eyes 'Pain in the arse that one. Mind out fer the ma but – she's even worse.'

The child knew she was being talked about and skipped towards them. Her strawberry blond hair was caught up in bunches tied with red satin bows and someone had painted large freckles all over her nose. Her gingham dress was far too short and on her feet were ankle socks and the inevitable white tap shoes. She removed a bright red lolly from her mouth.

'What are you called?' she said.

'Irene.'

'Irene what?'

'Irene Goulding.'

She pulled a face. 'That's not a very good name for the stage.' She held out the edges of her skirt and twirled. 'My name's Twirly Semple and I sing like Shirley Temple, so I do. D'ye wanna hear some?'

'Not really, no.'

Too late, Twirly was off tapping and skipping across the room. 'On the good ship *Lollipop*,' she sang.

'Fifteen minutes to curtain up. Make sure you check the running order behind the door. Oh yes, and another Goulding Sister has arrived.' Derek had acquired a clipboard and a sense of urgency.

'Thank goodness Sheila's made it on time,' said Pat. 'She'll be able to catch her breath too; we're not on until the second half.'

Twirly Semple had reached her finale and was turning cartwheels across the room towards Martha. Suddenly, the child panicked, struggled to right herself and, as she did so, vomited all down her gingham dress. At the same time an ordinary-looking woman stood up and began to yodel. Martha looked from one to the other and let out a cry. At that moment, the door opened and Peggy stood there smiling broadly.

'Aah, have you come to wish us good luck?' Irene assumed the best of Peggy.

Pat said sharply, 'What are you doing here?'

Martha didn't need to say anything, she knew exactly why her

42

self-centred daughter had appeared and, in a rare moment of selfishness, she was so glad to see her.

'Where's the programme? What time are we on?' Peggy was taking off her coat. 'Mammy, let me have your blouse. God, I hate mauve, so I do!'

'Don't move, Mammy,' Pat commanded. 'Now you listen here, Peggy Goulding. You're not a part of this. You can't just walk in here and go on the stage with us. We've rehearsed all this and you haven't. So you are not playing in this concert.'

Peggy ignored her and turned to Irene. 'You know Mr Goldstein, from the shop? Well, he's here, in the front row, he gave me a lift.' Peggy paused for them to be impressed then added, 'In his car.'

'So that's it, is it? Out to impress your boss. Well, I don't care about Mr Goldstein, you're still not performing,' Pat shouted. At the sound of raised voices the dressing room fell silent as they watched the sisters face each other, hands on hips.

Irene, being the eldest, stepped between them. 'We can all perform. Sure it'll be great fun, the whole family up there together.'

Just then Derek stuck his head round the door and said, 'Awfully sorry, ladies – change in the running order. We're having to sponge down Shirley Temple and she won't be dry 'til the second half. So, Goulding Sisters, we've switched you and her. You're on in twenty minutes.'

'But Sheila isn't here yet,' wailed Irene. 'What are we going to do?'

'It's quite simple.' For the first time since she'd entered the Grosvenor Hall, Martha felt in control of herself and, more importantly, her daughters. 'You three are the Goulding Sisters. It was you they invited to sing here. That's how it's meant to be. So, stop arguing – just go out there and perform.'

Pat was furious. There was no questioning her mother's logic, but that didn't mean she forgave Peggy for her behaviour. Once again, she had been awkward and stubborn, but still got exactly what she wanted.

Then Derek was in the doorway again, looking bewildered.

'Another Goulding Sister's arrived. Are they coming out of the woodwork?'

Sheila stood drenched to the skin, her shoulders heaving as she sobbed. Martha hugged her. 'Thank God you're here. What was I thinking about, allowing you to travel all the way here on your own? You're soaked. Get that wet coat off you.'

Sheila undid her sodden scarf and revealed her once bouncy curls plastered to her scalp. The elocutionist shyly offered a towel. Sheila stood shivering; her mauve blouse was now purple where the rain had beaten down through her coat.

'Am I too late?' she asked as Martha rubbed her hair vigorously.

'You're just in time, love,' said Martha. 'You're on in twenty minutes.'

Sheila lifted her head and noticed Peggy. 'What are you doing here?' Her tone wasn't challenging, just curious.

'I've decided to perform. So don't worry, you don't have to go on. Neither does Mammy.'

'But I'm not too late, am I? I ran and ran to get here.'

'I know,' said Peggy, 'but I'm here now to do it.'

'But I've rehearsed every night. Sure I know all the songs and everything.' Sheila's voice was rising steadily. The whole dressing room had stopped to watch the final act of the drama play out. Peggy was about to explain again when Martha put her arm around Sheila's shoulders.

'Of course you're going to sing. There are going to be four Goulding Sisters on the stage tonight. Aren't there girls?' She looked at her other three daughters. Irene clapped her hands in delight. Pat looked at Peggy and said, 'Of course Sheila's got to sing.' Peggy said nothing.

Since Sheila's arrival, the concert had been going ahead at a cracking pace. Performers came and went while they tried to get Sheila dried and Peggy dressed. The yodeller, who introduced herself as Ethel Crawford, had the idea of putting Sheila's blouse on the hot water tank she'd seen in the toilets. 'We won't put it straight on the tank, or it'll get marked. We'll lay it on this underskirt of mine. Sure it's only an oul thing.'

When Myrtle came off stage, she took one look at Sheila's hair and said, 'I know just the thing, a French pleat.' She swept the wet hair back from Sheila's face, expertly folded it over and over and secured it tightly with hairpins.

Just enough hair had been left outside the pleat to arrange in a cascade of curls on the top of her head. Martha took off her blouse and gave it to Peggy.

'The work skirt you've on you will do you rightly. You know what you're playing don't you?'

'Of course I do. Sure haven't I been listening to it for the last fortnight?'

'Look, you concentrate on the piano and let Sheila do what she's rehearsed. Here's the music.' Martha handed her the brown leather music case with the brass bar fastening.

'I don't need the music.'

'I know you don't normally, but this isn't a normal performance.'

Peggy shrugged and took the music with no intention of using it. With two minutes to spare, Sheila's mauve blouse was rescued from the hot water tank.

'But, Mammy, it's all creased down the back,' she wailed.

'Ach it'll do rightly. Sure a blind man would be glad to see it!'

Harry Ferguson always played his hunches. He'd followed the pretty dark girl with the good legs from the City Hall to the music shop where she worked and chanced his arm a couple of times, enough to get her interested. He'd waited, sheltering in a doorway across the road, for her to finish work and been disappointed to see her emerge with the old man. The thought that he might be her sugar daddy crossed his mind, but he figured it was unlikely, given the space between them as they walked round the corner to his car. No, they were going somewhere together he was sure, but where? Then he remembered the poster in the window. What had he to lose? Maybe they were heading for the Grosvenor Hall. Even if they weren't, he'd nowhere better to go for a few hours until the card school got going down Sandy Row around eleven.

'And now, ladies and gentlemen, a real treat. With some wonderful singing, please welcome The Goulding Sisters!'

45

They came on in a line and bowed quickly to the welcoming applause. Peggy settled herself behind the piano and Pat, Irene and Sheila made a half-moon shape towards the front of the stage.

Peggy played the introduction to 'Zing! Went the Strings of My Heart' a little livelier than Martha, Pat thought, but it felt good and she began to sway in time to the beat and Irene and Sheila did the same. Pat's voice was the strongest of the sisters and they followed with harmonies where she led. Sheila seemed unfazed by the audience and was doing brilliantly. Peggy added a little extra of her own between the verses. At the end of the song the applause was wonderful. They were doing it! Singing in the Grosvenor Hall!

The applause died down and they stepped forward again for the second song, 'The Mountains of Mourne'. They waited for the opening bars. Come on Peggy, thought Pat, keep up the pace. The opening notes began and she realised they were from 'Whispering Hope', the third song on the programme. What was Peggy doing? Had she made a mistake? Pat took a deep breath: 'Whispering Hope' it is then. She prayed it hadn't thrown Sheila. The song was melodic and so uplifting that Pat always let some of the emotion she felt when singing it creep into her voice. The slower pace and the fact that she had sung it hundreds of times meant that she could listen to her sisters. Sheila was doing well, exactly like they'd rehearsed. Irene was Irene; her voice was never strong, but it was tuneful and well-rehearsed.

Peggy, too, was singing and she could hear the extra voice lift the sound to fill the huge hall. Loud applause followed and the girls looked at each other in amazement at the sound of cheering. It would have made a great finale. Now for 'The Mountains of Mourne', thought Pat, but Peggy had other ideas. She began to play and Pat realised it was something else entirely. She looked quickly towards Irene and Sheila and the panic in their eyes told her they had no more idea than she had. She missed the cue ... what she was expected to sing? Peggy seamlessly picked up the opening bars again, giving them another chance to begin. Pat had only a few seconds to recognise it before the audience would surely realise something was wrong. Of course, that was it! Pat raised her head, heard her note and swung into the opening of 'T'aint What You

Do (It's the Way That You Do It)'. They'd sung it plenty of times at home; Irene and Sheila gave it everything. At the front of the stage they clicked their fingers and swayed in unison. Peggy improvised as only she could. The audience were swaying too and clapping along. On the last high note, it felt like the roof, cornices and all, was lifting off. They took their bow, all four of them holding hands at the front of the stage to thunderous applause and cheering, then ran off waving and smiling as the curtain closed for the interval.

'What on earth were you doing out there,' yelled Pat. 'In front of all those people you want me to guess the tune?' A rash of pink had spread over her chest and up her neck to cover her face in anger.

'You didn't want to sing that boring "Mountains of Mourne" rubbish,' Peggy said matter-of-factly. 'We needed a big closing number.'

'We were supposed to close with "Whispering Hope". They loved that,' shouted Pat.

'Yes, but "T'aint What You Do" was miles better. They're out there now drinking their cups of tea, talking about us and how good we are.'

'I don't care! You can't just change the programme!'

'Leave it for now, Pat,' said Irene. 'Let's go and find Mammy. She was in the wings watching us. Did you see her?'

'I couldn't see anything,' said Sheila. 'I was too scared to look anywhere but the back of the hall. Wasn't it brilliant?'

Pat marched off backstage, but Peggy lingered as though reluctant to sever her connection with the stage and the performance.

'You two go on. I'll see you in a minute.' She had revelled in the final applause and her eyes had swept the audience, taking in their excited faces as they cheered, including a tall, dark figure who rose to his feet with applause and a smile just for her.

Backstage Martha was bursting with pride. If only Robert could have been there. She had been as shocked as the others by Peggy's switch of songs and had a difficult moment watching the girls struggling to recognise the introduction. She'd have a few words to say to Peggy when she got her on her own. Pat would be angry, of course, and would no doubt give Peggy a piece of her mind, if she hadn't done so already.

At the end of the evening the Reverend Lynas made a point of seeking Martha out to thank her for allowing the girls to take part. 'We're going to need plenty of community spirit, before this war is over. Morale-boosting events like this could be our secret weapon, Mrs Goulding, believe you me. Well, I must be off before it gets too dark to see. I don't think I'll ever get used to the blackout.'

Peggy appeared. 'Mammy, come and meet Mr Goldstein.'

He smiled broadly, his eyes crinkling behind his gold-rimmed glasses, and offered a neat, well-manicured hand. 'I am delighted to make your acquaintance, Mrs Goulding.'

'Nice to meet you, Mr Goldstein. Did you enjoy the concert?' asked Martha.

'I thought it excellent entertainment and best of all were the Goulding Sisters. You must be very proud of them.'

Martha blushed. 'Yes I am.'

Goldstein went on. 'Now, it is getting late and the rain continues to fall very heavy outside. So, if you ladies do not mind being a little cramped, I could offer you a lift home.'

'Oh no, we couldn't take you out of your way,' Martha said politely.

'Not at all, I live on the Antrim Road. It is but a little detour. I insist.'

Chapter 5

Pat stood in front of the iron railings of May Street National School and watched the boys at one side of the playground kicking a small bundle of rags around, jerseys marking out the goals. On the other side the girls were playing games Pat recognised from her childhood: hopscotch, giant steps, the farmer wants a wife. Two girls broke free from a circle and ran up to her. 'Can we help you?' they sang in unison.

'I've come to see Miss Goulding.'

'We'll take you,' said the one with a pudding-basin cut.

'We know where she is,' said her friend with pigtails.

Her friendly guides led Pat down a long echoing corridor with half-glazed walls which gave her a view of the classrooms on the other side, then up a winding staircase.

'She's in here.'

Pat was amazed to find herself in what looked like a parlour. Kathleen stood in front of an open fire and around her half a dozen pupils were dusting, sweeping and polishing.

'Good afternoon, Pat.' If Kathleen was surprised to see her, she didn't show it. Instead, she added without a moment's hesitation, 'You're just in time for lunch.' They went through to the next room where children were laying a damask-covered table with crystal glasses and silver cutlery.

Kathleen shouted out instructions. 'Come on now, John, I'm sure you can remember where the soup spoons go. That's right, girls, set a napkin in its ring next to each place.'

'Miss Goulding, we've arranged the flowers in the centre piece, so can we put it on the table now?' asked a girl, who was pale and fragile, and wearing a faded dress several sizes too big for her.

'Yes, Joan.' Kathleen touched the child's matted hair. 'But ask Audrey to help you. And children, we have a guest today for lunch. This is my niece and she's also called Miss Goulding. John, will you set an extra place, please?'

Pat was surprised. Could this be the fierce Aunt Kathleen who gave her family short shrift and was famous for not suffering fools gladly?

'I didn't know you had somewhere like this in school,' said Pat.

Kathleen smiled. 'I had this attic space made into a flat a few years ago so that the children could learn how to hold their heads high in polite society. They may come from poor homes, but good manners cost nothing.'

'And they learn how to wait at table?' asked Pat.

'Yes, as well as which cutlery to use and how to hold a knife and fork.'

Pat watched the children take their places. One boy in a filthy shirt and trousers held up with string pulled out a chair for a girl to sit down before taking his place next to her. He then removed a napkin from its ring, shook it and placed it on his lap.

'Did the school provide the cutlery and glasses?' asked Pat.

'No,' said Kathleen in her dismissive way, 'they're mine.'

Pat cast her eyes around the cosily furnished flat and realised most of the furniture looked familiar.

They ate a good lunch of leek soup, Irish stew and fruit salad, no doubt provided by Kathleen. The conversation was often initiated and managed by her, but Pat was very impressed by the confidence of the pupils. Their accents were strong, but they discussed a wide range of topics and inevitably the talk turned to war.

'Do you think we'll be evacuated, miss?' asked one girl with her front teeth missing.

'I don't know,' answered Pat, 'but I think probably not. The Germans aren't likely to bomb us here.'

'Nonsense!' said Kathleen. 'You know my views on burying our heads in the sand. The Germans will bomb Belfast. They'd be fools not to and, believe you me, Hitler is no fool.' And with that she clapped her hands. 'Right, let's get all this cleared away and we'll join the rest of the class for some arithmetic.'

When the children were busy with their chores Kathleen gave Pat a long hard stare. 'Well, Patricia, out with it.'

'I've come to ask you a favour.'

'Have you now?'

'I'd like you to train my voice.'

'You have a lovely voice, Pat, very pleasant on the ear,' said Kathleen.

Pat detected a note of condescension. 'But I feel I could do more with it.' She struggled to express the dreams she had of standing in an opera house, maybe in Covent Garden or even La Scala, and singing to the tiered galleries. 'Aunt Kathleen, you did it. You learned to breathe the right way, to use your voice to move people. All those stories you told me about singing in music festivals. The time you went to Milan to sing. Please help me.'

Kathleen looked at her second oldest and favourite niece. There was so much in Pat that reminded her of herself. Not just the physical characteristics – the full mouth and toothy smile, the ample bosom – but she also saw in Pat a sensitivity that set her apart.

'Pat, it takes years.'

'I've got years. I'm only nineteen.'

'I'm not trained as a singing teacher.'

'But someone taught you. You know what needs to be done. Please, Aunt Kathleen, couldn't we try it for a few months? I'll work so hard.'

In the few moments it took to think about Pat's proposition, Kathleen saw the chance to take one of Robert's daughters under her wing. 'Very well, you're to come to my house one night each week after work and each Saturday afternoon at two o'clock. You must not miss a single lesson.'

Pat's face broke into a broad smile and, despite herself, Kathleen's did the same.

'Listen to this,' said Irene. She was sitting in the armchair by the window, catching the last of the light to read the *Belfast Telegraph* before they had to draw the blackout curtains.

'Wanted. Entertainers to join a fund-raising troupe. Auditions to be held at the Grand Central Hotel, Royal Avenue.' She looked towards Pat and Sheila who sat opposite each other on the settee. Sheila held a hank of pale blue wool taut between her wrists and Pat was winding it into a round ball. 'We could go.' Irene added.

Sheila's eyes lit up. 'Brilliant!'

Pat stopped winding. 'A troupe?'

Irene could see the possibilities. 'It'll be just like the Grosvenor Hall, singing on stage, raising money for the war effort. It'll be great! What do you think? Should we audition?'

'We have to go – Mr Goldstein's expecting us,' said Peggy without looking up from the book she was reading.

'What's Mr Goldstein got to do with this?' asked Irene.

'He's arranged the whole thing.'

'Did you know about this advert?'

'Of course I knew about it. I helped write it.' Peggy raised herself from her prone position on the hearth rug, sat crosslegged in front of them and carefully turned down the corner of the page she was reading. 'He got the idea when he came to the Grosvenor Hall; a group of entertainers willing to put on concerts to raise money and keep morale high. He's going to organise everything and I'm going to help him.'

Martha, who had been sitting quietly in the corner chair mending a stocking stretched over a wooden mushroom, looked up. 'Wait a minute. Don't you be getting carried away here. What does it involve exactly? I'm not having you girls out late at night in the blackout, gallivanting here, there and everywhere with goodness knows who.'

'Mammy, we're old enough to take care of ourselves,' said Irene. 'Anyway there's four of us so we'll be together. We'll come to no harm.'

'A troupe of entertainers,' said Martha dismissively. 'Imagine the type of person you'd be mixing with. Remember, if you lie down with dogs, you'll rise with fleas!' She was getting more and more agitated. These girls of hers had no father and she had to keep them on a tight rein. 'I'll hear no more about it, thank you.'

Less than a week later on a drizzly Wednesday evening Pat and Irene hurried along Royal Avenue towards the Grand Central Hotel. They'd plotted the deception the day after reading the notice in the paper and decided to tell their mother they would be going to the cinema straight from work to catch the early house. If she was suspicious of the coincidence that they were going to be in the town on the evening of the audition she didn't say anything. They'd had to exclude Sheila. They wouldn't normally take her out with them, especially on a school night.

The outside of the hotel lived up to its name, with revolving doors and a liveried doorman who touched his peaked cap and smiled at the girls as they entered. The outside was impressive, but they had walked past it many times and given it little thought. Inside, however, was a different matter. They had never seen, let alone imagined, such style: thick red carpet; highly polished wood panelling; elegant chairs and sofas; large displays of tastefully arranged flowers. They paused a moment to take it all in, then Peggy came rushing towards them looking elegant in her shop clothes: a slim navy skirt with a crisp white blouse and her hair piled on top of her head to show off a string of pearls and matching earrings.

'You're here at last. Come on, I'll take you upstairs. Lots of people are already there. I've been taking names and addresses.'

The room was a good size, with a small stage at one end, a piano to one side and a small dance floor in front of it. People sat around chatting quietly. Suddenly Irene began waving. It was Myrtle and her Templemore Tappers, ready in their black tap shoes, short red taffeta skirts and white embroidered gypsy blouses. Pat and Irene joined them and kept a seat for Peggy, who was still welcoming newcomers and taking their details. The girls passed the time until the auditions began by scanning the packed room trying to guess what sort of act each person might perform.

Then a young man arrived and sat across the aisle from Pat. She studied him closely: smartly dressed with fair, neatly cut hair. He straightened his cuffs and Pat was impressed to see a flash of silver cufflinks.

'He's a comedian,' said Irene, following her sister's gaze.

'No, he's a musician, I think.'

'But where's his instrument?' asked Irene.

'Where do you think?' whispered Myrtle, and Irene threw back her head and laughed. Pat didn't. Truth be told, she found Myrtle a bit common.

'He's a pianist of course. He'll play the piano over there.'

By the time Goldstein stood up in front of the microphone it was well after seven. He looked dapper in his pinstripe suit, set off by a crisp white shirt and a paisley dicky bow, which gave him a jaunty air. He appeared a little nervous as he juggled his papers and gold spectacles, eventually putting the papers down temporarily to adjust the spectacles.

Despite his accent, he spoke excellent English with the formality of a BBC announcer. 'Ladies and gentlemen, thank you for coming tonight to what I hope will be a momentous occasion.' He paused and looked over his spectacles, eyes sweeping the room, giving everyone present the feeling that he was speaking directly to them. His voice became grave. 'We are at war ... at war with a tyrant. One who will not easily be defeated and we are all soldiers in this struggle, but not all of us will carry guns. This is a call to arms, but we will arm ourselves with music and dance and laughter; a company not of infantry, but of entertainers.'

Pat could sense a stillness fall over the room; all shuffling, whispering, coughing ceased as everyone gave Goldstein their full attention.

'Imagine a troupe of variety artistes using their talents to raise the spirits of a city as it faces the ordeal of war. Imagine if in doing so, they could also raise funds to help those in need, or to support vital services.'

Yes, Pat could imagine that quite easily. It was the natural thing to do, not to be a part of it would be squandering their talent.

'So, ladies and gentlemen, I am looking for twelve excellent acts to join this company. The auditions will begin in five minutes. Good luck to you all!'

Goldstein left the stage to thunderous applause. If this was his audition for inspirational leader, he had won the part, not to mention the hearts of all there. He made his way to a small table set out at the front of the room. Before sitting down he straightened his papers, produced a silver fountain pen from his inside pocket and carefully arranged everything on the polished surface. Almost immediately, a young man with unfashionably long dark hair jumped up on to the stage. 'Let's get started, ladies and gentlemen. I'll call each act in the order in which they signed in tonight. Good luck everyone. Our first act is Lizzie Riley.'

Peggy leaned towards Irene and whispered 'That's Horowitz, a friend of Goldstein's. The two of them will decide on the twelve acts.'

'He's quite good looking in a sort of foreign way isn't he?' said Irene. 'Is he married?'

'How would I know? I only met him tonight!' hissed Peggy.

Lizzie looked about sixteen and was clearly flustered at being the first to perform. She was painfully thin and her navy pinafore, drawn in at the waist with a belt, made her look as though she had come straight from school. She heaved a sizeable instrument case on to the stage, unclipped the fastenings and pulled out a piano accordion, glistening red and gold. With it strapped over her shoulders, she looked in danger of toppling over on to Goldstein's table. She bent her head and carefully placed her fingers over the keys and buttons. Pat wondered if every note would take as long to find. Lizzie straightened up, fixed her eyes on the back of the room, took a deep breath and began to play a lively reel, tapping her foot energetically to keep time. Slowly, the pained look of concentration gave way to a bright smile and her delicate fingers danced over the keys. Soon the audience were tapping their feet too and Goldstein leaned in towards his young friend, spoke into his ear and both nodded. Lizzie finished her audition to loud applause, but by then the smile had disappeared and was replaced by her anxious look.

The Templemore Tappers were announced and there were squeals of excitement and a rustling of taffeta as they tapped on to the stage where they immediately formed a straight line with their backs to the audience. Meanwhile Peggy, who had agreed to accompany any acts who needed music, had crossed to the piano and began their introduction. There was a gasp from the audience as all six dancers bent forward from the waist to reveal their frilly black knickers. Goldstein's mouth gaped, and from the back of the room a strong Belfast accent shouted, 'You show 'em, girls!'

The stage was a bit too small for their ambitious routine of fast tapping with lots of joining of arms and high kicks, and at times there was some discreet pushing as they jostled for space.

For the finale each dancer pirouetted in turn and ended with her arms held high. Myrtle was last in line and by the time the rest had finished, she found herself with nowhere to place her trailing foot and pirouetted off the stage landing with a thud, legs in the air, giving the front row a final look at her frilly knickers. The room erupted with loud cheers and whoops and Myrtle, red-faced, took her own bow from the floor as the Tappers hurried in confusion from the stage. Irene was shaking with laughter, rocking back and forth, shoving Pat. 'Did you ever see ...' but Pat had on her affronted face.

'Irene, for goodness sake, that's so, so ...' She struggled to find the word.

'What Pat? Common?' Irene could barely get the words out as she wiped away the tears.

By the time Myrtle returned to her seat she had moved from embarrassment to basking in the attention. Irene patted her on the back. 'Well, I don't think Goldstein will forget the Templemore Tappers in a hurry!'

'No, not if the look on his face was anything to go by.'

Myrtle laughed. 'Mind you, I don't think we're quite what he's looking for, do you?'

Horowitz jumped on stage smiling broadly. 'Well, that'll be a hard act to follow! Next we have Walter Burns.'

'Ooh, he's a handsome man.' Irene was watching Walter fix the wooden head on to his ventriloquist's dummy.

'I know you'd fancy anything in trousers, Irene, but I thought even you would draw the line at a lump of wood with his head on the wrong way!' Myrtle was out to enjoy the show, now that she'd had her audition. Walter's dummy, Wee Shouie from the shipyard, had them all laughing so much they didn't notice that sometimes Walter brought his hand up to his mouth to cover words beginning with the letter B. There was something about Shouie that put Pat in mind of Jimmy McComb – maybe it was the ginger hair sticking out from under his greasy cap, or the blue boiler suit – but even she couldn't help but smile at his silly notions.

There followed several more acts: dancers, singers, musicians, comedians, even conjurors and an illusionist. Some good, some dreadful, some where opinion was divided, but every one keen to be included in Goldstein's new venture. After each performance Goldstein and Horowitz conferred and made notes.

'Ok, it's us next,' said Peggy. 'Let's show them what the Gouldings can do!'

The opening bars of 'Cheek to Cheek' played. Pat and Irene swayed, picking up the rhythm and their cue as though they'd been practising for weeks and not just in their half-hour dinner break at the mill. In the middle of the song, where Peggy improvised several bars, Irene held out her hand to Pat and both of them danced Fred and Ginger style round the small dance floor, returning to the piano in time to sing the final verse. They finished to enthusiastic applause and Irene risked a look at Goldstein and Horowitz as she raised her head from their bow, to see both of them smiling and applauding warmly.

Irene turned to Pat and Peggy as they left the stage and whispered, 'Let's get out of here. If we run we'll catch the last bus.'

'We can't do that. I promised Mr Goldstein I'd stay to the end. Anyway there's another singer to come.' Peggy indicated silver cuff-links. 'I have to accompany him.'

'But we'll have to walk all the way home. Mammy'll be raging,' insisted Irene.

At that moment William Kennedy was announced and Pat watched him rise and move towards the stage. 'Don't fuss, Irene,' she said, and without taking her eyes off him, she felt for her chair and sat down.

William Kennedy exuded not arrogance, but a quiet confidence. A man used to succeeding. He had what Pat, on the long walk home, would describe as breeding. 'Mark my words' she would say as they crossed Carlisle Circus and headed towards the Cliftonville, 'that fellow had good breeding written all over him. Oh, it's difficult to describe, right enough, but unmistakable once perceived.' And Peggy rolled her eyes, just as she had done half an hour earlier when William Kennedy Esquire had passed her his music and she read the title: 'Nessun Dorma' by Puccini.

For a tenor he was not large, but his voice had an unexpected resonance that filled the room. His breathing and phrasing indicated at least some training and his gestures suggested he had stage experience. Pat was enthralled. His inclusion in the company would raise the tone considerably, but would they want someone with a classical repertoire? She glanced at Goldstein who was sitting quite still with no expression on his face. Then she concentrated on the sound, thinking about the story of the cruel princess and her suitor with the mysterious name.

As the applause for William Kennedy died away, Goldstein climbed on to the stage. 'Ladies and gentlemen, what can I say? My friend, Mr Horowitz, and I have been overwhelmed by the talent we have witnessed this evening and we thank you from the bottom of our hearts.' He then began to read out the names of the successful acts. Each name was cheered enthusiastically, none more so than the Templemore Tappers. Myrtle jumped up and down and hugged Irene, who was still waiting anxiously with her sisters to hear if they had been chosen. Eventually, when they felt sure he must have read the names of at least a dozen acts, he said, 'And the excellent trio, the Golden Sisters.' There was a moment's confusion as he hesitated and corrected himself.

'Forgive me, I mean the Goulding Sisters.' Irene whooped with joy and hugged Pat and Peggy, but Pat quickly disengaged herself and turned again to the stage, where Goldstein was waiting for the cheers to die down. 'Last but not least,' he said, folding up his spectacles, 'a very talented tenor, Mr William Kennedy.'

Irene and Peggy were astonished to see Pat lean across the aisle to shake the tenor's hand.

Chapter 6

Irene bent her head over the linen tablecloth and fastened it taut in the wooden frame. She smoothed the weave to check for loose thread or lint, then loaded the fine squirrel-hair brush with pale blue, the colour of the flax flower. With tiny arcing strokes she outlined the delicate petals before lightly filling them in. A cluster of six and the first was soon dry enough to trace thin veins in a stronger colour. Complete all six again and an even finer pointed brush of soft yellow added the stamens. A siren broke the silence. The posy would have to wait until Monday for leaves and a ribbon. Now it was Saturday dinnertime, work was over for the week and Irene had plans for the weekend that would begin as soon as she collected her wages from the office.

'What are you doin' the night?' Theresa asked as they queued to collect their pay packets.

'I'm going to see my friend Myrtle on the Newtownards Road. Remember, I told you about her? She's a dancer.'

'The one with the knickers?' Irene had given Theresa a full account of the auditions.

'Yeah, she's a geg.'

'Have youse told your ma yet about the audition?'

'No, we're waiting until we hear about the first concert. We think she might let us go to that if we say Goldstein is short of an act and then, you know, she might get used to the idea.'

Theresa looked at her in surprise. 'You mean you're not going to tell her you went to the audition?'

'What's the point?'

'The point is she's goin' te find out sooner or later; mammies always do. It's a fact of life!'

Irene didn't have an answer to that and was glad of the distraction of signing for her envelope and putting it in her bag.

'You're a bit dressed up. Are ye goin' out on the town?' asked Theresa.

'Aye, there's some Hallowe'en dances. We might go to John Dossor's, or maybe the Dundela Ballroom. What about you?'

'Me ma says I've to help her with our Marie's first communion frock. We could be sewin' an' stickin' pins in ourselves the whole weekend.'

They parted at the mill gates. Theresa headed up the Falls Road and Irene down town to the shops. Although it wasn't much past one o'clock in the afternoon, the sky was grey and murky with a hint of mist that made her camel coat clammy to the touch. A quick look in her pay packet showed she had thirty six shillings, the extra six for the overtime she'd worked on a special order of tablecloths and napkins for the Masonic Lodge. She decided to keep that for herself. Mammy would never know.

She suddenly felt guilty: it was another deception to add to the lie about the audition and she didn't tell her she was going to a dance either. Never mind, she'd be able to buy a lipstick of her own, go dancing, and have a laugh with Myrtle. She calculated it might be thruppence on the tram, a shilling to get into the dance, another tuppence for a drink. With six shillings she was a woman of substance, and she pushed open the door of Robb's department store with all the confidence of an heiress. The woman on the Max Factor counter was very elegant, all in black, blonde hair pulled back in a neat bun. Irene couldn't help staring at her eyebrows, or the lack of them! The thin arched pencil line gave her a look of perpetual surprise.

'Can I help you, madam?' Her smile revealed tiny white teeth.

'I'd like some lipstick, please.'

'Yes certainly, what shade would you like?'

'Red, please.'

The smile didn't move. 'Well, we have scarlet, crimson, cherry, and then there are the dark pinks, geranium, fuchsia ...'

'Oh, I don't know ... what colour are you wearing?'

'This is our latest colour, Pink Lady, very suitable for younger women. Would you like to test it?' Without waiting for an answer she had turned to the rows of tiny wooden drawers with brass handles behind her, produced a gold lipstick and handed it across the counter.

Irene pulled off the fluted top and saw the colour of the carnations Mr Harper grew in his front garden. She could almost smell their scent as she moved to the mirror and pouted her lips.

'Stop!' shouted the assistant. 'That's not how you test lipstick.' She took the lipstick, reached for Irene's hand and drew a test streak across it.

'Oh it's lovely,' whispered Irene. 'How much is it?'

'Two shillings.'

Irene's face fell.

'Is this your first lipstick?'

Irene nodded.

'I'll tell you what, I've used this a few times as a tester, but it's nearly new. I could let you have it for one shilling if you like.'

Irene caught the Holywood bus out of the city and, as it crossed the Queen's Bridge, she saw the shipyards along the Lagan where her father had been apprenticed and spent all his working life. In the weeks since his death they had settled into only slightly altered routines: they didn't set his place at the table; they peeled a few less potatoes; his boiler suit didn't flutter on the washing line. In some ways he'd been a distant father. Often tired when he got home, he liked a quiet mealtime and a rest in his chair with the paper. He'd always been strict about manners – no elbows on the table, remember please and thank you – and responsibilities – cleaned rooms, shared chores. It was different when they were younger and he was stronger.

Sundays were family days and after church, if the weather was fine, they would travel all the way to Holywood to picnic and play on the beach. He'd organise races, giving head starts to each child according to age, and he taught them to skim stones. Later, settled on an old blanket to eat their egg pieces, they'd ask him to tell again the story of the unsinkable boat he'd helped to build and how it came to grief in an icy sea.

She felt tears prick her eyes at the memories and understood for the first time since his death that she missed him just being there. Even so, one thing she knew for certain was that she'd not be wearing lipstick or going to a dance if he were still alive – and his girls would certainly not be allowed to join a troupe of entertainers.

Myrtle was waiting at the Templemore Avenue stop and waved both hands as she spotted Irene on the platform of the bus.

'Myrtle, what are you wearing?' Irene gasped as she hopped on to the pavement.

'Oh, ye like the trousers?' Myrtle stuck her hip out and put her hands behind her head like some Hollywood film star.

Irene laughed. 'And the turban!'

'I've just come from work. Ye have to wear trousers in the aircraft factory. Did ye not know that? They can't have girls climbin' ladders in skirts, can they, or the men would never do any work.'

'But don't people stare at you in the street?'

'Not round here, they know we're from Shorts. Anyway, when we go out on the town the night, I promise I'll wear a dress so you're not embarrassed. Now come on, ye eejit.' Myrtle linked her arm through Irene's and they set off along a street of red brick terraced houses. On one corner some young men were standing about smoking and bantering.

'What about ye, Myrtle?' one of them shouted as they walked past. 'Are ye not gonna introduce me te your friend?'

'Ach, catch yerself on, Frankie. What would she want to know you for?'

'Oh ye'd be surprised what good-lookin' girls want to know me for, Myrtle.'

She pulled on Irene's arm, quickened her pace and shouted over her shoulder, 'You've a dirty mouth on ye, so ye have, Frankie Burns.' Then she whispered to Irene, 'Thinks he's God's gift t' wemen, but they wouldn't pass the time a day wi' 'im.'

The door to number fifteen was open and Irene followed Myrtle into the dimly lit front room.

'Ye all right there, Grannie?'

Irene could just make out the shape of someone lying on a settee against the far wall. In the grey tiled fireplace to her right, a few coals glowed and above it, just catching the light through the cream lace curtain, King William looked down in triumph from his rearing white horse.

'Ach, hello darlin', is this your wee friend ye were telling me about?'

'Aye, this is Irene, Grannie. She's come fer her tea, mind?'

The old woman struggled to sit up. 'Oh aye, I mind. Me legs might be bad, but I'm still *compos mentis*.' She looked at Irene and offered what sounded like an oft-repeated explanation.

'Ulcerated, the doctor says. Aye, an' sure why wouldn't they be? Me standin' on that fish stall, all weathers for thirty years.' At the sound of her voice a budgie in the cage behind her began to sing, quietly at first, then louder and more urgently. 'Would ye shut up, Joey, we've visitors can't ye see!' She reached back towards the cage and retrieved an old towel. 'Here, Myrtle, cover 'im up for God's sake. Give me head a bit a peace.' Then Grannie closed her eyes and in the darkness Joey did the same.

Myrtle put her finger to her lips and motioned Irene to follow her. The stairs were steep and narrow with worn oilcloth nailed to them.

'I share a room with me sister, she's only six. Think she's out playin'. Anyway, I've told her she's te stay out of the room while we're here. Me da an' our Tom sleep in there.' She indicated the room on the left and pushed open the door on the right and went in. Suddenly, there was an evil laugh and a dark figure with a hideous face jumped out of the wardrobe. Myrtle screamed and grabbed the figure roughly. 'Jesus Christ, Tom, ye wee messer! I told you to keep outta the way, so I did.'

64

Tom removed the cardboard mask and grinned. 'Youse are right scaredy baas, 'fraid of an oul false face. Is this your friend then?'

'It is.' Myrtle dragged him by his collar and pushed him out the door. 'And this, Irene, is my wee get of a brother Tom, fourteen goin' on five-an'-a-half.'

'Me da won't be home 'til late and he says you've te make me tea.'

'Aye, well I say you're an ugly brute, even without the false face, an' ye can make your own tea,' and she slammed the door.

Irene sat on the faded gold eiderdown; the bed was hard and sagged in the middle. Myrtle reached for her handbag, pulled out a packet of five Woodbine, pushed up the bottom and offered one.

'Here ye are.'

'Oh, I don't smoke.'

Myrtle laughed. 'Course ye do. Here I'll light it for ye.'

Peggy had suggested to Goldstein several times that he should employ a Saturday assistant, but he wouldn't hear of it.

'You do very well, Peggy, takings are always good. And you can put up the closed sign and have your lunch, can't you?'

She'd tried telling him that profits would go up if they could serve the customers quicker, but he shrugged his shoulders.

'How so? If a customer wants some sheet music he will not mind whether it takes five or ten minutes to buy.'

Then she tried explaining that she spent all her time selling records and sheet music and so couldn't deal with customers who were interested in the instruments or wirelesses.

'Persons wanting to purchase a wireless do not come to buy on a Saturday afternoon,' he explained as though talking to a ten-year-old.

Peggy wanted to say that even a ten-year-old who spent a Saturday in the shop would be hard pressed to see the logic in his argument, but she bit her tongue for once.

At twelve o'clock Peggy hung the 'Closed for Dinner' sign on the door and drew the blinds. In the pokey little kitchen at the back of the shop she put on the kettle and unwrapped her piece.

Meat paste again. How many times had she told Mammy she'd rather have plain bread and butter? She'd a good mind to throw them in the bin, except she was famished. To cap it all, the wee bit of milk saved from yesterday was sour and she'd have to drink her tea black. Still, it was good to take off her high heels and after she'd eaten her dinner, she stretched out sideways on the battered leather armchair, with her legs dangling over one arm and her head resting on the other. She could feel her eyes closing and thought she could trust herself to take just five minutes …

… She was on a swing, wearing a beautiful white dress and gazing out over the Tara plantation thinking of Ashley Wilkes …

No she wasn't! She was in the shop, the bell was ringing and that was a customer who couldn't read. In seconds she was on her feet and through the door.

'I'm sorry we're …'

He was leaning on the counter smiling.

'Closed, yes, I saw the sign.'

'You're not supposed to be in here. The shop's …'

'Closed, but I don't want to buy anything.'

Peggy smiled. 'Oh, I thought maybe you'd come back for the gramophone.'

He laughed and nodded as if acknowledging the point went to her. 'Ach no,' he confessed and looked serious. 'I've come back for you.'

'But I'm not for sale.'

'I know, but maybe I could take you out on loan.'

'You want the Central Library up the street.'

He laughed. 'In that case, could I just take you out?'

Peggy deliberately misunderstood. 'I think Mr Goldstein might object to the loss of trade if I went off gallivanting on a Saturday afternoon.'

'Not now,' he said quickly. 'I was thinking about tomorrow. You don't work on Sundays do you?'

Peggy put her head on one side as if considering his invitation. She was actually working out how she could go out with him without her mother finding out. 'I could meet you at two o'clock tomorrow.'

He grinned. 'Where?'

'Do you know Cliftonville Circus?'

'Course I do, been round and round there many a time.'

Just then the phone in Goldstein's office began to ring.

'I'll be back in a minute,' said Peggy. It was Goldstein reminding her to put dust covers over the pianos.

'I don't even know your ...' she said as she came back into the shop, but the door was open and he was nowhere to be seen.

It was around three o'clock when she realised it was gone: a small Bush wireless with a square walnut case and brass knobs. She was in the middle of selling 'Anything Goes' by Ethel Merman when, for no accountable reason, she found herself looking at an empty space on the shelf. It looked odd and it was a moment before she realised why. She finished serving the customer, then crossed to the door and hung the 'Closed' sign.

She had managed to stay completely calm as she served the remaining customers, but soon she was alone and staring at the spot where the £9/19/11 wireless should have been. How long had it been missing? It was definitely there this morning first thing; she remembered dusting it. Somebody must have stolen it, but when? She pushed aside the feeling of panic. She'd have to tell Goldstein. Oh God, he'd take the money out of her wages.

What would she tell Mammy? He might even dismiss her. Then how would they manage with a wage missing? There again, it wasn't her fault it was gone, hadn't she told him so many times how busy it was?

Goldstein listened without comment when she telephoned him, then said simply, 'I will be there shortly.' Well, she'd be ready for him. Just let him try to blame her and she'd give him a piece of her mind. While she waited for him to arrive, she went through all the sales receipts on the spike, remembering each sale, each customer, trying to build up a picture of who was in the shop and who went near the wirelesses. She couldn't remember anything unusual. Maybe it had happened at dinnertime while she was in the kitchen. No, she'd have heard the bell. No one came in, except ...

Goldstein had rung the police from his home before leaving and a constable arrived just before he did. He was tall and heavily built

67

with a ruddy complexion. Peggy thought he looked like a farmer's boy and his accent confirmed it. She showed him through to the office where he asked her to sit, then he seated himself behind Goldstein's desk.

'Name, address and age please, Miss.' He didn't look up when she answered, just wrote the details in his little notebook stopping every now and again to lick his pencil stub. Goldstein came bustling in just as Peggy was explaining how she noticed the wireless was missing.

'Why is the bolt not on the shop door? Already I have lost one valuable piece of stock; are we inviting thieves in to strip the place bare?'

Before Peggy could speak, the constable stood up and extended his hand. 'You must be the manager?'

Goldstein drew himself up to his full height. 'I,' he emphasised, 'am the owner.' Then he removed a pile of ledgers from an ancient dining chair and sat on it with his feet stretched straight out in front of him, his arms folded, clearly put out that his own seat had been commandeered.

The constable continued to question Peggy. 'And at no point did anything unusual happen?'

'No, nothing.'

'Did you see anyone acting suspiciously?'

'No. It was just an ordinary day.' She looked at Goldstein and added, 'Very busy.'

'What about lunchtime? What happened then?'

'I made myself some tea and ate my sandwich.'

'In here?'

'No, there's a kitchen in the back.'

Goldstein sat up in his chair. 'The bolt – did you bolt the front door?'

Peggy turned, didn't blink. 'Of course I did,' she said and looked him straight in the eye.

'So, tell me about this fella a yours.' Irene and Myrtle sat on the bed with a plate of jam sandwiches cut like door steps between them, nursing cups of tea you could stand a spoon up in. 'He's a kiltie, isn't he?'

'Well, he comes from Scotland, but he doesn't wear a kilt!'

A mouth full of jam and bread didn't slow down Myrtle's relentless questioning. 'How'd ye meet him then?'

'It was funny the way it happened. I shouldn't have been there really.'

'When was all this?'

'Last twelfth of July.'

'Was he over for the parade, in a band? Was he one of them that throws the pole? See me, I love those kilties. Best bit a the whole parade, so they are.'

'No he wasn't at the parade.' Irene thought again about the twist of fate that had taken her away from home that day. 'Neither was I.' She took a long drink of her tea and stared straight ahead. Myrtle settled back on the pillow sensing that the whole yarn was about to unravel without any questions.

'It was Theresa, you know, the Catholic girl I told you about?' Myrtle nodded. Irene went on. 'I always watch the parade from outside the King's Hall. Best place, always great fun in the crowd. Theresa stays at home up the Falls and doesn't go anywhere near the Orangemen. She says to me the week before, "Me and Mary," that's another wee Catholic girl we work with, "are going away for the day on the Twelfth."

'Says I "Where are you going?"

'"Scotland," says she. "Me an' Mary are goin' to Stranraer for the day." So I says, "Is that not awful far?"

'"Course it's not, anyway the boat trip's the thing. Great fun, loads a fellas, music and craic. The bar's open all day, none of your Ulster Protestant drink laws, and they're not fussy about who they serve."

'Well, the upshot of it is, Mary eats a plate of bad herrings and spends the eleventh on her outside privy and Theresa talks me into leaving the country.' Irene paused, remembering how her legs wobbled walking up the steep gangplank; the crowds of people loaded up with rugs and bags; the rows of packed wooden benches and the banter going nineteen to the dozen.

'It was a lovely day, the sea was calm, thanks be to God, and we went out on deck. We sailed down the lough past the Cave Hill and Carrickfergus and out into the sea. And you know what the funny thing was?' Myrtle shook her head. 'I was there in the middle of all those Catholics and I was a bit scared. I thought they'd look at me and know … but they were just ordinary people, out to have a good time with their friends and family.

'We met some boys Theresa knew and had a Guinness with them – tasted nice. When we arrived in Stranraer they went off to carry on drinking, but Theresa told them we hadn't come all that way to sit in a bar, we wanted to see what Scotland looked like. So, we took our picnic and found a nice grassy bank overlooking a wee beach. We didn't notice them at first, we were too busy laying out the blanket, unwrapping sandwiches, cracking open the hard-boiled eggs. They were on the path above us, leaning over the railing. I don't know how long they'd been watching us before one of them shouted: "Hey there, save us a bit of that!"

'There were two of them in uniform, RAF. One tall and quite dark; he jumps up on to the railing and sits there swinging his legs and he's the one doing all the shouting. His friend turns away, has his back to us, saying nothing. He's shorter, kind of sandy auburn hair. Well, Theresa's not a bit backward in coming forward and she shouts, "Why, what's it worth?"

'"What will you take?" says the dark one.

'"Away on with you! I don't even know you," Theresa shouts back.

'Next thing, the dark one's over the rail and running down the slope towards us, while his friend walks the long way round and down the steps. They've got fish and chips. You know how it is, when you smell the newspaper wet with vinegar and you start to drool and you'd do anything for a chip.'

'Oh aye …' Myrtle nodded her head in a knowing way.

'No, it wasn't like that. We shared the food and they had some beer and we had some brown lemonade. The dark one was called Tommy and his sandy friend was, you've guessed it, Sandy. They were based just outside Stranraer.'

'God, were they pilots?' asked Myrtle.

Irene laughed. 'No, they weren't posh or anything. They were radio engineers.'

'Sounds posh enough to me. So, what happened then?'

'Tommy was really taken with Theresa and after a while Sandy said he was going down to the harbour to look at the fishing boats. He nodded at me as if to say come on. I knew what he meant, Theresa and Tommy had forgotten we were there sitting like dummies, while they made eyes at each other.'

'And did you like this Sandy?' Myrtle leaned forward now as if Irene might be about to reveal some secret.

'Ach he was nice enough, a bit quiet. We walked along the harbour wall. He had his hands in his pockets looking at his feet. He told me he was from the north-east of Scotland. Right enough, his accent was very strong, hard to make out sometimes. He stopped and talked to some wee boys who were fishing. I watched him. He looked happy, down on his hunkers looking at the fish they'd caught, helped one boy get a fish off the hook. He stood up then and smiled at me, a nice smile, one that you'd give a friend.'

The light had faded, but Myrtle was reluctant to draw the blackout curtains and turn on the light, feeling that it might signal the end of the story. Irene went to the window and leaned her head against the pane, trying to conjure up Sandy's face.

Finally, she turned.

'Time to get ready, eh?'

'Aye, in a minute,' said Myrtle. 'Finish your story. What happened then?'

'Nothing. It was time to get the boat home. We walked back to Theresa and Tommy, but just before we reached them he stopped and said, "I'm going to be posted overseas again soon. Can I write to you?"

'I wondered what he'd find to say in a letter, when he'd hardly spoken to me in the hour we'd spent together, but he had a nice smile so I said yes.'

'So really he's a penfriend?'

'That was the idea. Trouble is, he never wrote.'

'Ah well, sure never mind,' said Myrtle. 'Come on, let's get

71

ourselves dolled up and see what make of man we can meet the night.'

John Dossor's was one of the best nightspots in Belfast: resident band, dancing, even lessons for those wanting to do more than shuffle round the floor. It was on the corner of Victoria Street, close to the Albert Clock, which leaned like the Tower of Pisa on its sandy foundations. Above the door was a banner proclaiming: 'Grand Hallowe'en Dance' and inside a flight of narrow, dimly lit stairs ran up to the first floor where an elderly lady in a hair net with rouged cheeks sat behind a table, taking the money and stamping hands.

'Keep on the right side a her,' whispered Myrtle, 'if ye don't want te be barred.'

On the first floor there were dance studios, and posters advertised lessons at one and six an hour. 'Up again to the dance,' said Myrtle. Irene turned to follow her then stopped dead. The stairs were lined on either side with young men, some of them wearing ghoulish false faces making spooky noises, laughing, calling to them to come up the narrow space. At that moment, Irene would gladly have fled, but Myrtle grabbed her by the arm and pulled her up through the loud jostling youths and into the sanctuary of the ladies' toilets. Inside was already packed, noise levels were high and the smell of disinfectant was slowly being replaced by Midnight in Paris and 4711 cologne. Myrtle found a spot in one corner that gave her a chance of seeing the edge of a mirror and carefully reshaped the waves in her hair. Irene reapplied the carnation lipstick and offered it to Myrtle, who slicked on an extra layer.

'Here, let's get into the Hallowe'en spirit. Look what I've got.' Myrtle pulled out two cardboard eye-masks, one black with white lace, the other pink with black lace. 'Choose,' she said, offering them.

'I don't know, you pick.'

'You have the pink, then. I'll be more daring in the black.'

She slipped the shirring elastic over her head and grinned as Irene did the same.

'Now we can say an' do whatever we like and no one will know it's us!' Myrtle's laugh was infectious and soon both of them were giggling away in the corner.

'God, Myrtle,' said a thin girl with long black hair, holding a bottle of sweet sherry. 'How much have you had?'

'Nothin' at all – we don't need drink in us te have a good time.' She took Irene's arm and led her back into the corridor. Out of earshot she whispered, 'She'll be paralytic in an hour and outside throwin' up in two.'

The dance hall was bathed in yellow light. At the far end there was a six-piece band playing 'Red Sails in the Sunset'.

Several couples were waltzing around the floor, some of them made up of two girls dancing together. Round the outside of the room were wooden tables and chairs. Soft drinks were being sold from a hatch. Young men were standing about in groups at the edge of the dance floor, chatting and laughing as they sized up the girls. Several of them were wearing Hallowe'en masks which, combined with the yellow light, gave them a sinister look.

'Don't they dance?' asked Irene after they'd bought themselves bottles of Ross's orange with paper straws and found an empty table.

'Some of them don't bother. They try an' get ye to talk te them, then the next thing ye know, they want ye te go outside with them.'

'So you don't get many dances with a boy then?' Irene couldn't keep the disappointment out of her voice.

'Ah, there's some of them can dance, some very well.' Irene wasn't convinced she'd be doing much dancing and sighed.

'Look,' said Myrtle, 'we'll have some of our drink an' then we'll have a couple of dances together. It's never very long before one of them lifts ye.'

'Lifts you?'

'Aye, lifts ye. Comes up te ye while you're dancin', taps ye on the shoulder, an' when ye turn round, they start dancin' with ye.'

There was an interval while the band took a break, during which some of the boys Myrtle knew from Shorts came over to say hello, then the band returned with a singer.

'This is more like it,' said Myrtle. 'Some of those fellas will ask us te dance now, just ye wait an' see.' Sure enough, they were just getting into the swing of a quickstep when they simultaneously felt taps on their shoulder and turned round to the shock of green cardboard Frankenstein masks. Irene gasped, but before she could say anything, she felt a vice-like grip around her waist and was whisked away at great speed. When the song ended Irene faced her partner and clapped. 'Thank you,' she said and turned to walk away. Just then the music started up again and her partner reached after her and took her hand, swinging her around in a circle, back into his arms; a waltz this time and a chance for her to catch her breath and speak to him.

'Why don't you take your mask off?'

'Why don't you?'

Irene's hand went up to her face. 'I'd forgotten I had it on,' she smiled, and added, 'anyway, mine just covers round the eyes.'

'Well, you can see my eyes too.' They crinkled up, smiling. 'They say the eyes are the windows of the soul.'

'That's all very well, but I don't know who you are.'

'Yes you do!'

'No I don't, who are you?'

The blue eyes glittered. 'Course you do. I'm Frankenstein!'

'Then shouldn't you be in a lab somewhere, instead of waltzing round John Dossor's?'

'I sneaked out to find a mate.'

'You'll never find one,' Irene laughed. 'You're far too ugly!'

'I'm not underneath. I just need someone to kiss me and I'll turn into a handsome prince.'

'You're in the wrong story for that.'

'No I'm not; just kiss me and you'll see.' He stopped waltzing, bent his head and pulled her closer.

Irene stood on tiptoes, put her lips on the green cardboard and made a kissing sound. Frankenstein laughed and pushed the mask to the top of his head and Irene found herself looking into the very handsome face of Theresa's brother.

'Sean!' She stared in amazement. 'I never guessed it was you.'

The band switched to a tune with a fast rhythm. 'Can you tango?' he shouted.

'Can I what?'

'Tango. Come on, I'll show you.'

Irene did her best to follow his lead, but the steps were so strange and unpredictable that she quickly realised she needed to relax and let Sean take control and guide her movements. The beat was throbbing in her head, he held her firmly, and she felt herself pushed and pulled. Slowly she began to sense the pattern of steps and the drama conveyed by the shape their bodies made.

Suddenly, Sean stopped abruptly and arched her backwards from the waist until she found herself staring at the ceiling. The music ended and he bent over and kissed her. Irene could hear applause and cheering a long way off, but she kept her eyes on Sean's face as he helped her up and pulled her towards him. Her head was light and she closed her eyes. When she opened them, Sean had turned away to listen to a man in a serpent's mask who was speaking urgently in his ear. As she watched, he nodded several times before turning back to her.

'I'm sorry,' he began, 'I'm going to have to go.' He paused as though struggling to shape his words. 'Something's happened. I need to ...' He gave up trying to explain, kissed her quickly on her cheek and followed the serpent out of the building.

Across town in their shop on Manor Street, the McCrackens – John, Aggie and Grace – were entertaining Sheila and Martha. Martha had arrived after tea to buy her groceries and spend a couple of hours with her cousins before she and Sheila went home. Inevitably, as they settled in front of the fire with tea and homemade cake, the talk turned to war.

'The fact is that we're totally unprepared. Belfast will be tried and found wanting in this war. You mark my words.' John had talked of nothing else for weeks.

'But sure, John, we have the ARPs like yourself,' said Martha.

'Let me tell you, it would take thousands of trained, I say again, trained men to protect this city, but people won't hear the call.' He shook his head and bent to poke the fire into a blaze. 'We're too few and there's no training to speak of at all.' His sisters fell silent and busied themselves with their knitting.

Martha ventured an opinion she'd heard in the queue at Carson's butchers that morning. 'We're a powerful distance from Germany. How would they ever get themselves away over here?'

'I'll tell you this for nothing, Martha, there'll be planes coming up the lough dropping firebombs like apples out of a basket and they'll be falling on our heads.' John got into his stride. 'We've neither anti-aircraft guns, nor bomb shelters. Sure we haven't even got hoses to put out fires. They have us practising with baths full of water and stirrup pumps.'

'It said in the *Telegraph* they were going to provide Anderson shelters for workers in the shipyard and the aircraft factories.'

Martha tried to be positive. John slumped back into his chair as though he suddenly realised that Martha and his sisters had no concept of the scale of the disaster he felt certain would befall them all. After a moment he stood up and took down the family Bible and found a passage about Joshua and the walls of Jericho and read it to them. When he had finished they sat there quietly, each thinking about their city lying in the path of danger. Then Sheila began to sing softly 'Abide with me ...' One by one they joined her, finding comfort in the familiar words they'd known all their lives. Suddenly a banging on the back door made them jump, the notes cut in their throats. John was on his feet in an instant shouting, 'Who's there? What do you want?'

'It's Ted Grimes come to see if Mrs Goulding is still here.'

'Wait. I'll turn the light out and open the door.'

Martha had never seen him so agitated. Ted stepped quickly into the room.

'Aye it's a bad do all right.'

'What is? What's happened,' she asked.

His face was grave. 'Young man from Cullybackey not long since joined the force; they've taken him to the Mater Hospital. God knows what they can do with a bullet in his chest.' He took a drink of the strong, sweet tea Aggie handed him.

'Anyway, Martha, I thought as I was going off duty, I'd call and see you and Sheila safe home; there's a lot of people on the streets, both sides, very angry. There'll be trouble before the morning, so there will, especially if there's more internment of these IRA men the night.'

Chapter 7

Sunday dawned with overcast skies threatening rain, but by the time Peggy set off to walk the ten minutes to Cliftonville Circus, a stiff breeze had sent the clouds scudding over the Cave Hill and the sun was making a half-hearted attempt to break through. Peggy, never one to be rushed, had taken her time getting ready and tried on two or three different skirts before deciding on her A-line navy one with the inverted pleat at the front and neat rows of covered buttons up either side of the hips. It went well with her blue and cream striped jumper. She had only one coat, brown tweed flecked with green, with wide lapels.

She hated it and wondered whether she could get away with not wearing one. In the end, she decided to wear it open, so that the first impression would be of her skirt and jumper. She tried her black work shoes, but they'd be too high if they went for a walk, so she settled for her dark blue suede ones with the low heel.

She came downstairs and saw herself revealed slowly, from the feet up, in the large mahogany mirror in the hall. She was happy with how she looked until she saw her hair. It was pulled back to the nape of her neck and fastened with a tortoiseshell clasp. Maybe she needed a headscarf, but hers were horrible. Pat had a nice one, though, Chinese-looking with heavy-headed chrysanthemums …

She could hear the roar long before she saw the car. It shot out of the Oldpark Road and round the circus, a low two-seater with the top down. It went round twice then headed up the hill and made a U-turn, finishing up alongside her. He leaned across, opened the door and greeted her with a dazzling smile.

'Hello there, hop in.' He was wearing a dark blue suit, white shirt, no tie. 'Is that a scarf?' Peggy nodded. 'Put it on then. You're going to need it!' he shouted as he put the car into gear and they roared off. 'Thought we'd head out the Shore Road, see how far we get, eh?' She nodded again.

'Cat got your tongue, Miss Goulding?'

'How d'you know my name?'

'It's what your boss called you the day he interrupted our Ella Fitzgerald moment,' he laughed, 'but I can't call you that all day, can I? What's your first name?'

'At least you know one of my names. I don't know any of yours.'

'That's true.' He took his right hand off the steering wheel and held it out to her. 'I'm Harold Ferguson, but you can call me Harry. How do you do?'

Peggy shook his hand. 'Margaret Goulding, but you can call me Peggy.'

They turned left on to the Shore Road and followed it along the north side of the lough. There were few cars about; not many wanted to use their precious petrol for Sunday afternoon trips to the seaside. Harry chatted on and Peggy studied his profile. Very dark hair; strong, almost Roman nose; firm jaw; smiled a lot. His hands on the wheel were long and thin, the nails clean and neat. Elegant, a pianist's hands, she thought.

Last night, as she lay in bed thinking about him, she had decided to ask him straight out about the wireless, but today, sitting next to him in the car speeding along, she really didn't care whether he had stolen it or not. Maybe she'd ask on the way home. Meanwhile she relaxed into the leather seat and enjoyed the rush of wind in her face. 'Do you play the piano?' she asked.

At Carrickfergus they walked along the sea front and Harry offered her his arm. A family sat on the scrap of sand with brightly painted tin buckets and spades scattered around them.

Two small children had taken off their shoes and socks and were daring each other to run into the brown sea.

'You'd never believe there was a war on, would you?' said Peggy.

'No, everything's just the same. That's why they're calling it a phoney war.'

'So it won't really happen then, bombs and invasions and everything?'

'Oh, it'll happen all right. It'll just take a while to get going.'

He stopped and pointed over the lough towards Bangor. 'Did you know in the last war there was a prison ship anchored out there full of German prisoners of war?'

'Away on with you!'

'It's true, honest, and I've heard they're thinking of doing the same thing again, only this time they're going to intern IRA men on it.'

'Can they do that?'

'It's already started. There's a bunch of them in the Crumlin Road jail already, and after the shooting and trouble there was last night, I wouldn't be surprised if the RUC didn't round up quite a few more.'

They climbed over the rickety iron bridge to the castle and passed under the raised portcullis into the inner courtyard. They looked into the dank rooms with earth floors and crept down a narrow spiral stone staircase to see the dungeons. All the time Harry treated her as if she was fragile, supporting her arm, taking a hand to help her up or down. In one tiny room there was virtually no light. Harry went in first and pulled her in after him.

'Oh, it's freezing in here.' Peggy shivered.

He wrapped his arms around her and lifted her off her feet.

The last of the light caught her face and he kissed her full on the mouth. She didn't resist, but when he set her down she said fiercely, 'Who said you could do that?'

'You did.'

'When?'

'Just then when you half-closed your eyes and pouted.' His smile mocked her a little.

'I did no such thing!' Peggy stormed out into the daylight.

Harry hurried after her. 'I'm sorry, Peggy. I didn't mean … Look I was only …' Peggy turned away, pulled her coat tightly around her. Harry circled her to look into her face. 'I think I made a mistake.' No response. 'Peggy? Peggy?' He tried another tack. 'I'm very sorry,' he said. 'Will you forgive me?'

She looked at him, as if weighing up the advantages and disadvantages of accepting his apology. 'Very well, I forgive you.'

And she took his arm again and they walked back to the car in silence.

'I've a surprise for you,' said Harry, as he unlocked the boot.

Peggy's mood turned on a sixpence again. 'Oh, I love surprises!'

Harry produced a travel rug and a bag and, even though it was November, they went down on to the sand. When they were settled, he removed a Thermos and some china cups and a large round tin from the bag. He served her coffee then opened the tin. Peggy gasped in delight. 'It looks delicious, is it home-made?'

'Yes, I made it just for you.'

Peggy laughed.

'No, really. I did.'

'Did you?' Peggy was incredulous. The fruit cake was beautifully iced and had little sugar violets scattered across the top.

'I did. I'm a baker.' He grinned. 'I work at the Ormeau Bakery.'

Peggy threw back her head and laughed. 'You're full of surprises, Harry Ferguson.'

Harry saw the delight in her face. 'So are you, Peggy Goulding, so are you.'

When they returned to the car, Peggy got in and watched him in the wing mirror as he replaced the rug and bag and slammed the boot. She was surprised to see that he had a brown envelope in his hand and, as she watched, he opened it quickly and fanned out a wad of money as though checking it was still there. Unaware that she was watching, he put it into his inside pocket and joined her in the car.

'I've a wee message to do on the way back,' said Harry. 'Just need to drop something off.'

They drove away from the sea front and turned into a narrow

street where the houses on either side looked like they would fall down if they didn't have each other to lean on. Harry stopped the car outside a house with its windows boarded up and knocked on the door. Peggy watched him glance nervously up and down the street and more than once his hand patted his inside pocket. He was about to knock again when the door was opened by a short, thick-set man who wore a shirt without a collar and braces hanging down by his sides. He was chewing and wiped his hand across his greasy lips before greeting Harry with a nod. Within seconds, the envelope was handed over, the door slammed and Harry was back in the car turning it towards the main Belfast road. The light was failing fast.

'What do you think, Peggy? Should we stop and put the hood up, or will we beat the rain?'

Peggy shrugged.

'Ach, sure we'll leave it down and race back,' said Harry and put his foot down.

They were just turning into the Cliftonville Road when the first drops of rain began to fall. Peggy had been quiet since they left the house in Carrickfergus. Harry was just the opposite, chatting all the way, glancing across at her every now and again trying to elicit more than a monosyllable in response: 'What do you think, Peggy? That's a good one isn't it? Peggy?' They pulled up at the end of Joanmount Gardens and Harry turned to face her. 'Cat got your tongue again, Miss Goulding?' He laughed. She didn't.

'Something happened in the shop yesterday after you left.'

'Oh, what was that then?'

'I noticed there was an empty space on the shelf; a wireless was missing.'

'Missing? What do you mean?'

'Gone. Stolen.' She saw the thoughts move across his face.

'What did you do?'

'Telephoned Mr Goldstein, of course, and he telephoned the police.' Heavy drops of rain splattered on the windscreen.

'Wait a minute ...' A worried look settled on his face. 'You don't think I took it?'

'You were there. I didn't see you leave. You could have taken it.'

Harry stared at her in disbelief, oblivious to the rain now falling on his face and clothes. 'You do, don't you? You think I took it. Walked in there to ask a girl I like to go out with me' – his voice was rising steadily – 'and when her back was turned, stole a wireless!'

Peggy scowled. Who did he think he was, shouting at her like that? 'Well, you made a quick enough exit,' she snapped and wiped the rain from her eyes.

'I had to be somewhere. I was late. You were on the telephone.'

'Just for a couple of minutes!'

'And so you told the police about me, did you?' No answer. The rain began beating on the streets. 'I take it they've a full description … out combing the back streets of Belfast as we speak, are they?'

'I didn't tell them about you.'

'Well, now you'll be able to give them a name and a place of work.'

Peggy screamed, 'I didn't tell them!'

'No doubt they'll turn up at the bakery in the morning and haul me off to Mountpottinger. Thank you very much!'

Peggy's arms were stiff by her sides, fists clenched. 'Would you listen to yourself? Shouting like that at me. I'm only telling you what happened, so there!'

'And I'm …' Harry put his face close to hers, his dark hair falling over his eyes, rain running down his face. 'I'm only telling you what didn't happen. I didn't steal your bloody wireless!'

'Don't you swear at me!'

'Don't you call me a thief!'

'I did no such thing.' She opened the car door. 'I never heard the like.'

In a split second he had reached over and slammed it shut and grabbed her arm.

'Just a minute, you didn't tell them? Why not?'

'Because I … I …' She stopped and looked down at his hand gripping her arm. 'Let go of me.' She spoke each word slowly, individually. Something in her icy glare made Harry unsure. He pulled his arm back. Peggy was out of the car in an instant, eyes blazing and shouted, 'Of course there's always tomorrow.' Then she turned and ran.

Harry sat in the rain a while, then slowly got out of the car, put the hood up and drove back into the blackness of the city.

In the morning Goldstein was waiting for Peggy when she arrived at work.

'What do you notice, Peggy? What do you notice?'

'You're more than usually excited to be in work on a Monday morning?'

'No. On the shelf, on the shelf!'

There it was, the £9/19/11 missing wireless.

'You got it back?' Peggy's eyes opened wide.

'The police rang me at home on Saturday night and told me they had it. I picked it up first thing this morning.' He raised his hands, palms upwards, as if to say, 'Can you believe it?'

'But how did they find it? Who had it?' she asked.

'Saturday night, around closing time, the police had a call from Mr Kavanagh.'

'Mr "I-Buy-Anything" Kavanagh?'

'The same. He is in his shop on Smithfield Market and someone comes in to sell a wireless. He can see it is brand new with no dust on the valves inside. Also, it is a new model, one he has not seen before. It seems Mr Kavanagh has built his reputation on being an honest trader. If he suspects he is being offered stolen goods, he telephones the police. They come.'

Peggy could hardly contain her excitement. 'So, they caught him on Saturday night?'

Goldstein shook his head. 'Unfortunately it was not that simple. When Kavanagh made an excuse to go into the office to use the phone, the young man became suspicious and ran away.'

Peggy interrupted, 'But Kavanagh saw him clearly? Could describe him?'

'Wait, there is more.' Goldstein paused as though trying to remember the sequence of events as described to him by the police. 'Kavanagh is on the phone to the police when he hears the shop bell ring as someone comes in; he shouts that he will be there in a moment. There is sound of a scuffle, followed by noise of something falling. Mr Kavanagh runs into the shop and sees an elderly gentleman on the floor with a hat stand on top of him. The shop door is wide open and so is the till. The thief has gone; so too has the day's takings.'

Peggy closed her eyes; it all made sense. The envelope full of money ...

'Is something the matter?' asked Goldstein. 'You are happy the wireless is returned, yes?'

Peggy forced herself to smile. 'Yes,' she whispered, 'I'm very happy.'

Goldstein gave one of his rare laughs. 'But not as happy as you are going to be. I have two other pieces of news we must discuss, but not yet. First we will have a cup of tea. I will have mine in the Crown Derby as usual.'

Peggy was scarcely aware of what she was doing as she prepared the tea. She'd hardly slept, going over and over in her mind what she'd said, how he'd responded, the hurt look on his face, his anger. By the time she'd got up for work she was convinced he was innocent. When Goldstein said the wireless had been recovered she was sure of it. But then there was the money. Oh yes, the money changed everything. Goldstein sipped his tea, put his cup back in the saucer and turned to Peggy.

'I had a letter this morning from my sister.'

'In Poland?'

'Indeed,' he sighed. 'Things do not go well for her and her family. Their shop has been closed. They are forced to stay indoors most of the time and there are rumours.' He paused as if imagining the fears of his sister.

'What kind of rumours?'

'The worst kind: Jewish families arrested in the middle of the night and taken out of the city. To where, they do not know.'

He shook his head and Peggy thought he shuddered. Then he seemed to brighten.

'But that is not my news. My news is good.' He went on, 'You remember I told you about my niece. She is close to your age. Her name is Esther.'

Peggy nodded.

'Well, Esther has left the city.'

Peggy put her hand to her mouth, but Goldstein, realising she had misunderstood, went on quickly. 'No, no, she was not taken away. She managed to get on a train going west to Holland. A family, not Jewish, friends of my sister, agreed to take Esther with them. They got her a ticket by saying she was employed by them as a … what is the word? Ah! Governess. Once in Holland, Esther will try to get a boat to England. When she arrives there I will send her the money to come here to me in Belfast.'

'That's wonderful; I'm so pleased for you.'

'You can also be pleased for yourself, Peggy, because Esther has worked in the family music business in Warsaw since she was fourteen and when she comes here she will be able to help you in the shop.'

Peggy could see the possibilities and it was as if Goldstein read her mind.

'Then we will see trade increase and you will have an assistant in the shop, while I concentrate on launching the Barnstormers!'

'Barnstormers?'

'Yes, our troupe of entertainers. That's what they will be called. I was telling my very good friend, who is a lecturer at Queen's, about you all and how I was trying to think of a name and he said, "A group of strolling players, wandering the country entertaining people to keep spirits up? Such people used to be called barnstormers!"'

'That's brilliant.'

'And the best bit of news is that the Barnstormers' first public performance will take place in just over two weeks' time in the Central Hall.'

'So soon! Is it all set up? Is there …'

Goldstein put up his hand. 'One thing at a time, Peggy. I have already got things moving. I contacted the *Belfast Telegraph* office this morning. They were very interested – it is a change to have some positive news – and will send a reporter round this morning to interview me about our group and the concert.'

'We're going to be in the paper?'

'Of course, that's the quickest way to let everyone know about the event. We also need to get some posters printed and I want you to organise that. Here are all the details, so go quickly to McCann's in North Street. They're expecting you. Tell them we need one hundred eye-catching posters by Wednesday.'

'And Peggy,' Goldstein shouted, as she went out the door, 'on the way back buy some plain postcards and twelve stamps. I will need to write to the performers about rehearsals.'

When Peggy returned, Goldstein was deep in conversation with a man in a tweed overcoat and a trilby (which he hadn't removed), with a camera around his neck. 'Ah, here she is,' Goldstein exclaimed, 'one of the talented Barnstormer performers.'

The reporter eyed her up and down. 'I think I've got all the detail I need. Now, how about a picture?'

On his afternoon off, Ted Grimes spruced himself up and left his house, closing the door quietly behind him. His wife Vera had earlier complained of palpitations, which he suspected were caused by his suggestion that the cupboards could do with a good redding out, and she had taken to her bed leaving Ted to take himself up the Oldpark, yesterday's *Belfast Telegraph* under his arm, to visit Martha. He was a man with decent manners, so he rattled the side gate before coming round the back of the house past the kitchen window and in through the back door.

'Hello, anybody home?' The kitchen was neat and tidy, cosy with the little stove lit. The table was set for the evening meal and there was a meaty smell coming from the oven. 'Hello, Martha! Are you in?' He heard quickening footsteps above him followed by the sound of someone coming down the stairs.

Martha's face appeared round the door.

'Well, well, would you look who's here,' she said. 'Not at work the day, Ted?'

'Ach no, sure it's my afternoon off.'

'Oh, that's grand. We'll sit in the front room. Will you take a wee cup of tea?'

'Don't mind if I do, Martha.' He eased himself into the armchair to the left of the fireplace.

'I was very grateful the other night when you came to collect us from the McCrackens,' shouted Martha from the kitchen.

'Not at all, not at all.' Ted looked around the neat room, noted the bust of Beethoven on the piano, and was that Tchaikovsky on the china cabinet? Martha was a woman with unexpected depths.

'Nice and strong, just how you like it,' said Martha, handing him the tea, 'and you'll take a bit of fruited soda as well, won't you? It's still warm from the oven.' Back in the kitchen, Martha removed her overall and returned with a thick slice of buttered soda and her own tea and sat opposite Ted. 'Did they get the one who shot the policeman?'

'Well, they've taken a few Catholic fellas from the Falls Road into custody. That caused a lot of bother itself; people out on the streets protesting and throwing stuff.' He shook his head. 'Internment's the only answer in my view.'

'That's all very well, but what about the families? It's them I feel sorry for without the man's wage. I know how hard that is.'

'Ach, Martha, never you worry yourself about them.'

'God knows, Ted, it's hard to put food on the table.' Martha looked away as though she'd said too much already. The last thing she wanted was Ted Grimes to think she was crying poverty. They sat in silence for a while. From the street came the strangled cry of the herring man. 'Ardglass!'

'Have you thought any more about evacuating Sheila?' Ted changed the subject.

'Ah no, she's safe enough here for now.'

'A lot of the primary school childer have gone. The offer's still there you know. My cousin Edna would welcome help on the farm in exchange for board and lodging.'

'Aye, I know that, but she needs to finish her schooling. She could get a decent job, you know. She's talked about working in an office. She's bright as a button.'

'Is that going to matter do you think?'

'What do you mean?'

Ted leaned forward to press home his point. 'You know she's a lovely girl. I'm guessing when she's old enough she'll find herself a young man and stop work altogether, if you get my drift.'

'Your drift seems to be to get me out of the way to provide cheap labour for your family in the country.' Sheila stood in the doorway, hands on hips. She turned to her mother. 'Mammy, why are you listening to him? What's he doing here anyway?'

'Now, Sheila, don't you be rude to Mr Grimes.'

'We talked about this and you agreed I could stay here. I'm not going anywhere!' She snatched the cup, saucer and plate of half eaten soda out of Ted's hands. 'But you are!'

'Sheila, how dare you speak to a guest like that!'

Ted stood up, towering over the two women. 'It's all right,' he said quietly to Martha. 'It's time I was getting back anyway. Oh, by the way, I brung you yesterday's *Telegraph*, chance you hadn't seen it already.' He set it on top of the piano and turned to Sheila. 'As for you, miss, you've far too much to say for yourself.'

Martha didn't draw the blackout curtains. There was no need; she hadn't switched on any lights. Upstairs, too, was in darkness. After she had sent Sheila to bed, Martha listened to her sobbing until, eventually, there was silence. Later, as darkness fell, she crept upstairs to find her lying fully clothed on her bed fast asleep. At half six, Irene, Pat and Peggy arrived home together.

Irene was first through the door.

'Mammy, what are you doing in the dark?' Without waiting for an answer she leaned over the draining board and drew the curtains and Pat crossed the kitchen ready to turn on the light as soon as Irene finished checking there were no gaps.

'Is the tea ready? I'm starving.' Peggy went to hang their coats in the little back hallway.

'Where's Sheila?' asked Pat.

'What's for tea?' asked Irene, bending down to look inside the stove.

Martha didn't move. 'It's nearly ready; Sheila's upstairs asleep; stew, mashed potatoes and cabbage, but that can wait until we sort something out.'

Irene stood up from the stove, Peggy paused in the doorway, Pat stopped at the sink, a glass in one hand, her other reaching out to the tap, each struck by the strange tone in their mother's voice.

'Sit down, all of you.' Martha waited while they sat. 'Did I, or did I not, forbid you to join that troupe of entertainers?'

The girls looked quickly at each other. Irene was the first to answer, trying to be honest. 'Yes, yes, you did.'

'And now I hear you're going to sing in a show next week.'

'Who told you that?' asked Irene.

'Never mind who told me. What I want to know is … is it true?'

'Well, it's sort of true …' Irene hesitated.

'Sort of, what do you mean, sort of?' Martha raised her voice.

Peggy intervened. 'What Irene means is that we said we'd do one show, because Mr Goldstein's been let down by one of the acts.' Pat gave her a sideways look, but Peggy carried on.

'Someone can't perform that night … a singer it is. So, he asked us.'

'And that's all, is it? One show?' asked Martha, looking sternly at each daughter in turn. Irene looked embarrassed; Pat was looking at Peggy, her face flushed. Peggy nodded, smiling.

The *Belfast Telegraph* was on the high mantelpiece above the stove. Without a word, Martha retrieved it. It had been folded to show the picture of Peggy leaning on her elbows, one hand laid flat over the other supporting her chin, her face beautifully made-up and smiling, looking for all the world like a Hollywood starlet.

Martha began to read, 'Peggy Goulding (pictured) and her two sisters Irene and Pat are members of the new company.'

Martha paused and looked at them over the paper, then continued. 'Peggy told our reporter, "We've always dreamt of being entertainers and as members of the Barnstormers we'll get lots of opportunities to perform."' Martha pursed her lips and looked at them. 'So, one concert is it?'

'We were going to tell you, Mammy, honestly.' Irene was close to tears.

'Oh, aye, and when was that? Next Saturday as you went out the door, all dolled up like this one in the photo? Or when you arrived home at midnight and me worried sick?'

'Ach, Mammy, we're old enough to look after ourselves,' said

Peggy. 'And anyway there's three of us. We wouldn't be anywhere on our own.'

'That's not the point. I'm your mother and you girls defied me.' Martha was on her feet, leaning across at them, knuckles on the table.

'Mammy, we were going to tell you.'

'Oh were you now.' Martha faked an understanding smile. 'Would that be like you told me about going to the audition?'

Martha pointed her finger at each daughter in turn. 'Deceit is a dangerous game. I never thought I'd see the day my daughters would stoop so low. Not only have you lied to me, but you've got yourself involved with some low music hall characters.'

'Mammy, that's not fair,' said Irene. 'You don't know these people. They're really nice.'

'Irene, don't be so naive. Before you know where you are, m'lady, you'll be out smoking and drinking in some back street dance hall. And if you think I'm standing for that, you've got another thing coming!'

Irene thought of Saturday night with Myrtle and said no more.

Peggy waded in then. 'But Mr Goldstein is a respectable businessman. Sure you know he owns a shop in Royal Avenue.'

'I'm sure he is respectable, it's not him I'm worried about,' argued Martha.

'Do you not trust us, Mammy?'

'I thought I could, but now I'm not so sure. I wonder sometimes what goes on in your head, Peggy. And as for you' – she turned again to Irene – 'you're the eldest. What on earth were you doing, encouraging your sisters to get involved in something like this?'

'Mammy, we just wanted to do something different. Something that was' – she struggled for the word – 'something exciting.'

'Dear God.' Martha sat down again and put her head in her hands. 'Exciting isn't for the likes of us. We've to work to keep a roof over our heads and food on the table, you know that. And since Daddy died it's harder than ever. And now there's a war.'

She shook her head. 'Is the threat of bombs not excitement enough for you, but you have to go out in the blackout to God knows where, with God knows who?'

'But we'll be helping the war effort, Mr Goldstein said so. We'll keep people's spirits up, so we will,' argued Peggy. 'And you never know,' she went on, 'we could become famous.'

Martha laughed out loud. 'Peggy Goulding you are unbelievable. Listening to music all day in that shop has turned your head. Who do you think you are?'

'Somebody who isn't going to waste their life cooking and cleaning and raising we'uns!' Peggy shouted.

At that moment, Pat, who had listened without comment to her mother and sisters arguing, spoke up. 'Will you stop it! We shouldn't be arguing like this. Look, Mammy, we were wrong. We shouldn't have gone to that audition without telling you. I'm ...' She looked at her sisters. 'We're sorry. But you know this war is going to take young fellows off into real danger. We can't go and fight, but we should do something. It's about morale and carrying on even though there might be danger. And you know we can do this, Mammy. You saw us at the Grosvenor Hall. You heard the Reverend Lynas say how important it was to have more events like that. That's what we want to do.' She reached across the table and put her hand on Martha's. 'And we want to sing, Mammy. You know that. We want to sing.'

'Sure I know that, but this isn't the odd concert in a Christian church hall. Your Daddy would never have agreed to this and I'd never forgive myself if something happened to you.'

'Mammy, we'll be all right.' Pat took her hand. 'Sure haven't you brought us up to know how to behave? You need to trust us.'

'That's all very well, but do you think I'd trust some of these men? I don't want any of you letting me down. You know what I'm saying now, don't you?' She looked at each of them in turn. They nodded.

Martha stood up, seeming to shake herself, as though shedding such distasteful thoughts. 'I'm going to have to think about this. So that's an end to it for now. Let's get this meal served before it's spoilt altogether.'

The following day Martha left home at twelve o'clock and caught the trolleybus into Belfast, alighting on Royal Avenue just across the road from Goldstein's music shop. She waited there until one o'clock, when she saw Peggy leave and walk towards the nearby Queen's Arcade, no doubt to spend her lunch hour looking in the windows of the expensive shops inside. Almost immediately after, Goldstein appeared at the shop door where he turned the sign to show it was closed. By the time he had bolted the door Martha had crossed the road and was knocking on the window. He looked startled and was about to indicate the closed sign when he looked more closely and recognised her.

'Mrs Goulding,' he said as he opened the door. 'I am afraid you have just missed Peggy. She has gone for her lunch.'

'I know,' said Martha. 'It's you I've come to see.'

If Goldstein was surprised, he didn't show it. Instead, he nodded and ushered her into the shop. 'Of course, Mrs Goulding, follow me.'

Martha was struck by the formality of the office with its heavy mahogany desk and matching filing cabinets.

'Please sit down.'

Martha sat on the edge of the chair, her back completely straight, clasping her handbag on her knee.

'Can I offer you a cup of tea?'

'No thank you. I'll come straight to the point, Mr Goldstein. I'm here about my daughters joining your entertainment troupe.'

Goldstein smiled. 'You mean the Barnstormers?'

'Yes. I will be perfectly honest with you, I'm concerned about the wellbeing of my daughters, about them keeping company with what sound to me like music hall acts.'

Goldstein leaned back in his chair, made a tent of his hands, and observed Martha for a few moments. 'What exactly are you concerned about, Mrs Goulding?'

Martha blushed, took a deep breath and addressed her words to her handbag. 'Let us say, shall we, that my daughters are innocent, naive even, and might be easily led astray by undesirable people.'

'Aah.' Goldstein nodded slowly. So that was it. He appeared to consider his words carefully. 'Peggy, it seems to me, is a very strong-willed young woman. She likes to get her own way and once she makes up her mind there is no changing it. Am I right in that judgement?'

Martha managed a grim smile. 'Indeed you are.'

'I doubt whether she could be influenced by anyone,' said Goldstein. Martha said nothing. He went on. 'Pat I have met only twice, but she struck me as a serious young woman, dignified and sensible. Is she?'

'Strait-laced, you mean? Well, maybe she is,' Martha conceded.

'Now, Irene is friendly and enjoys company. She is the eldest, is she not?'

Martha was well aware of where all this was going. 'She is.'

'She would want to look after her sisters, would want to set them a good example I'm sure.'

'She would, Mr Goldstein. And I've no doubt that my daughters would behave correctly. After all, they've been well brought up. As I said before, it's not their behaviour I'm worried about. It's the behaviour of the men they'd be mixing with.'

Goldstein folded his arms, pursed his lips and stared at the ceiling. Martha sat perfectly still as the silence stretched into a minute then two. Suddenly, Goldstein leaned across the desk and smiled warmly.

'I am very glad that you came to see me, Mrs Goulding. It is important that I look after the very talented young people who have volunteered to join the Barnstormers. I have an idea. I'd be interested to know what you think.'

While her mother was deep in conversation with her employer, Peggy walked the length of the Queen's Arcade, ignoring the temptations of the dress shops, and emerged on to Fountain Street where she turned right towards Smithfield. Within minutes the quiet street gave way to a noisy, busy area, crowded with stalls that spilled second-hand goods on to the pavements and out into the road. Hawkers stood on street corners. One, a wizened man with a humped back, was trying to press packets of razor blades into the hands of passers-by. Another had a wooden tray covered with handkerchiefs hung with rope around his neck. Peggy ignored everything and walked purposefully to the shop at the far side of the market. She paused a moment under the sign 'I buy anything', took a deep breath and pushed open the door. The air was musty, like a room closed up for years. Towards the back of the shop heavy sideboards, tables, chairs and settees were piled in crazy configurations, like some stairway to the grimy skylight. Elsewhere, the contents of a hundred houses had seemingly been abandoned in the shop, proving that Kavanagh was true to his word. The man himself was sitting in a leather-covered chair with horsehair stuffing escaping from the arms. He acknowledged Peggy with a curt nod assuming, because she wasn't carrying anything to sell, that she intended to look around the shop. Peggy had worked out exactly how to get the information she wanted.

'Good afternoon, Mr Kavanagh?'

'It is, surely,' he replied. 'What can I do for you?'

'I work for Mr Goldstein of Goldstein's Music Shop.' She smiled warmly and held out her hand. Kavanagh, a little taken aback, quickly wiped his hand on his waistcoat and shook hers.

'I've come to thank you for recovering the wireless that was stolen.'

'Sure it was nothing. People need to know I don't handle stolen goods. That's how I build my reputation.'

'The thing is, Mr Kavanagh, I have a feeling I might have seen the thief in the shop, but I'm not sure enough to mention it to the police. Could you tell me what he looked like?'

'Oh aye, saw him as plain as day. Tall fella he was.'

Peggy's heart sank.

'About seventeen, eighteen, I should think.'

Her hopes rose.

'Ginger hair, a right ugly bake on him he had.'

Peggy couldn't stop herself grinning. 'Is that right?'

'Is that the same man you have in mind?' he asked.

'Oh no, that's not him,' she laughed. 'Not him at all!'

Chapter 8

Irene could sense an atmosphere as soon as she passed through the gates of the Ulster Linen Works. Small groups of men stood around talking quietly and there was none of the usual banter as they queued to clock in. In the finishing room Theresa's place at the table was empty again. In contrast to the sombre mood, Alan Briggs seemed buoyant. 'Come on, you lot! We've a big order for tray cloths to finish. And would ye look at that, we're one brushie down! Maybe she's took herself out for the day, eh?' he sniggered. 'Round to Crumlin Road jail, I've heard.'

'What's going on?' Irene whispered to the girl next to her.

'We found out why Theresa hasn't been in.' She paused and looked behind her. Alan Briggs was busy sorting out a new delivery of paint. 'Saturday night, the peelers raided a load of houses up the Falls.'

'I heard,' whispered Irene. 'There was a policeman shot, wasn't there? But what's that to do with Theresa?'

'Theresa's da was taken away.'

'Arrested?'

'Not exactly, they call it internment. Gets suspected IRA men off the streets.'

'But Theresa's family wouldn't be involved in anything …' Irene caught her breath, 'and Sean, what about him?'

'Nothing.'

'What do you mean, nothing?'

'Got away, disappeared. Some say they're lookin' for him.'

Alan Briggs appeared behind them. 'Come on now, you two, get to work. Don't ferget, I'll be countin' how many each of youse has done by the end of the day.'

At the dinner break Pat reminded Irene of her plans. 'I'm going to see Mr Goldstein after work. Do you want to come with me?'

'Sure he doesn't need to see me. It's about you doing a duet or something, isn't it?'

'I don't know. Peggy just gave me the message, she wasn't for discussing it. I think maybe her nose was out of joint, but that's nothing new. Now Irene, you go straight home. Don't be thinking of taking a wee trip up the Falls, will you?'

'But maybe Theresa …' Irene struggled to explain why she wanted to see her friend. 'I just need to show her that I …'

Pat spoke sternly. 'Listen, there's nothing you can do. Keep out of this. Don't even risk showing your face up there. They'll know you're not one of them.'

'Oh for goodness sake, Pat! It's not about them and us. She's my friend.'

'I'm telling you, no good'll come of it. Leave Theresa and her family be.'

They finished their lunch in silence, then painted tray cloths all afternoon listening to the rain thrattle on the skylights above their heads until the hooter sounded the end of the working day.

Pat was one of the first out to keep her appointment with Goldstein. Irene dawdled, unsure of what to do, but the torrential rain that met her outside and the swish of the trolleybus stopping a few yards away settled it. She could always see Theresa tomorrow night.

Goldstein was just locking up when Pat arrived at the shop.

She was surprised to learn that Peggy had already left.

'I sent her home early so that she could call at the GPO to post some sheet music.' He was wearing a wide-brimmed, high-crowned

97

felt hat, the style of which Pat had never seen. 'I thought we might have a bite to eat. The Pam Pam is very good. You know it, on the corner of Donegall Place?'

Pat did know it – it was new and stylish and she'd only half a crown in her purse. She hesitated. 'I don't think I can stay that long ...'

'Nonsense, the service is quick.' He shook out his umbrella, pushed it up and took her arm, adding with a smile, 'Besides, I like to treat beautiful young ladies.'

The Pam Pam was very modern and very crowded. Goldstein helped her out of her wet coat. She wished she'd been wearing something with a bit more colour, but at least the navy dress was neat and, thankfully, slimming. Goldstein spotted someone in the far corner and waved and Pat followed him as he zigzagged across the room.

'Miss Goulding, you remember William Kennedy, I hope, from the auditions?'

'Of course, the tenor. How nice to see you again.' Now she wished she'd combed her hair.

They shook hands, each a little surprised to see the other.

She was impressed to see he wore a suit and tie.

Goldstein insisted on ordering for all three of them. 'It will save time,' he said, 'and we can get on with our discussion. Patricia, William, I want you to be an extra act. Of course, William, you will still have your own spot, as will you with your sisters, Patricia. But you will also sing together.' He looked from one to the other and hurried on. 'You are familiar with the famous Hollywood couple Jeanette MacDonald and Nelson Eddy?'

They nodded.

'Well, I have the sheet music. I will find you the costumes ... the Mountie ... the Indian girl. You will be a sensation!' He beamed with delight at his idea.

Pat had a sudden image of herself dressed as an Indian squaw. 'Mr Goldstein, I don't think ...' she hesitated and turned instinctively to William.

His tone was reasonable but confident. 'They have fine voices, especially when they use them to sing opera ... Puccini ... Verdi.

Perhaps we could look at their wider repertoire to find something suitable for our voices.'

At that moment their food arrived and the talk turned to the arrangements for the Barnstormers' first performance, at the beginning of December, just a month away. Goldstein had found them a place to rehearse and was arranging all the publicity.

They would take Belfast by storm, he was sure. He ate quickly, chatting between mouthfuls about the performers, the venue, the ticket prices ... then he wiped his mouth vigorously with his napkin and stood up.

'Now I must dash. But you please stay and discuss what you will sing when you are Jeanette MacDonald and Nelson Eddy. I will get the bill at the door. I look forward to seeing you at the rehearsal on Sunday.'

They watched him leave. Pat was the first to speak. 'I'm not too sure about all this, are you?' She felt a little embarrassed sitting in a restaurant with a man she hardly knew to discuss how they were to become the famous American Sweethearts.

'Actually, I think I need to be getting home now.' He stood up.

'Yes of course, me too. I'm not really used to being out in the blackout.'

He seemed to find his manners. 'I'm sorry, I wasn't thinking. I'll walk you to your stop.'

'There's really no need.'

'No, please, I'd like to.' He helped her on with her coat.

Outside the rain had stopped and a full moon mocked the idea of a blackout as they strolled along Royal Avenue trying to remember the songs from the films of MacDonald and Eddy.

Around the time Pat was digesting the news that she had a new singing partner, Irene turned into Joanmount Gardens and was just passing the corner shop when she heard someone call her name. A shadowy figure was standing beneath an overhanging privet hedge.

'Sean ... is that you?' She moved closer. He had no coat, was soaked to the skin and wearing the same clothes he'd worn on

Saturday night at John Dossor's. 'What are you doing here? I think the police are looking for you.'

'I know, that's why I can't go home. I need you to get a message to Theresa.'

'What's going on, Sean?'

'You remember the boys found me in Dossor's? Well, they told me there were going to be raids. We wanted to stop them. There was talk of barricades, but it was too late. When we got there they were puttin' me da in the Black Maria. I stood on the corner and watched; they didn't see me. I wanted to run out and hit them, scream at them, but I just stood there and let them take him. Then me an' the other lads went somewhere in the Bone, an oul woman's house where the peelers wouldn't look.'

His voice began to rise. 'Now they're searchin' everywhere for me and I've got te get out of Belfast.'

The shop bell tinkled behind them and a tall man with an upright stance emerged. In the seconds before he closed the door against the blackout, Irene recognised him. In a flash, she reached up and drew Sean's head down to kiss her.

Ted Grimes paused for a moment to take a cigarette from the new pack and light it, before hurrying home to Vera and his tea.

'I'm sorry,' she whispered. 'I know him, he's a policeman.'

'He didn't see me, did he?' Panic was in his voice and Irene felt him shivering against her.

'No, I don't think so. What do you want me to tell Theresa?'

'Just that I'm all right … and tell Mammy not to worry. I'm goin' over the border tonight. Just say I'll be in Donegal, she'll understand.' Then he brushed his lips against hers in the most fleeting of kisses and walked quickly away. Over the Black Mountain thunder rumbled and heavy clouds obscured the moon.

Irene could smell the stew as soon as she pushed open the back door. Martha was at the ironing board, smoothing out some cloth.

'What's that you've got there?'

'It's a remnant, end of a roll.' Martha held up the huge piece of turquoise cotton. 'Vera Grimes sent it up with Ted. There must be over five yards here. She thought I could make some use of it.'

'That was nice of her. What will you make with it?'

'I was thinking it would do nicely for three matching blouses. You know, the sort that would look good on stage.'

Irene's face lit up. 'You mean we can sing at the concert?'

'Aye well, why not?'

Irene hugged her. 'What made you change your mind?'

'Mr Goldstein.'

'Goldstein?'

'We had a long talk and the upshot of it was he asked me to act as chaperone.'

'What's a chaperone?'

'I'm to be there keeping an eye on the young women. Looking after them backstage; seeing they come to no harm.'

Irene felt a stab of disappointment. She'd been looking forward to being a Barnstormer, going out in the world, a bit of freedom, but now …

Just then Peggy arrived, soaking wet and in high temper.

'Jesus, Mary and Joseph, will you look at the state of me! A lorry drove in a big puddle next to the kerb, right over my head it went.'

'Peggy, there's no need to blaspheme!' Martha chided her. 'The fire's lit in the front room. Away in there and get warm the pair of you. You can put your coats over the fire guard too or they'll never be dry for the morning. I'll get you some towels as well.'

While they dried themselves, Irene told Peggy about the chaperoning.

'My God that's all I need, puts the tin hat on it. What a day I've had!'

'Why, what else has happened?'

Peggy was certainly not going to tell her nosey sister about her trip after work to the Ormeau Bakery looking for Harry Ferguson. Nor how angry she'd been to find he'd worked the early shift and left at dinner time. Then there was Goldstein's big plan for Pat and that miserable-looking tenor. Stars of the show indeed!

They'd finished the stew and potatoes by the time Pat arrived home. She seemed delighted with the news that her mother would be attending each concert. 'So we'll be able to sing after all and, Mammy, you'll be there to watch us!'

Peggy rolled her eyes.

Pat went on, 'And did you hear about me singing duets as well?'

'Aye, but who is this William Kennedy anyway? What do you know about him?'

Pat reeled off a list of his attributes. 'Very well spoken, works in an office, I'm told.' Irene and Sheila looked at each other and made an 'Ooooo' sound. Peggy tutted. Pat carried on.

'Good manners, smartly dressed, cufflinks.'

'Cufflinks,' said Peggy. 'Well, he must be all right then!'

'Don't use that mocking tone with me, Peggy Goulding!' Pat snapped.

'Oh don't you be getting on your high horse, just because you've got the chance to sing a few more songs. Don't forget you could easily end up singing them unaccompanied!'

'Will you girls stop it? This was supposed to be a nice evening … sorting out what you're going to wear and everything.' Martha had brought the turquoise material from the kitchen and spread it out over the settee. It was just like when they were children and she'd stop their bickering with a distraction.

'Now then, Peggy, you've an eye for fashion,' Martha said. 'What style of blouse do you think you should have?'

Peggy allowed herself to be flattered and knelt down to feel the material. 'I assume we'll stick to the black skirts; we've all got one.' They nodded. 'Now this material's plain so the shape will need to give it style. I'm thinking something dramatic.'

Alan Briggs was waiting for the brushies when they arrived for work the following morning, arms folded across his chest, a basket of painted tray cloths at his feet and a face on him that could sour milk.

'Right, listen youse uns.' He pointed at the basket. 'Them's a load of rubbish. Youse wasted yer day yesterday. There shoulda bin two hunred done and yer thirty short.'

'Aye but, Mr Briggs, we were one down yesterday; Theresa was away,' someone shouted from the back.

'D'ye think I care if yer woman was swinging the lead? Anyway, the colours isn't right neither. The centres should've been magnolia cream with magenta petals on the outside. Not the other way about.'

There was uproar, all the women shouting at once that he'd given instructions to paint them like that. In the midst of the noise Irene noticed that Theresa had slipped in at the back. She looked drained and her eyes were red. Irene moved through the shouting women until she was next to her friend and leaned over to whisper in her ear.

'I saw Sean last night.' Theresa's eyes opened wide and she made to speak, but Irene cut her off. 'He asked me to tell you ...'

Theresa listened, nodding, then mouthed 'Thank you'.

'Well, would you look at what the cat's dragged in?' Alan Briggs seized the opportunity to distract attention from himself.

The women turned to stare. 'And has your brother shown his face as well? If he has, we'd best ring Mountpottinger police station, I think there's a few questions they'd be wantin' te ask him.'

Irene could see Theresa was close to tears. 'Mr Briggs, Theresa's had a hard time over the last few days. I'm sure she's just glad to be back to work.'

'That's as maybe, but I'm afraid there's no work any more for somebody who misses two days because they're in trouble with the police.'

There was another loud protest from the women, but he shouted them down. 'Now look here! Youse had better quit arguing. This is insubordination!' The grumbling continued, but the volume was lower. 'If ye don't like what goes on in this building then maybe youse need to find yersels an alternative place of employment.' He pointed at Theresa. 'And you, Miss, can go and collect your cards right now. They have them ready for ye. An' if there's anyone thinks that's unfair, well, ye can go with your Fenian friend and collect yours too.'

The room was silent. Theresa turned to leave. Pat caught Irene's eye and shook her head in warning, but it was too late. Irene turned on her heel and followed Theresa out of the room.

The mill office was on the top floor, far above the clattering of looms, the lint-heavy air and the smell of sweating workers.

Irene pressed the brass bell and when a woman appeared she spoke for both of them.

'We're here to collect our cards,' she said, adding quickly, 'and our wages.'

The woman showed no surprise. Instant dismissals were common. 'Names?'

'Irene Goulding and Theresa O'Hara.'

She scribbled on a slip of paper and hurried away.

Theresa sat on one of the bentwood chairs, her head in her hands. 'You shouldn't have walked out, Irene. I knew they'd sack me, but you shouldn't have got involved.'

'What was I supposed to do? It's not fair them sacking you like that. You've done nothing wrong.'

'God, Irene, Briggs is a bigot and he's been looking for an excuse to get rid of me since I started here. I think me da hauled off by the police and me brother on the run was too good an opportunity to miss, don't you?'

They sat in silence a while then Irene said, 'You know what, Theresa? It's a matter of principle, so it is. You have to stand up to bullies whether it's Adolf Hitler or Alan Briggs. We've struck a blow for freedom here ...' She stopped and laughed, suddenly struck by the absurdity of it all. 'And that's what I'll tell Mammy when she hits the roof tonight after I tell her I've no job!'

Theresa hugged her. 'You're a good friend, so ye are. Will ye get in awful trouble?'

'No, there'll be no trouble at all.'

'Why's that?'

''Cause I won't tell her!'

'You'll have to tell her. There'll be no money.'

'Look, it's Thursday so I'll only lose two days' pay and I've a bit of overtime to come. That's this week sorted and I'll take myself down the town now and find another job. Go round the shops asking. I'll get something. Why don't you come too?'

'No, you go on. Ye'll have a better chance of getting something if you're on your own. Anyway, I've an uncle runs a bar on

Northumberland Street. He's always asking me to work evenings. I'll be all right.'

Outside the day was brightening up. 'I've been wondering,' said Theresa, 'why Sean found you to pass on the message.'

'Well he couldn't risk going anywhere near a Catholic area, but nobody would think to look for him where I live, would they?'

'But he …'

'He knew no one would expect him to contact me,' Irene went on quickly. 'Now promise me you'll keep in touch.'

'I will.' Theresa hugged her. 'And, Irene …'

'What?'

'Thanks … for everything.'

'And you're to sing two duets in this concert, is that correct?'

'Yes Aunt Kathleen, but William, I mean Mr Kennedy, and I are not sure what to sing. That's why we need you to give us some advice.'

'Your voice has developed over the six lessons you've had, and you are certainly capable of giving a passable account of yourself, but Mr Kennedy is the unknown quantity.' She paused to consult her silver pendant watch. 'I hope he will be punctual. This could take some time.'

At that moment the long case clock in the hall chimed the hour and there was a knock at the door. In the hallway, Pat made the formal introductions and Kathleen shook William's hand.

'Tell me, Mr Kennedy, are you one of the Lisburn Kennedys?'

'No, I'm afraid I'm not. My family come from Ballymena.'

Kathleen stood a little taller. 'Do they indeed? I'm not acquainted with any Ballymena Kennedys.' She pronounced the word Ballymena as though it was something she would want to keep at arm's length. 'Do come into the drawing room.'

Kathleen sat at the elegant upright piano and ran through some warm-up exercises. 'Good, good, now let me see what you are thinking of singing.' Pat produced the sheet music from her music case and Kathleen looked through it quickly, making two piles.

'Suitable and unacceptable,' she said, reaching for the smaller of the two piles. 'We'll start with these.'

'But Mr Goldstein particularly wants us to sing "The Indian Love Call",' said Pat, rescuing it from the unacceptable pile.

'Good gracious, no. That's pantomime music! You can do better than that.'

She set a duet from Puccini's *La Boheme* on the stand in front of her and played the introduction. Pat and William moved closer to read over her shoulder.

When they had finished, Kathleen swivelled round in her seat. 'Pat, your voice is strong, but does not convey sufficient emotion. Mr Kennedy, your breathing is at fault. Have you forgotten you have a diaphragm?'

And so it went on. All afternoon they sang and Kathleen criticised. When the clock struck four, she announced that they would have a final run-through of what she considered their four best songs. There was no doubt her coaching had made a difference and when the final note ended Pat and William were smiling with the exhilaration of it all. After Aunt Kathleen, two hundred paying customers would be easy.

'Excellent,' said Kathleen, standing up to shake them both by the hand. 'You know, I think I'll buy a ticket myself, just to check the quality of the final performance.'

'Irene, you knew when you walked out of the mill that we couldn't manage without your wage.'

'But, Pat, I was sure I'd have another job by Monday.'

'Oh aye, and now it's Sunday and you're still unemployed. And you know what the worst of it is? I'll tell you – deceiving Mammy. Pretending to go out to work and coming home at the normal time.'

'I've spent every day wandering the town looking for a job.'

'Well, you'll have to tell her now, won't you?'

'Maybe not, something could turn up next week and by Friday I could have a wage to give her.'

Pat shook her head. 'I doubt it.'

'You won't tell her, will you?'

'Irene, she'll find out anyway. Mammies always do.'

The noise inside York Street Presbyterian Church Hall was deafening.

'Can you please be quiet ... we need to make a start!' Peggy shouted from the stage.

No response.

At that moment the compere, Sammy Reid, gave a shrill whistle through his teeth. The room quietened and with a wave of his hand he left the stage to Peggy.

'Mr Goldstein will be along at two o'clock, and a full run-through will begin then. I've pinned up the running order at the back of the hall. So, I suggest you spend the next half hour practising.'

Myrtle flopped down in the seat next to Irene. 'My God, ye look like you've lost a pound and found a ha'penny.'

'Aye, well, you're not far wrong,' moaned Irene. 'Trouble is, next week I won't even have two ha'pennies to rub together.'

'Why, what's happened?'

Irene told her about Theresa and how she'd lost her job.

'I've been tramping round the town for the three days and there's no work to be had at all. I tell you, if the rag man offered me a job yelling from his cart I'd take it.'

Myrtle laughed again.

'It's no laughing matter. You haven't heard the worst of it.' Irene's voice faltered. 'I ... I haven't told Mammy yet.'

'Can ye climb a ladder?'

'What? Myrtle, this is serious. Without my wage we won't be able to pay the rent.'

'I know, but answer me this, can ye climb a ladder? And I don't mean clingin' on for dear life. Could ye run like a whippet up and down wi' your hands full?'

'Why?'

'If ye can do that, ye could have a job same place as me – the aircraft factory.'

Irene's eyes lit up. She could get a job and Mammy wouldn't

know she'd been sacked. She'd just tell her she'd got a new, better job. Only one problem; she'd never climbed a ladder.

It was dark and dusty at the back of the stage. Myrtle led the way. 'I'm tellin' ye, they do plays here and ye see thon lights.' She pointed to the ceiling above the stage. 'Well, they need a ladder te reach them and if we can find it ye can have a wee go.'

It took four of them ten minutes to manoeuvre the ladders on to the stage. They'd have done it more quickly if they'd had a better sense of right and left and hadn't collapsed with laughter every time someone got caught in the side curtains. Then it took an age for them to stand the twelve-foot ladders upright.

Finally, Myrtle stood back and surveyed the scene.

'Right Irene, go and put these on.' She threw her a pair of trousers. Irene nipped behind a curtain and took off her skirt.

The coarse material felt strange against her legs and fastening the fly buttons was even stranger, but walking on to the stage she felt a sense of freedom, or was it confidence? Whatever it was, she needed it to face the crowd of people, who, on hearing what Irene was about to do and why, stood waiting for her to appear.

'All right, up ye go. Quick as ye can!' shouted Myrtle.

There were a few shouts of encouragement and Irene took a deep breath. She could do this. People climbed ladders every day. She gripped both sides, tested the steadiness, put a foot on the first rung, then the next and the next …

'Go on, ye can do it!'

'Keep going!'

Up and up she went, always looking at the top of the ladder, never down. She was aware of some noise, but kept moving one arm, one leg, other arm, other leg. Start again, one arm, one leg … then there were no more steps, only a flat square of wood, just right for sitting on.

Down below, people were clapping and cheering. There was Pat and Peggy, and Myrtle waving her hand in a turning motion and shouting, 'Turn round now, Irene, and come back down. Careful, turn round …'

She swung out of her seat and felt for the rung with her foot. There it was. Easy. She watched the top move further and further away. At last, her feet touched the floor and Myrtle threw her arms around her. Everyone was clapping and cheering loudly and Irene, finding herself on the stage at the end of her performance, smiled and took a bow.

From the back of the hall came Goldstein's booming voice. 'What have I missed, a trapeze artist?' He made his way to the front closely followed by Horowitz. Then he saw Irene's trousers. 'Or is it one of those Burlington Bertie impersonators? Now, let's clear the stage and get rid of the ladders.'

Minutes later everyone was sitting quietly in the hall.

'In five minutes we shall start the run-through.' Goldstein paused, and waited for two Templemore Tappers at the back to stop talking. Someone nudged them and he went on, 'These instructions are very important: everyone on in the first half will be backstage and ready. Sammy will be our compère and introduce you. Come on quickly and perform. Then you will bow and leave the stage. If anything goes wrong do not apologise, simply carry on as though nothing has happened. Then we will have the interval, when you can have something to eat and I will give notes before moving on to the second half. Five minutes, everyone!'

Sammy Reid was a good choice for compère: broad Belfast accent, plenty of jokes and he gave each act a big build-up before announcing their name. Goldstein sat a few feet from the stage and occasionally shouted out some directions to the performers.

'Louder! … Smile!'

The Goulding Sisters were the last act before the interval. 'Now, ladies and gentlemen, three girls and a piano … the lovely Golden Sisters!'

Irene hesitated and turned round to Pat mouthing the words 'Golden Sisters?' Then Peggy pushed them forward and they almost fell over each other on to the stage.

Peggy stuck to the agreed songs in the right order and their rehearsal went without a hitch. As they took their bow Goldstein stood up. 'Wonderful, wonderful, but your entrance was ragged. You have to walk on stage with purpose, looking at the audience and smiling.'

'Sorry, Mr Goldstein, it was my fault,' said Irene. 'I thought

Sammy called us the Golden Sisters.'

'You are right, he did.' Goldstein turned to Sammy who checked his copy of the running order.

'Oh sorry, should have been the Goulding Sisters, shouldn't it?'

'Maybe not,' said Goldstein, and he spoke the name softly to himself. 'Golden Sisters, I like that. It sounds right.'

'But, Mr Goldstein,' Pat began, 'it's our family name and we've been know as the Goulding Sisters since we ...'

Goldstein interrupted her. 'That's as maybe, but a name needs to send a message to the public about what to expect and I think Golden will suit you very well.' Then he turned to speak to the rest of the performers. 'That first half was adequate. No more. Let's see how good the rest of you are. Five minutes break, then I'll give the notes.'

Pat was furious. 'He's got no right to change our name like that. What will Mammy say?'

'But Golden's a better name, so it is,' snapped Peggy. 'People will remember it. Everyone gets Goulding wrong. Remember when we were at school?'

'But can't you see what he's doing? Goldstein ... Golden ... it's like we belong to him. We're not us anymore! You understand don't you, Irene?'

Irene understood that Peggy and Pat would never agree. 'I don't think we should worry about the name right now. Mammy'll be here shortly and we can talk about it then.'

Pat gave her a furious look and, picking up her music, stormed off backstage to get ready for her duet with William.

In the second half Goldstein was constantly shouting, 'Pace, pace!' The Templemore Tappers, including Myrtle, seemed under-rehearsed, lagging behind the music. The conjurer too was hesitant, fumbling a trick, giving away the fact that the string of brightly coloured handkerchiefs was not coming from the top hat, but was being clumsily pulled from his inside pocket.

'And now, ladies and gentlemen, a real treat! Belfast's answer to Jeanette MacDonald and Nelson Eddy – Miss Patricia Goulding and Mr William Kennedy!'

Pat's voice began softly, the Italian sounds echoing strangely around the Belfast church hall. She turned to look at William, remembering all of Kathleen's advice about conveying emotion in her voice. He sang in reply, at first lifting his head towards the audience, concentrating on his breathing, then looking at Pat and taking her hand. He held it while she sang, her eyes directed at the floor as though his boldness made her shy. His voice came back stronger, then hers too. Now she looked up into his eyes as their voices blended together; two distinct sounds weaving in and out. In the hall no one moved or spoke. Irene, close to the stage, watched her scarcely recognisable sister holding William Kennedy's hand and singing of her love.

Oh my God, thought Irene, can everyone see this? She looked sideways at Peggy, who sat stony-faced. Goldstein on the other hand was enthralled, but maybe it was simply the music.

The duet reached a crescendo, both voices powerful and complementing each other, and Pat and William turned to face the audience for the final moments. As the last note ended there was silence. Pat stood looking upward towards the roof, seemingly unaware of her surroundings, and then suddenly everyone began to clap and she looked startled then quickly recovered and bowed on William's cue.

'Bravo! Bravo!' shouted Goldstein, jumping to his feet. 'Now we must hear "Indian Love Call" before the finale.'

Pat and William looked at him blankly.

'You must finish with that. I gave you the sheet music, remember.'

'We're not going to sing that,' said Pat.

'What? You must sing it! It's the American Sweethearts' most famous song.'

Pat was about to repeat herself when William interrupted.

'We haven't rehearsed it properly. It's not ready to be heard yet.'

Goldstein pouted, weighing up their conflicting replies, but it was getting late and he decided to press on. 'Right, everyone on stage for the finale.'

Chapter 9

A sharp November wind cut into Irene's face as she crossed the Queen's Bridge. Around her men walked briskly, their caps pulled down, mufflers around their necks, carrying piece boxes under their arms. No doubt some, like her, were heading for the aircraft factory, but thousands more were making for the shipyard. There were hurrying women too. The office workers took care to hold their coat flaps in place to stop their skirts from blowing up, but the girls in trousers had no such trouble.

They linked arms, chatted and laughed. Irene shifted the cloth bag containing an old pair of her father's trousers over her shoulder and fell in behind them, and as she did so she said a silent prayer that, when she crossed the bridge in the opposite direction, she'd be one of them.

She rounded the corner and there it was in front of her, a long, single-storey building. The ground level was solid brick, above which were tall glass windows topped with a series of steep roofs, running like zigzag stitching against the sky into the far distance. Irene hesitated a moment, but was quickly carried along by the flow of hundreds of workers behind her. At the main entrance she was relieved to see Myrtle, cigarette in hand, waving frantically at her.

'Right, Irene,' she said as they went inside and queued for her to clock in, 'we're goin' te see James McVey. Mind, I told ye about him?'

'Aye.' Irene remembered he was in charge of hiring and sweet on Myrtle.

'I've already spoke for ye. So ye should be in with a good chance of gettin' taken on.'

James McVey was middle-aged and balding. He wore a suit that was too tight on him with shiny patches at the elbows and cuffs.

'Now then, Myrtle, this is your wee friend, is it?'

'Aye, Mr McVey, this is Irene.'

'How old are you, Irene?' He looked her up and down.

'She's twenty, same as me, Mr McVey.'

He nodded, but didn't take his eyes off Irene.

'Where'd you work before?'

'Ulster Linen Works.'

'A stitcher were you?'

'No. I painted the linen goods.'

'Oh, so you'd be good with your hands then? A delicate touch comes in very useful in an aircraft factory. Isn't that right, Myrtle?'

Myrtle blushed.

'And why would you want to work here?'

'I need the money.'

'Is that so?'

Irene nodded.

'You see thon ladder?'

Irene nodded again.

'Well, let's see you get yourself up that. Quick as you can now.'

Irene looked at Myrtle, who didn't meet her eye.

'I've my trousers in my bag. Should I go and put them on?'

'Not at all, there's no time for that. Just take your coat off. Here,' he said, moving to the base of the ladder, 'I'll hold it steady for you.'

Irene had no choice. She wasn't going home to tell Mammy she'd no job. She took a deep breath and, without hesitating, she went straight up and down the ladder, with McVey looking upwards the whole time.

'Well now, I'll tell you what I'll do. I'll give you a month's trial. General skivvying duties in the Stirling section. Myrtle'll keep an eye on you. You can go there now with her to have a look around and you can start tomorrow at seven.'

Irene followed Myrtle through the factory, which was nothing like she'd imagined. There were people working at benches, others handling huge sheets of metal and everywhere was the strange smell of what she would later learn was hot metal and solder. There were deafening sounds, too, of metal being cut, beaten and riveted into a thousand different shapes. Eventually, they arrived in one of the hangars where light flooded through the high windows on to a huge half-built structure, catching and glinting its angles.

A Stirling bomber. Irene had never seen anything more beautiful.

Peggy had a quiet morning in the shop, then just before lunchtime she made a sale – the Bush wireless. In a way she was glad to see it go. Every time she looked at it, she was reminded of Harry Ferguson. It had been a mistake to go to the Ormeau Bakery looking for him. If he'd got in touch after that, she would have told him the wireless had been returned. She might even have apologised, but now …

It was still blustery as she nipped into Robinson and Cleaver's to look at the pearl necklaces like hers for Irene and Pat to wear at the concert. At the jewellery counter she saw a string just the right length and asked the assistant how much they cost.

'Five shillings, Madam.'

'Oh, that's a wee bit more than I expected.'

'You could try Woolworths.'

Peggy was affronted. The fact that she couldn't afford them was irrelevant. How dare a shop assistant speak to her like that?

Woolworths indeed! She leaned against the heavy door and was about to push when it swung outwards. She marched out.

'I'm sorry, what did you say?' came a voice.

She was aware of someone holding the door to her left.

'Nothing!' she snapped.

'You know I could have sworn you said, "Thank you".'

There he was, smirking at her.

'Oh it's you, is it?'

'As charming as ever I see, Miss Goulding.' Harry tipped his hat.

'Shall I call you a policeman, so you can have me arrested?'

'Don't be ridiculous.'

'Oh, ridiculous is it now? It doesn't matter that I stole your wireless then?'

'You didn't steal the wireless.'

'Well, I'm glad to hear that. And there was me ready to flee the country with my ill-gotten gains.'

She began walking up Donegall Place and he fell into step beside her.

'Maybe, now that my unblemished character has been restored, you might like to come out with me one evening?'

She stopped walking and looked directly at him. That was the trouble with him. He always seemed to be mocking her. How could she tell when he was serious? Anyway, he might not have stolen the wireless, but he had been up to something that day at Carrickfergus. Something that involved a lot of money.

'I'm very busy these days,' she said.

He looked sceptical. 'Busy, is it?'

Peggy walked on. 'Aye, I'm rehearsing in the evenings for our next concert.'

'The one advertised in Goldstein's shop?'

So, he'd been past, seen the poster in the window.

'That's it. It's going to be even bigger than the last one. We've got a new company together.' He probably knew that too.

He raised his hat. 'I'll bid you good-day then.'

She watched him go. Good riddance, she thought.

When Pat came through the back door that night she noticed two things: the smell of fresh paint and Jimmy McComb, large as life, drinking tea in the kitchen. She hadn't spoken to him since their disagreement after her father's death.

Martha greeted her. 'Ah, Pat, what do you think? Young Jimmy here came round after work and painted that wall in the bathroom that looked such a mess.'

Jimmy smiled awkwardly. Pat didn't acknowledge him, but turned to her mother. 'I didn't know we'd any paint for that.'

'That's what's so good about it. Jimmy had some left over from painting his bathroom and he brought it round here for us.'

'That's very good of you, Jimmy.' Her tone was frosty.

'Well, I'll be away now, Mrs Goulding. Thanks for the tea.'

'Not at all, Jimmy. Thanks for the painting and don't forget about the concert, now.'

'I won't. Cheerio.'

When he'd gone Martha noticed the look on Pat's face.

'What's the matter with you?'

'Why have you invited him to the concert?'

'Sure he's a family friend, Daddy's apprentice.'

'Ach, Mammy, can you not see he's round here trying to get in with me. I told you about him asking me out, didn't I?'

'Pat, what's the matter with you? Jimmy's a nice boy, good family. You could do worse.'

'Look, he can paint all the walls he likes and mend as many fences,' said Pat, 'but I am not going out with Jimmy McComb and that's an end to it!'

At that moment, a hundred yards away, Irene was hurrying home when Ted Grimes in full Royal Ulster Constabulary uniform called out to her.

'Irene, a word please, if you don't mind.'

She was startled to see him, but tried not to show it. 'Hello, Mr Grimes, have you been to see Mammy?'

'No. No.' He did his usual staring into the distance and spoke over her head. 'It's you I need to speak to, Irene.'

Something in his tone sounded at once formal and sinister.

She struggled to keep her voice steady. 'What is it?'

'I'll not go round the houses. Fact is you've been seen with a wanted man, wanted on the gravest of charges. Do you understand?'

Irene thought about denying it, but what was the point, he'd clearly seen her with Sean. Then she remembered; dear God, he'd seen her kiss him! She lowered her head, her voice barely audible. 'Yes.' Her heart was thumping. He'd tell Mammy. Or he'd take her to the police station. She didn't know which was worse. But she'd done nothing wrong, had she?

'Ye realise that man is a Roman Catholic.'

'Does that matter?'

'Don't ye get clever with me, young woman!' Then his tone changed, softened. 'Now I need to know what your involvement is in this matter. Ye need to tell me everything. We'll start with how ye know him and then ye can tell me where he is now.'

'Honestly, Mr Grimes, I only know him to see. I worked next to his sister. He wanted me to tell her not to worry about him, that he'd be all right.'

His hand shot out and grabbed her arm. As he spoke he squeezed it harder and harder as if to emphasise each word.

'Only know him to see?' Squeeze. 'Ye were courtin' an' kissin' him.' Squeeze. 'A disgrace ye are.' Squeeze.

'Mr Grimes, you're hurting me. Please.'

'Please is it? I'll give ye please. He shot a policeman. You knew that and ye stood there wi' your arms round him.'

'No, he didn't. He didn't. He was just scared and ran away. And I don't know where he is now. Honestly, I don't know!'

He let go suddenly. 'Now, listen you here, I know what you've been doin', but for your mother's sake I'm goin' te say nothin' for now. But you'll keep in with the sister and find out where he is and then come an' tell me. Do ye hear?'

Irene nodded and rubbed her arm.

'And make sure ye do, or you'll get what's comin' to ye. Now get out of my sight!'

Irene hurried away, great sobs shaking her. She had to stop for a minute or two to compose herself before she went round the back of the house and in the door.

Martha was at the stove finishing off the bacon and cabbage and Sheila was setting the table when she came in.

'What's the matter with you?' asked Sheila.

'I wasn't well on the bus. I was nearly sick.'

'You're as white as a sheet, so you are.'

Martha looked her up and down. 'Away and splash some water on your face. You'll be as right as rain. This'll be ready in five minutes. Oh aye, and there's a letter for you on the mantelpiece.'

Irene did as she was told, not wanting to arouse any suspicions. A few minutes later she came back and sat at the table, just as Sheila shouted up the stairs to Pat and Peggy to come for their tea.

'There's a letter for you on the mantelpiece,' said Pat as she sat down.

Then a moment later Peggy arrived and asked, 'Did you know you've a letter?'

Irene looked at her wearily. 'Oh have I? Where would it be, do you think, on the mantelpiece maybe?'

Sheila laughed and Irene shot her a look.

It's not like Irene to snap at people, thought Martha. 'Leave her alone now,' she said. 'Can you not see she's unwell?'

The chat round the table was lively. Sheila described a bomb shelter being built close to the school. 'It's so small and dark; nobody would want to sit in there.'

Peggy told them about the expensive pearls. 'Never mind,' said Pat, 'we'll save up. Now what are we rehearsing tonight?'

Irene sat through it all without speaking and eventually, when she'd eaten enough of the bacon and cabbage so as not to upset her mother, she excused herself. 'I think I'll go up and lie down for a bit.'

'Don't forget your letter!' they chorused together and, in spite of herself, Irene smiled.

'Yes, I remember. It's on the mantelpiece, isn't it?'

It bore no stamp, only a smudged franking mark, impossible to read. She didn't recognise the handwriting and turned it over. Nothing. Inside was one page of neat script.

Dear Irene,
I hope you remember me. We met at Stranraer in the summer.

It was him, after all this time.

I'm in a city called Karachi. It's an amazing place. Teeming with people and so hot it's like standing in an oven. We only work in

118

the morning. The rest of the time we try to stay out of the sun. But yesterday, Tommy and I went for a walk and found a market. Everywhere was colour: people's clothes; the fruit and vegetables, most of them we didn't recognise; rugs and silks hanging everywhere. I hope you don't mind, but I bought something for you. It will probably arrive after this letter because it's a parcel. Will you write and tell me if you like it?
    Sandy

Irene read it again and again. He hadn't forgotten her. He'd gone to the other side of the world and thought of her. He was even sending a present – she couldn't wait! She tried to conjure up an image of him in his RAF uniform, slim, thick auburn hair, but she couldn't bring his face to mind. She remembered his eyes were brown and knew she'd liked his gentle smile, but his face wouldn't come. She put the letter under her pillow and went downstairs. In the sitting room she found Pat, Peggy and Sheila standing in their underwear and Martha handing out turquoise blouses.

'Finished the last one today. I didn't want to show them to you until I had them all done. Now get them tried on to make sure they fit. You're just in time, Irene. Are you feeling better?'

'A bit,' said Irene. 'You made four, then?'

'Aye, there was just enough material. So I did one for Sheila as well, even though she's not singing.'

'You never know,' said Sheila. 'I might be singing in the future. Isn't that right, Mammy?'

'Now we're not going over all that again, Sheila. You've your schooling to finish. There'll be plenty of time to sing after that.'

'Look at this,' said Peggy. She was standing on tiptoe looking in the mirror that hung over the fire. 'Do you see how nice the pearls are with this style and the colour? I wish we could all have them.'

Pat spoke sternly. 'Well, we can't and that's an end to it.'

Irene tried on her blouse. She loved the sweetheart neckline, the peplum and the deep cuffs. Peggy was right, the style was dramatic.

'Right, come on,' said Peggy sitting down at the piano. 'Let's get on with rehearsing. What will we start with?'

'How about Irene's mysterious letter?' said Sheila.

Irene found herself blushing. 'What?'

'What do you mean, "What"? The letter from the mantelpiece, are you not going to tell us who it was from?'

'And what it was about?' added Peggy.

'I suppose I might as well tell you,' said Irene, and she couldn't keep the smile off her face. 'You remember when I went to Stranraer in July and I told you we got talking to two RAF boys? Well, it was from one of them.'

Everyone seemed to talk at once.

'What's he called?'

'Where's he from?'

'Why's he suddenly writing now?'

Irene laughed. 'Sandy, he's from Scotland and he's been posted to India.'

'India?' said Sheila.

Peggy laughed. 'Perhaps you should be learning the "Indian Love Call" instead of Pat.'

'That's not funny,' snapped Pat.

'It is when you sing it!'

'For goodness' sake, girls, don't start all that again. Peggy, you know how Pat feels about having to sing that song. Don't rub it in.' She turned to Irene, who knew what was coming. 'What do you know about this airman, besides his name, nationality and present posting?'

'His rank and serial number?' whispered Peggy.

Martha glared at her.

'Nothing really,' admitted Irene. She was going to say his smile was nice, then thought better of it, and added, 'He's sending me a present.'

'Bless us,' said Martha, 'a present! Well, I suppose he's harmless enough … in India.'

It was easy for Irene to sneak out of the house half an hour earlier than usual the following morning for her first day at Short and Harland. She could hear her mother snoring gently as she crept downstairs and knew she wouldn't rise until eight to make a quick breakfast for Peggy and Sheila. She left the door on the snib knowing Pat would close it properly when she left at their normal time. She had decided not to tell her mother about her new employment. Sacking was a disgrace in Martha's eyes and working in a factory was a long way from the refined occupation of painting linen. Pat knew, of course, and would have nothing to do with deceiving their mother.

'It's underhand, Irene. I hate lying.'

'You're not lying. You're just not telling her. It's different.'

'Not in my book it isn't. What if she asks me something about you at work?'

'She won't. Why would she?'

'Well, if she does, I'm not making anything up.'

Myrtle met her at the gate as before and showed her how to find her card and clock in. 'Have ye your trousers and scarf in your bag?' she asked.

'Aye, I didn't want to risk anyone seeing me in them,' said Irene, then added quickly, 'not yet anyway.' There was just time to get changed in the toilets. Myrtle took the scarf from her and folded the square into a triangle.

'Bend your head over' – Irene looked puzzled – 'so your hair falls forward.' She demonstrated. Irene did as she was shown and Myrtle took both ends of the triangle and tied them at the front, tucked Irene's hair neatly in the pocket made, and drew the final point of the triangle up to meet the tied ends. Then, with a few deft touches, she tucked in the whole lot.

As instructed by Mr McVey, Myrtle took Irene to number four hangar and left her with the foreman. He looked her up and down.

'I hope you're quick on your feet and nimble with your hands, Missy, or you'll not last long!' Irene said nothing and he went on, 'I'll start you off counting rivets. Follow me.' He led her to a bench with a high stool. Stacked high along the lefthand side were dozens of small tins; on the right, a box full of metal rivets each half the size of a farthing.

'Fill every tin with twenty-four rivets, get the lid on tight and put them on the cart behind you. You'll need to get a move on: all tins to be full in one hour and exactly twenty-four a tin, mind.'

With that he was gone, striding the length of the hangar, shouting as he went, 'Right, lads, get stuck in, it's a long time 'til tea break.'

Easy enough, thought Irene, as she reached into the box and counted one at a time. In five minutes she'd filled five boxes. A quick bit of multiplication told her she'd be less than halfway through in an hour. There must be a quicker way. She tried two at a time, still too slow. Then six lots of four. Eventually, she threw a pile of rivets on the bench and separated out four lots of six at a time, held the tin to the edge of the bench and swept them in. She finished the last tin as the foreman reappeared.

'Good enough, good enough,' he said. 'Now, away you go with the cart and see every riveter gets two tins and collect any empty ones and bring them back.'

'Then do I fill them again?'

'Oh don't you be getting ahead of yourself, Missy! Next duty is to sweep the floor. Cleanliness is next to godliness in the work place. That's my motto.'

The hangar was the length of Joanmount Gardens and twice as wide. The brush was huge and difficult to manoeuvre; she was also given a scraper to remove the bits of solder. Irene was exhausted by the time she finished and her back ached from the frequent bending. Once, she narrowly missed being burnt when a large drop of liquid solder splashed on the floor next to her. By the time the hooter sounded for tea break, she felt she'd already done a full day's work.

In the canteen, Irene queued for tea and bread and jam then joined Myrtle, who was sitting with a group of women.

'This is Irene, she just started today.'

An older woman, with a faded green turban and a cast in her eye, asked, 'Are you skivvyin', love?'

'Well, I've been counting rivets and sweeping the floor so far.'

'Then you're bloody skivvyin' and you'll know the worst of it when you go back to collect the bloody shavins before your dinner, then do the whole friggin' lot again 'til clockin' off time.'

Irene hid her surprise at the woman swearing and laughed with everyone else. Within minutes the hooter went and she took a quick bite, gulped down a mouthful of tea and followed the rest of the workers back to hangar four.

'Missy!' The foreman was waiting for her. 'You've to take yourself away to the tool shop and tell them I sent you for the long weight. Mind, don't you come back without it.'

The tool shop was at the far end of the factory. When Irene told the man who came to the counter what she'd come for, he said, 'Sit yourself down there and I'll see you get one.' Then he disappeared behind the racks of shelves that stretched far into the echoing space beyond. Irene watched the grey sky through a high window above her and, as she waited, clouds of darker grey scudded past. Occasionally, through a break in the clouds, a shaft of sunlight fell on the worn oilcloth at her feet. Once the man put his head round the shelves and said, 'Are you still waiting?' But he was gone before she could ask how much longer. Then the door opened and a girl came in, wearing a red turban with green leaves.

'Hello, you're new aren't you?'

'Aye, I just started today.'

'So, have you been waiting here long?'

'Well, it seems like ages' – Irene shrugged her shoulders – 'but the foreman said I wasn't to come back without it.'

'Without what?' Red Turban raised a questioning eyebrow.

Pause. Understanding spread across Irene's face and she nodded. 'I suppose they do that to all the new workers?'

'Only if they can get away with it.'

Irene had no problem seeing a joke, even if it was on her.

Besides, chances were she'd escaped the 'bloody shavins' because dinner time couldn't be far off. The foreman hailed her as she returned and Irene could sense those in the know looking at her, expecting some reaction. The more annoyed or embarrassed she was, the more amusement there would be, no doubt. Well, she'd show them neither.

'Did you get the long weight, then?' The foreman grinned.

'No, I didn't,' said Irene looking him in the eye. 'They'd none left, but it's all right: the storeman said I'd be welcome to come back every day until they got one in.' Irene paused and looked around her. 'But tomorrow I'll bring myself a book to pass the time while I'm waiting.'

Just then the hooter went for dinner.

Irene had no need to recount the story of the long weight to the other women. Red Turban was just finishing the tale when she sat down. 'Good on you, girl!' said the faded green turban. 'He deserved taking down a peg or two.'

Irene wasn't so sure. 'I'd better keep my head down, or I'll not make it to that pay packet at the end of the week.'

'What pay packet's this? Don't you know you have to work a week in hand?'

'You mean I won't have a wage for a fortnight?' Irene was dismayed. 'What am I supposed to live on?'

'Maybe your family could help ye out,' suggested Myrtle.

'Your ma would understand, wouldn't she?'

'I don't think so.' Irene was beginning to panic. 'I still haven't told her I've left my other job.'

The women fell silent, each understanding how tight money was. How they too had struggled with the week-in-hand rule.

The foreman was waiting for her when she returned from dinner. 'You've a lot of catching up to do, Missy. Take the cart round now and collect the metal shavins. Up the ladders, quick as you can, carry down the bags of shavins and empty them into the cart.'

Irene looked down the length of the hangar. People had been running up and down the ladders all morning. Now it was her turn. They were higher than the one Mr McVey had asked her to climb and much steeper than the one in the theatre. The foreman read the look on her face.

'Not afeared of heights, are you? Or you're no good to me.'

One ladder was much like another, thought Irene, climb one and you can climb them all.

'Mind the shavins, them's sharp, Missy,' the foreman shouted.

She was aware of him watching her, no time to hesitate.

Foot on to the first rung, a moment to test its steadiness then she was off. Hands and feet synchronised, a steady climb. The top was tricky; she'd never had to climb off a ladder before. She leaned forward and eased herself over the lip of the cabin door and scrambled on all fours inside. She looked down at the foreman and a few other workers who stood looking up, no doubt hoping for a bit of sport. She gave them a wave and disappeared into the fuselage in search of 'bloody shavins'.

She worked her way up the length of the plane. The shavins were slivers of metal trimmed from the welded joints that collected at the feet of the workers. Some of the men, seeing a new face, stopped for a moment to ask her name, or tried a bit of banter. Her bag was about half full when she noticed a piece of metal caught in the space between two spars. She reached for it and pulled. It was stuck fast and her hand slid up the length of the sharp metal. She let out a cry and watched as one red globule of blood after another appeared in a line across her palm. She felt a lightness in her head and sat down quickly, cradling her hand in her lap. The man nearest to her called for a first aid kit and seconds later one appeared.

'Looks like a clean cut; not so deep. I don't think you've damaged anything.' He raised her hand, placed a pad of cotton wool over the wound then bandaged it tightly. All the time he spoke to her in a soft voice. 'Don't worry, love. You'll be all right. It's Irene, isn't it?' She nodded. 'We'll need to take you to the first aid post. There's a nurse there will sort you out.' He got her up on her feet. 'You can lean on me.' But before her head reached his shoulder, black spots appeared before her eyes and her knees buckled.

'Irene ... Irene ... listen. I'm going to carry you down. Just stay completely still.' And, with that, he swung her over his shoulder in a fireman's lift. She closed her eyes tightly and endured the weird sensation of descending head first, holding her hand in the air, bouncing all the way. Back on the ground he set her upright and Irene opened her eyes to see the foreman scowling at her.

'Well, we didn't get much work out of you the day, did we?'

Then Myrtle arrived. 'My God, Irene, what happened?'

'The shavins, Myrtle, the bloody shavins!' she replied.

Chapter 10

'You'll have to tell Mammy now, Irene.'

'No, why should I?'

'Don't be daft. You've a cut hand that's still dripping blood, for one. And number two, you've no wages coming for a fortnight.'

Irene had met Pat as she got off the bus outside Deerpark post office, to walk home with her as though they'd been to work together. If she had expected some sympathy from Pat as a result of her injury, she was mistaken.

'I'm going to say I cut it on a packing case; you know how Mr Briggs sometimes asked us to unpack deliveries of paint when he couldn't be bothered.'

'Irene, I'm not lying to Mammy! And even if she believes you about the hand, what idea have you to explain the lack of wages? Tell me that!'

'I don't know.' Irene was close to tears. It had been an awful day and in a few minutes it could get a great deal worse.

The smell of onions frying greeted them as they came through the back door. Martha was removing a piece of raw liver from a shallow dish of pink milk. She didn't look up, intent as she was on transferring it to the pan without drips.

Sheila was setting the table and greeted them excitedly.

'Irene, you'll never guess what! Wait here.' She threw the cutlery in a heap and ran into the sitting room, returning in seconds with a parcel. 'Your present from India. It must be.' She thrust it into Irene's hands. 'Open it, open it!'

The brown paper was thick and crumpled as though it had been handled many times. The string was rough and fraying, held together with misshapen blobs of sealing wax at its knots.

Irene held it, as if the parcel itself was the gift to be explored and marvelled at. And indeed it was, for she had never before received a parcel of her own. But there, as if to prove its validity, was her name in capitals across the brown paper, weaving in and out of the string.

Martha broke the silence. 'What have you done to your hand?'

'Oh … I don't know … I think I cut it at work emptying some packing cases.'

'What do you mean "you think"? Don't you know what happened?' Irene had turned away and was trying to open the parcel.

'Pat, did you see what happened to her hand?'

A moment's hesitation. 'No. No, I didn't. I wasn't there.'

'Come on, Irene,' cried Sheila. 'Open it. Let's see what's in it!'

'Don't do that!' shouted Martha, momentarily distracted by the sound of ripping. 'We'll need to save the paper and string.'

She took the parcel from Irene and carefully worked the knots loose, only handing it back for the paper to be removed to reveal the gift. The moment had passed, the hand was forgotten and Irene breathed a sigh of relief.

First there was the colour which drew gasps. Blazing like an orange split open to glisten in bright sunlight. Irene touched it.

'It's so soft. What is it, silk?'

'Let me feel,' said Martha. 'Aye, it's silk all right. Just like your Aunt Anna's favourite scarf, only this is finer, softer.'

'Indian silk, then,' said Pat, as though she knew.

Irene stood up with the end of the silk in her hands and walked backwards as Martha began to unwind the bolt of cloth revealing a border of silver embroidery. Irene reached the end of the room and Pat took up the cloth and followed in Irene's footsteps. Meanwhile

Irene walked round to the far side of the table. Sheila took up the next unwinding following Pat, who followed Irene as she circled the table. Eventually all the silk was revealed winding from sister to sister like a broad, bright ribbon around the Belfast kitchen; an exotic visitor, brightening their lives. No one spoke. The clock on the mantelpiece ticked. The liver sizzled gently in the pan.

The back door opened and Peggy came wearily into the kitchen. 'What's going on? What's all this?' A wave at the silk.

'It's Irene's present from India,' Sheila said excitedly.

'Oh, very nice, I'm sure,' said Peggy, making her way around the outside of the silk circle.

'Is that all you can say?' asked Sheila.

'No it's not,' said Peggy. 'I'd also like to say, what on earth is it? And where's my tea?'

The spell had been broken. Martha turned her attention to the liver. 'Right let's get all this put away and the table set. Tea'll be ready in five minutes.'

Around the table, talk of the silk continued. 'What will you do with it, Irene?' asked Pat.

'I don't know. Keep it, I suppose, and look at it now and again.'

'It's a lovely thing, right enough, but neither use nor ornament, if you ask me,' said Martha.

'I wonder what he thought you'd do with it,' said Sheila. It was the first time the sender had been mentioned.

Peggy said bluntly, 'I wonder why he sent it. I mean, to someone he only met for a few hours.' All eyes turned to Irene.

Only she could answer that. The truth was that she was as mystified as the rest of them. She'd been surprised when he mentioned a gift in his letter and now that she had received it ... What she did know that they didn't, was that the gift was not all that had been in the wrapping paper. In her pocket was an envelope that had been folded into the first section she unwrapped. She had put it away quickly when all eyes were on the silk and was saving it to read when she was alone.

Pat leaned back in her chair and folded her arms. 'I've a notion what it is.' They stared at her. 'What it's used for, I mean.' They waited. 'In India that is ...'

128

Sheila could contain herself no longer. 'What, Pat. What is it?'

But she would only say, 'After we've washed the dishes, we'll have a little experiment.'

Pat took charge of the second unwinding of the silk. 'Draw the curtains, Sheila. Now, Irene, move away from the fire and you'd best take your jumper off.' Then she took up the first yard's worth and, wrapping it in half lengthwise, she draped it across Irene's left shoulder. 'Right Sheila, you get hold of the rest of the material and follow me, feeding it out as I need it.'

Pat proceeded to walk clockwise round Irene, winding the silk as she went, until Irene was wrapped like an Egyptian mummy in orange and silver.

'Now this is the tricky bit,' said Pat. 'There's something that happens with the arm ...' She hung the remaining material over the crook of Irene's arm. 'There you are! I think it's called a sari. Now you're dressed like an Indian woman.'

'Not quite,' said Peggy. 'Get me some warm water in a bowl, Sheila.' Peggy took a comb from her bag and dipped it in the water, smoothing down and slicking back Irene's dark hair.

Then she pulled it into a tight bun at the nape of her neck and fastened it with some clips.

'Well, I never saw the like!' said Martha.

'How did you know what it was?' asked Sheila.

'Saw it in a film once,' said Pat.

'*Elephant Boy*,' added Peggy.

'I'm going upstairs to look at myself in the mirror,' said Irene. 'That's if I can climb the stairs.'

'Then we'll need to get rehearsing,' said Peggy pulling out the piano stool. 'It's less than two weeks to the concert, don't forget.'

Upstairs, Irene carefully removed the sari and folded it in yard lengths, then held it to her face and breathed deeply. When the parcel was first opened she'd been aware of a faint smell.

None of the others appeared to notice, but now it seemed the warmth of her body had drawn out a lovely but unfamiliar scent, one that would forever remind her of her silk sari, a faraway land and an airman whose face she could not quite bring to mind.

There was a soft knock on the bedroom door and Sheila came in.

'Peggy says to hurry up.'

'Well that's rich coming from her!'

'And I've got this for you.' Sheila held out an envelope and Irene immediately recognised the Free State stamp. 'I answered the door to the postman when he delivered the sari and he gave me this as well. I thought … I don't know … maybe you might not want Mammy to see it.'

'Will you two get a move on!' Peggy shouted from the bottom of the stairs.

Irene took the letter. 'Thanks, Sheila. You did the right thing.'

They rehearsed the three songs: 'Stormy Weather', 'Pick Yourself Up' and 'I'll Take Romance'. Then Peggy insisted they try a new song. Goldstein had given her the sheet music and she'd practised it a few times in the shop when there were no customers. 'Tuxedo Junction' was a simple enough song and Peggy was comfortable playing it. Pat successfully followed the music, but it was difficult to work out the three-part harmony.

Martha listened to several attempts, but it was clear to her that it didn't work. It was getting late. Maybe tomorrow it would come. In the room she shared with Pat, Irene waited until her sister had fallen asleep then crept downstairs in her dressing gown, the two letters in her pocket. Which to read first? Sean's letter, for it must surely be from him – she knew no one else over the border – or Sandy's letter accompanying the beautiful sari? Sean's was probably the most urgent and short. Sandy's was to be savoured like his gift. She ripped open the envelope, and found a hastily scribbled note inside.

Tell Theresa I'm fine. I'm on the hill overlooking the Atlantic as I write this. She'll know the place. Tell her not to write. It's better that way.

Simple, then: she had only to memorise the message and find Theresa in a bar on Northumberland Street, maybe tomorrow night after work. Sandy's letter was longer: the script was carefully formed as though this was a fair copy and, like his speech, there were no wasted words.

Dear Irene,
I wanted to send you a gift that would be like sending a piece of India …

'Well, I didn't expect to see you the day, Missy.' The foreman was standing at the entrance to hangar four watching the workers arrive. 'Made of sterner stuff than I gave you credit for.'

'The nurse said yesterday I'd be all right to work, but I've to see her at tea break and she'll have a look at my hand and maybe put another bandage on it.' Irene knew if she hadn't shown up for work today she'd not even get to complete the month's trial she'd been promised and she certainly wasn't going to tell him that her fingers were stiff and aching. Luckily the cut was on her left hand so she was able to manage the rivets with her right.

The sweeping was a bit more difficult, but she gritted her teeth and got it done. Later, when she collected the shavins, the men teased her a little.

'Have ye rung fer the ambulance yet, Dave?'

'He's been on standby all mornin', Joe.'

'Hey, Dave, why're they called bloody shavins?'

'Cause that's their colour when some people's finished with 'em.'

Irene sought out her rescuer who was welding at the far end of the plane. 'Hello,' she said.

He turned off the blowtorch. 'Hello. How's the hand?'

Irene showed her bandage. 'Still there, I think.'

He nodded towards the cabin door. 'You can manage the ladders then?'

'Oh aye, couldn't have done yesterday, mind you, so thanks for what you did; carrying me down.'

'Ach, that's all right. It's not the first time I've carried someone down a ladder. I used to be a fireman, but you were one of the lighter ones!' He held out his hand. 'I'm Robert.'

She shook it. 'I'm Irene.'

'Yes, I know.'

'How?'

'Myrtle.'

Irene laughed. 'Of course, everyone knows Myrtle.'

'You're new on hangar four then?'

'I'm new to Shorts. They've given me a month's trial.'

'So how's it goin' so far?'

'Oh great, yesterday was my first day. I did two hours' work, gave cheek to the foreman and went home two hours early with a cut hand that stopped all work in the hangar, while the workers had a good laugh watching me being carried head first down a ladder!'

Robert threw back his head and laughed. 'Well, sounds like a good start to me!'

'I'd better get on with my work, if I'm to last the day. Thanks again.'

'Anytime you need a fireman's lift …'

The Short and Harland nurse was a large bustling no-nonsense woman. Her green serge uniform was stretched tightly across her ample bust and the white apron, which strained with every movement, was held in place with a large safety pin on one corner and an upside-down watch on the other.

'There's a lot of dried blood under this bandage, but it'll need to come off. We'll try it the easy way first.' She filled a basin with hot water and nodded in its direction. Irene gingerly put her fingers in and quickly withdrew them.

'Good heavens, what's the matter with you, girl. Get it in there!' she said, as she plunged Irene's hand into the boiling hot water and held it there. Irene cried out in pain and the basin turned red. After a minute the nurse withdrew Irene's hand. It was clear that most of the bandage had loosened, but in one place it was still clinging. In one swift movement the nurse ripped the rest of it off and Irene screamed again. It was even worse when the nurse wiped it with iodine.

Her hand continued to throb for the rest of the day and it was clear that some fresh blood was seeping through the new bandage the nurse had applied. The long afternoon dragged by and, knowing the foreman was watching her closely, she tried to ignore the pain and worked with all the enthusiasm she could muster.

At the end of the day, she desperately wanted to go straight home to bed, but she had asked Pat to tell her mother she was going to a friend's house for her tea. That would give her a couple of hours to get to Northumberland Street, find Theresa and deliver Sean's message.

Night was falling as she crossed the city centre, but as she went north along Divis Street she was amazed to see lights blazing in some shops and houses in defiance of the blackout.

The people she passed looked much the same as those elsewhere in the city. A mother came towards her with four children piled in a dilapidated pram. 'Haud yer wheesht,' she chided the snivelling boy who, too old to ride in the pram, ran alongside holding the handle. The mother's coat was thin and offered little protection against the sharp wind whipping up the hill. A cotton headscarf framed her thin, gaunt face. She was probably no older than twenty-five, but was stooped and aged beyond her years. Here, too, young men stood on street corners, hands in pockets.

'What about ye, love!' one shouted as she passed.

'Ye not stapping fer a wee chat the night, then?' from another.

Anything to get her to look, but she hurried on. Two girls stood outside a sweet shop with their backs to her, gazing at the pile of Yellowman, no doubt wishing they had a farthing.

'Excuse me,' said Irene. They turned slowly, half an eye still on the sweeties. 'Do you know where Northumberland Street is?'

'Aye missus, sure that's it there, the next road.'

There was a public house on the corner; she'd try there. It took a moment for her to adjust to the dark interior and the smell of beer, stale cigarette smoke and the lingering stench of men whose only chance of a good wash was an occasional trip to the local baths. She was conscious of a few men in the corners and a couple standing at the far end of the bar. She knew all eyes were on her, but the barman, who was polishing a glass, didn't look up.

She stood in front of him and waited. He held the glass to the light and said without looking at her, 'The lounge bar's next door. It's men only in here.' He reached up and put the glass on the shelf.

'I don't want a drink,' said Irene. 'I'm looking for someone.'

'Missus, if one a these uns is your man, you're welcome to him, fer there's none of them has the price of a glass of stout.'

'I'm looking for Theresa O'Hara.'

'Don't know her.'

'She told me she was going to work for her uncle who worked in a bar round here.'

'Don't know him neither.'

The smell was making Irene feel nauseous and her hand was aching again.

'Look, it's really important I speak to her. Do you know Theresa?'

'And who are you exactly?' he demanded.

'I'm Irene Goulding.'

'That doesn't sound like an Irish name.' Irene was confused; was he making fun of her? 'How do you know Theresa O'Hara?'

'I worked with her at the Ulster Linen Works,' she said, adding, 'and her brother, Sean.'

He leant across the bar, his face so close to hers she could smell his foul breath. 'What do you know about Sean?'

Irene's head, already throbbing, began to spin and she felt the bile rise from her stomach. The bar was fast disappearing into the encroaching blackness – only the man's threatening face was left.

'I know where he is,' she whispered and slumped on to the rush matting on the floor.

'I'll wait 'til ten, then get my coat on me and go looking,' said Martha. She was standing at the window watching the street as she had been, on and off, since eight o'clock.

'Mammy, she's probably missed the bus and she'd have to wait a while for the next one at this time of night,' said Sheila.

'She might have decided to stay the night at her friend's,' said Peggy, who had been restless all evening, demanding to know why Irene had gone off gallivanting instead of staying in to rehearse.

'Ach away on with you, Irene wouldn't do that when we're expecting her home,' said Martha, without turning from the window.

'Mammy, come and sit down, you're getting yourself in a state standing there,' said Pat.

'Who did you say this friend was?'

'Her name's Theresa. She and Irene used to sit next to each other at work.'

'Used to?'

'Aye well, Theresa left last week.' Pat looked uncomfortable.

'Theresa? Is that that wee Catholic girl she went to Stranraer with?' Martha had turned away from the window, suddenly aware of possibilities she hadn't previously considered. 'So, where does she live?'

'I don't know,' said Pat, wary of where the conversation could lead.

'Somewhere up the Falls, wasn't it?' Martha held her breath.

'Aye, somewhere round there, but she'll come to no more harm there than she would up the Shankill. You know that.'

'Given the choice I'd rather she wasn't either place, but home in her bed!' With that, Martha went and got her coat and headscarf. 'I'll walk down as far as Cliftonville Circus. It's better than standing here doing nothing.'

'What the hell did ye bring her down to the cellar for?'

'For Christ's sake, she knows where Sean is and I've never seen her before in my life.' The barman's voice betrayed his nervousness, 'Sure she fainted on my floor, out cold. What was I to do? Ring for an ambulance to take her away?'

Irene felt the hard cold floor beneath her and was aware of the strong smell of beer mixed with damp. She tried to raise her head, but the world tilted and fell away again. Her mouth was so dry her tongue stuck to the roof of her mouth, her eyes so heavy they had to close.

Martha waited in the doorway of Carson's Butchers from where she could see any passing bus, but only one had come by and that was empty. Late on a cold November night, it seemed wise people were at home by their own firesides. A few shadowy figures passed, but none of them had the build or gait of her eldest daughter. A dog howled over towards the Waterworks and was answered by another close by. A figure emerged out of the darkness, unmistakable. Pat had come to find her.

'Is she home? Did I miss her?' The words tumbled out in a rush of hope.

'No, Mammy. She's not come home. Peggy and Sheila have gone to bed, it's after eleven. Should you not come home and wait?'

'Where is she, Pat? It's not like her. Something's happened. I know it!'

'Mammy, there's something …'

Martha wasn't listening. She turned to Pat, her eyes bright with sudden hope. 'Ted Grimes. He'll find her for us. Sure isn't he in the RUC?' She began to walk quickly in the direction of his house.

'Mammy, what can he do?' Pat shouted after her. 'She'll be home soon. I'm sure of it.'

'Well, you away on home then and wait for her. Me, I'm going to find her!'

'What did you say her name was?'

'God, Michael, I don't know! Irene somebody, I think.'

'Don't ever think of applyin' for the intelligence unit. You'll never pass the entrance exam.'

Michael Todd, sergeant in the 2nd Belfast Brigade of the Irish Republican Army, knelt down beside Irene and shook her roughly by the shoulders. 'Irene, Irene, wake up! D'ye hear me?'

Irene gave a low moan, then muttered some slurred lyrics of 'Stormy Weather' before whispering something that sounded like 'bloody shavins, Myrtle … brown paper and sealing wax'.

He put his hand to her forehead. 'She's running a fever; we'll get no sense out of her.'

'Why don't we just dump her out on the street, like she's never been here? Somebody'd call an ambulance.'

'Aye, then in her next ramblings she mentions Sean's name! We can't risk it.' He stood up. 'Where are they? They should be here by

136

now. Go and see if there's any news. Then bring some cold water and a cloth. We'll try and bring her temperature down.'

Ted Grimes had come off duty at ten and Vera had left his dinner on a low light as usual. She was fast asleep and snoring by the time he turned his key in the lock. He took off his tunic and hung it behind the kitchen door. Then he undid his collar studs front and back and removed the stiff white collar, which had been annoying the boil on the back of his neck all day, and set it on the dresser. The dinner of bacon, cabbage and fried potato was just as he liked it, crisp around the edges, and the buttermilk he fetched from the pantry was cool to wash it all down.

He had just let out a huge belch when there was a pounding on the front door. He knew Vera wouldn't wake and he was in no hurry to answer it. Instead, he remembered his training.

Turning out the light, he took his revolver from its holster, cocked it and moved silently to the back door. Outside he looked from right to left. Then silently, gun at the ready, he crept around the side of the house. He crouched low and peered through the darkness at the small figure already lifting her hand to pound the door again.

'A strong sweet cup of tea, that's what you need.' Ted Grimes couldn't believe his luck; a distressed Martha Goulding in his back kitchen close to midnight. He'd played the strong supportive friend, arm around her shoulders, leading her round the back. Once inside, he had the coat off her and persuaded her to sit close to the fire.

'Gone missing, ye say?' He took control. 'Now, Martha, when did you last see her? Who's this friend she went to see? Falls Road, ye say?'

Martha was flushed; heat was rising from deep inside her.

'Something's happened to her, Ted, I know it.' She looked up at him, tears in her eyes – one blink and they'd fall. 'Help me find her.'

'Martha, I already have some information about Irene's friend and her family through, let me say ...' he cleared his throat, '... official sources.'

'You have?'

He sat down at the opposite side of the fender, facing her.

His expression was the one he used to break bad news to relatives. 'Theresa O'Hara and her family are well known IRA sympathisers. Father's in the Crumlin Road jail and the brother fled the city after the young policeman was shot.'

'Dear God,' whispered Martha. 'But Irene only went there for her tea. Why would she not come home?'

'It pains me to say this, but Irene also had' – more clearing of the throat, – 'an affiliation with the brother.'

'A what?' Martha stood up. 'An affiliation!' She spat out the word. 'What are you saying? My daughter's run off in the middle of the night with some Catholic boy accused of murdering a policeman!'

Ted realised he'd made a tactical error. 'No, no, Martha, I'm not saying that. It's just that she knew him too, because he worked at the mill.'

'Affiliation, indeed!' Martha refused to be placated. 'She wouldn't just take herself off. I've not brought up my girls like that!'

'I know that, Martha. I'm only saying ...'

'Something's happened. She's had an accident, that's it. Knocked down maybe and ended up in hospital.'

'In that case the police would have been informed and asked to contact the relatives.'

Martha's thoughts rushed ahead. 'She's unconscious; can't tell them where she lives. Now what you need to do, Ted, is check the hospitals. You'll have the contacts, I know. The Mater and the Royal would be the best bet.'

This wasn't what he had envisaged when Martha showed up on his doorstep not ten minutes before. He meant to take control, have her in his debt.

'Now you sort that out and I'll go back home. Come and let me know when you've found her.' She raced on. 'And get the address of the O'Haras while you're at it, in case she's not in hospital. That's where I'll go next.' She grabbed her coat. 'Right, Ted, get cracking; quick as you can, now.'

'Irene, Irene, wake up.'

Irene's eyes flickered and opened briefly.

'It's Theresa. Wake up … please.'

'Theresa?' Irene tried to focus on the face above her. The smell told her she was still in the public house and now her hand was throbbing to the same beat as her head. 'Theresa … you're here.'

'Yes, I'm here. You were looking for me?'

'Am I still in the bar?'

'Yes, downstairs. You fainted … they took you down here where it's cool.'

'I needed to find you. There's a message from Sean.' Irene was suddenly very thirsty. 'Can I have a drink of water?'

Theresa nodded to the barman. 'Yes, there's one coming.'

'There were two men shouting.' Irene remembered. 'Then I felt ill …'

'Don't worry about that now, Irene, tell me about Sean.'

The water arrived and Irene gulped it down. 'What did Sean say?'

Irene was wide awake suddenly and her mind seemed to clear. 'He sent me a letter … said to tell you he's fine.'

'Did he say where he was?'

'Yes, he did. He sent me a parcel too.'

'A parcel? Where is he, Irene? Tell me.'

'Orange … silk … for me to wear …' Michael Todd moved closer. 'You drape it over your shoulder.'

'A sash?' the barman whispered and Michael shrugged his shoulders.

'But where's Sean, Irene? Do you know?'

'Oh yes.' Irene's eyes stared into the distance. 'The sky is the brightest blue; the sun a huge yellow orb, burning his back through his uniform. The market is busy with all the merchants pressing their wares into his hands: silver jewellery; glistening oranges; sweet tea, even rugs from faraway Persia …'

'My God, where is he?' asked the barman.

'Don't be stupid! Can't you see she's rambling?' said Michael scornfully. 'Trouble is we've no way of knowing where the grains of truth are amongst all this storybook nonsense.'

'Well, you'd better make up your mind what to do. We can't keep her here any longer.' Theresa was holding Irene's hand and the bandage was coming away seeped in yellow, foul-smelling pus.

'We can't let her go and risk her telling someone where Sean is,' argued Michael.

'You can't keep her here and let her die!' shouted Theresa.

No answer.

'For God's sake, Michael, she didn't tell anyone the first time Sean sent us a message to say he was in Donegal. I've told you, she's a good friend. She even got the sack sticking up for me. Why would she betray us now?'

'Maybe she wouldn't deliberately, but you've heard her rambling. She could say enough for someone to put two and two together.'

'Who, for instance? Do you think a nurse or a doctor will be standing around trying to piece together a load of nonsense in the hope it might lead them to the dangerous Sean O'Hara? Or might they be more interested in saving a girl's life?'

'I can't be sure what'll happen. I won't be there!'

'No, but I could be. Think, Michael, she came to visit me, she felt ill, I took her down to the Royal. Like a good friend, I'd want to stay with her, wouldn't I now?'

Michael stared at Irene's pale and sweating face.

'Come on, Michael. Sean trusted her; he liked her.'

'It's up to you, Theresa, he's your brother. But none of this must come back to me, the bar, or the brigade. Do you understand?'

Martha went straight to the foot of the stairs and shouted, 'Pat, come down here this minute!'

Sheila appeared first in the kitchen as Martha was attempting to poke the fire back to life. 'Away you upstairs and tell Pat she's to be down here in two minutes. Then get yourself back to bed.'

'But what about Irene, have you found her yet?'

'Nearly ... now do as you're bid and tell Pat she's wanted.'

Martha put half a shovel of slack on the embers; it might be a long night. Pat appeared at the door in her brown felt dressing gown. It was clear she'd been crying.

'Now, my girl, you sit yourself down and we'll have the truth this time – none of your blarney.'

'Mammy, honest to goodness, I haven't told any lies about Irene.'

'Aye, well that's as maybe, but you haven't told the truth either. So this wee girl Irene went to see is Theresa O'Hara. Now, you tell me about her brother and what he has to do with our Irene.'

'Sean? I know who he is. He used to work at the mill, but he's nothing to do with Irene.' Martha raised an eyebrow and Pat went on, 'Look, all I know is he disappeared the night his father was interned, same night the policeman was shot.'

'Ted Grimes seems to think Irene had some sort of an affiliation with him.'

'Affiliation? What does that mean?'

Martha looked embarrassed. 'He implied she was ... carrying on with him.'

'Away on, she was not. Sure I'd have known!'

'Are you telling me the truth now, Pat?'

'I am, Mammy.' Pat looked away. 'Well, I am about Sean ...'

There was a rapping at the window and the back door opened. It was Ted Grimes, now in full uniform. Martha paled and stood up.

'We've found her, I think.'

Martha stifled a sob and closed her eyes as if in prayer.

'Is she all right?' asked Pat quickly.

'Well, she is, but ...'

'But ...'

'She has blood poisoning. She's unconscious.'

For all Ted Grimes' fussing about his contacts and the RUC interest in what had happened to Irene, no one at the Royal seemed to be expecting them. A nurse was dispatched to find out where the unidentified patient was and Martha and Pat were left in the waiting room with their RUC escort. The early morning sun was just beginning to cast long shadows through the high windows as they sat on the hard wooden chairs.

Eventually, the nurse returned with the news that the patient had been transferred to a surgical ward, but they could see her immediately to confirm her identity. They followed the nurse along a deserted corridor, where the smell of carbolic clung to every surface, and up a concrete staircase on which their footsteps echoed.

The stillness of illness had settled through the night and lingered on in the ward. The matron was at her desk and stood as they entered, but her eyes moved beyond Martha and Pat to the uniform behind. 'I'm sorry, close family only permitted.'

'I'm here in an official capacity,' said Ted.

'Official or not, I cannot permit you to see the patient. You must wait outside.'

She nodded to Martha and Pat and they followed her, treading softly, scarcely breathing, past curtained beds to the far right-hand side of the ward.

Irene lay completely still and from her arm a drip snaked upwards to a bottle of clear fluid. Her eyes were closed, her face pale, her hand heavily bandaged.

The matron turned to Martha, who nodded her head. 'Yes, it's my daughter, Irene.'

Martha and Pat sat either side of the bed. 'It's that cut hand she got unpacking the cases that's the cause of this,' Martha said angrily. 'I've a good mind to go down to the Ulster Linen Works and tell them what it's done to Irene.'

'You can't do that, Mammy.'

'We'll see about that!'

'No, you can't …'

'But they're responsible.'

'No they're not,' said Pat. 'Short and Harland are to blame.'

'What are you talking about, Short and Harland?'

'I've tried to tell you, Mammy, Irene left the mill. She's been working at Shorts since Monday. That's where she cut her hand.'

'What?' Martha was dumbfounded. 'What are you talking about?

Irene at Shorts! Why wasn't I told this?' Martha's voice was rising. 'You've got some explaining to do, my girl, and you can start with why she left a perfectly good job.'

'She didn't leave, Mammy, she was sacked.'

'Dear God! This goes from bad to worse.'

At that moment the curtain around the bed parted and the matron came in, followed by a young woman.

'This is the person who found your daughter, Mrs Goulding.'

'Hello, Pat,' said Theresa.

Martha opened her mouth to speak, but the matron turned to her and went on, 'The consultant has just come back on duty and would like to speak to you immediately. Follow me, please.'

Martha looked again at Irene lying motionless, then at Pat who didn't meet her eye and followed the matron out of the ward.

The doctor, a Scotsman, was brusque; he spoke quickly, seemingly unable to look her in the eye. 'Your daughter has acute septicaemia. The cause is a serious hand wound. I intend to operate this morning to amputate her hand. It's the only chance of saving her life.' He pushed a piece of paper across the desk. 'As the patient's next of kin you are required to sign the consent form.' He handed her a pen.

'Is there nothing …'

'There is nothing else we can do. Life or limb is the choice.'

Martha stared at the pen.

'Mrs Goulding …'

Somewhere close by, a church bell began to ring.

Martha stood up. 'Excuse me. I'll be back shortly.'

'Mrs Goulding, there's no time …' But she was out the door and halfway down the corridor, before the doctor had come round his desk and shouted after her '… to waste!'

Two elegant towers, silhouetted against the pink dawn sky, drew Martha to the doors of St Peter's. The interior was cool and she sat at the back and clasped her hands in prayer, but no words came. A movement to the right caught her eye. A young priest walked purposefully up the aisle and into a confessional box. Martha followed.

'Father, can you help me?'

'Do you wish to confess your sins?' he asked in a soft brogue.

'I'm not sure … I just need to talk …'

'Sure that's grand.'

'My daughter is in the Royal.'

'Aah, I see.'

'I'm not a Catholic.'

'God listens to all who need his help.'

Martha recounted the story as she now understood it.

'I was going to sign the paper, Father, but then I heard your bell and I thought if I prayed, it would give me strength, but no words would come.'

'God knows what is in your heart. He doesn't need words. Would you like me to pray for Irene?'

'I would, Father, thank you.'

On her way out, Martha stopped to light a candle. Then she noticed that the young priest was at her side.

'I was wondering what made you come here, to our church?' he asked.

'I heard the bell ringing.'

'I thought that's what you said.' He smiled and added, 'We have twelve bells at St Peter's, but none has been rung this morning.'

As Martha approached Irene's bedside, she saw the matron lifting the sheet to cover Irene's face and she stifled a cry.

'No, no …' said the matron. 'Look.' She turned the sheet back to tuck it under the mattress, revealing colour in Irene's cheeks and her eyes flickering open.

'Mammy, I don't need an operation do I?'

'We've been giving her a new sulfa drug since she was admitted, and about twenty minutes ago it began to take effect,' explained matron. 'Of course we can't be sure if it has halted the spread of poison.'

Martha put her hand on Irene's forehead. 'No, Irene, there won't be any operation. You'll be fine, my love.'

Chapter 11

'How many's in now, Sammy?'

'Not enough for a football team, but more than you'd need for three-han' whist,' came the reply. 'An' seein' as how they're me Mammy, Daddy and three sisters, it looks like none of the rest of ye mentioned it to anyone.'

'But it was in the *Telegraph*, so why has nobody turned up?'

'Word got round you were in it, that's why.'

'Ach, save your wit for the payin' customers, why don't you?'

'Because, right now, I've a bigger audience in the dressin' room than I have in the theatre!'

Horowitz, stage manager for the concert, put his head round the door. 'Fifteen minutes to curtain-up, everyone.'

'Mr Horowitz, is it true there's no one coming to watch?'

'Of course not – they're just a bit slow selling the tickets, that's all.'

Sheila, who had been sitting in the corner of the dressing room, caught up with Horowitz. 'Do you think I could help?' she asked. 'Maybe with the tickets or something?'

'You're not a performer?'

'No. I'm just here ...' she shrugged her shoulders. It was too complicated to explain about her mother chaperoning and being unwilling to leave her at home.

'Well, the hall has its own people to sell the tickets, but between you and me, I don't think they've done this kind of show before.' He shrugged his shoulders. 'So why don't you just go out front and see what you can do?'

The entrance hall was quite small and the audience members were squeezing through half the double doors a few at a time to buy tickets from two elderly ladies seated in their coats and hats behind a small table. 'Now where would you like to sit, love? Near the front? Let's see what we can do.'

Sheila approached the nearest ticket seller. 'Can I help?'

'That'd be grand, love. The tickets are two shillings. Do you want to pull up a chair and sell some?'

'Maybe in a minute,' said Sheila, going straight to the double doors and opening the closed side. In the seconds before the crowd realised there was another way in, Sheila took in the rain falling heavily from a moonlit sky and a crowd of people queuing a hundred yards down the street.

'Just take the money and let them sit where they want, please,' she called to the ticket sellers. Then seeing their puzzled faces she added, 'There's not enough time. We need to get them inside quickly.'

Backstage the Templemore Tappers had arrived in a giggling rush, late again, as they had been to every rehearsal.

'You're here! I can't believe it!' Myrtle screamed when she saw Irene. 'God, ye look awful. Are ye all right?'

'Thanks for that, Myrtle. Maybe I need a bit more rouge.' Irene pinched her cheeks. 'I'm fine. I get tired easily, but I've been asleep most of today, so I'm raring to go.'

Myrtle pulled Irene into the corner next to a costume rail.

'Listen, Irene, I spoke to Mr McVey about you.'

Irene's face fell. 'They wrote to me saying that they couldn't keep the job for me.'

'I heard that, but I told him it wasn't fair ye lost the job. It was your first day and someone should've been showin' ye what te do.'

'What did he say?'

'Told me te sling me hook, but then I sent for the cavalry!'

'What did you do?'

'Told Robert.'

'The fireman?'

'The very same. Took a shine to you he did. What with him havin' you over his shoulder!'

'But what could he do?'

'Not what he could do, but what he's done.'

'Why, what's he done?'

'Got ye your job back, no less. Not a trial, mark ye, but a proper job.'

Irene's eyes opened wide. 'How did he …'

'Ach, it's not what ye know, it's who ye know.' Myrtle winked. 'Robert's other name is McVey.'

'McVey?' Realisation crept over Irene's face. 'Like the man who took me on?'

'Yes, Robert's his son, so he spoke up for ye.'

At that moment Horowitz reappeared carrying a huge bouquet. 'Ten minutes to curtain-up,' he shouted. 'And Peggy, these are for you, just been delivered.'

Peggy giggled in delight and scanned the room to check who was watching her as she took the flowers.

'Secret admirer, eh, Peggy?' said Horowitz.

'Works in a funeral parlour, does he?' added Sammy.

Peggy shot him a withering look and took the card from the flowers. The message was simple, an instruction. 'Meet me in White's Tavern, round the corner, after the show. I'll give you a lift home, Harry.'

Who did he think he was, giving her orders and wanting to meet her at a tavern of all places? She'd a good mind not to go! But the flowers were beautiful, from a shop in Shaftesbury Square. Expensive.

'And who might they be from?' asked Martha.

'Just somebody I know, a customer from the shop,' said Peggy and turned away to slick on another layer of red lipstick.

Martha watched her uneasily.

In the corridor near the stage door, Pat and William had found a quiet place to warm up. Scales first, then the first verse of each song they were to sing. 'It's always a bit nerve-wracking singing in front of people you know, isn't it?' said Pat.

'It can be.'

'It's Kathleen I'm worried about. What about you?'

'We just have to do our best. It's been fine in rehearsal.'

Pat pressed on. 'Have you sold many tickets to your family and friends?' There it was; she'd said it. William had never mentioned his family and she'd formed the opinion he lived with his mother, but couldn't be sure. He'd never mentioned friends either. He wasn't secretive, it was just that he never volunteered anything and Pat was too polite to ask.

'No, not many.'

'How many?' The question slipped out. Pat was horrified at her boldness.

'None.'

'Oh …'

'Starters in the wings please, curtain-up in three minutes.'

'You don't have a big family, then?'

'No.'

'And your friends?'

'Don't have any of them either.'

Pat stared at him. 'No friends?' Then she caught the look in his eye. 'Oh, you're joking me, I see!'

They hurried back to the dressing room and Pat was glad to see that someone had rigged up a curtain to provide separate sides for men and women. She had costume changes for both her duets and had been worrying about how to manage them and still retain some modesty.

The Templemore Tappers opened the show with their usual high-kicking display; the bigger stage ensured there were no mishaps. The applause and whistling could be heard in the dressing room. Sammy's jokes, a mixture of war and Belfast humour, went down well. Two more acts, a piano accordionist and a yodeller, then it was the Golden Sisters. Both Pat and Martha were still not sure about the change of name, but Irene, Peggy and Sheila were enthusiastic. 'It's more modern, Mammy,' said Irene and Peggy added that

Mr Goldstein thought it would stay in people's minds better.

They wore the turquoise blouses over slim black skirts. The colour was strong and stood out on stage. The design was also distinctive; Peggy had been right about the need for something with real style. They had done each other's hair in soft rolls and, because they were on the stage where, as Peggy pointed out, 'the lights could drain you', Martha had agreed that they could wear some make-up: a little powder to stop the shine; a little rouge to bring out the colour in their cheeks; a little lipstick to define their mouths. Irene was still under-rehearsed because of her illness, but she knew her sisters would carry her.

'You've heard of the Andrews Sisters from Minnesota. Well, these girls are from Belfast and they're even better. Ladies and gentlemen, please give a warm welcome to – the Golden Sisters, the girls with the golden voices!'

The girls ran on stage, smiling broadly. Even with the stage lighting they could see the hall was packed. Peggy was quickly at the piano playing the opening bars. Thank heavens, thought Pat; it was the song they'd rehearsed. She and Irene swayed to the beat then looked at each other and right on cue they were into 'Tuxedo Junction'. The harmonies had finally come together at the last minute and it was only the previous night that they made the decision not only to include the song, but to open with it. The response from the audience was palpable; they swayed in their seats and tapped their feet and at the back of the hall a young couple started dancing.

Next they changed tempo for 'Stormy Weather'. Peggy had a solo section halfway through and the audience listened carefully to her interpretation of the melody. When she finished there was a warm round of applause. Finally, what they hoped would become their signature tune, 'I'll Take Romance'. It was going so well that Peggy went for an extra verse, but Pat was ready for her (she'd tried the same trick in rehearsals) and Irene followed where Pat led. On the final note the audience were on their feet applauding and calling for more. In the wings they hugged each other. 'Best yet,' said Irene, and the others agreed. Then Pat dashed away for a quick change before her first duet with William in front of a paying audience.

William waited in the wings, a little uncomfortable in his dinner jacket and bow tie. The magician on stage was into his final and most dramatic trick, the appearance of a white dove from the folds of his black cloak, when Pat slipped quietly through the small group of people watching backstage and stood at his side. Sensing her there, William turned and his eyes widened.

Pat was transformed. She wore a stunning empire style evening dress in soft grey silk. The bodice was covered in silver and coral beading. Her rich auburn hair had been swept up on top of her head, with trailing tendrils that framed her face. The magician, having made his dove fly through a series of hoops, made his exit and Sammy bounced on to the stage to introduce them. Pat was aware that William was staring at her, but she modestly lowered her eyes.

'Time for some culture,' Sammy began. 'Who says Belfast hasn't got class? Ladies and gentlemen, Miss Patricia Goulding and Mr William Kennedy!'

William took her hand and led her on stage. They smiled and bowed to the audience who gave them a warm reception.

The music began and they turned away from each other, Figaro to measure out the space for a bed, Suzanna delighted with her new hat and desperate for Figaro to pay her some attention.

They had never sung better, their voices swooping and soaring in Italian, the language of love. Towards the end they came together, voices weaving in and out, first one then the other dominating, then in perfect unison. As the last note died away Suzanna and her Figaro faced each other. The audience were silent a moment, unwilling to break the spell. It was William who moved first, taking Pat's hand and pressing it to his lips, and the audience burst into applause. They bowed together then William, still holding Pat's hand, invited her to take the applause.

She sank low in a deep and perfectly executed curtsey as if she had been doing this all her life. Truth was, in her imagination, she had. William led her off stage and stopped in the wings, his face flushed with excitement. 'You were wonderful,' he said. Pat dropped another quick curtsey to hide the colour in her cheeks and looked up at him through her lashes.

'Pat, I …' He hesitated and at that moment Sammy, who had missed his cue, rushed between them and on to the stage.

'Yes?'

William looked uncertain, as though he had misplaced the words he had been ready to speak. He smiled. 'I hope our next song goes just as well.'

In the audience, Aunt Kathleen glowed with pride. Pat had looked every inch the opera singer and, what's more, every inch a Goulding. She had been right to lend her the grey silk and she smiled at the memory of wearing the gown herself at a benefit concert at the end of the Great War. She hoped they had decided to sing the Schubert in the second half, as she had then. She had detected one or two technical faults, but nothing the audience would have noticed. On the other hand, in front of an audience, unlike rehearsal, it was clear there was something between the two that added a certain frisson to the performance. Had anyone else noticed, she wondered?

Two rows back Jimmy McComb had read the same signs. It could have been part of the act, that look on Pat's face as she sang, but it was exactly the way he longed for her to look at him.

At the interval, Martha was surprised to see her sister Anna and her husband Thomas in evening dress chatting to a group of important-looking people. Anna had indeed written to her after Robert's funeral and, although her tone had been one of sympathy, Martha had not replied. She considered slipping away to avoid any awkwardness, but Anna caught sight of her and waved her over.

'Martha, the girls have done so well tonight. We were just saying to Councillor Craig that they have always been musical and entertained us many a time at family gatherings.'

Goldstein arrived at that moment with Martha's cup of tea. 'Mr Goldstein, may I introduce you to my sister Anna and her husband Thomas Wilson.'

Goldstein gave one of his quick formal bows. 'How do you do? You are enjoying the concert, yes?'

'Very much so,' said Anna. 'In fact we were just remarking to Councillor Craig how accomplished the performers are.'

'Indeed, they are very talented.'

151

'Mr Goldstein has produced and directed the show,' explained Martha.

'Well, Councillor Craig, who is very high up in the city council' – Thomas puffed on his large cigar – 'he has the ear of Lord Craigavon, you know, and was just saying that Belfast will need more events like this to keep up morale during these difficult times.'

'You are quite right, but it seems to me,' said Goldstein, 'that the council could also improve morale by giving more relief to the poor of the city.'

Thomas tipped back his head and blew a stream of smoke towards the ceiling. 'Well, that's one opinion, but I'm a member of the Belfast Board of Guardians and it's our view that young men should not be encouraged into idleness by receiving handouts from the ratepayers.'

'Lack of opportunity to work breeds resentment,' countered Goldstein. 'I have seen such things on the continent. Then those with extreme views take hold. Just look at the rise of Nazis in Germany.'

Thomas eyed Goldstein coldly. 'Goldstein? You're a Jew, I take it?'

Goldstein nodded.

'Didn't Hitler try to prevent the Jews taking advantage of the German people?'

'What do you mean ... advantage?'

'Lending money at high rates; monopolising some areas of commerce.'

'You are mistaken. Jews are honest business people, making a living. They fulfil a public service.'

'Like pawn shops, you mean?' said Thomas with contempt.

'You ridicule an honest trade.' Goldstein was struggling to maintain his composure. 'Sometimes it is the pawnbroker who keeps starvation from the door.'

'Work, sir, is what prevents starvation,' countered Thomas.

'Indeed, Mr Wilson, and Belfast has record unemployment. As I said before, those who rule this province have a lot to answer for.'

The bell rang for the end of the interval and Goldstein immediately excused himself. 'I must go and speak to the performers before the start of the second half.'

'Well,' said Anna. 'What an odious little man!'

'No, Anna,' said Martha. 'He's a good man, trying to make a difference by lightening people's lives and he's right about there being so many people living hand to mouth. But you wouldn't know anything about that, would you now?'

Thomas saw the colour rise in his wife's face. 'Now then, Martha,' he said. 'Leave the politics to the men and you'll not embarrass yourself in polite society.'

'Don't you speak to me like that, Thomas Wilson.'

'Mr Goldstein, please. I can't possibly wear this costume.'

'Of course you can. You must trust me; the audience will love it.'

'I'll look ridiculous!' said Pat. 'It's … de … demeaning.'

Goldstein smiled. 'No, Pat. It is de … lightful! Especially the lovely plaits.'

Pat was close to tears. 'Why can't I wear the gown I wore in the first half?'

'Because you will look ridiculous in that, next to William as a Mountie! Now let us have no more histrionics, please.'

After the Golden Sisters' second spot of the evening Peggy was first off stage to find her mother. 'Mammy, some of the others are going out for a while after the show. Is it all right if I go with them?'

'Peggy, it'll be half ten before this show is finished, quarter to eleven before we get away. We'll have to rush to get the last bus and even then we'll have to walk part of the way.'

'But sure I'll get a lift. Mr Goldstein is going to be there. He's invited everyone along to the Grand Central Hotel. Please, Mammy.'

'Well, Sheila and I won't be going and, Irene, I don't think you should go. You'll have exhausted yourself tonight and you need to get your strength back. But if Pat wanted to go then there'd be the two of you and I'd be much happier about that.'

Peggy turned eagerly to her sister. 'Oh come on, Pat. It'll be great. Everyone's going!'

'I'll think about it.'

Peggy thought that sounded like a no. 'I'll be all right, Mammy, honestly. You can trust me.'

Martha eyed Peggy, the daughter she was least likely to trust, but maybe she was being overprotective.

'Are you sure you're getting a lift home?'

'Oh, yes,' said Peggy. 'It's all arranged.'

'Final call for "Indian Love Call",' shouted Horowitz.

Pat stood in the wings in her buckskins and listened to the catcalls and jeers as Walter the ventriloquist and his wee pal Shouie died on stage. Sammy had a job to quieten the audience after such uproar and as a result he rushed their introduction.

'You loved them in the first half, now Belfast's Sweethearts are back again – Pat Goulding and William Kennedy!'

William went to take her hand and found it stiff and unresponsive by her side. 'Come on, Pat,' he urged. 'Pat, we're on.'

'How dare he!'

'Who?'

'Goldstein, of course. Belfast's Sweethearts indeed! How could he!'

'Pat, it's only an introduction. It doesn't mean anything.'

Then Sammy was in the wings with them. 'What's the matter?' he hissed, 'you're on!'

'No, I'm not!' said Pat and she pulled the plaits, feather and all, off her head and marched off.

The slow hand clapping began.

'What'll we do?' asked William, panic rising in his voice.

'You'll have to go on,' said Sammy.

'Are you out of your mind? It's a duet.'

'Never mind, just get out there and sing. I'll get her back.'

The slow hand-clap was deafening. Sammy pushed William on to the stage so hard he almost fell. The opening bars played.

William, ashen-faced and suffering from stage fright for the first time in his life, missed his cue. Meanwhile, someone in the audience, having recognised the music, started whooping an Indian war cry. William looked in desperation at the wings hoping to see Pat there, but there was only Sammy mouthing the word, 'Sing!'

'*When I'm calling you oo-oo-oo, will you answer too oo-oo-oo?*'

To his surprise there came an answer, but not in Pat's voice. It was Sammy singing falsetto. The audience saw William's confusion, took it as a joke and began to laugh. William could do nothing but carry on. The next moment Sammy had minced on to the stage looking very coy. He had rescued the plaits and feather from where Pat had thrown them and sang her next line.

The audience clapped in delight, especially when Sammy wrapped his arms round William and fluttered his eyelashes at him. William took a deep breath and did the only thing he could do; he played it absolutely straight. The audience roared with laughter, as much at William's discomfort as Sammy's antics. At the end Sammy leapt into William's arms and was carried off stage to whistling and cheering from the audience.

During the impromptu duet Horowitz had the presence of mind to gather the whole cast in the wings and as soon as William carried his Rose-Marie beyond the sight line, the finale began as act after act ran on stage to take their bow at the front during a rousing chorus of 'It's a Long Way to Tipperary'.

The show ended with the whole company on stage, save one weeping squaw who was alone behind a costume rail in the empty dressing room. Sammy then led the audience in a final singsong, during which Horowitz gave the signal and a huge banner unfurled across the stage showing in red and gold letters one word: 'Barnstormers'.

Chapter 12

The moon was just a sliver of yellow, affording very little light in the blackout, but Peggy knew the centre of Belfast well and in minutes she was pushing open the door to White's Tavern, 'the oldest inn in Belfast'. He was leaning on the bar, foot on the brass rail, one hand in his trouser pocket and the other round a glass of porter. It was a moment before he was aware of her at his side. He turned slowly, blinked and focused his eyes.

'If it isn't one of the girls with the golden voices!' He leaned back, both elbows on the bar. 'Didn't expect to see you here.'

'You asked me to come,' said Peggy. 'You sent me flowers.'

'Did I? Oh yes.' He looked her up and down. 'Where are they then?'

'My mother took them home for me.'

'Oh well, now you're here, would you like a drink?'

Peggy had never tasted alcohol, but she wasn't going to let him know that. 'I'll have ...' A Bombay Gin advert caught her eye. 'I'll have gin, please.'

He laughed. 'A spirit drinker, eh?' He ordered her drink and another glass of porter. 'Better put some tonic in that gin,' he called to the barmaid, and winked at Peggy. 'You don't want to end up worse for wear.'

'Did you enjoy the show?' Peggy asked.

'Only saw the first half, had some business to see to. Thought you girls were very good.'

Peggy sipped her gin and shuddered.

'Why don't you and me go out to a dance one night?'

'Yes, all right,' said Peggy.

He drank the rest of his porter without stopping. 'Well, if I don't see you through the week, I'll see you through the window.'

'What?'

'I need to go now; another spot of business. You know how it is.'

'No, I don't know how it is,' said Peggy, her voice rising. 'You asked me to meet you here. I've only just arrived and you're out the door.'

'I know, but we'll go out dancing another time. I was thinking about next Saturday at the Plaza, maybe.'

'But you said you were going to give me a lift home.'

'Aye, I was.'

'And now you're not?'

'Sure I've no car.'

'So you expect me to walk home on my own in the blackout?'

'I could walk you as far as Peter's Hill if you like?'

'Don't bother yourself!' shouted Peggy.

The lounge of the Grand Central Hotel was furnished with large chesterfields and winged armchairs around low mahogany tables. A heavy crystal chandelier hung from an ornate ceiling and strategically placed standard lamps added to the stylish ambience. Late at night, the wealthy citizens of Belfast would call in for late night coffee and a nightcap after a show or dinner in one of the few good restaurants in the city. Goldstein had ordered coffee for the members of the company who, still full of performance adrenalin, wanted to extend the evening. Pat, at first reluctant, had been persuaded by William to join them.

'We need to talk about our next performance,' he said. 'To decide what we want to sing.'

They had just sat down when Goldstein joined them. 'Well, what have you to say for yourself, Miss Goulding?' His voice was not unkind.

'I couldn't do it,' said Pat. 'I don't know why, I just couldn't.'

'But it is a very popular song; they loved it when Sammy did it.'

'Mr Goldstein, Sammy is a comedian; he doesn't mind being laughed at.'

'No one would have laughed at you, Pat.'

'It's just not what I want to do, Mr Goldstein.' She was close to tears.

'Well, I have to confess the duet between William and Sammy was an unexpected hit. So much so, that I would be prepared to have them perform the little routine again. What would you say to that, Mr Kennedy?'

William hesitated. 'I don't know. It's not the kind of thing I do either.'

Goldstein leaned forward. 'I want the song in the show. Pat does not want to do it. If you agree to perform with Sammy then she does not have to.'

William looked at Pat. 'I suppose I could do it, but we'd need to rehearse it properly.'

'Of course,' smiled Goldstein. 'It will be even funnier next time when Sammy wears the full costume!'

'There's something else,' said Pat.

Goldstein leaned back in his chair, arms folded.

She deliberately didn't look at William. 'I didn't like the introduction.'

Goldstein raised an eyebrow.

'Belfast's Sweethearts.' There, she'd said it. She was surprised when William answered.

'Don't worry about that, Pat. It doesn't mean anything. It's just a role, a part to play for the audience.'

'Yes, that's it.' Goldstein beamed. 'A little bit of romance. The audience will always respond to that.'

'I'm not sure it's a part I could play,' snapped Pat.

Goldstein stood up. 'But you are doing it. We could all see that tonight when you sang the Mozart. Nothing more is required!'

When he'd gone Pat said, 'You didn't need to agree to do the song. He couldn't make you do it.'

'That's true,' said William, 'but I agreed because I didn't want you upset anymore.' He moved closer to her. 'Pat, I don't know how to explain this, but singing with you tonight was … it made me feel … different.' He paused. Pat was tempted to say she understood the feeling he was trying to describe, because she had felt it too.

'Pat, I could stand on the stage and sing with you forever.'

'And what would you sing?' She turned to face him.

'Anything but the "Indian Love Call"!' he laughed.

At midnight, Goldstein came to ask Pat if she wanted a lift home.

'Is there room for Peggy and me?'

'Peggy?' said Goldstein. 'Peggy is not here.'

'What do you mean, not here?'

'She did not come to the hotel.'

Pat hadn't given a thought to Peggy, so absorbed had she been in her discussion with William about their repertoire. She turned to him in panic. 'Where can she be?'

'Don't worry, she'll have gone straight home, you'll see.'

Pat stood up and quickly gathered her belongings. William also stood and, to her surprise, took her hand and once again put it to his lips. 'Goodnight, Pat. I've had a lovely evening.'

When Pat came through the back door, she was surprised to see the kitchen light on and Martha sitting in her dressing gown, her hands round a cup of tea. Peggy's flowers lay on the table. She stood up as Pat came in and her eyes moved to the darkness behind her.

'Where's Peggy?'

'Is she not home?'

'No, she was with you, wasn't she, at the hotel?'

'She didn't come to the hotel.'

'God save us! I can't keep up with you girls. I don't know where you are half the time.' She paced the kitchen. 'The business with Irene was bad enough, without another one of you going missing!

159

What did she say to you?'

'That she was going to the hotel. She left before me.'

'And you didn't notice she wasn't there? Or was she there and she left? Did she leave with someone?'

'I didn't see her. There were lots of people there and I was talking to …' She stopped at the sound of the gate rattling.

Seconds later, Peggy came through the kitchen door.

'Where have you been?' demanded Martha.

Peggy looked quickly at Pat who gave a barely perceptible shake of her head. 'Out with some friends,' she said calmly.

'You lied to me and your sister when you said you were going to the hotel.'

'I didn't. I just changed my mind.'

'What friends were you with and where have you been 'til this hour?'

'Just some friends I know from work,' said Peggy, as she crossed the kitchen taking her coat off.

Martha shouted after her, 'And I take it you met him in White's Tavern and he gave you a lift home?'

Peggy turned to face her mother, caught sight of the flowers and realised her mistake in not removing Harry's card. Her chin went up. 'The truth is I didn't meet him. I waited but, if you must know, he didn't show up, so I got the bus home. Only how was I to know it only went as far as Carlisle Circus and I had to walk the rest of the way.'

'On your own in the blackout?' Martha was appalled.

'I wasn't on my own. I met a couple of girls I know and walked most of the way with them.'

'And you expect me to believe that? For all I know you've been out half the night with some man.'

'Think what you like. I've told you the truth.'

'Now you listen to me, young woman! If your father was here, you'd feel the sharp end of his tongue and his belt I dare say!'

Peggy bristled. 'Mammy, Daddy isn't here and you're not going to tell me where I'll go and who with!'

'How dare you speak to me like that. I'm the mother here and you'll do as I say!'

'I'm old enough to be out without your approval!'

'You're not twenty-one yet and you live in my house, so you'll do as I say! Wee girls who carry on like this end up in trouble and you know what I mean, madam. I'll not have you bring disgrace on this family.'

'Ach, catch yourself on, Mammy. That's not going to happen. Anyway, I'm entitled to have some fun.'

'Fun is it? Well ...' Martha reached across the table, grabbed the flowers and in one swift movement, opened the top of the range and plunged them into the fire. 'That's an end to that nonsense! Now get yourself to bed, before I take my hand to you.'

'Irene, are you awake?' whispered Pat.

'Yes. What was all that shouting?'

'Peggy went off with someone instead of coming to the hotel and Mammy found out.'

'Serves her right. Did you have a good time?'

'I think so,' Pat hesitated. 'I talked to William.'

'Oh really!' Irene, suddenly interested, sat up in bed, eager to hear all.

'Keep your voice down,' said Pat. 'Anyway, it wasn't like that.'

'What was it like then?'

'We talked about what songs we'll sing. Goldstein says I don't have to sing the "Indian Love Call", because William agreed he'll do it with Sammy.'

'Did you find out anything more about him? Where he lives and who with?'

'No.'

'Didn't you ask?'

'I didn't want to intrude.'

'Pat, that's just normal conversation. People always talk about things like that when they're getting to know each other. So what did he have to say?'

'He said he could sing with me forever.' Pat's voice was matter-of-fact.

'What?' Irene clapped her hands. 'He didn't!'

'He just meant he enjoyed singing duets.'

'No, he didn't. Pat, are you daft? He really likes you. Anyone can see that.'

'Do people think so?' She considered, shook her head. 'No, it's all an act. He said it's a role we have to play, a performance, that's all.'

Irene yawned and pulled the eiderdown over her shoulder,

'Well, you think that if you like, I know different.'

Within minutes she was asleep, but Pat lay awake staring at the ceiling reflecting on how little she knew about William Kennedy.

December was murky and damp; day after day the grey mist rolled in off the Lough and crept through the city streets. Irene and Pat took to walking to work to save money. Peggy joined them for the first few days then complained that she couldn't walk that far in her high heels and went back to an extra half hour in bed and catching the bus. Soon the shop windows on Royal Avenue and Castle Place were decorated for Christmas.

In Robb's, children were promised a magic sleigh ride to visit Santa at the North Pole, while on York Street, the Co-op offered a walk through Fairy Land to Santa's workshop.

In the music shop there were no decorations. Instead, each day Goldstein would light a candle on the menorah in the window.

'Is there no word of her yet?' asked Peggy.

'Alas, no. I had hoped Esther would be here for Hanukkah and now the last candle is lit.'

'Sheila, what are you doing in there?' shouted Martha.

From under the stairs came a muffled answer and the sound of a tin bath being dragged.

'Tell me what you're looking for. I'll know where it is.'

'I've got it!' There was the sound of boxes being moved and Sheila appeared in the doorway carrying an old Crawford's biscuit tin.

'Oh Sheila, do you think we should be bothering with all that this year?'

'What do you mean "all that", Mammy? It's Christmas Eve tomorrow. We've got to have some decorations and if no one else is going to put them up then I will.' She put the box on the table and removed the lid.

'Don't be getting all that stuff out!'

'What's the matter with everyone in this family? Pat and Peggy have been miserable since the concert, Irene's got no energy for anything, but at least that's understandable, and you usually love getting ready for Christmas.' Sheila stopped. 'You haven't made the Christmas cake yet. You've always made it by now.'

Martha turned away to rinse her cup in the sink. 'It's different this year ... you can't get all the ingredients.'

'That's never stopped you before. We have to have a cake!'

Martha stood with her back to Sheila, wiping her hands on her apron. 'I don't want a cake, or decorations. In fact, I don't want Christmas at all,' she said softly.

'Mammy, what's the matter?'

'I can't face it. I just can't!' Martha covered her eyes with the heels of her hands. Sheila watched her mother's shoulders heave as each sob escaped her lips. When she spoke again her voice was low and Sheila strained to catch her words. 'I don't want Christmas ... all the cooking, cleaning, trying to make everyone happy. For two pins I'd lock myself in my room and not come out 'til January.'

'But sure you love all the fuss and the preparations. Remember last year when Daddy said not to bother yourself with Christmas pudding and trifle? And you said: Christmas comes but once a year and didn't Jesus' birth warrant a bit of effort.'

Martha spoke softly. 'And now Daddy's gone, what kind of Christmas are we to endure without him?'

Now Sheila understood.

Martha went on, 'What are we to do? Put on paper hats, pull crackers and sing carols round the piano without him?'

'Yes.' Sheila held her mother's damp hands. 'Yes, that's exactly what we'll do and we'll imagine that Daddy's here somewhere at home with us, smiling and watching everything we do. And he won't be sad when he sees us. He'll be happy that we are living our lives and his dying isn't hanging over us like a black cloud.'

Martha looked at her hands clasped in Sheila's and not for the first time she was taken aback by the eloquence of her youngest daughter. 'But it'll be so hard.'

'That's why you have to make up your mind to do it. You have to show us how to behave; how to deal with the fact that Daddy isn't carving the turkey or leaning on the piano singing "O Come All Ye Faithful". We've got through these last few months because you've shown us how.'

'Aye, that's as maybe, but there's something else. I didn't want to tell you girls … I kept hoping something would turn up.' Sheila heard the hard edge to her mother's voice.

'What is it, Mammy, what's happened?'

Martha crossed to the high mantelpiece and felt for the brown envelope she'd hidden there. Without speaking, she handed it to Sheila who removed the white sheet of paper. The typing was sparse and in capital letters, full of its own importance.

Beneath the heading 'Royal Victoria Hospital' it read 'Reminder', followed by 'Unpaid Invoice'. Sheila had never heard the word invoice before, but a quick scan of the remaining words and the total £5/10/- at the end made the letter's purpose clear.

'Why do we owe all this money?'

'We have to pay for the treatment that saved Irene's life and the advice of the consultant who wanted to remove Irene's hand which, thank the Lord, we didn't take!'

'Do we have to pay it?'

'I'm afraid so and within five days.'

'Why can't we just ignore it?'

'Because, Sheila, you have to pay your debts in this life, for sooner or later they'll catch up with you and twice the size they were.'

'But have we got the money?'

In reply, Martha again stood on tiptoe, took the coronation tea caddy from the mantelpiece and emptied the contents on to the table. 'There's nearly four pounds there in change; I've been saving a little each week since last Christmas. Lately I've had to dip into it, but I thought four pounds wisely spent would make Christmas a bit more bearable. Now it'll have to go towards paying the bill.'

'Ach, Mammy, sure we don't need special things at Christmas. A plate of champ will do rightly. We can make our own entertainment like we always do. It'll be fine, so it will.'

Martha breathed deeply and wiped her eyes with the corner of her apron. 'Aye, well it'll have to be, won't it? I'll go down town tomorrow to see what I can pick up cheap at the last minute before the shops close. Now promise me you won't say anything to your sisters about this.' She replaced the bill on the mantelpiece. 'Especially not Irene.'

'Of course I won't. We'll manage, I know we will and I'll take a run down to the McCrackens this afternoon; they're putting together people's orders for tomorrow, they might pay me a little bit to help. Should I put the kettle on for a wee drink of tea before I go?'

'Thanks, you're a good girl. I'll just get a breath of fresh air.'

Martha went out the back door and into the garden.

Sheila busied herself with cups and saucers, but images of a bleak, miserable Christmas flitted in and out of her head. So too did the realisation that her mother had shared her worries with her as though she was a grown up, an equal. While the kettle boiled, Martha made a tour of the garden, stopping to check on some staking, then turning to look back at the house from chimney to doorstep. Sheila, at the window, raised the teapot and Martha acknowledged it with a wave of her hand.

The days had grown steadily colder as Christmas approached. Outside the City Hall flower sellers supplemented late autumn chrysanthemums with sprigs of holly and mistletoe, and the man who played the saw offered carols in return for loose change. But Peggy's routine was unchanged. She sat on the bench under Queen Victoria's statue in the gardens and seethed at the sight of meat paste on her sandwiches.

'You've a bake on ye like someone who's lost a ten bob note an' found a ha'penny!'

She turned away from the voice and studied a flock of starlings taking off from the lawn into the darkening grey sky.

'Cat got your tongue, again?'

She felt the slats under her shift as he sat down, sensed the slide of his arm along the back of the bench and his weight leaning into it.

'You got home all right then the other night?'

'No thanks to you!' she screamed in her head.

'Peggy, pet ... I don't know what to say. I had something important to do ... just couldn't get out of it.' He gave a quick nervous laugh. 'More than my life was worth.'

The starlings wheeled in a wide arc and disappeared behind the green dome.

'I'm sorry, Peggy, really sorry. Do you think you could give me another chance?' The slats shifted, his arm moved further along the bench. 'I've got tickets for the big Christmas Eve dance tomorrow at the Plaza Ballroom. Like gold dust they are.'

He rushed on, promise following promise. 'We'll go for a meal, drink champagne. What do you say, Peggy?'

The starlings reappeared, stretched to a streak of black, then regrouped to swoop towards the lawns again. It seemed to Peggy that something else had also lifted and settled with subtle shifts imperceptible to all but her. She turned to Harry. 'On Christmas Eve I'll be at home with my family, not gadding about the city with the likes of you.'

Martha spent the afternoon mopping the oilcloth and washing down the paintwork with a damp cloth dipped in carbolic. Around four, Betty rapped on the kitchen window and, with a wave of her arm and a tilt of her head in the direction of her house, invited Martha to join her. At Betty's back door lay a bundle of glossy green holly tied up with twine.

'That's for you to take home. Jack cut it this morning. Best crop of berries in years he says and you know what they say about berries on holly?' Martha looked uncertain. 'It'll be a long, hard winter! As if it won't be bad enough with a war on, shortages of food and, Lord bless us, maybe bombs too, without being up to our oxters in snow as well.' Betty's tone changed.

'I've a wee treat for you, so I have.' On the table was a tray set with two tiny glasses. 'Will you have a glass of port with me?'

Betty was already pouring when Martha exclaimed, 'Oh no, I couldn't, sure you know I don't drink.'

'Well, I wouldn't normally myself, but my brother bought it for me and it is nearly Christmas.' She handed Martha the glass and, as there was hardly more that a tablespoonful in it, Martha took a small sip.

'Were you doing a bit of sewing there, Betty?' A man's shirt lay on top of a needlework box on the table.

Betty pulled a face. 'Never much of a seamstress at the best of times and here I was tryin' to turn the collar on Jack's favourite shirt. Sure the whole thing was frayed and the shirt itself as good as new. I got the collar off all right, but getting it back on the other way around has me beat!'

'Let's have a look at it.' Martha had given many of Robert's shirts a new lease of life by turning the collar and it wasn't long before she'd unpicked the clumsy stitches and started again with new thread in a smaller needle and a copper thimble on her finger. As Martha worked, Betty relaxed, sipped her port and chatted about Jack and his vegetable garden. Around five Martha finished the collar. 'There you are, Betty. Good as a ten shilling new one from Spackman's!'

'Oh you're a marvel, Martha, right enough! Hang on a wee minute. I've something for you.'

Irene was the first to arrive home. She bounded up the stairs two at a time shouting 'Mammy' at the top of her voice. Martha was getting the good tablecloth out of the hot press.

'I see you've got some of your energy back today.'

'I have and something else as well. Close your eyes.'

'Ach come on, Irene. What is it?'

'No. You have to close your eyes.'

Martha played along.

'Now hold out your hands.'

'Irene, what …'

'No, you have to do it.'

Martha's squeezed her eyes tight; her hands shook a little in anticipation. She felt something being placed across her palms and waited for the instruction.

'You can open them now!'

The notes were grubby and crumpled, but their value unmistakable. Five one pound notes. A fortune.

'Irene, where did you get …'

'I pawned the sari.'

'What!' Martha looked from the notes to Irene. 'Why?'

'I know about the hospital bill. I found it on the mantelpiece … I couldn't let you pay it.'

'But we'd have managed.'

'Not at Christmas, Mammy. It'll be hard enough as it is.'

Martha hugged her eldest daughter. 'You're a good girl, Irene. We'll find a way to get you your sari back, I promise you. Now come downstairs and I'll show you what Betty's given us.'

Martha opened the cool cupboard under the sink to reveal carrots, sprouts and potatoes, the latter still caked in earth.

'That's two gifts today,' she laughed. 'I can't wait to see if there's a third on its way!'

The sitting room was cosy and festive by the time Sheila arrived home. Peggy, wearing an old pair of leather gloves, had trimmed and shaped the holly and hung it in graceful boughs from the picture rail. Irene had begged a branch from the spruce in the McKee's garden and she and Pat were decorating it with baubles.

Sheila stood in the doorway, giving off the chill of the outside air. Her navy nap coat was buttoned right up to her collar. They hardly looked at her, intent as they were on the decorations. She smiled uncertainly and carefully untied her headscarf. Pat stepped away from the tree and turned to choose a bauble from the tin. She froze. She stared. The warm languid air was instantly charged as each of them turned to the stranger in their midst. She looked much younger, her eyes huge, ears tiny and perfectly shaped so close to her head. Her hair was darker and cropped like a boy's. Martha was the first to move, instinctively knowing what had happened and why. Sheila held out a tin of biscuits. 'The McCrackens sent you these, Mammy.'

Martha took them from her, set them down and began unbuttoning Sheila's coat.

Peggy was the first to speak. 'What have you done to your hair?'

'Cut it.'

'But why?' asked Pat. 'You had lovely hair.'

'Just cut it.'

Martha was removing her coat as one would a child's: lifting each arm upright; pulling the sleeve off; then peeling it from her shoulders. Sheila didn't help; didn't seem to notice.

'Never mind, it'll soon grow again,' said Irene.

'Course it will,' said Martha, 'and in the meantime it shows off your lovely face.'

'Why didn't you tell us you were going to do it?' Peggy was never one to understand the value of silence. 'We could have persuaded you …'

'That's enough now, all of you.' Martha took control. 'I think Sheila looks really tired. You'd best get off to bed, love. Have a good night's sleep. It's Christmas Eve tomorrow.' Martha led her youngest daughter away from all the questions, upstairs to bed. Downstairs the speculation continued; each sister trying to imagine the circumstances in which they would part with their own long hair and all agreeing the chances of them ever doing so were remote. Upstairs, it seemed Sheila had just enough strength to reach her bed and close her eyes, but moments later as Martha was hanging up her coat, she spoke.

'In my coat pocket, Mammy, there's money. Four pounds they gave me for my hair … said it was thick and strong. And five shillings from the McCrackens; a Christmas bonus, John said, and Aggie gave me the biscuits.'

Martha stroked her daughter's shorn head. 'Sssh, go to sleep now. We'll talk about it in the morning.'

'I'm sorry it's not quite enough to pay the bill, Mammy. But it'll help won't it?'

'Yes Sheila, it's a big help.'

'And we won't tell Irene, will we?'

'No, love, Irene will never know.'

Chapter 13

Martha did not begrudge a penny of the money she paid over the counter at the offices of the Belfast City Health Board. Irene had been a whisper from death and although sound reasoning would have it that the the sulfa drug had caught her in time, Martha didn't doubt that God had heard her in St Peter's for, after all, what was the drug but God's latest work in the field of medicine.

One debt paid; two more to go.

Smithfield Market covered half an acre in the city centre, tucked away behind the pretentious shops that lined the best streets, like some wide-boy who might not be entirely honest in the eyes of the law, but who never knowingly cheated a poor man in search of a bargain. She had memorised the name on Irene's pawn ticket, assuming she might have to ask directions but, as luck would have it, she emerged from Kelly's Entry and within yards picked out the three gold balls high above the shoppers' heads with the name 'Blumfeld' swinging underneath.

Coming in from the chill December wind, the shop was a warm fug of dusty air and the unmistakable smell of paraffin. In front of Martha was a low wooden counter and, stretching up from it towards the roof, a strong metal grille. Beyond this were racks and racks of clothing and shelves piled high with an example of every possession known to be worth a few shillings to the desperate. The man behind the counter was as exotic to Martha as the inside of his shop. His complexion was sallow, emphasising the whiteness of his teeth as he smiled a welcome.

'Good day to you, missus, how may I help you?' He turned slightly and swept his hand to indicate all the goods in his keeping. Martha noted the small black cap fastened to the back of his head and the strings hanging below his tight waistcoat.

'Are you here to pawn, redeem or to buy?'

'Perhaps all three, depending on the arrangement we come to,' said Martha.

When she emerged from the pawn shop twenty minutes later, Martha's opinion of Jewish businessmen, already strong as a result of her dealings with Goldstein, had been further enhanced by the honesty and charm of Jakob Blumfeld. She was delighted to have, safe in her bag, a large parcel; a very small parcel; a new pawn ticket and, in her mind, the thought that two more debts had been repaid.

From Smithfield she made her way to St George's Market, a large red brick building with a corrugated iron roof, where the sound of noisy Christmas bargain hunters and pushy stallholders shouting their wares soared into the rafters to join the squawking and chirping of the birds who made their home there. Martha held her shopping bag tight and her purse even tighter, not daring to open it to find the list she had made. No matter, she could remember everything on it. From a fruit stall she bought four oranges and half a pound of mixed nuts. The box of dates with the lid showing a caravan of camels crossing the desert was more expensive than last year, but, at sixpence, was still worth the treat.

She already had a present for each daughter. At Easter time she had seen a new modern pattern for a jumper in the wool shop and started knitting right away. The lady who owned the shop had laid aside the wool, a different colour for each girl, and Martha had paid a little each week towards the cost. The jumpers had been finished for over a month, but she had still to add three small buttons across each shoulder. At the haberdashery stall the range of buttons threatened to overwhelm her. How to choose? In the end she decided on small clear ones with a pattern like cut glass. Three buttons per daughter, times four daughters made twelve buttons, which at tuppence a button came to two shillings.

There was a long queue at the butchers. She had never bought from the market before, always preferring Carson's closer to home, but lately his prices had risen steadily. Martha watched as each customer entered into a discussion, then some kind of haggling, before meat was finally produced from under the counter and quickly parcelled up.

'Hello, Mrs Goulding. How're ye keepin'?' It was the mother of Thelma, Peggy's cinema pal.

'Not too bad, Mrs Boyd, and yourself?'

'I'll be a lot better when I get all this Christmas palaver over with, I can tell ye!' She set her baskets down either side of her and flexed her fingers. 'Them begs is cuttin' in tae me, so they are.'

'Have you got all your messages then?'

'Aye, just got a turkey. Have ye seen the price of them? Scandalous it is! All ye get from them is, "There's a war on, what do ye expect!" Says I, "A war, my backside, youse uns is just profiteerin".'

'Why, how much are they charging?'

'Sure didn't he want ten bob for a scrawny wee critter! I told him te catch himself on, turned on me heel an' left.'

'So where did you get your turkey then?'

Mrs Boyd leaned in close. 'There's a farmer from Knocknagoney, over in the left-hand corner there, will sell ye one for five bob. Take a quick look in me bag and ye'll see why.'

Martha caught a handle and leaned over to peer inside.

There was a loud shriek from the bag, which shook furiously and an ugly scaly head with yellow eyes and a sharp beak came within inches of Martha's face. In the time it took her to shriek as loudly as the turkey, Mrs Boyd had clamped the bag shut.

'Jesus, Mary and Joseph, what are you doing with a live turkey?'

'I'm takin' it home for Christmas dinner!'

Quick as a flash, a man in the queue shouted, 'Aye, give it a party hat and a plate of sprouts. It'll be no uglier than the rest a your family!'

'Are you going to kill it?' asked Martha.

'Well, I've not bought it for its company! Sure I grew up on a farm; saw me da ring the neck of fowl many's a time. Nothin' to it.' With that, she gathered up her belongings, living and dead, and waved her hand. 'All the best to you, Mrs Goulding.'

'The same to you, Mrs Boyd.'

Eventually Martha reached the front of the butcher's queue.

'I've not a lot left, missus. I could let you have a nice ox tongue and half a pound of beef sausages. How's that?'

Ox tongue! It was years since Martha had cooked a fresh ox tongue, not since the early thirties when times were really hard.

Still it was a tasty dish hot and delicious cold in sandwiches. She could do a lot worse. 'I'll take both,' she said.

The farmer from Knocknagoney was packing up when she got to his stall.

'Have you a fowl left at all?' asked Martha.

'I have, missus. This critter here is no great size, but I'll vouch for his meat, moist and tasty for sure. You can have it for five shillings if you've a mind to take him as he is.' He spat on his hand and held it out, a farmer's bargain, and Martha shook his hand on it then watched with some trepidation as he trussed its legs and taped its beak, and she prayed both would last the bus journey home.

An ox tongue was a disgusting article raw, but the knowledge Martha had of how to disguise its shape and cook it to perfection would turn it into a rare delicacy. She'd make sure the girls didn't see it until it was cooked. Over a foot long, it was unmistakably a tongue, from its rasping pointed tip to its ugly root where it had been anchored to the gullet. First, it must be scalded with boiling water and skinned, ready to roll it into a circle like a Catherine wheel, then tied tightly with string before being plunged into a large pan of boiling salted water to simmer for an hour. Finally, Martha set it on a plate, covered it with a tea towel and laid her heavy iron on top to press it. She was thankful all this was accomplished long before the girls were due home. Time enough to have a cup of tea and a think about the main course she'd left gobbling to itself in the bath.

Sheila's face at the window was a shock. Martha had completely forgotten about her hair, or lack of it.

'How was it at the McCrackens?'

'Very busy again, we ran out of sprouts, but John told everyone parsnips were great with a Christmas dinner, especially if you roasted them with the potatoes. I've brought some home so we can try them.' She put a string bag full of fat white parsnips on the draining board. 'What have you been doing?'

'I went shopping at St George's Market, then came home and cooked some pressed tongue and made a Madeira cake. I thought we could ice that instead of the Christmas cake. There's tea in the pot if you want some.'

Sheila busied herself getting some tea. 'I could ice the cake for you, if you like.'

'That'd be great and while you're doing that, I could try making a Christmas pudding. I remember a recipe of my mother's that doesn't need so many ingredients and steams in half the time.'

The two set to work, each concentrating on their chosen task. Outside the light began to fade and neither heard the sound of the gate rattle or the back door open. Suddenly there was a piercing scream from the bathroom, followed by a startled cry from Sheila as she dropped the palette knife she was holding. By the time it hit the floor Martha was out of the kitchen and rattling the bathroom door.

'Peggy, Peggy are you all right?'

Another shriek – less startled than terrified this time.

'Peggy, open the door! Open the door!' Martha rattled the doorknob.

Now Sheila was at her side.

'What's happened? Is Peggy all right?'

'Of course she is. She's just seen the turkey, that's all.'

'What turkey?'

'Peggy, open this door!' Martha shouted with all the authority she could muster.

There was the rattling of the key and another scream as Peggy squeezed herself through the narrowest of openings and slammed the door behind her.

'Calm down, Peggy. It's just a turkey. Sure it's all tied up. It can't hurt you.'

Peggy had blanched as white as the turkey's breast feathers; her eyes were wide with fright. 'I needed to go to the toilet. Switched on the light and it came at me. Its wings were flapping trying to get out of the bath; its claws scrabbling over the side; coming straight for me!'

Sheila gasped. 'How'd a turkey get in our bathroom?'

Martha tried to calm her hysterical daughters. 'It's our dinner, for tomorrow.'

'What!' Sheila and Peggy looked at her as if she was a mad woman and indeed Martha was beginning to think that sometime in the afternoon in St George's Market she must surely have taken leave of her senses.

'Oh, Lord help us!' she whispered and covered her face with her hands. 'What have I done? Christmas Eve and a Knocknagoney turkey has taken over our bathroom and I'm damned if I'm the one to get him out!' She took her hands away and bit her lip just a little and smiled, slowly at first, looking from one girl's face to the next. Sheila smiled too, then Peggy, in spite of the fright she'd had. They turned their backs on the bathroom door, went back into the kitchen, sat at the table and looked at one another smiling and laughing a little, then laughing a lot. And when they stopped, it only took one of them to look in the direction of the bathroom for the laughter to start again. They were still sitting there when Pat and Irene came through the back door and fortunately Martha had the presence of mind to shout out, 'Don't go into the bathroom!'

'There's nothing else for it,' declared Martha. 'We just have to wait until Jack and Betty come back. They've probably nipped out for a few things. They'll be home for their tea.'

'But Mammy, I don't think I can wait 'til then. I need to go now!' said Peggy.

'She's not the only one,' added Irene. 'I haven't been since lunchtime.'

'What I don't understand is why you think Jack Harper can help,' said Pat.

Martha spoke confidently. 'Sure doesn't the man have a way with birds?' Her daughters stared at her in disbelief.

'Mammy, Jack keeps budgies! He's never wrestled with an eight-pound turkey on Christmas Eve!'

And then they were laughing again; everyone except Peggy, who stood up, crossed her legs and howled at the floor, 'Oh! Don't make me laugh! Please don't make me laugh!'

At that moment there was a knock at the front door. 'I'll get it,' said Pat.

'And if it's Jack Harper tell him he'll need a large piece of cuttlefish and a very strong swing,' shouted Irene. Pat left them shrieking and returned moments later to hear Irene warming to her theme by painting a picture of the turkey flying around the Harpers' sitting room and landing on Betty's head. It was a few moments before anyone noticed Pat had returned and behind her, smiling broadly, stood Harry Ferguson.

'Hello Peggy. Looks like I've arrived in time for a good laugh.' All eyes turned towards him, faces full of laughter smiled a welcome. Couldn't have timed it better if I'd tried, he thought.

He reached across the table and held out his hand to Martha.

'I'm guessing you're Mrs Goulding, but I may be wrong.' He smiled warmly and made a point of looking round the daughters then went on. 'I'm Harry Ferguson, a friend of Peggy's.'

Martha stood up, the smile still playing on her lips. 'Pleased to meet you, Mr Ferguson, you've arrived at a very strange time.' Harry raised an eyebrow.

'Why don't we go into the sitting room and we'll tell you all about it.'

'It's no problem, Mrs Goulding, no problem at all. I may be a master baker by trade, but I've helped out in my uncle's butcher's shop since I was twelve years old.'

'But Mr Ferguson, you're all dressed up. Were you on your way out somewhere?'

Harry was already removing his jacket, but didn't miss a trick. 'To tell you the truth, Mrs Goulding, I was hoping to ask your permission to take Peggy to a Christmas Eve dance tonight.'

Martha took the jacket and held out her hand for the tie that quickly followed.

'Oh, is that right? Peggy didn't mention it.'

Harry rolled up his sleeves. 'Now then, lead me to the beast.'

The Goulding women stood in silence in the kitchen listening to the noise of claws scrabbling on a cast iron bath and the flapping of wings against walls. Then suddenly all was silent.

The door opened slowly and Harry Ferguson, looking very handsome with his dark hair falling over his eyes, poked his head out.

'I'll be needing a very sharp knife, some string and as much newspaper as you can lay your hands on, if that's all right, Mrs Goulding.'

'Of course it is, Mr Ferguson. I'll fetch it right away.'

Half an hour later, he emerged and put a newspaper parcel on the table. 'That can all be thrown out.' A second parcel followed. 'That's your giblets; good for making gravy.' Then the turkey plucked and trussed was on the table. 'All sorted now, just needs stuffing and it's ready for the oven.'

'You're a life-saver, so you are!' Martha was delighted. She looked from him to the turkey then back again. That's when she noticed his shirt. 'Oh no, it's ruined, or it will be if you don't get it in cold water right away. Quickly, get it off you,' she ordered.

Martha filled the sink with cold water liberally sprinkled with salt. 'The best remedy for bloodstains,' she assured him, and plunged his shirt in the sink. Only then did she turn around and, with a jolt of surprise, saw a young man stripped to the waist in her kitchen and her four daughters wide-eyed and mesmerised by the sight.

An hour later, wearing Robert's only decent shirt, albeit a little tight around the collar, Harry Ferguson left Joanmount Gardens in his borrowed sports car with Peggy at his side on their way to a dance and her entire family waving them off.

Harry had promised to have Peggy back before midnight and Martha had surprised herself by believing him. Of course she

177

decided to wait up, but she passed the time, not by worrying, but by adding the final touches to the girls' presents.

She sewed the buttons on their new jumpers and wrapped them up. Hanging from the fireplace were four Christmas stockings, each filled with an orange, some nuts and a different coloured comb for each daughter. Just before midnight, Martha heard the back door open. Peggy bustled in flushed and smiling.

'Well,' said Martha, 'did you have a good time?'

'Oh yes, yes. First of all we had some supper at a restaurant on Chichester Street, very nice, Harry knew the owner.' Peggy didn't mention the glass of champagne she'd drunk, the amazing bubbles and the lightness in her head. 'Then we went to the Plaza Ballroom. There was a full orchestra, can you believe it, and singers. It was wonderful and the dancing …' She could tell no more, there was too much going on in her head, image after image, moment after moment. She searched for words to explain. 'Oh Mammy, it was wonderful!' was all she could manage.

Later as she lay in bed waiting for sleep to come, she heard again the rich sound of an orchestra and felt Harry's arms around her as they danced; no baby grand or angry boss to contend with this time. She remembered how he had leaned down to whisper in her ear; she looked up at him wondering if she had heard him right; and saw again his smiling eyes as he kissed her.

It was after one o'clock when Martha checked on her daughters. She laid the orange sari, redeemed from the pawnbroker's, over Irene's bed. Next door, on Sheila's side of the dressing table she left a small box wrapped in Christmas paper with a tag that said, 'For Sheila, who has the most beautiful ears.' At last Martha climbed into bed, weary but content. Since she was a child she had believed Christmas Eves were full of magic. As she got older that belief never changed, but each year brought a different kind of magic and this Christmas Eve had been one of the strangest ever. It seemed that Robert had been with her all day, had given her permission to pawn their ring. No ordinary wedding ring, Robert had explained that Christmas Eve long ago when he had placed it on her finger, but a ring of rubies. Even the turkey came from Knocknagoney where she and Robert used to walk out together on warm Sunday afternoons. And nothing seemed more unexpectedly natural than to lend Harry Ferguson Robert's best shirt to take their daughter to a Christmas Eve dance.

Christmas Day dawned with a sharp frost. Martha was first downstairs to start cooking the turkey. Next she lit the fire in the sitting room, so it would be warm when the girls came down to empty their stockings and share the opening of the presents. Finally, she put the porridge on. Irene was first up and came into the kitchen all smiles and hugs.

'Thank you so much for my sari. I never thought I'd see it again. How did you …?' Irene's eyes were brimming with tears.

'That's all right, love. It means a lot to you doesn't it?'

Irene nodded, unable to express the sadness she had felt when she thought she'd lost it forever.

Pat and Peggy quickly followed and all were sitting at the table chatting and eating porridge when Sheila came into the kitchen. She posed in front of them, turning her head from side to side to show the pearl in each ear lobe.

'Thank you so much for my earrings. They're the best present I've ever had. Are they from you, Mammy?'

'They're from all of us, Sheila. You deserve them.' If the other sisters were surprised at the fact they were the givers of such a beautiful present, they didn't show it. Instead each marvelled at the appropriateness of the gift and the stunning effect the earrings had on Sheila's appearance.

The sharing of gifts was a simple, but organised, ritual. Each in turn would give out her gifts and in turn they were opened and exclaimed upon, and then the recipient thanked the giver. That way everyone shared in the opening of every gift and consequently each gift and giver received equal attention.

Soon it was time to leave for church, with everyone well wrapped up against the chill wind blowing from the east and each Goulding girl in a cosy new jumper. The carols were sung with gusto by all, but the sermon brought the whole congregation back to the reality of a Christmas at war. The Reverend Lynas took as his theme the people of Europe united against evil.

Christmas dinner was a huge success and at the centre of it all was the now infamous Knocknagoney turkey. The parsnips, roasted as suggested by the McCrackens, were pronounced delicious. Finally, the girls thought that Martha's simple version of the plum pudding served with custard was an improvement on every pudding they'd ever eaten. Pat and Irene volunteered to wash the huge pile of dishes, provided Peggy and Sheila did the same on Boxing Day when the whole meal would be repeated.

Martha, after all her culinary efforts, was relaxing in the front room, enjoying a cup of tea when she was surprised by Goldstein's car drawing up outside. As she watched, he jumped out and hurried to the passenger door to help someone out. Martha caught her breath at the sight of the figure that emerged: a frail-looking young woman with unkempt hair, wearing just a thin cotton dress. Her face, as she turned towards the house, struck Martha to her core. The girl's eyes were wide and staring, her face grey and drawn.

'Mercy me,' whispered Martha as she watched Goldstein support the girl in taking hesitant steps, as though she had only lately gained the use of her legs. Sheila, who had been sitting on the rug in front of the fire cracking nuts, heard the horror in her mother's voice and joined her at the window.

'Who is it, Mammy?'

But Martha was already out the door, having paused only to shout upstairs, 'Peggy, come quickly!'

Martha ran to the girl's side and supported her, so that between them she and Goldstein practically carried her into the house. Peggy was in the hallway as they helped the girl over the threshold.

'What's happened, Mammy?' Then in a moment her eyes took in Goldstein and the weight he and her mother were carrying.

'Mr Goldstein, is this …?'

'Yes, Peggy, this is Esther.'

They took her into the kitchen and settled her in Robert's chair close to the warm range. Irene drew up a chair close to Esther and held her hand, all the time speaking softly to her, explaining where she was and introducing everyone, knowing that Esther understood little of what was said, but hoping she might sense the kindness surrounding her.

Meanwhile, Pat made tea and prepared a plate of turkey sandwiches. Peggy went off to look for a warm dress and cardigan. Sheila sat opposite Esther and smiled their welcome.

In the sitting room Goldstein was as close to tears as Martha had ever seen a man. 'Forgive me, Mrs Goulding, I did not know what to do. I am her uncle, but it is not enough … I could not …' He stopped wringing his hands and held them open. 'I brought her to you.'

'Of course, of course,' said Martha. 'It was the right thing to do. We'll see to her, don't worry.'

'She arrived in Belfast early this morning off the Liverpool boat. Some passengers, a business man and his wife I believe, had become concerned for her, because of the state she was in. She had no luggage and didn't respond to their questions, so they took her to the harbour police. She had a scrap of paper with my address on it in her hand.' He paused then as though remembering the sequence of events. 'The police arrived at my house and asked me to identify her. I do not know … I could see the suspicion in their eyes. I tried to explain she was probably my niece. I have never seen Esther, you understand. I left Poland many years before she was born. And of course, to the policemen my accent sounded, you know …' He struggled to explain. 'I could have been a German for all they knew. I told them right away that I was Polish, but…' His voice trailed off again.

'But they must know your shop and you've papers, I'm sure,' said Martha.

'Oh, yes, but at seven in the morning with two policemen in my house and a young woman in a distressed state … I don't know … I became confused.' He paused and shook his head as if to rid his mind of what could have happened if at that moment the young woman had not lifted her head, looked at him through eyes that were identical to his sister's and whispered 'Shalom'.

'She is my niece, I told them. They were kind men at heart and maybe they understood something of what she had been through. Since then she has not said a word. I did not know what to do.

Then I thought of you and your girls.'

Just then Pat put her head round the door. 'Excuse me, Mammy, I've made her something to eat and a drink of tea, but she won't touch them and I'm sure she's starving.'

Goldstein stood up. 'I think I know why.'

In the kitchen, Goldstein spoke to her in Polish. At the mention of the word 'Kosher' she looked quickly at her uncle.

He nodded and Esther began to eat.

Meanwhile, Peggy ran her a bath adding some of the Yardley freesia bath salts Irene had given her for Christmas. She laid out towels and hung a blue flannel dress of Sheila's (guessing she was closer to Sheila's size than any of the other sisters) and a beige cardigan of her own on the hook behind the door. When Esther emerged from the bathroom she was certainly cleaner, and her cheeks had regained a little colour, but Sheila's dress was hanging loosely on her and still she said nothing.

'I think she probably wants to sleep. I'll take her upstairs and she can lie on my bed.' Peggy returned five minutes later. 'Fast asleep. I don't think she's slept properly for days.'

'Mr Goldstein, why don't you leave her here, she'll probably sleep for hours,' said Martha. 'You could get a bit of sleep yourself. Come back later.'

Goldstein knew that Esther couldn't be anywhere better than under Martha Goulding's roof. So, with much shaking of hands and thanks, he took himself back up the Antrim Road.

As twilight fell there was a rap at the kitchen window and Jack and Betty came in to wish their neighbours a merry Christmas.

'How was your dinner?' Betty asked.

'Very good,' said Martha, 'especially the excellent vegetables!'

'There'll be plenty more where they came from in future,' said Jack, lighting his pipe. He said no more until he had sucked and sucked so that the tobacco in the bowl began to glow and the room filled with aromatic Old Holborn. 'I've decided to dig up my garden to grow my own vegetables. Mind you, I'm likely to have that many carrots, potatoes and the rest that I'll need the help of a few neighbours to make sure they don't go to waste, if you get my drift.'

Betty smiled encouragement at her husband. 'Tell them about your other idea, Jack.'

Jack checked his pipe, risked pressing the tobacco a little tighter and puffed again to make it catch. 'I've a mind to get a few chickens too.' He smiled his pleasure.

The entire Goulding family avoided each other's eyes.

'Sure, Jack, you're famous for having a way with birds,' said Martha.

Twilight had given way to the night and the girls were lighting candles when there was a knock at the door. Peggy jumped up. 'I'll get it.'

Harry Ferguson came into the room like a man who felt his appearance was not only expected, but eagerly anticipated.

'Good evening, Mrs Goulding, and a very merry Christmas to you.' He shook her hand and swept the others with a smile. 'I won't interrupt your evening.' He went on, 'Just thought I'd return the shirt you lent me.' He handed over a brown paper parcel. 'All washed and ironed.'

'That's very considerate of you,' said Martha. 'Stay a while, why don't you?'

'No I couldn't. I've just brought you a wee present. I hope you enjoy it.'

Martha took the tin from him. 'Am I to open it now?'

'Of course, you can even eat it now, if you like.'

'Goodness me!' exclaimed Martha as she gazed at the beautifully iced Christmas cake. The thick royal icing was peaked into a snowy landscape across which two Eskimos raced on a sleigh towards Father Christmas and around the edge the words 'Merry Christmas' were written in red and finished with a sprig of holly.

'You made it yourself, didn't you Harry?' said Peggy.

'Oh yes, you're a baker aren't you?' said Martha. 'Well, what a wonderful present. Now you'll have to stay while we all taste it. Sheila, get Mr Ferguson a chair.'

'Please, call me Harry.'

The cake delighted everyone.

'It's very rich,' said Martha.

'Is there a bit of sherry in there?' asked Betty.

'The marzipan is just the right thickness.'

'And so almondy.'

After a while the conversation died a little and Peggy opened up the piano lid and began to pick out the opening bars of 'Away in a Manger'. Very softly in the candlelight someone hummed, a voice added the words. On the second verse more voices joined in. The last notes died away and Peggy moved quickly into the next song. Jack led the singing of 'Rudolph the Red-Nosed Reindeer' with gusto and Martha was the only one who heard the quiet knock at the door.

Goldstein had returned.

'Esther's been asleep since you left,' explained Martha in the hallway. 'We keep looking in on her, but she hasn't stirred. I'll go up and check on her again.' She opened the door to the sitting room. 'Come in and join us.'

Jack's singing had gone from bad to worse. He was stuck on the names of the rest of the reindeers and the others were shouting out as they remembered them. He had just finished the song amidst loud cheering, when the door opened and Martha led Esther into the room.

Goldstein stood up and took her arm and, with her eyes still on the ground, she whispered to him.

'May she have a drink of water?' he asked.

Sheila fetched the water, together with a piece of Harry's Christmas cake. She drank and nibbled a little. Again she spoke and Goldstein translated. 'She says to thank you for your kindness and that she cannot believe she is here with her uncle and his friends.'

Esther gave a half-smile. Then slowly, with Goldstein translating, she told her story: 'I left Warsaw on 26 September …'

The night we sang at the Grosvenor Hall, thought Peggy.

Chapter 14

Snow! It arrived in dark clouds that settled over the city as though they could go no further with such a heavy load. From the Cave Hill across the lough to the Holywood Hills it fell through the night in thick white flakes as big as half crowns. It seemed, on that Sunday morning in early January, that the people of the city rose late from their beds. The snow had deadened the usual early morning sounds by which they registered the new day and the blackout curtains had kept the light from their bedrooms.

Martha, who slept at the front of the house, was the first awake, disturbed by the sound of children's excited laughter in the street outside. Bernard Murray already had a good slide going. He climbed up the hill a little then launched himself down the middle of the road, body and feet turned at right angles, and skimmed across the slippery surface for twenty yards using his arms stretched out from his side to keep balanced.

'Come on youse uns!' he shouted. 'The more we use it, the slippier it'll get.'

From the kitchen window, as she waited for the kettle to boil, Martha marvelled at the transformation in the garden. The wind had blown small drifts here and there; at the back door it was a foot high covering the steps. The branches and twigs were heavy and thick with it. On the path were the prints of a bird that had moved this way and that as it searched for food. There'd be no church for her this morning; she hadn't the footwear for the twenty minute walk there and back in thick snow.

By mid morning, with no sign of a thaw, Peggy had disappeared into the shed at the back of the house and after much shifting of its contents she emerged triumphant, hauling behind her the Joanmount Flyer. The other sisters who had been working as a team in the garden to build the biggest snowman ever, left him without a second thought, his tiny unfinished head at his feet.

Sheila clapped her mittened hands in delight. 'It's Daddy's sledge!'

'I didn't know we still had it,' said Irene. 'Do you remember how he made it for us when we were small?'

'Mammy didn't allow us to go on it by ourselves.'

'Now, Robert, you're to promise me that you will always be in control of the sledge.' Peggy did a passing impersonation of her mother at her most protective.

'Aye, Martha, don't fret. I can sit two of them on it with me.'

Martha had joined them in the garden and spoke aloud her husband's words. 'Rest assured, they'll come to no harm.'

'You remember, Mammy, the fun we had on this sledge?'

'Indeed I do, a fine sledge built by a carpenter for his children. Now I wonder how you're going to spend the day.'

She raised an eyebrow.

'Come with us, Mammy, it'll be great,' pleaded Sheila.

'Ach, away on with you, I've plenty to be doing here without risking my neck up the Carr's Glen! I presume that's where you're going.'

Half an hour later, in their warmest clothes, the girls had left the houses far below them and reached the top of the Ballysillan Road, where in summer the meadows were full of clover and cowslip and heavy with the sound of insects. This morning, it was more like an Alpine village with dozens of figures trekking up and sliding down the slopes on makeshift sledges.

'It's just like *Heidi*!' exclaimed Sheila.

One or two groups had recognisable sledges, but others were sliding down on tin trays or bits of wood. There was even a tin bath. They found a space at the top with a clear run for fifty yards.

'I'm the one who found it, so I'll go first,' said Peggy.

'Have you forgotten it's a two-man sledge?' said Irene. 'And I'm the eldest, so I'll go down with you.'

'Suits me,' said Pat. 'I'm not sure whether I want to do this at all.'

'Don't be such a scaredy ba,' said Sheila. 'You and I'll go down together next. I'll be at the front.'

Peggy lined the sledge up. 'You see this?' she said, holding up the tarred rope fastened to the sledge like reins on a horse. 'I'll use it to steer.' She braced her feet on the cross bar. 'Now get yourself on, Irene. Quick as you can!'

Irene sat on the wooden slats behind Peggy, glad that she'd worn her work trousers. She held on to Peggy's waist, but couldn't quite figure out where to put her legs. She felt the sledge begin to move beneath her. 'Wait, Peggy, wait!' But with Peggy, whether it was songs on the piano or sledging on snow, there was no stopping once she'd made up her mind. The sledge tipped forward and Irene saw below her what looked like a sheer drop. She had the oddest sensation that she was about to fly over Peggy's head and land in front of the sledge as it careered downward. Her legs were stuck out at acute angles and it was all she could do to keep her feet off the ground. Suddenly, she had the weird sensation of lifting off into the air. Too late she realised that her backside had left the sledge. For an instant it was only her grip on Peggy's waist that prevented her from flying down Ballysillan unaided. Then the sledge lifted to meet her crashing down. The breath was knocked out of her and they were rushing headlong again. Snow spraying in her face … eyes squeezed tight … mouth open, but she couldn't catch another breath. Once more she rose in the air over a bump and back on to the slats with a thud … then a sensation of turning sharply, the sky twisting above her … a sudden jarring that turned her sideways and dumped her in a white pit, her mouth full of snow.

She was aware of shouting all around her and that high-pitched laugh that Peggy did when she became over-excited. Hands pulled her to her feet. She shook her head free of snow and felt an ache at the base of her spine as she put weight on her legs.

Then she was laughing too. A group of boys had gathered round them, pulling her and, more importantly, the sledge from the snowdrift that Peggy had steered them into.

'My God, I've never seen anything like it!'

'What a speed!'

'Where'd ye get a sledge like that?'

Back at the top of the slope, Pat and Sheila waited anxiously, having witnessed the reckless progress of the Joanmount Flyer.

Pat cupped her hands around her mouth and screamed, 'Are you all right?' and was glad to see first Peggy, then Irene wave back.

Sheila, on the other hand, yelled, 'Hurry up! Bring it back for our go!'

'Are you mad?' asked Pat. 'That thing's dangerous!'

The boys pulled the sledge back up, hoping, no doubt, to get the opportunity to have a go themselves, but Sheila had other ideas.

'Right, Peggy, my turn.'

'Look,' said Peggy, 'aim for the right of where we went down. It looks a bit less bumpy over there. You could probably slow it a bit as you get near the bottom by pulling it to the right in an arc. You see those boys down there? How they're slowing down, sort of sideways into the snow?'

Sheila nodded. 'Yes I see. I can do it and if it goes wrong I'll just fall off into the snow.'

'You won't have time to think about that,' laughed Irene.

'Come on, Pat!' Sheila climbed on the sledge. 'Get behind me.'

'I can't!'

'Yes you can. It'll be great!'

'Go on, it's really good,' said Irene.

At that moment Pat saw a familiar figure coming towards them, pulling a sledge almost as big as theirs. He raised his hand and called out. Instantly, Pat was on the back of the sledge, shouting in Sheila's ear, 'Right! Go! Go!'

Sheila pushed off and they went hurtling down the slope leaving Jimmy McComb a lonely figure at the top, disappointed again.

Ever persistent, he was still waiting when, cold, miserable and nursing a wrenched shoulder, Pat returned. 'Well, that's the last time I'll risk my neck for that experience.' Her words were angry, but her tone was one of pride that she'd done something a little reckless.

'Some experience, isn't it?' Jimmy was beside her, a Thermos flask in his hand. 'Would you like some tea?'

She looked at his earnest face, ruddy with the cold, and the cup of steaming tea he held out to her and felt a little embarrassed by the way she'd rushed off. 'Thanks, Jimmy.' She took the cup in both hands and sipped the hot tea. 'You came well prepared for the cold.'

They stood side by side gazing out over the city towards the docks where dozens of giant cranes scraped the low grey sky.

'Do ye see that crane, fourth one in from the left?' Jimmy pointed. Pat nodded. 'That's on the opposite bank to where I work. It unloads sugar from the boats for the Tate & Lyle factory. Mind you, there's not been many of those since the war started.'

'Aye, there hasn't been sugar in the shops for a few weeks now.'

'We probably won't see it again 'til the war's over.'

The silence stretched between them; neither was much practised in small talk. Eventually Pat took a deep breath:

'Look, Jimmy ...'

'Pat, I'm sorry we got off on the wrong foot.'

'No, no, I'm sorry. I shouldn't have been so angry with you.'

'Can we be friends then?'

'I suppose so.' She smiled and handed back his cup.

He screwed it back on the flask, and packed it away in his haversack, chattering nervously. 'Would you like a ride down on the back of my sledge? I'm on the run over there. You can see it's not as steep.'

'No thanks, I'll just get back to my sisters.' She turned to walk away, but he fell into step beside her.

'Pat, do ye think we could start again, you and me?'

She stopped and faced him. 'Jimmy, there is no you and me. There won't ever be a you and me.'

'Why not?' His tone changed. 'Am I not good enough for you?'

'Don't be silly. I don't want to fall out with you. You're a very kind person, but there's nothing between us.'

'It's because there's someone else, isn't it?'

'Look, Jimmy, there isn't anyone else. And even if there was, it would be none of your business.'

'It's him you sing with, isn't it?' His voice began to rise.

'What?'

'I saw the two of you together on stage, you looking into his eyes, the way he kissed your hand at the end!' Some of the others standing on the hill were turning to stare. Pat lowered her voice.

'Jimmy, you don't understand, that's a performance, an act. There is nothing between me and William Kennedy.'

'Oh yes, I know that's his name, saw it in the programme, and that's not all I know about him.'

'What do you mean? What is there for you to know about him?'

'I know he has a wife and child!'

Pat took a step backwards, and for a moment looked like she was going to argue, but instead she turned and walked quickly down the lane.

Sheila saw her go and ran after her. 'Wait Pat, wait for me!'

Pat's hands were deep in her pockets, her mind deep in thought. Sheila caught hold of her arm.

'Leave me alone. I'm going home!'

'It's Jimmy, isn't it? He's upset you again. Look, just tell him you don't want to go out with him and he'll have to leave you alone.'

Pat turned to face her sister. She was catching her breath in gasps and when she spoke, the words escaped one at a time.

'You ... don't ... know ... what ... it's about. It's ... not that ... simple.' Pat breathed deeply and tried to calm herself. 'He says ... he's married!'

'Jimmy's married?'

Having to explain seemed to calm Pat a little. 'Not Jimmy ... William.' She began to sob and Sheila took off her mittens and wiped her sister's face.

'William? What's this got to do with him?' But even before she'd finished the sentence, Sheila understood. She guessed, too, that the reason for Pat's distress was not her dislike of Jimmy, but her growing love for William Kennedy.

'Ach, how would he know anything about William? Sure he's just made that up to upset you. Can't you see?'

'No, it's true, I'm sure of it. Why else does he keep his life a secret? I don't know anything about him. Where he lives … who he lives with … nothing – and now I know the reason why!'

'Well, I wouldn't believe Jimmy if I were you. You know what I'd do?' Sheila didn't wait for an answer. 'I'd just ask William straight out! You can do it on Friday night at the rehearsal.'

'I can't just walk up to him and ask him is he married! What would he think of me?' And she began to cry again.

From the hill above them floated the excited sounds of the sledgers who hadn't a care in the world beyond staying on their sledges. Down on the lane, Sheila hugged her sister and some of Pat's despair transferred itself through the layers of warm coats, scarves and mittens to Sheila's warm heart. Bit by bit Pat's sobbing subsided and her shoulders relaxed a little.

Then Sheila took her hand. 'Come on, let's go home, and if we slip on the way down the lane at least we can catch each other.'

Goldstein was already seated in a booth in the Ulster Milk Bar when Martha arrived. 'Mrs Goulding, thank you for coming to meet me. I have already ordered for us both. Do you know this is the only place in Belfast where they make a good pot of fresh coffee?'

Martha didn't know that, nor did she know why Goldstein had sent Peggy home with a handwritten note asking for a meeting. The coffee when she tasted it was a surprise. So too were Goldstein's words.

'You know that Esther and I had to report to the police immediately after Christmas to register her as an alien. How I hate that word! Well, they have allowed her to stay in my care, provided I take full responsibility for her.'

'Yes, Peggy told me she could stay.'

'You may not know that she worked in our family music shop

in Warsaw and she was looking forward to working here. But, try as I might, I have been unable to acquire for her a work permit. Unfortunately, I have … what is that saying again?' His eyes moved from side to side as if searching for it in Martha's face. 'Ah, I have come to the brick wall.'

Martha smiled in spite of his serious expression.

Goldstein smiled back. 'Then it came to me! I could ask you to help.'

'Me?'

'We need someone with considerable standing in this city, to speak for Esther.'

'But no one would listen to me.'

'Maybe not,' Goldstein leaned across the table, 'but what about your brother-in-law?'

'Thomas Wilson?'

'Yes, I remember him saying he was on the Board of Guardians.'

'Aah, I see.' Martha nodded.

It was growing dark when Martha crunched up the gravel drive that swept in a semicircle in front of the large grey Edwardian villa. The last time she had been here was when she had been paid to clean the house in preparation for a large dinner party.

Anna raised an eyebrow at the sight of Martha on the marble steps. 'Heavens above, Martha, to what do we owe this pleasure and at this hour of the day?' She ushered her into the wide entrance hall just as a grandfather clock began to strike, and Martha waited until the sixth stroke had died away before replying.

'I've come to see Thomas, if that's possible?'

'Come through, come through.' Anna didn't suggest Martha remove her coat and Martha didn't expect her to. Nor did she expect to be shown into the drawing room. Instead, Anna led her towards the rear of the house to the morning room, chatting as she went. 'How are you, Martha? What about the girls? How's Irene's new job?'

Martha waited nervously while Anna went to fetch Thomas, going over in her head the words she'd rehearsed.

'Hello Martha. You're a stranger in these parts.' He took a puff of his cigar and eased himself into an armchair. Martha realised that was the extent of the formalities and took a deep breath, praying her tactics would be the right ones.

'There's a young woman,' she began, 'a friend of Peggy's. She's from Poland. After Hitler invaded she managed to escape the country and travelled across Europe alone. She's now with relatives in Belfast.'

'And what does she need that brings you to my door on a dark winter's evening?'

'She needs to be able to work, Thomas, and that means a work permit. Could you … would you … use your influence to get her one?'

He brought the cigar to his lips again, rolled it between finger and thumb as he thought. 'What's the girl's name?'

'Esther Silverman.'

He nodded. 'Tell her to go to the issuing office the day after tomorrow. If my influence is worth anything the permit will be waiting for her.'

'Thank you, Thomas.' Martha stood up.

'Sit down, Martha, there is something you can do for me, for us, in return.' She lowered herself back into the chair.

'I'm travelling to England on a business trip early next month and Anna would like to come with me. We need you to stay here for a week to look after Alice and Evelyn. That wouldn't be a problem, would it?'

'Myrtle! Myrtle, wait'll you see what I've got!' Irene was waving a blue airmail envelope. 'It was there for me when I got home from work.'

'Is it a letter from Sandy?'

'It's better than that. It's a letter and a photograph!'

Myrtle shrieked with delight. 'I can't wait to see what he looks like!'

'It was taken at Christmas. He's having his Christmas dinner in a place called Ambala.' She looked at the photograph again

193

quickly as she took it from the envelope and handed it to Myrtle.

'Guess which one's him?' The photo had been taken from the end of a long table. Those nearest the camera leaned back while those furthest away leaned inwards, like some exercise in perspective.

'How will I be able te guess?' laughed Myrtle. 'Sure didn't you forget what he looked like and you spent a whole afternoon with him.'

'He's on the right.'

'Well, that narrows it down a bit and they're all good looking down that side.'

'He's there, third one along, smiling.'

'They're all smiling, Irene. It's a photograph.'

'There, there!' She leaned over and jabbed the photo.

'Oh that one,' said Myrtle, bringing the photo closer to scrutinise it. 'Did I say they were all good looking? I meant, all except that ugly one, third down on the right!'

Irene laughed and punched her in the back. 'I'm glad he's not your type. You'd only be after him too.'

Myrtle waved the photograph towards the rest of the Templemore Tappers. 'Hey, do youse want te see Irene's RAF fella?'

Martha had watched Irene's excitement with some apprehension. The correspondence between her and this young serviceman had been limited, but the arrival of the photograph today seemed to ignite a spark in Irene, as though seeing his face had put the relationship on a new footing. There was even talk of her having a photograph of herself taken to send to him. Not for the first time, Martha felt guilty for the sense of relief she felt in knowing that he was thousands of miles away.

Just then Goldstein arrived and behind him, still looking frail, but smiling shyly, was Esther. They came straight to her.

'Esther has something she would like to say to you, Mrs Goulding.'

In halting, but understandable, English Esther said, 'Thank you very much for my work permit.'

Martha was delighted. 'You got it?'

'Yes,' said Goldstein. 'We called at the office this morning and it was there waiting. We can't thank you enough.'

'Don't mention it. I'm just glad I could help. So now, Esther, you'll be working in the music shop?'

Goldstein translated and Esther smiled, adding some words in Polish.

'She says yes, but that her uncle won't let her serve customers until she can speak better English!'

At the other side of the rehearsal hall, Sheila was talking earnestly to Pat. 'Now you know what you're going to say to him?'

'Yes, I'm going to say "Good Evening, William. Are you ready for a run-through of the songs?"'

'No! We've been through this and we agreed it was best to come straight out and ask him.'

'I didn't agree to anything. It's you who's been rehearsing this pantomime.'

'You can't not ask him!'

'The relationship between William Kennedy and me has always been professional. It is not personal. So, the man is married. What concern is that of mine? Is it going to affect our performance? I don't think so.'

Horowitz stood centre stage and called the company to order. 'Right everyone. Thanks for coming. First the details of the next Barnstormers' show: we're booked to play a benefit concert in a little under two weeks to raise funds for the Mater Hospital. The concert will take place in the main hall at the Belfast Institute. Before the rehearsal begins Mr Goldstein would like to say a few words.'

Goldstein stood centre stage, put his thumbs in his waistcoat pockets and addressed his company. 'It is my belief that each show is a dress rehearsal for the next and there are several things from our last performance that we need to improve.'

'But Mr Goldstein, the audience loved it. They were on their feet at the end,' shouted Sammy from the back of the room.

'The standard will not be judged by the audience, but by me and I want improvements.' His eyes swept the room daring anyone else to challenge him. 'Entrances and exits are still poor. Get on and off the stage quickly. No hanging around enjoying the applause! No changes to the programme and no ad libbing unless agreed by me.'

There was some noise and a suppressed laugh in the vicinity of Sammy, who could never resist an ad lib. Goldstein ignored it and went on.

'Templemore Tappers, still under-rehearsed. Some of you are finishing a good five seconds after the rest. Now the "Indian Love Call", there was a bit of confusion last time when Sammy and not Pat ended up singing a love duet with William.' Raucous laughter all round. Goldstein waited for quiet. 'So, Sammy, you have got the part of the lovesick squaw and you and William will work on it to make it even funnier.'

'Finally, the finale needs to be the moment you send the audience away thinking they have seen an amazing show. It needs a lot of work. We begin in fifteen minutes.'

'Go on, Pat, he's on his own.' Sheila pointed at William sitting on the stage steps. 'Speak to him now.'

'For the last time, I'm telling you I'm not going to ask him.'

'Well, if you won't, I will!'

But Sammy in the Indian headdress got there first. 'Okay, Mr Mountie, time for us to work on our routine.'

Never mind, I'll see him later, thought Sheila. In the meantime she had business of her own to discuss with Mr Horowitz. She found him chatting to the man in charge of lighting.

'Could I have a word with you when you have time, Mr Horowitz?'

'Yes, of course. I've just finished here.' They walked out into the entrance hall.

'Do you remember at the last concert,' Sheila began, 'all the delay selling the tickets and refreshments?'

'I certainly do. You helped out, didn't you?'

'Yes, and I've been thinking about how to organise things at the Belfast Institute concert.'

Horowitz looked closely at the girl in front of him. Noticed her unusual appearance; hair cut close to her head; huge eyes that barely blinked as she explained her ideas. 'You're one of the Golden Sisters aren't you?'

'I'm one of the Goulding sisters,' she corrected him. 'I'm Sheila.'

'So, Sheila, how would you like to do Front of House?'

'What does that mean?'

'It means being in charge of everything you've just described. Think you can do it?'

'Oh yes, I could manage that.'

She left Horowitz and went in search of Pat and was surprised to find her backstage directing Sammy and William.

'At this point, Sammy, you need to look really sad, because you think he's gone forever.' Dramatic hand-wringing and miserable weeping sounds from Sammy. 'Then you think you hear him, but look doubtful. Suddenly, you see it is him and your expression changes to joy.' Exaggerated excitement from Sammy. 'But then you realise the love between you can never be and you come together to sing one last time.' Sammy wrapped himself around William, sliding lower and lower down his leg.

William tried to leave and, in doing so, dragged Sammy screeching in full falsetto across the stage.

'Thanks, Pat,' said Sammy, straightening the feather in his headdress. 'We'll run through it again; see if we can get even more laughs out of it this time.'

'The idea,' said William, 'is for us to really look like we love each other, while the audience see how ridiculous it all is. Brilliant!'

Pat, without another word, turned and walked away.

Sheila waited until it was the Golden Sisters' turn to rehearse their new song and found William sitting at the back of the hall. She slipped into the seat next to him.

'It's good, isn't it?'

'Yes, it's catchy. The audience'll be clapping along.'

'It gives Pat the chance to show her range too.'

'Mmm …' William was listening intently, tapping out the rhythm on the back of the chair in front.

'You enjoy singing with Pat, don't you?'

William continued to tap. 'Mmm … yes.'

'She really enjoys singing with you. She told me.'

'That's good.' He used both hands to beat a more sophisticated rhythm.

'William, do you like Pat?'

'Yes, of course. She's great.' He slowed the rhythm.

'William ... are you married?'

'What?'

'I said are you married? And have you any children?'

'What's that got to do with you?' His expression changed. 'Did Pat tell you to ask me that?' A momentary pause. 'No, no of course she didn't. She wouldn't. It's you asking, isn't it?' He stood up and without a backward glance edged his way to the aisle.

Sheila went after him. 'Someone told her you were married and had a child.'

He turned sharply. 'Who told her that?'

No denial then, thought Sheila. 'Just someone she knows. He saw you.'

'Well, that person was mistaken.' The anger was clear in his voice. 'And that's what I'll tell Pat.'

His opportunity came towards the end of the rehearsal when he spotted her alone, going through her music at the back of the hall.

'Who told you I was married?' he demanded.

'It doesn't matter who told me. It makes no difference to me whether you're married or not. In fact it's not even worth discussing.'

'Well just for the record, I'm telling you I'm not married.'

'Just for the record, William, I don't care.'

'Pat, I'm telling you, I'm not married!'

'There is no need to shout. It doesn't matter.'

'It matters to me!'

'I'm glad it does. A wife is very significant, not to mention a child.'

'But I don't have a wife and child, that's what I'm trying to tell you!'

'And I'm trying to tell you, it doesn't matter if you have,' said Pat calmly.

'But all of this ...' William waved his hand in the direction of the stage. 'You and me singing together, I care about that. I don't want us to fall out. There's something special between us.'

'Yes there is – a professional understanding, a successful act.'

'Oh Pat! Face up to it we're ...' He struggled for a form of words that wouldn't offend her. 'We're attracted to each other.'

'I've never given you the slightest reason to think that!'

'You didn't need to. It's there for all to see. Everyone who bought a ticket for the last Barnstormers' concert could see it!'

'Well, I'll make sure that no one at the next concert makes the same mistake!'

Chapter 15

'And have we been good girls, Aunt Martha?' asked Alice. 'Daddy said if we were good all week, he'd bring us each a special present from England.'

'You've been no trouble at all,' said Martha as she helped her down from the chair she'd been standing on to wash the dishes.

The child had a tea towel around her waist, but it was likely she'd be soaked to the skin with the amount of soapsuds she'd created.

'I love doing the dishes,' said Evelyn, whose turn it was to dry. 'I'm going to ask Mummy if I can do them every day.'

Martha could imagine Anna's reaction on hearing her daughters had been allowed to help around the house. At the start of the week the girls had been restless, squabbling between themselves. They had a nursery full of expensive toys, including a coach-built high pram and beautiful dolls with porcelain faces and real hair, but it seemed they couldn't settle for more than ten minutes before they came to tell her they were bored. She'd cut up some dusters and they'd gone all through the house finding surfaces to dust. They'd polished some silver, trying to outshine each other. They'd shelled peas, made shortbread and, best of all, played shop.

'This was your cousins' favourite game when they were your age,'

Martha told them as she emptied the larder of all the tinned and packet goods. They set up the counter using some cardboard boxes from the garage. Alice remembered she had a cash register and some cardboard money in the cupboard in the nursery.

'I'm going to be a shopkeeper when I grow up,' said Evelyn.

'Well, when I grow up, I'm going to be the person who shops,' said Alice.

They were their parents' children, thought Martha with a wry smile; one making the money, the other spending it.

In the evenings the girls had a bath, and then came downstairs in their matching nightdresses and soft warm dressing gowns. Martha told them stories about their mother Anna when she was growing up.

'We loved bath nights when we were young, although we didn't have a beautiful bathroom like you.'

'What was your bathroom like, Aunt Martha?'

'We didn't have one!'

'If you didn't have a bathroom then where did you take a bath?' asked Evelyn.

'In front of the fire, of course. We had a tin bath and we boiled the water on the range and filled it up. Then we took turns to get in it and wash.'

'And how did the water get away? Was there a plug hole?'

'We took it outside and emptied it down the drain.'

Then Alice asked quietly, 'And where did you go to the toilet?'

'In front of the fire, of course,' said Evelyn.

'No!' laughed Martha. 'We went outside to a little room where there was a toilet.'

'But what about in the winter?'

'Just the same, except you got very cold.'

'And when all this happened, you were Mummy's big sister?'

'I still am,' said Martha. 'I was fourteen when she was born. Old enough to finish school and help my mother take care of Baby Anna!'

Alice and Evelyn giggled. 'Baby Anna!'

Baby Anna, thought Martha. Who'd have thought that that little mite, so weak and sickly, would end up in this beautiful house.

Now she's away to London with her husband, staying in a fine hotel and I'm here minding her children, just like I minded her.

There was no doubt Anna had been the prettiest sister, but wilful, everyone said. When she took up with Thomas Wilson, a man twenty years her senior, no one was surprised and when she married him a month later, everyone wondered what had taken them so long.

'When will Mummy and Daddy be home?' Evelyn had asked the same question every night for a week.

'They'll be here in the morning when we get up,' said Alice.

'They'll be getting on the boat tonight. That's right isn't it?'

Both girls looked to Martha for confirmation.

'That's right,' and she showed them again the list of instructions and information Anna had left. 'It says "We sail on the 8 February on the mail ship from Liverpool to Belfast. We will disembark" – that means get off the boat – "at about five and will arrive home about six."'

'Let's go to sleep then,' said Alice, 'and when we wake up, they'll be here with our presents.'

Martha picked Evelyn up and the child wrapped her arms around her neck, then she took Alice's hand in her own. The familiarity of it made her ache, remembering when her girls were small. Where had those little girls gone? Sometimes she felt their loss acutely. Once in a dream she had been talking to Irene, adult to adult, and a movement at her side had caused her to turn and, looking down, there was another Irene smiling up at her. How old? Maybe seven or eight ... but undoubtedly Irene ... exactly as she had been. She had knelt down then and hugged her little girl, knowing it was a dream, but for as long as it lasted her child was back, just the same, just the same. And she wept in her dream, but when she woke, her heart was thankful for those moments when she had held her little girl again.

At the same time as Martha tucked the Wilson girls up in bed and promised again that their parents would be home in the morning, Sheila was organising the front of house staff in the entrance hall of the theatre of the Belfast Institute. She explained the ticket prices to the two ladies who had introduced themselves as 'Friends of the Mater Hospital'. They quickly got their table organised with programmes and a cash box.

'I'll open the doors now,' said Sheila. 'Don't forget, two shillings to get in; sit where they like; the price includes refreshments at the interval. If you need me, I'll be inside making sure they all get seated quickly.'

She turned to Esther. 'All you have to do is to greet people at the door, smile and say, "Good evening", then point towards the ticket desk.' Sheila gave a short demonstration. 'Do you understand?'

Esther nodded enthusiastically.

In the ladies' dressing room things were not quite as well organised.

'We have to sing the songs printed in the programme. You can't go changing them!' shouted Pat.

Not this nonsense again, thought Irene.

Peggy had been in a bad mood since they arrived. 'I'm not playing "We'll Meet Again". It's turned into some sort of anthem. Everyone is singing it and, as soon as we start it, they'll all be joining in. I'm not some sort of pub pianist accompanying the audience while they have a sing-along!'

'Look, Peggy,' Irene reasoned, 'we'll have to sing it this time, but we'll speak to Goldstein and ask him if we can replace it in the next concert. How's that?'

Pat let Irene have her say, then rounded on Peggy. 'And don't you dare go changing everything when we're out there on the stage. I know you: Irene and I will be there ready to sing what's in the programme and you'll simply play something else, and if we don't want to look ridiculous we have to do what you want.'

'That won't happen, Pat. Peggy is a professional – she wants the show to be a success,' said Irene. 'That's right isn't it, Peggy?'

Peggy turned to face the mirror and dusted her nose with powder. It was as though the conversation had never taken place.

It wasn't the song that was the reason for her bad temper, although she did dislike it intensely. It was the fact that Harry had failed to meet her at lunchtime as promised, and that wasn't the first time he'd let her down. Earlier in the week, she'd spent an hour waiting for him outside the Capitol picture house and in the end walked home on her own. If he didn't turn up tonight at the concert, she didn't want to see him ever again. Actually, she might tell him that even if he did turn up.

Pat, too, was in no mood to compromise. She had been deeply embarrassed by her conversation with William at the last rehearsal. The last thing she wanted tonight was to deal with Peggy and her antics. No, on reflection, the last thing she wanted was to sing with William Kennedy.

With Alice and Evelyn settled in their beds, Martha had some time to herself. Another woman given free rein in Anna's house might have chosen to spend the evening in the drawing room with its elegant Gillow furniture imported from England. The settees were covered with Japanese patterned yellow silk, and there were Italian side tables of yew, inlaid with rose and cherry wood. On top of these were Belleek Parian table lamps with silk-tasselled shades in soft blue, and an oriental rug, bigger than Martha's sitting room, lay in front of the fire. But Martha preferred the modest morning room with its slate fireplace and comfortable cottage suite, which had a luxury the grander room lacked: a wireless. All week the news had been full of the possibility that Hitler was massing troops on the western border of Germany and fears were growing that he meant to sweep across Europe.

At the Belfast Institute concert, the rumour that a member of the Stormont government was seated in the front stalls had an immediate effect on the opening acts. Entrances and exits were sharper and the show moved along at a good pace. Sammy knew how to impress and had the audience roaring with laughter at the suggestion that the caves on the Cave Hill had been requisitioned by the government as bomb shelters. Unfortunately, he explained, the authorities didn't realise by the time people had climbed the hill, the all-clear would have sounded! One or two in the know who looked in the direction of the government minister were delighted to see him roar with laughter. Sammy also had a bit of fun with the sisters on stage when he introduced them:

'And this is Pat?'

'No, I'm Irene!'

'Then you must be Peggy?'

'No I'm Pat!'

'So where's Peggy?'

'At the piano!'

Sammy jumped in surprise at seeing Peggy, who had sneaked on behind him and seated herself at the piano.

'Time to go, Sammy.'

'Can't I stay with you girls?' He looked from one to the other.

'No!' they chorused and swung into 'Every Time We Say Goodbye.'

As they took their applause, Peggy scanned the stalls. She spotted the government minister right away – dinner jacket, dicky bow, red face – but her eyes swept past him to the rear stalls and beyond, where Harry Ferguson stood.

'Peggy, get a move on!' Pat hissed. Without thinking, Peggy felt for the notes and began to play. There was a quick glance between Pat and Irene and an inward sigh of relief from both in response to the unmistakable opening bars of "We'll Meet Again".

Martha had made herself a cup of Earl Grey tea, something else she'd got used to over the last week, and sat down with a couple of pieces of shortbread to listen to the news.

'Reports are coming in of the possible sinking of a ship in the Irish Sea. Enemy action is suspected. A rescue effort is underway somewhere off the coast of northern England.'

The shortbread on its way to Martha's lips never made it. She stood up and stared at the wireless.

A change of tone: 'In the House of Commons today, the Prime Minister …' No further mention of the ship. Had she heard correctly? Every nerve was telling her to move, go somewhere, do something, but what? She went into the kitchen and washed the cup, dried it and put it away. That was a start.

She went upstairs and looked into each bedroom. Alice and

Evelyn were sound asleep. She went to the bathroom, washed her hands and face in cold water and stared at the middle-aged woman looking back at her in the mirror.

She should check the note Anna had left her; there was a chance … there was no point … they were making the crossing by boat tonight. But there must be several boats crossing the Irish Sea every night … there was a chance …

She returned to the morning room, sat in the same chair, ate the shortbread and waited for the next news bulletin.

At the interval, Goldstein found Pat. 'I would like a private word with you, please. Your performance just now of the Mozart duet was not as good as it should have been.'

'Pardon?'

'The notes were the right notes, but something was missing. Last time that song was the best in the show, but tonight all the emotion was gone.'

Pat could feel the colour flood her face. Did Goldstein know about her and William?

He went on, 'You are a wonderful singer, but tonight you must prove what a brilliant actress you are. In your next song you must convince the audience of your passion. Passion, Patricia. Find it, please.'

She found him in the wings adjusting his bow tie. 'William, I apologise. I was a little abrupt with you earlier and at the rehearsal.'

'Please, Pat, don't apologise. I should have been more open with you.'

'Don't let's talk about that. We need to focus on the performance. I'm sure we can make our next song something special.'

'Of course we can. You will be Mimi, the love of my life.'

'And you will be Rodolfo, the love of mine.'

'And then later, after the show, can we talk? I'd like to explain.'

'No need to explain anything. Let's just give our best performance yet.'

'You're very understanding.'

'No I'm not. Look, let's forget everything and sing with passion?'

'Yes, Pat, passion sounds like a good idea.'

'Are you two ready?' asked Sammy. They nodded. 'Right let's give them some culture!'

With every expression, gesture, note of '*O Soave Fanciulla*', Pat was Mimi singing of her new-found love and Rodolfo was at her side singing of his. Then suddenly his eyes flickered from her to the audience, his focus lost. She too sensed sound and movement in the auditorium, where seconds before there had been the stillness of concentration. William sang his response, but his eyes did not meet hers. Their voices blended together, the movement in the auditorium ceased and William turned to her again. But the spell was broken; the audience remembered they were not in a Parisian garret. Instead, they wondered what news had been brought to a government minister who was enjoying a concert, that had made him leave in the middle of a performance.

Another member of the audience followed him out. The love expressed in Mimi's voice for her Rodolfo had been too much for Jimmy McComb.

Pat maintained her composure and took her bow to warm applause, but once in the wings she turned on William. 'How dare you! Where was your concentration? I've a good mind to ...'

He put his arm around her waist, pulled her close and kissed her. 'Sorry Pat, but I have to go.' And he left the building, still, according to Sheila, wearing Rodolfo's dinner jacket.

When the audience had left, Goldstein called for the cast to assemble on stage. 'During the performance,' he began, 'a message arrived for the minister informing him of a serious incident.' He lowered his head a moment as if shaping his words. 'The Irish mail boat with three hundred passengers and crew on board has struck a mine en route from Liverpool to Belfast.'

The company left the building in sombre mood. Outside Irene linked Pat's arm. 'Aunt Anna and Thomas were due to come home tonight; you don't think they could be on that boat, do you?'

'I shouldn't think so. They wouldn't be on a mail boat, would they?'

'No, I suppose not – the Wilsons are more likely to be crossing first class on the Queen Mary!'

'Good show tonight, girls.' Harry emerged from the shadows and fell into step beside Peggy. 'Hello Peggy, thought you might like to come out for a bit of supper.'

'Well, you know what thought did.'

'No, tell me.'

'Followed the binman and thought it was a wedding.'

He continued, undeterred. 'Did I tell you I have this friend, runs a restaurant in Shaftesbury Square? We could be there in ten minutes.' Harry went to put his arm around Peggy's shoulders, but she ducked and stepped sideways. He smiled and pressed on. 'Have you ever eaten brown trout from the Bann?'

No answer.

'I'll take that as a "No" then.' He caught her hand and held it firmly. 'In which case, you've a real treat in store.' Harry stopped at a black Ford Prefect parked at the side of the road. 'Your carriage awaits.' He gave a mock bow.

'What about the others?'

'I've booked a table for two.'

Peggy hesitated.

Harry pressed on. 'Candles, soft music …'

'Wait here,' said Peggy and ran to catch her sisters who had almost disappeared into the blackout.

The restaurant was tiny, just six tables covered with red and white gingham tablecloths; green wine bottles, encrusted with rivulets of melted wax, held burning candles. There were French posters on the walls. Harry's friend, dressed in his chef's whites, came out from the kitchen to meet them.

'What about ye, Harry?'

'Not three bad, Rodney.' They shook hands.

'And this is Peggy, is it?' He kissed her cheek. Her eyes widened in surprise. She'd seen men kiss women they'd never met like that in films, but in real life …?

'The meal's nearly ready. The waitress'll bring you an aperitif while you wait.'

Peggy leaned across the table and whispered, 'He has our meal nearly ready? How did you know I would come?'

'I knew.'

The drinks arrived. 'It tastes of aniseed balls!' laughed Peggy.

'It's the height of sophistication in Paris.'

'They drink this in Paris?'

'So I'm told.'

'Have you ever been there?'

'No,' said Harry, 'but I will someday.'

'I've never been anywhere.'

'Not even over the border?'

'No.'

'Tell you what, I might be going over to Dundalk next week. You could come with me, if you like.'

'Maybe I will.'

The food was delicious. The trout had crisp brown skin sprinkled with almonds.

'The potato has a strange flavour,' said Peggy.

'It's the garlic.'

'I'm not sure I like it.' She tasted a little more.

'Oh, you have to eat it, we both do.'

'Why?'

'Because then, when I kiss you, you won't taste it on my lips.'

When the wine arrived, Harry explained that one glass with her meal sipped slowly would have no effect on her, but by the time the dessert was served, her head was light. Rodney made a fuss of her as they left, kissing her on both cheeks this time.

'Come back again soon, Peggy,' he said. He shook Harry's hand and passed him a small package. 'See you next week.'

Peggy felt a little strange walking to the car and was glad to feel Harry's arm around her. 'What time is it?' she asked.

'Not too late. I thought we could go for a bit of a spin. What do you think?'

Peggy leaned her head against his shoulder. What did she think?

She thought it was the most exciting night of her life and who would know if she was a bit late home?

They crossed the Lagan and headed east along the south shore of the lough. Harry talked and she listened. The car was warm and the sound of the engine soothing. Sometimes she drifted into sleep, then back again to the sound of his voice ... his childhood ... school ... learning to bake ... how yeast worked ... the first day he saw her at the City Hall ... The miles slipped away and the moon crossed the sky.

She woke to the sound of the sea, not a gentle lapping but the crashing of waves against a harbour wall. He reached across and took her carefully in his arms. She watched his eyes, saw them close, hers did the same then his lips were on hers and she knew beyond doubt that what she had experienced tonight was what she wanted for ever.

Martha didn't wake with a slow realisation that it was morning. She went from oblivion to full awareness that something terrible had happened and she must begin to deal with it immediately. The clock on the mantelpiece said half past five. The last news before she fell asleep confirmed the sinking of the mail ship and reported that a major rescue operation was underway. She remembered reports, after the sinking of the *Titanic* nearly thirty years before, concerning the panic over the lifeboats: some severely overloaded; others half empty; lost souls floundering in icy water. She splashed cold water on her face and went to wake the girls.

'Are they home yet?' asked Alice sleepily.

'Have they brought our presents?'

'No.'

'Why not?'

'Because your Daddy has lots of business to see to and he might not have got it all finished.'

'But you said ...'

'It was in the note they left ...'

'I know, I know,' said Martha, 'but guess what? I've got a surprise for you.'

'What is it? What is it?' Evelyn was easily distracted.

'I'm taking you to my house so you can play with Sheila. You'd like that wouldn't you?'

'I want to stay here and wait for Mummy and Daddy.' Alice folded her arms and pouted. 'They might come home and wonder where we are.'

'That's all right,' Martha assured her. 'We'll leave them a note saying you're at my house, so your daddy can come and collect you.'

Harry and Peggy sat on the sea wall, buffeted by the sharp salty wind, and watched the dawn break. They didn't speak, but once in a while he would lower his head to kiss her. Soon it was time to follow the daylight back into the city. He held her hand as she walked the sea wall like a child on a Sunday School outing and, when they came to the road again, he reached up, swung her in the air and set her on solid ground. The car, so warm when they left it, was freezing, with ice inside the windows, and they drove the best part of three miles before it began to warm a little and Harry broke the silence.

'What will you say when you get home?'

'I've no idea.'

'Your mother …'

'She won't be there. She's at her sister's. What about you?'

'Oh they're used to me coming and going on different shifts. Are you in work this morning?'

'Supposed to be, but you'll need to take me home to get washed and changed.' She imagined her sisters' reaction when they realised she'd been out all night with Harry. Well, let them think what they like, she didn't care.

Irene was already dressed in her trousers and turban and was eating her breakfast when her mother walked in with Alice and Evelyn behind her. 'What is it, Mammy? Has something …?'

Martha shook her head in warning. 'Away upstairs would you,

Irene, and tell Sheila to come down quickly.' Then she turned to the girls, 'Now then, you two, shall we have some nice tea and toast to warm us up?'

'Wake up, Sheila. Wake up!'

'What is it?'

'Mammy's downstairs with Alice and Evelyn. She wants you to come down.'

Sheila sat up in fright. 'Is it about Anna and Thomas? Were they on that boat?'

'I don't know. Look, if you come down now and mind the children, I'll find out from Mammy what's going on. She won't talk in front of them.' She turned to go. 'Where's Peggy?'

Sheila stared at her sister's bed which clearly hadn't been slept in. 'She never came home.'

'We can't deal with that now,' said Irene. 'We'll just have to stop Mammy coming in here. Look ...' She pushed a pillow into the bed and ruffled the covers over it. 'If necessary we'll say she's sick.'

'That'll never work.'

'Well, can you think of anything better? No, so let's go and find out what's going on.'

While Sheila sat with the children in the kitchen, Martha slipped into the sitting room with Irene. 'Did you hear about the boat that hit a mine last night?' Irene nodded. Martha went on, 'Anna and Thomas were on it as far as I know. There's talk on the wireless of survivors.'

'What should we do?'

'I'm going down to the docks. Somebody there will know what's going on. There might even be some survivors brought in.'

'What can I do?' asked Irene.

'The best thing is for you, Pat and Peggy to go to work as normal. That way I'll know where you are if I need you.' Martha paused. 'Shouldn't those two be up already?'

Irene didn't hesitate. 'Pat's getting ready, but Peggy's having a lie-in. Goldstein said she didn't have to go in until ten.'

'I'm going to go now,' said Martha. 'I can't sit around waiting for news. Sheila will be fine with the girls, won't she?'

'Aye, course she will. You and I could go down town together. I'll leave you at the bridge and walk over to work.'

'Great, get your coat on then.' Martha followed Irene into the hall.

'Where are you going?' Irene asked as calmly as she could.

'To tell Pat and Peggy what's happening,' replied Martha.

'I'll do that,' said Irene over her shoulder. 'You tell Sheila.'

There wasn't much on the roads and Peggy and Harry made good time back into the city. As they rounded Cliftonville Circus, Harry asked, 'Will anyone be up at this time?'

'Irene maybe, but she sleeps with Pat so she won't know I'm not there. I share a room with Sheila and she won't be awake for ages yet, so I'll be able to sneak in, I think.'

'Peggy, I don't want to worry you, but isn't that your mother and Irene walking down the road towards us?'

'It is! It is!' Peggy shrieked.

'Get down!' Harry's arm shot out, caught the back of her head and pushed her down in the seat. At the same time he turned his head to the side.

'You know, Irene, that man in that car that just went past looked a bit like Harry Ferguson.'

Irene stared at the black Ford Prefect as it disappeared up the Oldpark Road.

'Ach I don't think so, Mammy. Sure doesn't he have a sports car?'

Chapter 16

The fog that had blown in off the sea in the middle of the night lingered like bad news around the docks. Martha was uncertain where to start her search, but close to Donegall Quay she saw a crowd of people hurrying towards the harbour building. 'Are you here about the mail boat?' she asked a woman.

'Aye, I've a son coming back from England on it. First they said conditions were bad, but now there's word of lifeboats being found and a few minutes ago we heard survivors were being brought ashore.'

A man in a naval-style uniform covered in gold braid appeared on the steps of the grey porticoed building and waited for quiet.

'Ladies and gentlemen,' he said in an English accent, 'some survivors from the mail ship which collided with a mine ...'

'Makes it sound like it's their fault!' shouted someone.

'... off the coast of the Isle of Man last evening, have been brought ashore and are now being cared for in the immigration hall at the back of the building. If you would please form an orderly queue we will take the names of the passengers about whom you are enquiring and we will confirm whether or not they have, as yet, come ashore.'

'They're round the back!' someone shouted. 'What are we waitin'
for?' People began to run, but Martha knew a quick walk would do
well enough for, whether joy or heartbreak awaited them, running
would not make a ha'p'orth of difference to the outcome.

At the rear of the building those at the front of the crowd stopped
suddenly and fell silent as they passed into the hall.

Over their heads, Martha could just make out a dimly lit space
and, coming from within it, the high-pitched scream of a baby and
the smell of the sea.

They filed in as silently as they would have into church. Those
at the back, like Martha, could not at first see what lay in front
of them. She moved to one side and round a pillar and almost
stumbled over a young woman leaning against it, a puddle of water
surrounding her. Her eyes were wide and staring, her face grey.
A child of four or five lay across her legs face down, vomit
trickling from his mouth. Beyond her sat an elderly man in his
shirt sleeves clutching a grip bag with trembling hands, beside a
girl hugging her knees, head bent, hair in rats' tails dripping down
her back.

On and on … some standing, some sitting, most lying, all with
faces grey from fear and the seawater in their stomachs. All drying
slowly in the chill of the February morning.

'God help us,' whispered Martha.

Slowly people began to move. Those searching stepped carefully,
like crossing a stream, finding little stepping stones of marble floor
in the sea of bodies. Those survivors who were stronger realised
what was happening and stood on tiptoe to see if a relative had
come to claim them. At first they searched only with their eyes,
then several began to shout out.

'John. John Buckley, are you here?'

'I'm looking for Mary Donaldson!'

Soon the cries were echoing round the high ceiling, and some
were heard and answered: 'I'm here! I'm here!'

'Where? Where are you?'

Martha didn't shout. She took her time and moved systematically
through the hall.

'I'm sorry. Excuse me. Could I come through there, please?'

All the while she forced herself to look into the faces, some of them cut and bruised, all of them full of pain.

Anna and Thomas were not there.

She made her way back to the front of the building and found the harbour master. 'Excuse me, I'm looking for my sister and brother-in-law. They were meant to be on the boat, but I can't find them in the immigration hall.'

'I'm sorry, but the rescue operation is still going on. People are being brought ashore all down the Antrim coast and some have gone to Liverpool. It could be days before we can account for everyone.'

'What should I do?' Martha was close to tears.

'Look, I've got the passenger list. If you give me their names I could at least tell you if they were on the ship.'

'Thank you. They're called Wilson, Thomas and Anna.'

He ran his finger down the sheet. 'Wilson ... Wilson ...'

Sheet after sheet. 'No, there's no Wilson here.'

'But they were booked on the mail boat. I know they were. Can I see the list?'

He looked sceptical, but handed it to her. 'Check if you like, but you won't find them.'

On the third page a name halfway down jumped out at her. 'Goulding' followed by 'T and A'. 'That's them!' she cried.

'But that's not the name you gave me.'

'I know, but it's them. I'm sure of it!'

'Well, I shouldn't really tell you this, but we're bringing some more survivors ashore. Down there in one of the Liverpool ferry sheds. You could have a look.'

She followed his directions to a large corrugated-iron building open to the elements at the front; beyond it was the coal quay and black hills of imported coal.

Martha heard Thomas before she saw him. She never in her life expected to be pleased at the sound of his pompous, badgering tone.

'And I'm telling you, I am not staying in this tin shed a moment longer! Now you, young man, need to telephone for a taxi to take me home.'

'Sir, I've explained already that the port authorities are required to record details of all those rescued.'

'I've given you my name and address. What more do you need?'

'I'm sorry, Sir, I haven't the authority.'

'Don't talk to me about authority. There's no one in authority here. This whole business is a shambles. God help us if they start dropping bombs. You'll expect names and addresses from the dead I suppose!'

'Thomas.' Martha spoke softly, fearing he might turn on her in his rage.

He ignored her. 'Now, if you'll tell me where I can use a telephone I'll call for the taxi myself.'

'Thomas.'

He stared at her as though she was some unwanted interruption.

'Thomas, it's me, Martha.'

'I can see it's you! What are you doing here? Where are Alice and Evelyn?' He looked anxiously around as though they might be nearby.

'I came to find you and Anna. I heard about the boat on the wireless. Alice and Evelyn are at my house.'

'Right, I want you to wait here while I find a taxi.'

'Thomas.'

'What!'

'Where's Anna? Is she safe?'

'Why wouldn't she be safe?'

'The boat sinking, Thomas, you remember?'

'Of course I remember. She's over there.' He waved his hand.

Anna lay on her side. The fox fur, wet and shiny, had been thrown over her. Martha knelt and spoke her name softly. She touched her glistening forehead expecting it to be wet and cold.

It was burning.

'Anna, can you hear me? It's Martha.'

Through cracked lips she whispered, 'Martha.'

'You're going to be fine, Anna. Thomas has gone to get a taxi to take you home.' The stone floor was cold and wet, but Martha sat and held her sister's hand as the certainty dawned on her that war had surely found its way to Belfast.

'Irene, you're the eldest, so I'm leaving you in charge. I trust you to make sure that everyone behaves themselves.'

'How long do you think you'll be away?'

'I don't know. Anna still can't get out of bed. It's like the strength's drained out of her. The doctor's there every other day, but I don't think he's any notion of what's wrong with her.'

'Sure we can manage, Mammy, don't you worry yourself,' said Pat.

'I'll do most of the shopping and cooking,' said Sheila.

'And so you should,' said Peggy. 'You've no work to go to.'

Martha turned on her. 'And I don't want you out with Harry Ferguson every night either. Weekends only, please.'

Irene shot a look at Peggy. She'd had a word with her about staying out all night with Harry, but Peggy had told her to mind her own business.

'I've left you some money on the mantelpiece for food and the rent man. Sheila, be careful what you buy. Better to eat bread and vegetables than some bit of a pig you'd not recognise.'

The rain set in soon after Martha left for the Wilson house.

The girls were glad they'd attended the morning service and could spend all evening at home in the warm. Pat had washed her hair and was kneeling in her slip to dry it in front of the fire.

Sheila was doing her homework at the kitchen table and Peggy and Irene were reading old copies of *Red Letter* that Betty had passed on to them. Thunder was rolling over the hills above them and almost drowned out the knock at the door.

Pat jumped up. 'Don't open it 'til I'm in the bathroom!' she shouted and ran out of the room.

'I'll go,' said Irene. 'It must be important to bring anyone out in this weather.'

Irene opened the door a little and peered out at a dark figure with hunched shoulders and a cap pulled down over his eyes.

'Hello, is that you Pat?'

'No, it's Irene. Who's there?'

'Hello, Irene. It's Jimmy. Is Pat in?'

Without hesitation Irene invited him in. 'Come on in, Jimmy. That's a terrible night, isn't it?'

In the sitting room he removed his cap and rain dripped from his hair. 'Missed you girls at church this evening.'

'We went this morning to sing in the choir, but we thought we'd give it a miss tonight,' said Peggy without looking up from her magazine.

'Do you want to take your coat off? We could dry it over the fireguard for a while,' said Irene.

'Thanks very much.' He handed her his mackintosh. 'I was hoping to see Pat.'

'Well, she's a bit busy at the moment, washing her hair I think. Peggy, away and see if Pat's finished yet. How're you keeping, Jimmy?'

'Oh, well enough.'

'And your mother?'

'The same.'

'Pat says she's washing her hair then she's having a bath. She's going to be ages.' Peggy picked up her magazine again.

'I could give her a message, if you like,' said Irene.

Jimmy hesitated. 'I don't know …'

'Is it something important?'

Jimmy looked sideways at Peggy. 'I suppose it might be.'

'Peggy,' said Irene, 'could you read that in your room while I have a wee chat with Jimmy?'

Peggy rolled her eyes and left the room.

Irene saw the sadness in his slumped shoulders, the tired eyes, the set of his mouth. He's a really nice boy, she thought, but Pat isn't what he needs even if she's what he wants. 'What is it, Jimmy?' she said gently.

He took a deep breath. 'I've enlisted, joined up. Start basic training in a fortnight.'

That I didn't expect, thought Irene. 'God, Jimmy, why? There's no conscription and, even if there was, you wouldn't be called, you're needed in the shipyard.'

He shrugged his shoulders.

'Is that what you really want, to join the army?'

'Might as well,' he said, looking at the floor. 'There's nothing for me here.'

'You've got your work. Time-served carpenter now, aren't you?' Irene tried to sound positive.

He took a moment to shape a reply. 'Look Irene, you know don't you?'

'What?'

'How I feel about Pat.'

'I know.'

'Well, it's just not going to be. I can see that now.'

Irene didn't argue. 'But there's lots of other girls. Ones that …'

'Are more my type?' His look matched the bitterness in his voice.

'I was going to say, who would love to have a man like you. You'll find someone else.'

'I don't want anyone else and I never want to see her with someone else! I've had enough of that at the concerts you keep inviting me to.' He grabbed his coat from the fireguard and put it on. 'Just tell Pat I'll never bother her again.'

Martha had settled into a routine at the Wilson house: waking Alice and Evelyn each morning; giving them breakfast before school; spending time with Anna; making her a light lunch.

Later, while Anna slept the afternoon away, Martha would clean.

In the evening she made supper for the girls and got them ready for bed. After that, she had the morning room to herself where she would read the *Belfast Telegraph*, maybe do a little sewing and, of course, listen to the wireless.

She was surprised at how little contact Thomas had with his daughters. He left early in the morning before they were awake. He sat with them while they ate supper then either went out, he didn't say where, or stayed in his study.

Anna was confined to her bed. At first the girls wanted to be with her, but Anna's lethargy meant she showed little interest in them and within a week they had grown bored and only went to her room to say goodnight.

The doctor too seemed to lose interest. Martha had overheard him talking to Thomas in the hallway. 'Physically she's fine. Fit as a fiddle, you might say, but there's no spirit there and I've no medicine to restore that.'

Martha knew of a herbalist on the Newtownards Road – Betty and Jack swore by him – and after lunch one day she went in search of his shop. The bell rang as she went in and moments later a small wiry man with prominent, yellow front teeth appeared.

'Lying in bed all day, you say?'

'Aye, she's the strength to get up, but it's as though she can't face it.'

'What about fresh air?'

'When I suggest a walk, she seems frightened and won't go over the doorstep.'

'Food?'

'Doesn't want it, eats a few mouthfuls and hardly chews.'

'Talk much?'

Martha gave a humourless laugh. 'One word answers, if you're lucky.'

The herbalist stood a while and sucked his teeth, while Martha stared at the advertisements behind him: 'Sloan's Liniment', 'Conde's Fluid', 'Surgical Stockings'. Eventually, he seemed to reach a decision.

'You're to make a pan of onion soup, fresh every day, mind. By the end of each day she needs to have two pints of it down her.' He waited for a response.

'Oh yes, I'll see to that, two pints.'

Satisfied with Martha's commitment he went on. 'Now I'll give you a mixture of herbs to go in the soup. Two full teaspoons, one for each pint.'

Martha nodded. 'That's sounds grand. I'll see she takes it.'

'Yes, you will, because you must be with her all the time she's drinking the soup.'

'Yes. Thank you,' said Martha.

'I haven't finished.' He paused for her full attention. 'Now this is the most important part of the treatment. You must talk to her the whole time. At first you'll probably have to do most of the talking, but by the third day, encourage her to talk. It doesn't matter at first what she talks about, but by the seventh day she should be ready to talk about what has happened to her. Let her speak of this for another seven days and she will be well on the way to a full recovery. Now will you remember all that?'

Martha assured him she would and left the shop with a bag of herbs and directions to the nearest greengrocers.

She was surprised to find Thomas home early and waiting for her when she got back. He called her into his study and asked her to sit down.

'Martha, I want to thank you for what you've done these last few weeks. To tell you the truth I don't know how we'd have managed without you. Unfortunately, Anna isn't getting back on her feet at all and there doesn't seem to be anything that can be done for her.' Martha didn't mention the herbalist and the onions. 'I'll come straight to the point. Would you be prepared to take on the role of housekeeper until such time as Anna feels up to running the house again?'

'I don't know, Thomas, my girls are older, but I wouldn't want to leave them to fend for themselves any longer than necessary.'

'But this would be a business arrangement – you'd be paid.'

'It's not that, Thomas.'

He carried on. 'How about we make an agreement for three weeks at a time, at a wage of three pounds a week? You could earn yourself a tidy sum in no time. What do you say?'

Three weeks, thought Martha, time enough for the herbalist's cure to take effect. Irene and Pat were sensible enough to run the house until then. She nodded. 'Three weeks it is and we'll see how Anna is by then.'

'Good, good,' said Thomas. 'Now I'm having some important visitors this evening. We'll be in the drawing room. Could you get a good fire going? Oh, and we'll need a bit of light supper around nine o'clock. Do you think you could make up some sandwiches and a pot of coffee for us, nothing fancy? There'll be a delivery of cooked meats and bread later this afternoon. Is that all right?'

'Yes, that's fine,' said Martha. Good old Thomas, she thought, always gets his money's worth. He'd be expecting her to call him 'Sir' next!

The men arrived around seven when Martha was upstairs reading a bedtime story to the girls. Thomas met them at the door. She checked on Anna around eight and, on her way downstairs, she was met by the smell of cigar smoke and the sound of raucous laughter.

She made the sandwiches, wondering how some people could still find thick cuts of roast beef and cured ham when there was so little in the shops. The nine o'clock news had just finished when Thomas popped his head round the door and said, 'Ready when you are, Martha.'

She carried the sandwiches into the drawing room. The men were relaxing, with typed papers lying about by their feet. The man in the armchair nearest the fire was the oldest and was somewhat old-fashioned in his dress. There was something familiar about the cruel downwards turn of his mouth and the bags under his eyes, and his air of authority. 'Look here, Wilson,' he was saying, 'I hope you told these Westminster people that we run our own show over here.'

When she brought the silver coffee set and fine bone china cups she sneaked another look at him and something connected in her brain. Of course, she'd seen his picture in the *Telegraph* just last week: it was Lord Craigavon, Prime Minister of Northern Ireland. The tray rattled in her hand as she set it on the table.

She straightened up and walked to the door. To her left, away from the others, a young man sat sorting papers. As she passed he lifted his head and Martha found herself staring into the face of William Kennedy.

They left about eleven and Martha went into the drawing room to clear up. Thomas was leaning back in his chair, legs crossed, glass in one hand, cigar in the other. The cut-glass decanter on the table next to him had about an inch of whiskey left in the bottom.

'Martha, that was a very important meeting here tonight.' He gave her a hard look and weighed his words. 'You know the warning posters, "Careless Talk Costs Lives"?' He waited. She nodded.

'You know what that means?'

'Of course I do, I'm not stupid.'

'No, no. I didn't mean that.' He tried a different tack. 'You recognised someone here tonight, didn't you?'

She knew he wasn't talking about William Kennedy. 'You mean Lord Craigavon.'

'Yes. Now look here, Martha, you must not tell anyone he's been here. Do you understand?'

'Of course.'

He paused, considering the need to explain further, and went on. 'Sometimes, I deliver messages on his behalf when I travel to England.'

Martha nodded. 'Was that why you were booked on the mail boat as Mr and Mrs Goulding?'

He looked at her sharply. 'So you know about that, do you?'

'I saw the passenger list. That's how I found you at the docks.'

'Well I'm trusting you, Martha. You know what I'm saying? These are troubled times.'

On Esther's first morning in the shop, Peggy showed her how to remove each section of records and dust down the shelves. Then they moved on to the rest of the stock; Peggy would say the English word and Esther would repeat it.

'Wire-less.'

'Wire-less.'

'Gram-o-phone.'

'Gram-o-phone.'

Then on to the instruments.

'Trumpet … saxophone … cello …'

Esther pointed. 'Violin.'

'You know that word?'

Esther nodded enthusiastically and took the violin and bow from the display stand. She positioned it under her chin, placed the bow on the strings, closed her eyes and began to play. The shop was filled with the sound of Vivaldi. She looked like a child, so small and thin in her pinafore dress, ankle socks and buckled shoes. Peggy had the strangest urge to hug her. Esther seemed to sense Peggy looking at her, stopped playing and opened her eyes.

'You know what, Esther, now you're working in the shop, I think your uncle should treat you to some suitably stylish clothes. We'll ask him when he comes back.'

The ladies' department at Robb's was an elegant place; carpeted in soft grey Axminster, with mahogany counters and shelving. Peggy had never had the money to shop there and might have felt intimidated, were it not for the fact that one of the sales assistants was Grace McCracken, sister to John and Aggie. Grace, a reed of a woman with strong features like John's, was behind a counter folding silk scarves when Peggy and Esther got out of the lift.

'Hello, Peggy, I haven't seen you in months. You're looking very well.'

'Hello, Grace, how are you?'

'Well, I'm a martyr to the rheumatism in this damp weather but, apart from that, I'm grand.'

'This is Esther, Grace. Did Mammy tell you about her?'

'Oh, the wee girl from Poland, indeed she did.' She shook Esther's hand. 'Thanks be to God that He kept you safe.'

Peggy explained their mission.

'Should we start with some measurements?' suggested Grace, removing the tape measure from around her neck.

'Now, these black skirts are what we wear in Robb's. They're very good quality and hard-wearing. Never show a mark. You'll also be wanting a couple of blouses,' and from one of the drawers behind the counter she took a plain white blouse.

Esther pulled at Peggy's sleeve and pointed to a mannequin dressed in a fuchsia pink blouse, yoked at the shoulders.

Peggy nodded. 'You're right – much more stylish.'

Esther went into the changing room a skinny schoolgirl and emerged, a few minutes later, a slim and stylish young woman.

Grace turned to Peggy and smiled. 'Well, I think that's the work clothes sorted.'

'Not quite,' said Peggy, pointing at Esther's ankle socks.

'Are we thinking silk stockings?' asked Grace.

'We certainly are,' Peggy replied.

Finally, they bought two dresses in a soft woollen material, one in a lovat green colour, the other blue as cornflowers. Grace wrapped everything separately, tying each parcel with string that ran from a spool in the ceiling to the counter, and as she wrapped each item Peggy named it:

'Skirt.'

'Blouse.'

'Dress.'

And Esther repeated each word.

At lunchtime Peggy and Esther ate their sandwiches together in the back office and as soon as they had finished Peggy got her comb out of her bag.

'Esther, would you like me to do your hair?' She mimed combing and shaping. Esther's hair was thick and dark, not unlike Peggy's. She wore it parted in the middle and pulled back into a bun. When she undid it, Peggy saw the potential for a very modern style.

She divided her hair into two sections, wove each one into a plait, then fastened both together on top of her head. The effect was startling, drawing attention to Esther's heart-shaped face and large brown eyes.

The following morning when Peggy arrived at work, Esther was already there in her fuchsia blouse and black skirt, with her hair plaited on top of her head.

Peggy clapped her hands. 'You look wonderful!'

'Wonderful ... you,' said Esther.

'Just one more thing.' Peggy delved into her handbag and produced a lipstick. 'Stretch your lips.' She demonstrated, Esther copied and Peggy applied a thin layer of pink lipstick. 'Perfect!'

'Perfect,' came the echo.

Between them Peggy and Esther could complete all the routine chores by mid-morning. Then it was quiet until lunchtime when workers from the offices and businesses in the city would call in to browse and listen to some music. During the lull Peggy would be the customer and Esther the shop assistant. They started with simple phrases: 'Good morning', 'Good afternoon', 'Thank you', 'Goodbye'. Over the next few weeks they progressed to 'May I help you?', 'Would you like to hear the record?' As soon as Esther learned to count in English they moved on to the prices. As with everything, Esther was quick and eager to learn and soon she could name everything in the shop and its price in English. Sometimes they even persuaded Goldstein himself to join in. He would try to catch Esther out by asking for some obscure item, but so thorough had been Peggy's teaching that Esther would smile and say, 'Yes sir, we have that in stock,' and she would fetch it and tell him the price.

After one of these sessions he announced, 'Now that both you girls are running the shop so efficiently, I can begin to relax a little. I might even devote more time to the Barnstormers. It's time we had another concert, don't you think, Peggy?'

'That'd be great and maybe Esther could play the violin. You always say we need more culture.'

'Indeed we do and now more than ever. I have received a letter from our tenor, William Kennedy, expressing regret that he can no longer continue as a member of Barnstormers as a result of work commitments.'

'You mean he's not going to perform again?' Peggy was shocked, 'How can work stop him? We practise at weekends and perform at night?'

'It would seem his profession demands more from him.'

'Why? What does he do?' asked Peggy.

'Don't know ...' Goldstein reflected. 'I got the impression he was a civil servant.'

'What about his duets with Pat?'

'I am not sure that would have lasted anyway. There was that little matter of him leaving before the end of the last concert, if you remember.'

'I don't think that was Pat's fault.'

'Maybe not ...' He paused. 'I wonder does she know he has left the company.'

'I'm sure she doesn't,' said Peggy.

'Then you must tell her before she finds out from anyone else.' He checked his watch. 'Now, girls, get on with making me a rich man! I am sure you will shortly sell one of those new radiograms and, when you do, there may be a small bonus in your pay packets.'

Harry watched Goldstein leave for his lunch, then waited for Peggy to finish serving a customer before he crossed the road to the music shop.

'And how are my two favourite shop assistants today?' He flashed his best smile.

'I bet you say that every time you go into a shop.'

'Of course, it goes down very well at Burtons!'

'Were you interested in some sheet music?'

'No,' he said bluntly. 'Are you interested in a trip over the border?'

'What?'

'Sunday, I've a bit of a job to do for Rodney. You know, from the restaurant?'

'And you want me to go with you?'

'Well, you did say you never go far. Here's a chance to widen your horizons.'

'But it'll take hours and how'll we get there? Have you a car?'

'Questions, questions! Of course I've a car, Rodney's Ford Prefect. It'll take about three hours to Dundalk, so I'll pick you up at seven o'clock.'

'Seven o'clock on a Sunday morning! Are you joking me?'

'Chance of a lifetime, Peggy.'

'What, a jaunt to the Free State?'

He leaned over the counter and kissed her. 'No, to spend all day with me!'

Chapter 17

Peggy stood in the sitting room watching smudges of grey fade in the early morning sky. A wood pigeon called to its mate. Then from somewhere round the corner and down the road came the soft noise of an engine. She stood on tiptoe to watch the black car pull up on the other side of the privet hedge. She left by the front door and banged it shut behind her as if to shout, 'See, I'm going!' She hoped it had woken Pat, serve her right for trying to tell her she couldn't go over the border with Harry. She threw the chrysanthemum scarf she'd sneaked out of Pat's drawer around her shoulders and smiled.

'Good morning!' Harry leaned across and kissed her on the cheek. 'You're a sight for tired eyes this time of day.'

They were soon on the Dublin Road heading south.

'Let's have a bit of your blather then, Peggy. What do you know, that's worth knowing?'

'Had a bit of a row with Pat last night.'

'Oh, aye?'

'You know that William Kennedy, who sings with Pat at the concerts?'

'Aye, looks a bit of a Mammy's boy if you ask me.'

'Well he told Goldstein that he was leaving the Barnstormers. Couldn't fit it all in with his busy job, he said.'

'Why, what's he do?'

'Don't know. Goldstein thinks he might be a civil servant.'

'Right enough he looks like one, doesn't he?'

'I don't know, never met one. Anyway, Goldstein asked me to tell Pat about him leaving, so I did.'

'She was a bit sweet on him from what I could see when they were singing.'

'Of course she was. That's why I said, "You'll miss him won't you, Pat." Well, she rounded on me, started shouting. "William Kennedy means nothing to me. I don't care if I never see him again!" Then she starts bossing us all about, complaining the house was a mess and she was going give us all jobs to do today to get it looking decent before Mammy comes home. So I said, for one I wasn't having her telling me what to do, she wasn't in charge, and for two, I wouldn't be in to do the jobs because I was going out for the day with you. She was raging. Wanted to know where I was going. That's when she started: I shouldn't be going over the border, it was too far, it wasn't safe, Mammy would never allow it. So, I told her Mammy wasn't here to say I couldn't go and she had no right to stop me. She'll tell her when she comes back, I know, but it'll be a bit late then. Anyway, Mammy's quite taken with you, isn't she?'

Harry grinned. 'And why wouldn't she be? Sure isn't cake the way to a woman's heart?'

By nine they were through Newry and in sight of the Mournes.

'I've never seen real mountains before. What's that on the top?'

'Snow, of course. There's a lay-by just along here. We'll stop and have a good look.'

Laid out before them was a patchwork quilt of green fields and, rising above them in stark contrast, dramatic peaks; in the distance the sea glistened in the March sunlight.

Softly Harry sang, 'But for all that I found there I might as well be, where the Mountains of Mourne sweep down to the sea.'

'And there they are, just like the song,' laughed Peggy, turning to look at Harry. His face was serious.

'What is it? What's the matter?'

'Peggy, in this place, in this moment, I love you more than anything.'

She opened her mouth to speak and hesitated; she had no idea what to say, how to analyse her feelings and give words to them. Harry put his finger to her lips.

'Don't say a thing. The words will come when you're ready.'

And he brushed his finger over her lips and replaced it with his mouth.

The border post was insignificant. A few road signs warned it lay ahead and Harry slowed the car. A Northern Ireland customs official stood outside a wooden building and as the car approached he waved them through.

'Is that it?' asked Peggy.

'Is anyone likely to be smuggling anything into the Free State?' Harry replied. 'Now we're in no man's land, neither one country nor the other.' He reached across to the glove compartment, removed a brown paper package and passed it to Peggy. 'Just keep that in your bag for me would you?'

'What is it?'

He laughed. 'Ask no questions, you'll be told no lies!'

The Irish border crossing a few hundred yards down the road was much the same as the one they'd just come through, except the signs were on a green background and written in Irish as well as English. Once again the guard waved them through.

'It's Sunday,' explained Harry. 'A lot of people from the North take a wee trip over because the bars are open here all day.'

Dundalk was the first town over the border. They parked the car on the main street and walked its length. There were plenty of people about in their Sunday clothes on their way to and from chapel.

'They look just like us,' said Peggy.

Harry looked at her in surprise. 'And why wouldn't they?'

'I don't know. I just thought …'

'They're Irish, we're Irish. Drawing a line on a map in London doesn't change that.'

'The town looks a bit old-fashioned though.'

'What do you mean?'

'Like when I was a girl. The shops are a bit pokey and the houses look old.'

'That's a city girl talking, all right. Have you ever been to Ballymena, or any other country town in the north for that matter? They're just the same as this.'

Harry stopped outside a bar. 'Come on, we'll go in here. The first thing you have to do when you cross the border is have a Guinness and a Sweet Afton.'

Later they ate lunch in the only decent hotel in town: damask linen, primroses in a china jug, silver service, Irish beef, tender and juicy, with colcannon and carrots.

'Peggy, I need to do a bit of business now, can I have the package from your bag?'

She handed it over and stood to go.

'No, you stay here, pet. I'll pay the bill and ask the waitress to bring you some ice cream – it said on the menu it was home-made – then some coffee, and before you know it I'll be back.'

Peggy looked uncertainly around the room. She was the only person on her own. The waitress brought the ice cream, the best she'd ever tasted, with fine shards of ice in it that crunched on her tongue, but she felt self-conscious eating it.

Why couldn't she have gone with him? The waitress brought a dainty coffee cup and filled it from a silver pot. The sugar was cubed and brown, the coffee bitter. What if he didn't come back?

Time crept on.

People left … their tables were cleared … she refused more coffee … a petal fell on the tablecloth.

The air stirred … movement behind her.

'Right, let's go.'

'Where have you been?' Her voice rose.

'Never mind that now. Come on.'

The car was parked outside the hotel, its engine running.

Harry opened the door for her and walked quickly round to the driver's side. Before she had closed her door, he slipped it into gear and they were off down the street.

'Now then, how was the ice cream?'

'You're asking me about the ice cream! Where have you been, leaving me sitting all that time on my own?'

'I told you I'd business to do. That's why I took this trip.'

'And here was me thinking you wanted us to spend the day together!'

'I did ... I do. That's why I asked you along.'

'The border's that way. There's a sign, you missed it.'

'Aye, well there's more than one way to cross the border. So don't start giving me directions.'

'Stop the car!'

'What for?'

'I want to get out!'

'Don't be ridiculous, Peggy, you've nowhere to go. You have to come home with me.'

'Where is it?'

'Where's what?'

'Don't treat me like an eejit. The stuff you're smuggling!'

'Honestly, Peggy, there's nothing ...'

'Don't talk to me about honesty, mister!'

Harry turned off the road and into a lane. They drove a while in silence. The lane narrowed and after a few miles it became pot-holed and stony. They drove slowly past a ruined farmhouse, its roof of thatch long gone. Harry stopped the car and reversed up the side of the house, then switched off the engine.

'You can get out now if you like.'

Peggy sat a while, then opened the door and stepped out into long grass. Round the back of the house fields ran away towards a small rounded hill in the distance, on top of which grew a fairy ring of trees. Inside the house, spindly purple weeds grew in clumps; yellow lichen clung to crevices; the chimney breast was blackened with the soot of dead fires.

'It might have been the famine.' Harry's frame filled the tiny doorway. 'Maybe they died here or in some ditch along the road.'

'Perhaps one or two made it to England,' said Peggy.

'Or America.' He came into the room, touched the gable wall.

'Show me,' she said.

'What?'

She nodded towards the car.

He removed the back seat and underneath, packed tightly on a tarpaulin, were cuts of meat: steaks, joints, shanks …

'Is that it?'

He opened the boot and uncovered the tyre well. Where the spare wheel should have been, there were packets of cigarettes.

'The whiskey's under the front seats,' he said.

Peggy shook her head and sighed, all anger gone.

'Peggy, listen, Peggy …' She turned away. 'Everybody does it.' He waved towards the car. 'This is small beer. People are bringing lorry loads over every night.'

She faced him again. 'It's illegal, Harry.'

'I only do it now and again.'

'And what about Carrickfergus?'

'Carrickfergus?'

'More money in an envelope, handed over. Was that to do with smuggling too?'

'No.' He looked at his feet. 'That was something different.'

'But illegal?'

'Yes.'

'And Saturday nights, Harry. Where are you when I'm sitting at home wishing I was out dancing?'

'At a card school.'

'Also illegal?'

'Yes.'

'I think you'd better take me home now.'

The light was fading as Harry drove slowly along the country tracks, zigzagging ever closer to the border. Darkness closed in, but he didn't turn on the headlights. Eventually, they reached a junction and turned right on to a proper road. Within a mile there was a sign in English for Newry and Harry reached across and switched on the lights. They drove back to Belfast in silence.

He stopped the car at the end of her street.

'Peggy …'

'Harry, you asked me earlier not to tell you how I felt about you until I had the words. I think I have them now.' She swallowed hard and fought back the tears. 'I never want to see you again.'

'God, Martha, how long have I been eating this onion soup?' Anna was sitting propped up in bed in her pink crocheted bed jacket.

'Nearly three weeks,' said Martha, 'and that's the first time you've mentioned the soup. You must be on the mend! Do you want me to take it away?'

'No, sit with me and we'll talk again.'

'Alice and Evelyn are going to a party at a friend's house after school today. They were so excited this morning. They'll want to tell you all about it later.'

'They're good girls aren't they?'

'They're lovely, Anna, a credit to you and Thomas.'

Anna took up the spoon and stirred the soup. After a minute she spoke in a voice that was soft and measured.

'When it happened, I thought I'd never see them again.'

Anna reached out and took the picture of her girls in their party dresses from the night table beside her.

'I caught their faces in my mind and held them there, pushing everything else away. I tried to bring their voices to me as well. Nothing came at first, just the faces. Then I heard Evelyn the day I dropped a plate in the kitchen. "You're a silly-billy, Mummy," she said and Alice laughed. I had their faces, now I heard them too. "You're a silly-billy, Mummy," and laughter, over and over. The sea would lift me up and I'd see them, I'd hear them. Then the sea would drop me and I'd fall and fall and fall, my stomach heaving, the salt water in my mouth and I'd bring them to me again, in their party dresses, smiling. "You're a silly-billy, Mummy" and the laughter. Rise and fall ... rise and fall ... water over my head ... in my mouth ... I'd bring them to me.'

Anna sat perfectly still, tears in her eyes and on her cheeks.

Martha reached into her apron pocket, took out her handkerchief and wiped them away.

'Then something hit me on the side of the head ... hands were pulling me upwards ... my back scraped over something hard ...

the hands released me and I fell backwards into nothing.'

Martha wiped the fresh tears.

'I remember the vomiting. Someone had rolled me on my side in the bottom of the lifeboat. I heard a retching sound and only realised it was me when the bile burned my throat. Then the girls stayed with me until they brought us ashore.'

Anna took the handkerchief from Martha and dabbed her eyes. 'I don't know what I'd have done without you staying with us, looking after Alice and Evelyn and being with me every day. Thank you.'

'You don't have to thank me. What are sisters for? Sure you'd have done it for me.'

'Would I, Martha? Do you believe I would?'

'Yes, I believe you would, but God grant you never have to.'

Martha left at the end of the week and Anna stood on the doorstep with Alice and Evelyn to wave goodbye.

Thomas drove her home with two crisp white five pound notes in her purse and best of all, on the back seat was her companion, the wireless from the morning room, a gift from her sister.

'Mammy, I'm so glad you're back,' said Irene. 'It's been really hard looking after these ones. I don't know how you manage it.'

'I'm sure it wasn't that bad.'

'It started with Sheila and the meals. They were all right to begin with, but then she kept giving us the same things. When we complained she started spending more time at the McCrackens. Some nights we had to get our own tea with whatever was in the house.'

'Well, that'll do you no harm,' said Martha.

'Then there's Peggy. She's been the worst.'

'Now there's a surprise.'

'Oh, not the usual stuff like shouting and falling out with people. She's just not speaking to anybody at the moment.'

'What?'

'You might as well know. Peggy went out for the day last Sunday with Harry and they went over the border.'

'Go on.'

'When she came back, very late, she went straight to bed and hasn't spoken more than two words since.'

Martha pursed her lips.

'Then there's Pat.'

'Pat?' Martha was astonished. 'Surely not!'

'Well, we found out that William Kennedy ...'

'What about William Kennedy?'

'He's left the Barnstormers. You know he walked out in the middle of the last concert and now he says he can't come back because of work commitments. More like family commitments if you ask me.'

'I am asking you,' said Martha. 'What family commitments does he have?'

Irene sighed. She'd said too much already.

'Out with it, Irene, come on.'

'Jimmy McComb says he's married with a child.'

'Humph! And how would Jimmy know that?'

Irene was embarrassed now, knowing that her mother hated loose gossip. 'He says he saw William with a young woman and a child getting into a taxi. And then ... then Jimmy went and joined the army.'

'Dear God, is that all of it now?' asked Martha. 'Or should I brace myself for the announcement that the Germans have invaded and Goebbels is billeted in my bedroom?'

March had roared in like a lion with high winds and thunderstorms, but true to the old saying it would go out like a lamb with soft sunshine, primroses in the hedgerows and daffodils in the borders of the Gouldings' garden. By Easter the girls had settled into a routine of work, eating their evening meal in relative peace together, rehearsing for the Barnstormers' next concert and, above all, listening to the wireless.

Martha was up early on Easter Sunday morning. She had saved up the coupons to buy real eggs, not for their breakfast, but to hard boil and decorate so they could roll them downhill at the picnic planned for the afternoon. She also made some ham sandwiches and put the bottles of lemonade and cherryade in saucepans of cold water in the back hallway to cool.

At morning service, Reverend Lynas preached a sermon about Daniel in the lion's den and the need for courage and faith in the face of danger. The parallels were obvious to all, with the Nazis beginning their push across Europe and the lack of strong government at home.

'Churchill's the man to sort this mess out.' Ted Grimes was holding forth in the spring sunshine outside the church. 'The sooner he's running things the better.'

'And what do you think he'll do if he becomes prime minister?' asked Martha, now able to hold her own in any discussion about politics, thanks to her wireless.

'Get the army over there pronto and stop Hitler in his tracks.'

'But is there time? Hitler could be in Paris before they train, arm and supply an army able to stand up to him.'

Ted looked sideways at Martha; she continually surprised him. 'You might be right, Martha, but something must be done or the Little Dictator will be sailing across the channel and, let's face it, if London falls, we all fall and there'll be Burgermeisters in the City Hall and Wagner every night at the Opera House.'

'What's a Burgermeister?' asked Betty.

The Belfast Waterworks was a twenty minute walk from Joanmount, a stretch of open land with reservoirs where, seventy years before, water was treated and pumped to the growing city.

Now it was a place of recreation with pleasure boats, bandstands and gentle slopes where families could roll and chase their hard-boiled eggs on an Easter Sunday.

Martha spread out the old blanket and set out the picnic.

Sheila and Irene went to paddle in a stream and came back with stories of jam jars, nets and sticklebacks.

'Honestly, the boys were catching them so easy,' said Sheila. 'They let me have a go with the net. On the end of a long cane it was. They said they're thruppence at the wee shop where they sell ice cream. Could I get one, Mammy?'

'Even if you got one, you haven't a jam jar.'

'I could come back tomorrow ...'

Their neighbours, the McKee boys, came past with some serious fishing tackle and stopped to talk to Pat and Peggy.

'They said we could go out in a rowing boat later if we wanted to, all of us.'

'Right,' said Martha, 'we'll have the picnic now because we don't want the sandwiches and lemonade to get warm. Then we'll go on the boats and last of all we'll have the egg-rolling contest. How's that?'

The sandwiches on pan bread were neatly made, even Peggy ate the crusts, and the bottles of mineral were passed round.

'You know what?' said Pat. 'I think this is going to be one of those special days that we'll remember forever.'

'Why's that?' said Irene.

'I don't know, but when we're old we'll say to each other, 'Do you remember that Easter Sunday in 1940 when we all went to the Waterworks for a picnic?'

They sat quietly and thought about that possibility.

'I think you might be right,' said Martha and she took a camera from her handbag.

'Where'd you get that?'

'Is there a film in it?'

'There'd be no point in bringing it if there wasn't. I borrowed it from Jack and Betty and the chemist put a film in it for me.'

They took it in turns to pose individually, then in twos, threes, and when the McKee boys returned from fishing they arranged themselves on the grass for a family photo; Martha in the middle, Irene and Pat on either side, and Peggy and Sheila kneeling up behind them with their hands on their sisters' shoulders.

The trip on the rowing boats didn't go as planned. Martha was standing on the jetty waiting to be helped into the boat when she suddenly decided she couldn't do it and no amount of persuasion or firm hands could get her to step on to the rocking boat. In the end, Pat stayed with her and the two of them waved every time the boats went by.

'Now it's time for the grand egg-rolling contest!' shouted Sheila.

The eggs had been boiled in tea to stain them and everyone had decorated their own using Sheila's old paints. Finally, they had put them all in a wicker basket decorated with ribbons. At the top of the hill, Sheila took control of the proceedings to ensure fair play. 'On the count of three, roll, don't throw. Then run after it and roll again. First to the bottom with a whole egg wins!'

'Wins what?' shouted Peggy.

'Wait and see,' said Martha.

They rolled and screamed and tumbled and cheated and accused and laughed all the way to the bottom.

'I'm the winner, so I am!' shouted Irene. 'What's the prize?'

'You get to eat the egg!'

'Ach no,' wailed Irene. 'I hate hard-boiled eggs.'

'Not that egg,' said Martha, 'this one!' And she held up a chocolate Easter egg with the faces of the Five Boys on the box.

There were shrieks of delight and Irene had to hold her prize in the air while her sisters leapt up and down trying to grab it.

'Where on earth did you get it, Mammy?'

'You'd be surprised at the very important people I know, who can lay their hands on a substantial piece of chocolate in a time of scarcity.'

'What?' said Sheila.

'I think that's a very grand way of saying she has some cousins who own a shop,' laughed Pat.

They ate the chocolate and no one spoke, for any distraction would reduce the pleasure of chocolate melting in their mouths. Afterwards, they lay on the grass in the warm sunshine and listened to the humming of insects, the birds and the children playing.

And the thought of war entered no one's head.

On the way home Sheila, not too old to hold her mother's hand, said, 'I loved today, Mammy. Can this be our new tradition? Next Easter Sunday can we come here and do everything again, just the same?'

'Of course we can, love. Why wouldn't we?'

Chapter 18

Pat hated working at the Ulster Linen Works. She hated the sight of it, the sound of it, even the very smell of it. She especially hated Saturday mornings when the foreman Alan Briggs gave back any work that he judged sub-standard. Payment for these pieces was deducted from wages and they had to be done again.

'These tablecloths for the Orange Order are a disgrace! Youse should be ashamed of yersels producin' work a thon quality fer such important customers.'

'Oh that's it, is it?' someone shouted. 'Feared you'll be drummed out a the lodge for the quality of your tablecloths, Mr Briggs?'

'Mightn't get te carry the banner in the parade,' someone joked.

Briggs was red in the face. 'Bad enough you spoil a load of good linen. Don't start insultin' my beliefs as well!'

'Ach, catch yersel on, why don't ye, it's not the end of the world. We'll do them again.'

'Excuse me, Mr Briggs,' said Pat. 'What exactly is wrong with the tablecloths?'

'I'll tell ye what's wrong with them. The paint looks like it's been laid on with a trowel, not a best quality squirrel-hair brush.'

'But, Mr Briggs, we told you the paint for this order was too thick as soon as you gave us it,' said Pat.

'Too thick was it? Well, why didn't you do something about it? Youse should a used the paint thinner on it.'

'We couldn't.'

'Why not?'

'Because you forgot to order any, Mr Briggs.'

Whoops of derision and cheering from around the room.

'You, Miss Goulding, are getting above yourself! And if yer not careful you'll be followin' yer sister and collectin' yer cards before long.'

Pat painted orange lilies all morning. She spoke to no one and no one spoke to her. The only good thing about Saturday was that, when the morning's work was done, she caught the tram up the Cregagh Road to Aunt Kathleen's for her singing lesson.

'Pat, what is the matter with you? This piece is adagio, not funereal!'

'I'm sorry, Aunt Kathleen, I'm afraid I just don't feel like singing today.'

Kathleen looked at her in amazement. 'I never imagined I'd hear you say that. What on earth has happened?'

'Oh, lots of things, one after the other.' Pat bit her lip.

'Why don't we take a break?' Kathleen swivelled round on the piano stool and without drawing breath went on, 'Is one of those things the fact that William Kennedy has left the company?'

'How did you know that?'

'Oh, you'd be surprised what I know.'

'Well, I'm sorry not to be singing duets with him, but that's all.' Pat felt the tears close to the surface. She swallowed hard.

'And there's work …' Pat told her about the tablecloths and about having to paint them all again.

'But it's not just that, is it? If I'm not mistaken you don't feel at ease with the people you work with.'

'They're nice enough, but …'

'They probably have conversations and you don't have anything to contribute. You listen, but can't connect. Is that it?'

'Yes, yes …' Pat lowered her eyes. 'Aunt Kathleen, what's the matter with me?'

'Absolutely nothing, Pat. You've been in that job since you left school, haven't you?'

'Yes.'

'So maybe it's time for a change. People like you have a sensibility, a need for company, conversation, a life that goes beyond the day to day. There are people out there just like you who could be your work colleagues, your friends. You just haven't found them yet.'

'But where am I supposed to meet these people?'

'You need to come out of that factory, maybe find work in business, the City Hall, an office.'

'But I've no experience or qualifications for anything like that.'

'You're bright as a button,' said Kathleen. 'You could do it, I'm sure. Look, shall I make some enquiries; find out where there are vacancies?'

'Would you do that for me?' Pat was amazed at the possibility that her life could be other than it was.

Kathleen was as good as her word and when Pat arrived the following week she greeted her at the door 'They're looking for clerks in the civil service. You'll have to take a test of course.'

'A test!' Pat was horrified.

'A simple test of reading and writing, probably a bit of mental arithmetic as well.'

'Mental arithmetic! Aunt Kathleen, I can't do that, it's ages since I left school.'

'Of course you can. I'll help you. You can write your application letter today and next week we'll prepare for the test.'

That night around the tea table Pat announced that she was going to try for a new job.

'It's in the civil service and I'll have to take a test. Aunt Kathleen said she'd help me prepare, but I'm going to start practising the mental arithmetic tonight, so can somebody help me?'

'I will,' said Irene. 'Better than rehearsing those same songs again. When is Goldstein going to fix up the next concert?'

'He's having a lot of trouble getting permission from the authorities,' said Peggy.

'What authorities? He's never had to do that before, has he?'

'That's because the concerts have never been for a military audience before.'

'No! Are we going to sing to soldiers?'

'I'm not supposed to tell anyone,' said Peggy, 'so you all have to swear to keep it a secret.'

'Where are we going to sing?' asked Pat.

'Probably Holywood Barracks,' said Irene.

'Or Balmoral Barracks,' said Martha knowingly. 'Have you seen the front of the *Telegraph* tonight? There's another battalion arriving there next week. The place must be bursting at the seams.'

'Can you imagine it?' whispered Irene. 'All that khaki!'

'I certainly can.' Peggy smiled.

That night when the girls were in bed, Martha settled down to listen to the wireless before the service shut down for the night. The news had been getting steadily worse all week. Belgium and the Netherlands had fallen. The British and French forces had been pushed further and further back and reinforcements were being sent across the channel. She recalled the conversation she'd had with Mrs McComb at church a few weeks before. Jimmy had completed his basic training and left for England expecting to be sent on active service almost immediately.

'You have to wear a costume for an interview,' insisted Peggy, 'and a hat wouldn't go amiss either.'

'She's not going to a wedding,' said Irene.

Pat slumped back on the settee. 'It doesn't matter. I don't have a costume, so I'll have to wear my Sunday frock and that's an end to it. I won't even get the job, anyway.'

'You've got to be confident,' said Martha. 'You're intelligent, you speak well, your handwriting is beautiful and you've a head for reckoning. What else could they want?'

'Somebody in a costume!' insisted Peggy.

'We must know somebody who could lend you one. Think,' said Irene.

'Aye, but it'll need to be someone Pat's size,' said Peggy.

Pat turned on her. 'What do you mean "Pat's size"? You keep your personal remarks to yourself!'

'Well, you're not my size, are you?'

'No, but that doesn't matter, because you haven't got a costume either!'

'Mrs McKee,' said Martha.

'What about her?'

'She has a very nice navy blue serge costume. She had it for her sister's wedding in ... when was it now? Nineteen thirty six. She's your size near enough, Pat,' said Martha. 'I'll go and ask her.'

The suit was a good fit, even if it was a little old-fashioned in style, and it came with a little navy straw hat with a red band.

'You could wear your turquoise blouse underneath – that'll brighten you up,' said Martha. 'Now, try the hat.'

Mrs McKee obviously did not have the same sized head as Pat.

'It looks ridiculous, perched on the top of your head,' said Peggy. 'Forget the hat, I'll do your hair for you in the morning. We'll sweep it back in a French pleat.'

There were fifteen people taking the civil service test that morning, all sitting at small desks in a stuffy room. It began with a comprehension test, followed by a writing test in which they had to answer a letter of complaint from someone unhappy about having to pay taxes, and finally the mental arithmetic.

Afterwards, they were shown into a room and given a cup of tea while they waited to be called for interview.

'Miss Goulding, would you like to come through now, please.'

An elderly man sat behind a large wooden desk. 'Please sit down.'

He asked some questions about the test and Pat realised that while she had been drinking tea it had been marked.

'Hum ... your mental arithmetic is good, spelling not too bad, some common sense shown in the letter you wrote.'

It sounded quite positive.

'Now tell me about your present employment.'

'I'm at the Ulster Linen Works,' said Pat.

'You're in the office there?'

'No. I work in the finishing room.'

'Finishing room?'

'I paint the linen goods.'

'Oh, I see …' He didn't hide his disappointment. 'What do you do in your spare time?'

'I sing.'

'Indeed, and what do you sing?'

'All sorts of things: modern, classical …'

'Classical?' He leaned forward in his chair. 'I'm fond of opera myself. Which composers do you like?'

Pat leaned forward too. 'I like Mozart, Puccini …'

'Ah, Mozart.'

'I sang the opening duet from *The Marriage of Figaro* at a concert recently.'

'Did you really? What concert was this?'

'It was to raise money for the Mater Hospital.'

'A very worthy cause in these troubled times.' He sat back in his chair. 'One final question, Miss Goulding.' He fixed her with an earnest expression. 'What do you think of the music of Gilbert and Sullivan?'

Without hesitation Pat replied, 'I love it.'

'You know, Miss Goulding, I think you're just the sort of young lady we need in the civil service.' He walked her down the stairs to the entrance hall. 'Details of the department you'll be assigned to will be sent in the post together with your starting date.'

'Thank you so much,' said Pat as he shook her hand at the door.

'Not at all. Did I mention there's a civil service choir?'

'You be sure and get that last bus home, or you'll have me to answer to!'

'Mammy, will you stop fussing. Everybody we know is at the Floral Hall tonight. We'll be fine.'

Peggy and Irene stood on the edge of the hearth looking in the mirror. The chill had gone from the early evening air as May drew to a close and for the first time in many months the fire hadn't been lit.

'I wish you wouldn't wear all that make-up. It's not decent.'

'Sure it's only a wee bit of powder so our noses don't shine,' said Peggy.

'And a slick of lipstick so our lips do,' laughed Irene, then added, 'Are you sure you don't want to come with us, Pat?'

'Yes, I'm sure. I told you, I don't want to spend any money because I'll have to work a week in hand when I start the new job.'

'We're away then. Just leave the key on the string behind the letterbox. We won't be late!'

The trolleybus let them off on the Antrim Road at the foot of a high grey wall with a banner stretched across it proclaiming 'Grand Summer Dance'. Steps were set into the wall at either side leading to the Floral Hall.

Peggy and Irene paid their shilling at the door and went inside. On the stage was a small orchestra: two trumpets, two trombones, a piano and a couple of snare drums. Several couples were fox-trotting around the dance floor. The tempo changed and Irene said, 'Let's dance a quickstep to this.'

Young men stood about watching the dancers and every time two girls went by dancing together there were whistles and catcalls. Irene ignored them and concentrated on leading Peggy round the floor, avoiding other couples. Peggy, on the other hand, was constantly looking around and smiling. When the music stopped she went to apply some more make-up and Irene made for the back of the hall where there were drinks for sale.

'Irene! Irene!'

At first all she could see was a hand waving, but she thought she recognised the voice.

'Theresa! Is that you?'

Her friend appeared through the crowd and they both spoke at once.

'How are you?'

'Haven't seen you for ages!'

Then Irene noticed someone at Theresa's side, holding her hand. 'This is my friend Michael.'

Irene thought he looked familiar. 'Do I know you?'

'I don't think so,' he said and turned away.

'It's so hot in here,' said Theresa. 'Let's get some fresh air.'

Outside there was a cool breeze and a wall to sit on.

'How've you been? How's your hand?'

'It's fine now. Are you still working in your uncle's bar?'

'Yes, but I'm not doing as many hours as I was. My mother's not well, so I look after her a lot of the time. What about you? Still working at Shorts, running up and down those ladders?'

'Still there, but the days are long and they're talking about shift work.'

'And how's Pat? Tell her I was asking for her.'

'She starts a new job next week, civil service.'

'That's great. The linen works wasn't right for her, was it?'

'How's Sean?'

Theresa lowered her head and spoke softly. 'He's never been back.' She sighed. 'You'd think a person could lose themselves in a city, especially when it's in complete darkness half the time. That they could walk the streets and nobody would stop them and accuse them of something they didn't do.'

'Is he safe, Theresa?'

'Yes, he's safe, as long as he stays where he is, but how can he settle when his ma's ill and his da's in prison and he might never see either of them again?'

'Why won't they let your father out? He hasn't done anything.'

'Ah, that's where they have us, don't they? They put you away for something they think you might do. And, even when your wife's dying, they keep you in a stinking prison ship, miles from your family.'

'A prison ship?'

'In Strangford Lough; takes nearly two hours to get there. I've been a couple of times, took our Marie, but he'll never see Mammy or our Sean again.'

'Maybe when the war's over …'

'Sean won't come back. He sends us letters to a friend's house. Last time he wrote he was talking about America.'

'Will you tell him I was asking for him?'

'I will. He liked you, you know, said you were brave not to say anything even when you were really sick.'

'Theresa, is Michael …?'

'Don't ask.'

'No, I mean you and him?'

'He looks after me.'

'I'm sorry we lost touch. Look, if you want to contact me, leave a message with our Peggy. You know she works in the music shop on Royal Avenue? We could meet up in town, have a good chat.'

'Aye, I'd like that.'

Theresa went in search of Michael and Irene found Peggy in the toilets where she'd met up with her friend Thelma Boyd.

'Hello, Irene. How ye doin?' Thelma was sitting on the floor, her back against the wall. Peggy was next to her and between them was a brown bottle.

'What's that you've got there, Thelma?' asked Irene.

'A bit a sherry.' Her voice was slurred.

'You'll not do much dancing with that inside you.'

'Oh you'd be surprised,' said Thelma. 'Anyway, I've shared it with my friend Peggy. Haven't I, Peggy?'

'Peggy, what are you drinking that for?'

'I like it. It tastes horrible, but it makes me feel happy.'

'Don't be ridiculous. Come on, let's go and have another dance.' Irene offered her hand and pulled Peggy up. Back in the hall they met up with the McKee brothers and some of their friends.

'Come on, Irene,' said Brian, 'I'll show you some of the fancy steps a bob's lesson can buy you at John Dossor's.'

'You've not been taking lessons, have you?'

'Certainly have. Got fed up standin' round like an eejit every time I went to a dance. Anyway you get to meet more girls this way!'

He was a good dancer with a sense of rhythm and not scared to lead. After the first dance they were going back to the others, but the music started again and it had such a beat to it that Brian pulled her back on the dance floor. 'This is great!' he shouted. 'The Lindy Hop is what they're doing in America now. Come on, I'll show you.'

Most couples, unsure about the fast pace, had left the floor, leaving more space for the more adventurous dancers. Irene saw right away that the steps were quite simple: the trick was to move all of the body, swinging the hips and the shoulders then moving backwards then forwards pivoting on the balls of the feet. Once she got the hang of that by mirroring Brian's steps, he took her hand and they moved together, shoulders, hips, ankles – all to the same rhythm. Then Brian shouted, 'Stand still, Irene!' and he picked her up at the waist and swung her over his hip and back to the floor again. 'You get it?' She laughed and nodded. 'Then let's go again ... only both sides!'

This time she was ready for it: he picked her up; she swung into the lift; catching the rhythm; back to the floor; the swivel and lift on to his other hip. Then down again. She heard cheering and the tempo quickened. Brian caught her hand and leaned right back, his free hand making waving movements in the air as he circled. Irene did the same; round and round they went, both of them twisting on the balls of their feet. Then back to the beginning to repeat the steps. As the end came, Brian grabbed her waist and shouted, 'Jump in the air!' She did so and he stepped quickly between her legs so that one went to either side of him and immediately he threw her up again to stand her on her feet as the music ended with the sound of cheering and whistling ringing in their ears.

The key was on the string behind the letter box when they crept in at eleven.

'Is that you girls?' Martha called from the sitting room.

She was sitting in the dark, the curtains hadn't been drawn.

Weak moonlight outlined her silhouette in the armchair next to the wireless. Pat was on the settee.

'You didn't need to wait up for us,' said Peggy. 'We got the last bus like we said we would.'

'What's the matter? Why aren't you in bed?' asked Irene.

'We've been listening to the wireless.' Pat's voice caught.

'The wireless? Why what's happened?'

Martha spoke softly. 'There's these troops, thousands of them.

They were supposed to be stopping the Germans from moving into France. They've been fighting and fighting, but the Germans have been so strong …' She searched for the words to describe the immensity of it all. 'They're being pushed back and back on to the beaches and there's nowhere else for them to go but into the sea.'

'They're stuck there,' said Pat, 'waiting to be killed or drowned.'

'Does this mean we've lost the war?' asked Peggy.

'I don't know. They're trying to rescue them,' said Martha, 'but how many boats would it take for all those men?'

'Where's Sheila?' asked Irene.

'We sent her to bed early,' said Martha. 'I think we should all go to bed now and pray for those poor men. We'll listen again in the morning to find out what's happening.'

By breakfast time, there were reports of heavy fighting as the British and French forces continued to fall back towards the coast. Martha couldn't get the image of desperate, exhausted men out of her mind and grew more and more anxious as the day wore on. She was glad when Ted Grimes arrived in the afternoon, straight from his early shift.

'Well, Ted, what do you think about this Dunkirk business?'

'It's a dark day and that's for sure.'

'Will they die, Ted, do you think?'

'Many of them will, Martha, unless they can find some way to get them off the beaches. They say two war ships left the docks early this morning. Not hard to guess where they're headed.'

By the following morning an appeal had been made for all civilian owners of seaworthy craft capable of crossing the channel to Dunkirk to transport military personnel back to England. In Belfast, for the first time in many months, apathy gave way to renewed interest in the war. For the next week, Irene heard Dunkirk discussed in the canteen at Shorts; Peggy heard it in Goldstein's shop; Pat heard it around the work table in the mill; Sheila's teachers explained it in school. Martha heard it in Carson's butchers as the woman in front of her in the queue discussed it with her friend.

'You can't picture that many people can you? What does over three-hundred thousand look like? My husband says they're lucky if they get two thousand at Glentoran for the football, so that's one-hundred-and-fifty football grounds full of men rescued.'

'That's all well and good, but my husband says they haven't told us how many died. He says that's propaganda for you; trying to turn a disaster into a success.'

'Aye, well there's one wee boy won't be coming home from Dunkirk, that's for sure.'

'What do you mean?'

'Jimmy McComb, lives just down the Cliftonville there, killed in action. His mother had the telegram yesterday.'

Martha saw the sawdust at her feet wet with the blood that had dripped from the beef carcass hanging next to her. Then she was outside in the warm sun retching.

They ate their tea in silence, the cheese on toast like cardboard that they could only swallow with mouthfuls of tea. Pat wanted nothing and went to bed early, for the next day she would start work at the Ministry of Public Security.

Chapter 19

'Did you get a postcard from Goldstein yesterday?' asked Irene as she joined Myrtle at tea break in the canteen.

'No, what'd it say?'

'Rehearsals this weekend and next, for a concert at Balmoral camp the week after.'

'So the army are goin' te let us perform?'

'Aye and Goldstein says it's our biggest show yet.'

'Think about it, all those soldiers.' Myrtle's voice rose with excitement. 'We could have our pick of them.'

'You could, but I prefer air force blue to khaki.'

'You're not still thinking about Sandy? I've told ye before, Irene, he's not here, so you're free to look around.'

'But what if I told you I've had a letter and he's coming back from India!'

'When?'

'Don't know. Might've left on the same boat as the letter. He could be here already!'

'So where will he be stationed?'

'He didn't say.'

'That's because someone might read it and tell the Germans

where to find our planes,' said Myrtle.

'How could they do that?'

'I don't know, but they say it happens all the time.'

'He got my letter with the photograph. I told you, didn't I? I sent him one of me taken on Easter Sunday at the Waterworks. He said I looked lovely!'

'Oooh, he could end up over here. He could come and find ye in Short's canteen one break time when you're eatin' your tea and scone and ...' Myrtle suddenly stopped speaking and stared over Irene's shoulder. 'Don't turn round ...'

'What is it?'

'I don't know ... it could be ... he's wearing a blue uniform ... he's lookin' this way ... searching.'

'Who, who?' shouted Irene.

'That ugly brute of a foreman in his boiler suit come to fetch us back to work!'

Esther stood at the shop window, her cheek against the pane as she squinted down Royal Avenue. 'He's coming,' she shouted.

Peggy shoved the sheet music she'd been sorting under the counter and rushed into Goldstein's office leaving the door slightly ajar. The shop bell rang and Peggy held her breath waiting for Esther to speak. 'Good afternoon, sir. Can I help you?'

'Yes, Esther.' A smile in his voice. 'You can call me Harry for a start.' He propped himself against the counter. 'I'd like to buy a record.' His eyes swept the shop and stopped momentarily at Goldstein's door. Peggy stepped back quickly.

'Which record, sir?'

'I think it's called "Who's Sorry Now?" Do you think I could listen to it?'

'Of course.'

The music began and Harry leaned back on both elbows and fixed his eyes on Goldstein's door. When the record finished, Esther lifted it off the turntable and put it back in its cardboard sleeve.

'Shall I wrap it for you?'

'No thanks, I'm not sure it's the one I want. I'll think about it.'

And he left the shop calling behind him, 'See you soon, Esther. See you soon, Peggy.'

'What is he playing at?' Peggy appeared. 'That's every day this week he's been in asking for a record to be played.'

'It's simple. "I Miss You So"; "Only Forever"; "I'll Never Smile Again". He tries to tell you something, Peggy.' Esther giggled. 'He loves you, I think.'

'Well, he needn't think he's going to get round me with a few love songs.'

'He is very handsome,' said Esther dreamily, 'with his dark hair and lovely smile.'

'You,' said Peggy, 'have too much English for your own good. Don't go practising it on the likes of Harry Ferguson!'

Irene and Peggy lay on an old blanket in the back garden surrounded by the sound of bees and the scent of floribunda roses rambling over the fence from the Harpers' garden. In the kitchen Martha was preparing the Sunday dinner, crying over the onions. There was the sound of something heavy being dragged and Pat emerged from under the stairs, red in the face and dripping with sweat.

'We'll have to clear this place out. There's stuff in here older than I am.'

'Pat, will you leave things be. I'm not having you throw out things that'll maybe come in useful.'

'But, Mammy, we're going to need some protection from air raids. Where were you thinking of going when the warning sounds?'

'Oh, I don't know,' said Martha, scraping the onions into a pan, 'out in the garden maybe.'

'In the garden!' Pat was appalled. 'That's the worst thing you could do.'

'Why's that? Sure it would stop the house falling on my head.'

'The house gives you some protection, provided it doesn't take a direct hit. Out in the open you've no chance. Did you not read that wee leaflet I brought home from the ministry?'

Martha sighed. 'No, I'm sorry to say I didn't.' She gathered up

255

the vegetable peelings and went outside to the compost heap. Pat followed her into the garden.

'It's called "Your House as your Air-Raid Shelter". It tells you how to create a safe area inside your house.'

Peggy rolled over on to her stomach and shouted, 'Look out it's the man from the ministry spreading panic again!'

'Don't be so stupid,' said Pat. 'I'm telling you, if the bombs fall you'll not be laughing, you'll be banging on the door of our shelter.'

'Are we having a shelter?' asked Irene.

'We are, because I'm going to make one and if you want to be in it, you have to help me.'

Irene jumped up. 'I'll help you. What do you want me to do?'

Pat's plan was simple. They'd remove everything from under the stairs. 'It's the strongest part of the house,' she told them.

'So we need to get it ready with things we might need to stay there all night.'

'There isn't room for all of us in there,' said Peggy, who joined them as they stared into the darkness. 'We'll die of suffocation long before the all-clear sounds.'

The late afternoon sunshine was a welcome sight after the drizzle of the morning, especially as the concert at the Balmoral camp was to take place in the open air.

'Imagine,' laughed Peggy, 'an entire regiment of soldiers and no Mammy to keep an eye on us!'

'It is most unfortunate that the military authorities refused her a pass because she's not a performer,' said Goldstein, 'but I have assured her that military discipline is tight and so is mine.'

He wound down his window as a guard, rifle at the ready, emerged from his sentry box. 'Now, get your passes ready, girls, and make sure you follow my orders at all times.'

They were directed to a low wooden building with a brass plaque on the wall engraved with the words 'Officers' Mess'.

The sound of dozens of conversations met them at the open door and as they entered the girls stopped momentarily, taken aback by the splendid navy and red plumage of a hundred officers in full dress uniform.

Likewise, at the sight of three young women in floral summer dresses in their mess, the men closest to the door paused in their war talk to stare and behind them more and more conversations fell silent. Then a young officer hurried up to Goldstein, his hand outstretched.

'You must be from the concert party.' The moment had passed, the conversation wound up again and he went on, 'I'm Captain Ayres, in charge of entertainment.'

'Thank you, we are delighted to be here,' said Goldstein. 'I wonder if it would be possible to speak to the quartermaster.'

'Of course, I'll find someone to look after the ladies and I'll take you over to the stores myself.'

Irene, Pat and Peggy were immediately surrounded by several officers. 'Are you performers?'

'Yes, we're singers,' said Irene.

A young dark-haired officer, so close to Irene she could smell the Brylcreem on his hair, asked, 'Do you dance too?'

'Not in the act, but there's a troupe of dancers performing. They'll be here soon.'

'Oh … that's a pity,' said another. He nodded at Peggy and added. 'I was hoping to win you in the raffle.'

'I beg your pardon?' said Peggy.

'What do you mean win us in a raffle?' asked Pat sharply.

'There's to be dancing in the mess after the concert.' His words tumbled out in his excitement. 'We've bought raffle tickets to dance with the performers.' He blushed then and added, 'The ladies, I mean, not …' His voice trailed off as Pat gave him a withering look.

'Dancing as well?' Irene was delighted. 'I hope someone wins me!'

The officer next to her whispered, 'I've bought a lot of tickets, but now I've met you, I think I'll buy some more.'

'Like a week's wages worth!' someone shouted, followed by hoots of laughter.

After tea and sandwiches, Captain Ayres offered to escort the

Barnstormers to the dressing rooms on the far side of the camp. As soon as they stepped outside there was the unmistakable sound of heavy boots on asphalt. They rounded the corner and were met by the amazing sight of several hundred men in discrete formations covering every inch of the parade ground.

'Gosh!' said Pat. 'How many soldiers are in the camp?'

Captain Ayres smiled and touched the side of his nose.

'That's classified information, I'm afraid, but I can tell you that when the *News Letter* estimated there would soon be seventy thousand British troops in Northern Ireland we didn't question their maths. Of course, they're not all at Balmoral.'

'But why are they here and not away fighting the Germans?'

'Because the enemy is not always where it is meant to be,' he said mysteriously.

'I don't understand,' said Pat. 'Surely you know where the Germans are. Don't you have reconnaissance planes tracking them?'

Captain Ayres looked sideways at Pat – it wasn't often he came across a young woman with an interest in the logistics of warfare. 'You seem to be very well informed, Miss … I'm sorry, I didn't catch your name.'

'Goulding, Patricia Goulding.'

'Well, Patricia, when two armies face each other it is known as a front. But one army can gain ground and outflank the enemy by moving swiftly to attack an area not protected, opening up another front. Hitler could seriously weaken Britain by suddenly moving up through Ireland to take the North with all its industrial power. So being here, we will disable such an attack or, better still, deter it altogether. Does that make sense?'

'Yes, it does, and in the meantime you have a safe area in a remote part of the country to train soldiers, ready to be shipped out when needed.'

'Precisely! And keeping up the morale of the troops while they wait is vital and that's where you and your fellow performers do your bit.' He stopped and pointed at the makeshift stage erected at the far end of the parade ground. 'It's not the Royal Albert Hall, I'm afraid, but it's the quality of the entertainment that matters, isn't it?'

'We're performing here?' Pat looked around. 'Where will the audience sit?'

'On the parade ground and right back as far as those transport trucks. We should be able to squeeze in about two thousand I think.'

'Two thousand!' Pat blanched at the thought. 'I expected …'

'Yes, I know there should be more, but we decided to restrict it. This is our first show of this kind, so we'll see how it goes.'

In the Nissen hut dressing room, Goldstein was waiting for them. 'Girls, I've had an idea for a costume change in the second half when you sing those military songs.' He dropped the kit bag from his shoulder and laid out three piles, each a complete uniform: trousers, battle dress, cap. 'I got the smallest size they had in the stores. They might still be a little big, but I'm sure you'll look the part.'

Irene immediately put a cap on her head. 'How do I look?'

'Ridiculous,' said Pat.

'Oh come on. It's just a bit of fun. Try yours on.'

Pat took the cap and placed it on her head, tucked her hair underneath and smiled in spite of herself.

The sound of the audience built up steadily over the next half hour, but instead of the usual pre-show excitement and nerves, the performers became more and more subdued.

'Are you all right, Myrtle?' asked Irene.

'I think so. I'm just a bit worried about whether they'll like us.'

'We just have to go out there and do our best.'

'But we're first on after Sammy. I can't decide if it's better to get it over with, or if those on later will get the best of it.'

'Who knows,' said Irene. 'This isn't like any other show. Anything could happen.'

'I'd better get these girls of mine fired up. They look like they're goin' te a wake.' She stood up, flounced out her tiny polka dot skirt and adjusted the gypsy blouse to show her shoulders. 'Right girls, let's run through those high kicks one last time and for God's sake, smile will ye!'

According to Sammy he'd played the Glasgow Empire on a wet Saturday night, after Celtic and Rangers had both been beaten by lesser teams, and witnessed the top of the bill being booed off the stage. 'It's all about confidence. Grab the audience by the throat. Show them you're not scared,' he told them.

He raced on to the stage, refusing the microphone offered and began the show with a loud 'Good evening, ladies and gentlemen!' Then stared across the footlights at the noisy crowd and bellowed, 'Oh! I'm sorry there aren't any ladies, and there aren't any gentlemen either by the looks of you lot!' The first twenty rows quietened and looked in his direction.

'I was talkin' to one of your sergeant majors earlier. He told me when you boys heard you were being sent to Belfast you said you'd sooner be parachuted into Berlin because you'd more in common with the Nazis than the Irish!'

In the wings, Goldstein watched anxiously as the boisterous good humour of the audience seemed to drain away from those within hearing distance. The rest were either noisily protesting that they couldn't hear, or completely unaware that the show had started. Something needed to be done, and quickly. 'Myrtle,' he shouted. 'Get the Tappers on right away!'

'But Sammy hasn't introduced us.'

'Never mind that, just get on there and make the audience notice you! I'll get your music started.'

Sammy tried a few more jokes about squaddies having long lie-ins and double rations. Several soldiers were on their feet heckling him so the Tappers' opening music and the sight of Myrtle in the wings ready to come on was all the encouragement he needed to exit stage right where, with shaking hands, he took a swift drink from the quarter bottle of Bells he kept in his breast pocket for the interval.

The girls filled the stage with colour and movement and the whistling and catcalls began immediately. Then the soldiers at the very back stood and surged forward. From the stage the girls could see the chaos as men struggled to keep their feet in an attempt to avoid trampling those seated in front of them. A moment's uncertainty and the dancers missed their cue to change formation and move downstage. Their rhythm had gone and with it their confidence. As if in slow motion their steps became fewer and fewer, until each girl stood motionless while the men in front of them became more entangled as they struggled to stay upright. Fortunately, Captain Ayres had the presence of mind and the power of command to push his way to the front of the stage and snatch a microphone.

'Attention!' he bellowed. 'This is an order. Attention!' Then he waited. The seconds ticked by as the soldiers slowly untangled themselves and stood to attention row by row, ramrod straight and totally silent. Still Captain Ayres waited. The last bars of the Tappers' music faded away and the only sound drifting over the parade ground was the click of the needle in the final groove. When he lifted the microphone for a second time, it was to address his fellow officers and NCOs.

'Please take command of your company. Those men standing beyond the parade ground will, on command, return to barracks. They will remain there until they are sent for. Those on the parade ground will be ordered one row at a time to sit and they will watch the first half.' He left the stage to the barking of commands and the rhythmic march of retreating feet, and went straight to Goldstein.

'I apologise for that. It won't happen again. Please organise your performers as quickly as you can. We begin again in five minutes and the audience will change over at the interval.'

In the dressing room Goldstein stood on an upturned crate and spoke plainly. 'The decisions we make in the next few minutes will make or break the Barnstormers. We stand on the brink of disaster, but triumph is also within reach. Now is not the time for clashing egos, but for teamwork. The previous running order is cancelled and replaced by another more suited to this unique audience. The shortened show will be repeated after the interval for the troops who have been returned to barracks.'

He looked around at his company, weighing up their strengths and weaknesses both as performers and personalities.

He turned to consult Horowitz who wrote, crossed out, moved names up or down the running order. Eventually, Goldstein announced, 'The new programme is as follows: to open, Corporal

Young, a soldier from the regiment; the audience know him and he'll get them back on our side.' One or two stole a look at Sammy, but his face showed no expression. 'Next, The Golden Sisters: get those uniforms on right away and I want you to use the two microphones available, it's the only way to get the sound loud enough to keep their attention.' The girls looked at each other; they'd never sung with microphones before. Irene shrugged her shoulders as though to say 'we might as well', but Pat, whose voice was twice as strong as the others, looked at her in disbelief.

'Tappers, you'll go on next, but keep it tight. You won't have any trouble with the audience this time, I'm sure. Then the crooner, followed by Jimmy on the harmonica, followed by Joan singing songs from the movies – I'll tell you which ones. Then we'll finish with Marie on the accordion for a sing-song and I'd like all of you on the stage singing your hearts out and encouraging the audience to do the same.'

He paused, knowing something more was needed to restore their confidence. 'I know many of you will be disappointed not to be performing. You are not to blame for what has happened, but we need to get this right to be offered the chance to perform at other camps in the future. Right, everyone, two minutes to curtain up, starters in the wings please!'

'These trousers are so itchy they'll give me a rash.'

'Stop moaning, Peggy, and get the uniform on.' Irene was already dressed and clipping the cap to her head.

'The legs are too long.'

'That's because you're in your bare feet; get your heels on.'

'I'm not wearing this hat! It took me ages to get my hair like this.'

'You have to wear it, so it's a complete uniform.'

'No I don't! Soldiers don't always wear them, they do this …' and Peggy folded hers neatly and slid it under the epaulette on her shoulder.

Only then did they notice Pat.

Irene was lost for words. 'Pat, you look …'

Peggy wasn't. 'Those soldiers will be drooling!'

'Don't be so uncouth,' snapped Pat, but she was well aware that the uniform showed off her figure in unexpected ways.

Someone had rigged up a wire to a speaker in the Nissen hut where the performers waited. After the disastrous false start and the hastily imposed discipline of Captain Ayres, the sound of the audience was reduced to a low buzz and Irene, Pat and Peggy were able to plan how to get the audience involved.

There was no time to rehearse, but at least they were all in agreement. The speakers fell eerily silent except for the soft swish of a broom and then the sound of a cockney voice singing quietly, '*Pack up your troubles in your old kit bag.*'

'It's the Corporal,' whispered Myrtle. 'I saw him gettin' ready, all padded up with a big bust, turban on his head and a fag in his mouth.'

The singing got louder and louder then stopped abruptly; howls of laughter followed. Clearly 'she' had realised she was not alone. 'Oh my Gawd! Where did you lot come from? They sent me on here to sweep up, said you'd been confined to barracks or was it shipped off to the Western Front for insubordination?'

'We're here for the show!' someone shouted.

'Tell you what, you'd never believe I used to do a turn down the music hall would you?' Some shouts of disbelief. 'Oh yes, I'll have you know I danced a bit too, showed a bit of leg. Would you like to see?' Catcalls and whistles followed.

'You don't mind a bit of knicker do you? I'll just tuck my skirt up here.' Loud cheering. 'Now then, you lot at the front keep back, a girl's got to have some secrets!'

The opening bars of 'My Old Man Said Follow the Van' began and the corporal sang falsetto with gusto, every now and again his voice breaking into a bass. 'Come on, you lazy buggers, you know the words, don't you?' Then all went quiet as he soft-shoe shuffled, calling out every now and again to some embarrassed young soldier, 'What do you think of these for a fine pair of legs? Would you like a squeeze? Excuse me, this is where I have to lean over, please cover your eyes, well one of them anyway.'

He left the stage to uproarious applause and cheers, but as he passed the girls waiting to go on they were shocked to see the sweat running down his grey face. 'Tough bunch, ladies. Best grip 'em early and get 'em involved or you're dead!'

Irene spoke quickly. 'We can do this. Keep smiling and fingers crossed I can get them to join in.' Then, without an introduction or music they ran up the steps and on to the stage.

Peggy went straight to the piano and, without sitting down, belted out a lively introduction to 'It's a Long Way to Tipperary'. Irene barked a command and she and Pat marched to the microphone where they marked time until their cue. The amplification of their voices caught them by surprise and they glanced quickly at each other and grinned at the power they had to deliver every word and note to the vast audience. In the middle of the song Peggy joined them centre stage and they encouraged the audience to clap in time, then on Irene's command the girls began to march. 'Eyes front, quick march! About turn, quick march!'

Finally, she led them to the back of the stage, where they turned and boogied up to the microphone and all three sang the final verse smiling and clapping with the audience. They finished with a sideways turn, right hands waving in the air and their left hands reaching out towards the audience who were immediately on their feet clapping and cheering.

Their second song was slower in tempo with Pat centre stage. 'When the Lights Come on Again All Over the World' was unashamedly sentimental and the parade ground fell silent.

She held the final high note for what seemed like an age then bowed her head. The cheers erupted. Pat raised her head, smiled and blew a two-handed kiss to the audience.

For their third song they moved the microphone over to the piano and all three sang 'Kiss Me Goodnight, Sergeant Major', but at the end of the first verse Irene left her sisters to sing while she moved down stage to scan the front row. A young soldier, smiling and singing along, looked a good sport. Irene beckoned to him to join her.

He stood up amid back-slapping and banter from his friends and climbed on to the stage. Pat and Peggy sang the refrain and Irene leaned towards the young soldier and pouted. Amid calls of encouragement he went to kiss her, only to find she had drawn back. A moment's embarrassment and he found Irene had stepped towards him again, this time offering to dance. Nervously, he took her hand and the two of them danced the polka round the stage. As the music ended, Irene leaned over and kissed him on the cheek, and he returned to his place wreathed in smiles. The girls took their bows to loud cheering and, waving their caps in the air, they marched in step into the wings.

Later, in the dressing room, Captain Ayres shook Goldstein warmly by the hand. 'Wonderful! Wonderful! What a great show. Your performers are a credit to you, sir.' No mention of the near-riot at the start, no criticism of the misjudged opening. 'Now, have you the energy to do it all again for the second house?'

Chapter 20

Irene had been waiting in a biting wind for over an hour when, at last, she heard the roar of a motorbike. She recognised him immediately in his RAF uniform as he came round the bend and swung the bike in an exaggerated sweep towards her.

'You came! I didn't know if you would. Got lost a few times on the way; lots of signposts missing. I spotted the castle on the map back at the base and I thought you'd know where it was.'

She had never heard him speak at such length, and even though his accent was still difficult to follow, she got the gist of it and smiled in response. 'Yes, I know the castle; I don't live far from here.'

'Joanmount Gardens,' he said, looking pleased. 'I remember. Should we go and look at it?'

'What, Joanmount Gardens?'

'No … Belfast Castle!'

Irene had never been on a motorbike before and was shocked at the intimacy of riding pillion. She couldn't avoid putting her arms around his waist during the steep climb up the hill and his body leant back into hers. The castle was built in a Victorian Gothic style with turrets, stained glass windows and armorial shields carved into the masonry.

'It's like Balmoral,' said Sandy as he got a clear look at it. 'You ken, the king's home in Scotland?' Irene nodded, though she was sure the king lived in Buckingham Palace.

There was a terrace with a formal rose garden where the bushes had been pruned back to short, thorny stems. They leaned on the wall looking out over the lough far below.

'Is that Bangor over there?' he asked.

She followed his line of sight to the opposite side of the water. 'No, I think that's probably Holywood. Bangor is further along the coast.' After his initial rush of conversation, Sandy seemed to revert to his quiet ways and Irene too fell silent and watched him.

'You look different,' she said at last.

'Do I, how?'

'I don't know, your hair, your skin maybe.'

'Oh that'll be the sun, or it could be the malaria.'

'Malaria? What's that?'

'It's a disease I had in India. Oh, don't worry,' he added quickly, 'I haven't got it anymore and you can't catch it. You get it from mosquito bites.'

'Were you very ill?'

'I was for a while. I lost a lot of weight, had to stay in hospital. No duties, no parades, just lying still in a dark room …' His voice trailed off as if remembering. 'That's why I didn't write to you when I promised I would. I'm sorry.'

'It doesn't matter. I thought you'd probably forgotten.' Irene smiled to reassure him. Sandy's face was serious. 'Oh, I never forgot, honestly, I thought about you all the time.'

Irene felt embarrassed by the sudden intensity in his voice and tried to move the conversation in another direction.

'What was it like in India?'

He relaxed. 'Very hot. It lightened my hair and darkened my face. It's full of sounds and smells the like of which you wouldn't believe. A lot of the time we were in camp working on the planes, installing radio equipment mostly, but we had leave and sometimes we'd take a trip; a few pennies would take you a long way on a train in India. Once we went to the Taj Mahal. Have you ever heard of it?'

Irene shook her head.

'Neither had I. It's the most beautiful building, white marble shimmering in the sun. Another time we saw the Ganges, the Indian people think it's a holy river. There were thousands and thousands there, some sort of religious festival, I think. People were bathing in the water all in orange robes and there were flowers everywhere. We felt like explorers. People would crowd around us wherever we went, they wanted to touch our pale skin and my hair, because … I don't know … maybe they hadn't seen red hair before.' He paused then as if he'd used up all the words he had in a sudden rush of description. Irene wondered if by speaking she would break his chain of thought, or whether he was waiting for her to say something.

'Were you frightened?' she whispered.

'No, they meant no harm; they were just curious, like we were. Lots of times we went to the markets; that's where I bought your sari. Did you like it?' His voice was anxious again.

'I love it. I have it covering my bed.'

'Do you?' He looked at her in surprise.

'I've worn it too, in the house, but I like to see it on my bed every day when I wake up.'

He smiled a little then and she knew he was pleased with her answer.

They walked away from the castle and the ground began to rise steeply. 'Are those caves up there?' he asked.

'Well, it's called the Cave Hill so they probably are. I've never been up there.'

'Do you think people live in them?'

'No, of course they don't,' she laughed.

'And there's all of Belfast below us. They have us studying it on maps and charts at the base. The ring of hills, and the lough a clear passage straight up from the sea to the city.'

They walked back to the motorbike and Sandy looked at his watch. 'I'm sorry, I'll need to get back soon, but I could give you a lift home.'

'No, it's not far, I can walk. If you take me home my sisters will want you to come in and then you'll never get away!'

They parted on the Antrim Road. Irene wondered if he might

kiss her and felt a stab of disappointment when he shook her hand and jumped on the bike.

'I'll write to you when I get another pass, I promise!' he shouted and opened the throttle. Irene waved until he was out of sight, but he never looked back.

The nights were drawing in and to save on coal Martha lit only a small fire each evening. 'When that shovelful is done there'll be no more tonight,' she'd say or 'Better get an extra cardigan on you, for I'm not burning money.' They took to going to bed before ten with a hot water jar, coats on their beds and bed socks on their feet.

As usual Martha locked up and checked the fire was safe. She was just looking in on Sheila to make sure she hadn't fallen asleep with a book in her hand when there was the beginning of a wailing sound that escalated to a loud mechanical scream within seconds. At first she thought it was coming from inside the house, then realised what it was.

Pat was quickly out of bed. 'It's the air-raid siren!' she shouted. 'Quick! Get downstairs into the shelter!'

Peggy was sitting up in bed. 'What is it?'

Pat grabbed her. 'Get up!' she shouted, but Peggy resisted.

'It'll be a test that's all.' And she fell back on to her pillow.

'Mammy, tell her!' screamed Pat and rushed to shake Irene awake.

'What's going on?' asked Irene.

'It's an air raid!' Pat pushed her mother towards the stairs. 'You go down, Mammy, and these ones'll follow you.'

'Where am I going, Pat?'

'Under the stairs, have you forgotten?' Pat looked at the bemused faces of her family and with all the force she could muster she screamed, 'Our home is our air-raid shelter!'

'Oh God help us,' moaned Peggy. 'The man from the ministry is back!'

Finally, with the siren still screaming, Pat got them to the bottom of the stairs, but instead of going through the door to the living room and on into the kitchen, Peggy stopped. 'I'm going to have a wee look outside to see if there's any planes.'

Pat grabbed her. 'You can't do that, stupid. If you can see the planes they've already dropped the bombs on you!'

'Oh don't be ridiculous, Pat.' Peggy unlocked the door and went out into the street.

Under the stairs the air was chill, but none of them had thought to take the coats off their beds. In the pitch black, Pat's voice sounded like something from the information films they'd been showing at the cinema for months. 'It's important not to panic. This is the safest part of the house. We'll remain here until the all-clear sounds.' She rummaged around in the dark.

'There's a torch here somewhere. Ah, here it is.' She switched it on and was shocked at their pale and frightened faces. 'There's blankets too. Here, wrap these round you.'

Martha could feel Sheila shivering next to her and put her arm around her. 'Don't worry, love, it'll be a practice, that's all.'

'But what if there's bombs dropping? What if they land on the house?'

'Sssh … it'll be over soon, you'll see.'

'I'm going to look for Peggy,' said Irene decisively and stood up, only to hit her head on the stairs.

'You can't,' said Pat. 'You have to wait for the all-clear – that's a completely different noise. You'll recognise it when you hear it. It goes like this … Woooo …'

'Oh for goodness' sake, Pat, move out of the way, so I can find out what's happening.'

Outside in the street, a group of neighbours were standing in the road chatting and occasionally looking skyward. Some children were running around, arms outstretched, pretending to be planes shooting at each other. Peggy was talking to Thelma and her family.

'What's going on?' Irene asked.

'We think it's a practice. The ARP warden was here a few minutes ago trying to get us to go indoors – apparently the biggest danger is from falling slates. But then he said there hadn't been any anti-aircraft fire from the guns down near the docks and there would have been if any planes had been sighted.'

'Well, it's too cold to stand out here. I'm going back in,' said Irene.

'Me too,' said Peggy, 'but I'm not spending the night under the stairs. I'm for my bed and you can wake me if you hear the guns.'

Irene wisely made a detour upstairs and collected coats and the eiderdown from Martha's bed: at least they would be warm while they waited. Then she went back to the others and told them what had been said. Pat was adamant they should wait for the all-clear, so they sat on in the cold and dark with few words to say between them, while upstairs Peggy slept.

The next day at the Ministry of Public Security, Pat was given the job of contacting police stations across the city to gauge the reaction of the public to the first air-raid warning. She could have written the report based on what happened in Joanmount Gardens or indeed what happened in the Goulding house: there was some fear and panic; some had taken earlier advice and had prepared a place to shelter; others wandered out on to the streets; quite a few had stayed in their beds.

Over the following weeks there were many more false alarms and the reports Pat made to her superiors revealed increasing complacency. Then at the beginning of December, Pat was summoned to the office of the senior civil servant in charge of air-raid precautions. She had never before spoken to anyone higher than her immediate supervising officer and wondered if her work was unsatisfactory. She had tried hard to be precise and accurate in her reports, but she knew that the results of her findings would not be well received.

In a part of Stormont reserved for senior-level civil servants, she followed the red-carpeted corridor to room sixteen and knocked on the door.

'Come in!'

The room was dominated by a large dark wooden desk behind which sat a man with his back to her looking out over Stormont's sweeping drive. He stood up and turned to face her, his hand outstretched.

'Hello, Pat, how are you?'

William Kennedy looked tired and his closely cropped hair made him look severe, but his smile was just as she remembered it.

Pat tried to match his tone, despite her surprise and confusion. 'Hello, William, I'm very well. How are you?' She knew she was blushing.

He invited her to sit down. 'Working hard, Pat, like everyone in this building. I've been appointed permanent secretary to John MacDermott to work on Northern Ireland's preparations for civil defence in the event of enemy attack.'

The mention of the minister by name surprised Pat, as did the implication of William's close connection to him.

He went on. 'I've been reading your reports on the public response to the alerts. Very thorough, you've a good grasp of what's going on out there. I'm told that people are very calm about the whole thing.'

Pat could see why he might think that was the case, but she explained. 'People don't panic, they take the false alarms in their stride, because that's what they always are … false alarms.

The trouble is they don't believe the Germans will ever attack us; they're concentrating on bombing London, Liverpool, Manchester, so why divert their efforts to Belfast?' She paused then, conscious that she'd expressed views that she'd never spoken aloud. Now here she was pouring them out to a permanent secretary.

'Maybe the people are right?' he ventured.

'Of course they're not! The Germans will come here. Not only because we build ships and planes, but because we're easy to bomb.'

William's face was grim and he nodded slowly. 'I fear you're right, Pat. All the soundings I've taken from those with some knowledge of the situation correspond to yours. We will be bombed and we are currently ill-prepared.' He folded his arms and leaned back in his chair. Time passed. Somewhere a door slammed. Somewhere else a telephone rang. Eventually William spoke. 'Pat, I've always admired your honesty and common sense and I'd be interested to know what you think would bring about a fundamental change in attitude.' Pat thought of Peggy with her flippant views and what it would take to alter them. 'I think the problem is that there is no evidence that those in charge believe there will be bombings. People don't carry gas masks and they break the blackout regulations, but nothing happens. Except for round the docks, there are no anti-aircraft guns installed and there are very few bomb shelters being built. It looks like those in the know aren't expecting bombs. Otherwise they'd have done something to protect us, wouldn't they?'

'Such things take time.'

'True, but has a start been made?'

'We wouldn't want to promote panic.'

'You've certainly avoided that, but what you've got instead is complacency.'

'You're right of course.' He looked at her across the desk and, to her surprise, he smiled. 'Pat, I know that we didn't part on the best of terms; there was' – he hesitated – 'some misunderstanding between us.'

That's one way of putting it, thought Pat.

'But I've found our conversation today very helpful and I hope you won't mind if I ask you to come and talk to me again. You give me a different perspective on a difficult situation and I value that.' He stood up.

'It was nice to see you again, William, and I'd be happy to help in any way I can.' Pat kept her voice light.

He walked her to the door. 'Are you still singing with the Barnstormers?'

'Yes, we're members of ENSA now, you know, entertaining the military.'

'Really!' He looked genuinely pleased.

'What about you?'

'I don't have a lot of time for singing, but I'm a member of the civil service choir. We'll be singing in a carol concert in the entrance hall just before Christmas. Why don't you join us? We could do with a good soprano.'

Chapter 21

The gunmetal grey clouds, heavy with snow, had gathered throughout the morning and by noon a luminous twilight enveloped the city streets. The first tiny flakes began to fall around two and by three o'clock the floor of Goldstein's shop was wet with melting slush. Esther had disappeared into the back of the shop as soon as Peggy began mopping up, but moments later she reappeared, buttoning up her coat.

'Where do you think you're going?' demanded Peggy.

'I've some errands to do.'

'Not again. You've hardly put in a full day this week!'

Esther stepped over the mop. 'Never mind,' she laughed. 'If I don't see you through the week, I'll see you through the window.'

Peggy swept the icy water out after her and watched her walk away. Within a hundred yards Esther crossed the road and went straight into the Ulster Milk Bar. The nerve of her, thought Peggy, she's just taking the afternoon off! She swept the pavement furiously causing passers-by to give her a wide berth. Then suddenly she stopped. What had Esther said? Peggy had taught her most of her English, but she could not recall teaching her that 'through the window' expression. In fact, there was only one person she knew who used that silly saying. Peggy left the mop in the doorway and, without bothering to fetch her coat, marched down the street. It took a moment for her to see through the condensation on the window of the café, but there they were.

Esther giggling and Harry Ferguson no doubt talking some nonsense. Well, she'd certainly seen them through the window.

When Irene arrived home from work that evening, she could hear Peggy screaming up the stairs at Pat. 'Will you stop singing those Christmas carols? I'm fed up listening to them!'

'I'm rehearsing.'

'Rehearsing for what?'

'Never you mind!'

Martha was in the kitchen and didn't acknowledge Irene's 'Hello' or her chatter about some cheek Myrtle had given the foreman.

'What's the matter with you?' asked Irene.

No answer.

'Are you annoyed about something?' Still no answer.

Irene went into the front room, where Sheila was curled up on the settee reading a book.

'You got more letters today,' Sheila whispered.

'Don't tell me,' laughed Irene. 'They're on the mantelpiece!'

Sheila looked at her quickly and shook her head in warning.

Too late. Martha was standing in the doorway wiping her hands on her apron and one look at her face was enough to confirm Irene's fears that she was in trouble.

'I think it's time we called a halt to all this letter writing, don't you?'

'What do you mean?'

'I mean, first post you've a letter from an airman we've never seen and another from someone in Donegal, and a third arrived in the second delivery this afternoon, posted in Belfast at eleven o'clock this morning.'

'Mammy, there's no harm in getting letters from my friends.'

'Yes, but who are these friends? I've never met them. They could be any kind of people.'

'Ach Mammy, catch yourself on. They're just people like you and me.'

'Don't you be telling me to catch myself on! If these were decent people, why haven't I ever met them? You'd think if they were friends of yours, they would be round the house once in a while.'

'Maybe it's not so easy for them to go visiting, especially where they're clearly not welcome!' Irene grabbed her letters and stormed out of the room.

'Well I never!' said Martha. 'What kind of behaviour is that?' She went to the foot of the stairs and shouted. 'Come back down here this minute.' Irene's answer was to slam the bedroom door closed and throw herself on the bed. She was in no doubt which letter to open first. She recognised Sandy's writing and had been waiting to hear from him for so long. After their meeting on the Cave Hill he'd written a short letter saying he had enjoyed seeing her and he hoped he'd be able to get to Belfast again soon. It had contained no clue as to how he felt about her and, as a result, her reply was equally non-committal, and she hadn't heard from him since. She unfolded the single sheet of writing paper:

Dear Irene,
I'm sorry I've not written sooner, all leave was cancelled and now I am being sent to England for more training. When I come back I promise you we'll have a night out in Belfast.
Sandy
P.S. Miss you.

What was she to make of it? Nothing, except the facts. If he was interested he would meet her some time in the future; if not, she doubted she would hear from him again. But he did say he missed her. He needn't have added that.

She opened Sean's letter next. It was a while since she had heard from him. The postmark told her he was still in Donegal.

It too was short.

Irene
I haven't heard from Theresa for a while, can you find out what's

going on and get her to write to me?
   S

She scrutinised the third letter and didn't recognise the writing; inside was a page torn from a child's jotter.

Irene
   I need to see you. Can you meet me outside the Co-op in York Street at two o'clock this Saturday?
   Theresa

Well that solved a problem. She could meet Theresa when she finished work and tell her to write to Sean. But why did Theresa need to see her in the first place?

The following morning Goldstein arrived late to open up the shop and Peggy was furious that she'd had to stand in the biting wind and sleet for half an hour. She was even more annoyed that she had shared the pavement with a delivery of sheet music and would be spending the rest of the morning on her hands and knees sorting it. Goldstein nodded curtly and unlocked the door, offering no explanation for his lateness.

'Is Esther not with you this morning?'

'You can see she is not.'

'Is she ill?'

'She would not get out of bed.'

'Why's that?'

'You tell me.'

'How would I know?'

'Because you are the reason she was out so late last night.'

'What?'

'I do not know where the two of you were at that time of night and in such bad weather.'

Peggy guessed where Esther had been, but it took her a few seconds longer to decide how to deal with the information. 'Mr Goldstein, I don't want to worry you, but I suspect there's much more to this than you realise. I'll be completely honest with you: I wasn't with Esther last night, but I know who she was with and I could make sure it won't happen again.'

'What!' Goldstein turned on her. 'She was not with you? You must tell me right now what is going on! Look here, if you are lying to me.' He paused, searching for possibilities. 'No ... she was lying to me. Who was she with?' His eyes widened. 'Was it some boy?'

'Not quite.' Peggy was shocked by the intensity in his voice, but she kept calm. 'You see, sometimes young girls can be foolish when a man –' she emphasised the word 'man', '– when a man takes an interest in them.' Peggy saw with delight the effect her words had on Goldstein. She went on. 'And for a sensible adult like yourself to chastise the young person, well, that might lead to them being more determined to do what seems forbidden.'

The processing of every word showed in Goldstein's face.

He seemed suddenly diminished. 'What is to be done?' he asked.

'I'll speak to her if you like. I can advise her.' She paused and added, 'Woman to woman.'

'You think that is best?'

'I'm certain it is. She won't meet this person again, I give you my word.'

'Peggy, I am so grateful to you. I am an old bachelor and, I will confess, I find it difficult to understand Esther at times. Do you really think you can persuade her against this' – he searched for the word – 'liaison?'

'Don't worry, Mr Goldstein, you can rely on me. Now would you like me to make us some tea? Then I'll get all that sheet music sorted.'

Just before three o'clock Peggy finished serving a customer and popped her head around Goldstein's office door. 'Would you like me to take the post along to the GPO, Mr Goldstein? Save you doing it on the way home?'

'Yes, that would be kind of you, Peggy.'

There was still some sleet in the air and she pulled her collar up against the bitter wind. She guessed that Harry had been working the early morning shift, leaving him with the afternoons and evenings free. At the milk bar she tried to see inside, but the windows were steamed up again.

'Well, well, if it isn't Miss Goulding, doing a bit of sleuthing.'

He was standing behind her in a tweed overcoat belted at the waist, his hat pulled down over his brow. Peggy gave little hint of the discomfort she felt.

'Oh, the very person. I want a word with you.'

He raised an eyebrow. 'How interesting. I'll tell you what. I'll take a walk down the street and back, while you send Dorothy in there back to Kansas. Then we can talk.' He raised his hat and set off towards the City Hall.

Esther had a face like someone caught with their hand in the sweetie jar. 'What are you doing here, Peggy? You should be in the shop.'

'I should be in the shop? Well, that's rich! I could say the same to you.'

'You've got to go. I'm … I'm meeting someone.' She looked anxiously towards the door.

'Your uncle thinks you're at home too tired to work after the late night you and I had. He'll be surprised when I tell him you had an appointment this afternoon with … who should I tell him you're meeting?'

'No one, no one you know – a friend.'

'Esther, I've just spoken to Harry and I can tell you he's not coming here to meet you.'

'That's not true. He said he'd be here.'

'He sent me to tell you he won't be seeing you again.'

'You're lying! Why would he say that?'

Peggy needed a good reason, one that would sever the link between Esther and Harry completely. Hadn't she promised Goldstein?

'Because he's just asked me to get back together with him and I said yes.'

'You're making this up! You hate him, you said so. All the times he's tried to get you to go out with him again and you were so … so horrible to him!'

'Esther, don't you see he was using you? It was me he was after.'

'No, he wants me to be his girlfriend.'

279

Peggy gave her a sympathetic smile. 'Esther, you're just not right for him, he told me so himself.'

Somewhere in Esther's mind a window opened on reality.

'Does my uncle know all this?'

'Of course not,' said Peggy gently. 'I told him you and I went to the pictures together. It'll be our secret.'

Esther stood up. 'I'm not going back to the shop today.' She was close to tears. 'I'm going home to bed.'

'That's a good idea,' said Peggy. 'You'll feel better in the morning.'

When Esther left, Peggy moved into one of the booths and waited. Ten minutes later he came in, ordered two cups of coffee and slid into the seat opposite her. 'Hello there, Peggy, nice to see you. How have you been? Still playing the piano?' She looked at him in disbelief, it was as though he had run into a passing acquaintance.

'Harry, what's going on?'

'What do you mean? Nothing's going on. We're just having a coffee, aren't we?'

'I've just upset a good friend, because of you.'

'Now why would you have done that?'

'Because you asked me to!' Peggy's voice rose and one or two customers turned to look at her. She quickly changed her tone. 'You wanted to talk about us.'

'Ah, would that be the 'us' where I chase after you for months and you ignore me, or the 'us' where I go out with someone else and you get jealous?'

'I am not jealous! I don't care who you go out with.'

'Is that why you told your good friend I didn't want to go out with her any more because I was going out with you?'

'I never ...'

'You did!'

'Why would I do that?'

'Because you're in love with me.'

'In love with you ... an underhand, deceitful, bookie's runner, smuggler ...'

'No I'm not!'

'Yes you are!'

'No I'm not! Look, if I could prove to you that I'm not any of those things anymore then would you admit you love me?'

'Don't be ridiculous.'

He stood up and at that moment the waitress arrived with the coffees.

'Harry, why don't you sit down and we'll drink the coffee while you tell me why I should change my opinion of you.'

The windows of the Co-operative Store had been decorated for the festive season with Christmas trees, streamers and huge paper bells, and as Irene waited she watched the excited faces of the children peering through the window at a giant cardboard Santa Claus surrounded by toys. Theresa arrived in a rush just after two, holding a little girl by the hand.

'This is our Marie,' explained Theresa. 'I promised her if she was a good girl and helped in the house I'd take her to see Santa. You don't mind do you? We can talk on the way.'

Irene laughed. 'Of course not, a good girl's never too old to see Santa!'

They bought a ticket for Marie and entered a dark forest of cardboard trees with cotton wool snow on the ground and stuffed animals lit by green spotlights. Marie stood for a while, picking out and naming creatures.

'I need to talk to you about Sean,' Theresa began.

'And I need to talk to you,' said Irene. 'He wrote to me asking me to find out why you haven't been in contact with him.'

'It's been really hard at home. Mammy's in a bad way. I keep trying to write, but I can't find a way to tell him. He and Mammy were very close.'

Marie, bored with the forest, pulled on Theresa's hand.

'Come on! It's the elves next.'

'The thing is, he'll want to see her, but they'll arrest him if he crosses the border.'

'He wouldn't do that, he knows the danger.'

'I'm not so sure he'd care. He'd want to see Mammy before …'

They moved on to a stable scene with reindeer and Santa's sleigh standing ready.

'The doctor says she may have a month at most, so I'll have to write to him soon. He'd never forgive me if I didn't. That's why I needed to see you, Irene: to ask you a favour.'

'Anything.'

'The police read all our mail and probably the mail of most people we know. So can I ask him to send his reply to you?'

'Of course you can.'

'If you get a letter, don't risk coming to my house, just leave a message at my uncle's bar. You remember where it is?'

'Do you think I'd forget that place after what happened last time?'

'Don't worry, you'll be safe. They know you're my friend.'

They rounded a bend in the path and there was the man himself, resplendent in his red robes. A fairy took Marie's ticket and led her by the hand to sit on Santa's knee where she whispered what she hoped to receive for Christmas, then chose a present from his sack.

All the way home, Irene couldn't get the image of the smiling Marie out of her mind.

'Just imagine,' said Irene, 'two whole weeks without rehearsals and concerts. What shall we do?'

'I've got my carol concert at Stormont tomorrow night,' said Pat.

'And I've got a dinner dance to go to on Christmas Eve,' said Peggy.

'You never mentioned that,' said Irene.

'I've only just been invited, that's why.'

'Where is it?'

'Who are you going with?'

'It's at the Carlton Hotel and I'm going with Harry Ferguson,' said Peggy. At the mention of Harry's name Martha appeared at the kitchen door.

'I thought you were never going to speak to him again.'

'I never said that.'

'You did,' they all shouted at once.

'I said, if I remember correctly, that I wouldn't be going out with him again until he had sorted himself out and had some decent prospects to offer.'

'Is that what you told him?' Pat was sceptical.

'I certainly did.'

'And now he has some decent prospects, I take it?' asked Martha.

'Well, we're going to the annual dinner dance for the Guild of Master Bakers. Harry's a member now and he's going to open his own baker's shop.'

'Are you sure it's not the Guild of Chancers and he's opening up his own card school?' said Pat.

'How dare you!' Peggy screamed. 'You're just jealous, because you've nobody to go out with over Christmas!'

'How do you know I haven't got somebody?'

'Oh, found another married tenor in the ministry choir, have you?'

'You've no idea who might be in our choir,' said Pat quietly.

Martha shook her head. 'You girls are beyond me. For two pins I'd stop all of you gallivanting, Christmas or no Christmas!'

The following day Pat left for work taking with her the grey beaded evening dress that Aunt Kathleen had given her when she sang the duet with William in the first Barnstormers' concert. She had some misgivings about wearing it again, but it was quite possible that William would not remember it and, besides, she had nothing else that was suitable.

After work she changed into the dress, pinned up her hair and put on a little rouge and lipstick. A light tea was to be served in one of the meeting rooms for those taking part in the concert.

The room was long and narrow with a grand fireplace at one end with a portrait of the late Lord Craigavon above it and at the opposite end a portrait of the king. Pat studied the ornate ceiling and the crystal chandelier that dominated the room.

There was a light touch at her elbow and she turned to find William next to her.

'Pat, you look stunning. Your dress is the one you wore the first time we sang together, isn't it?' He took her hand and put it to his lips. 'I think we need to talk, but there's no time now. Can we meet after the concert? Perhaps I could take you to dinner?'

Pat was astonished at his compliment and the invitation and struggled to reply to either. 'I don't know,' she said.

He raised her hand to his lips again. 'Don't worry, we'll talk later.'

The concert took place in the Great Hall with the choir arranged up the elegant staircase and the orchestra seated on the landing above them. Huge vases of holly and red and white chrysanthemums added festive colour. William had sent Aunt Kathleen a VIP invitation and she sat in the front row next to a middle-aged gentleman who was leaning towards her, chatting animatedly. She wore a dress of navy silk with pearls at her throat and in her ears, and around her shoulders was a stole of pale musquash. Pat acknowledged her with the merest inclination of her head and Kathleen responded with the same.

Although Pat had sung in the church choir since she was ten years old, she never failed to be moved by the precision of the joining and blending of voices. The more complex the parts, the better she liked it and tonight's arrangements of well-known carols were unusual and challenging. The string quartet began the concert with an arrangement of 'In the Bleak Midwinter'. The choir's first carol, 'Hark the Herald Angels Sing', showed off the acoustics of the grand entrance hall, with the sound rising towards the dome above their heads where it echoed and fell like a waterfall of sound. The soloists, a contralto and a baritone, gave polished performances.

The applause at the end of the concert went quickly from warm to enthusiastic and the audience, perhaps reluctant to venture out into the wintry night, lingered. Pat found Kathleen still talking to the man she had been sitting next to earlier.

'Hello, Pat,' said Kathleen, kissing her lightly on the cheek.

'Can I introduce you to John Andrews? We're old sparring partners from our days on the Board of Education.' Pat was astonished to find herself shaking hands with the recently appointed Prime Minister of Northern Ireland.

'Mr Andrews, this is my niece Patricia Goulding; she's one of your civil servants.'

'I'm delighted to meet you, Miss Goulding. In which department do you work?'

'In the ministry of public security, on the air-raid precautions section.'

'Indeed, very important work.'

'I've been telling Mr Andrews that he needs new blood in his administration. The likes of young William Kennedy would certainly get the British government to understand the danger to Belfast.'

'Still crusading, Kathleen?' the prime minister laughed. 'You should have taken my advice years ago and stood for parliament.'

'And what would be the chances of an Independent candidate getting elected anywhere in the Province, never mind a woman?' she replied.

'Well, voters are creatures of habit, thank goodness. Anyway, you know there is more than one way of getting your views heard.' He bent to kiss her cheek. 'And now I must excuse myself and seek out the excellent choir director. Nice to meet you, Patricia.'

'Well, Pat, who would have thought I would be here in Stormont watching a Goulding girl sing for the prime minister. I'm so proud of you. Now you run along and thank William for inviting me. Next year I expect you two to be the soloists!'

Pat had no intention of being so immodest as to seek out William, but as she crossed the room to join her friends from the office, he intercepted her.

'There you are. I've been looking for you. Wasn't it a lovely concert? Now look, I need to talk to you …'

'William, I'm not sure that's a good idea, given the circumstances …'

'But it's absolutely the right idea, why shouldn't I talk to you?'

'Because it's indiscreet.'

'Indiscreet? What do you mean indiscreet? You're a civil servant in my department; you've signed the Official Secrets Act, haven't you? I'm desperate to …'

'William, I don't think …' In the seconds it took Pat to speak the words, she realised the mistake she was about to make. She stopped. 'What exactly is it you want to talk about?'

'My plans for more shelters, of course. They're needed up and down the main roads radiating out of the city and in strategically important workplaces. I want to know your opinion. I was going to ask you to have dinner, but that might not be a good idea: 'walls have ears' and all that. Maybe I could give you a lift home?'

'No, that's not necessary. I already have a lift.' She tried to keep her voice light. 'Maybe we could discuss your ideas tomorrow at the office?'

Chapter 22

Christmas Eve of 1940 in Belfast was one of those rare winter days when the clouds had blown out into the Irish Sea leaving behind a sapphire blue sky and freezing temperatures. The streets were thronged with people shopping or meeting friends. The Salvation Army silver band played carols all day at the corner of Castle Place with the added percussion of rattling tins. In Goldstein's music shop 'White Christmas' played continuously.

They'd opened early – at eight – hoping to close around four, but the customers kept coming. Goldstein was delighted. 'We have never sold so much in one day in the history of the shop!'

They worked through lunch and, as four o'clock approached, Peggy asked, 'Mr Goldstein, are we going to finish soon? I need to get to Robb's to buy something and they might shut early too.'

'I cannot possibly close when customers still want to buy.'

'Then can I nip out for a while – I won't be long?'

'Stay until five, Peggy, and I will give you a little bonus. How does that sound?'

Peggy knew she wouldn't get her wages until the shop closed anyway so she smiled and secretly hoped the bonus would be enough to buy the elegant dress in Robb's window she'd been dreaming about all week.

The workers at the aircraft factory had also earned a bonus in the form of a Christmas dinner in the canteen. Irene and Myrtle sat with the other women in their paper hats.

'Call that a Christmas dinner? It's all potato! Sure that pick of turkey wouldn't fill your back tooth,' said Irene.

'Aye, well, it's more than I'll be eatin' tomorrow if I can't pick up something for next to nothin' in the shops,' said Myrtle.

'Are you going out tonight?'

'Later on I am. Robert McVey has asked me te the International Bar.'

'That sounds exciting.'

Myrtle pulled a face. 'Do ye think so? Depends who you're goin' with, so it does.'

'But Robert is so nice.'

'Oh yes, we all know you've had a soft spot for him ever since he put you over his shoulder and carried you out of that plane, but you've never been out with him. He's a bit boring.'

'Then you should find someone else.'

'Aye, maybe I will.' Myrtle winked. 'And what about you and the airman? Is it not time you found somebody who could take you on a real date?'

'Funny you should say that – I had a Christmas card from him.'

'Oh, and where is he now, the North Pole?'

'I don't know where he is, but I know where he's going to be on New Year's Eve!'

'Really?'

Irene nodded. 'Outside the City Hall at eight o'clock waiting for me.'

'That's great. Maybe we could make it a foursome – you and me with the invisible airman and the boring fireman.'

'You know, Myrtle, I think that's one of your better ideas. Sandy doesn't talk much anyway and you say Robert's boring, so at least you and I can have a good laugh together. What do you think?'

'I think I'll tell Robert he's to meet me outside the City Hall as well. We'll all go for a few drinks then maybe on to the Plaza to see in the New Year.'

Across the city, a meeting of the entire staff of the ministry of public security had been called for two o'clock on Christmas Eve. The girls in the office had been speculating about its purpose all morning. Pat kept her own counsel, knowing at least the gist of what would be said. The morning after the concert, she had been asked once again to report to the permanent secretary. William greeted her warmly and immediately explained his plans.

'It's not that we want to frighten people,' he explained, 'but they do need to know an attack will certainly take place and the consequences will be loss of life and property. Our aim must be to minimise the losses by ensuring people react speedily and sensibly.' He went on, 'You were right, Pat, when you said the lead must come from this ministry. If we're seen to be making preparations then people will believe in the threat. I'm thinking of recommending that we build more shelters.'

'That would be a start, but ...' Pat hesitated.

'But you're not sure?' he asked.

'William, the shelters are hardly ever used. No woman I know would go in one – you never know who'd be in there.'

'What if we had more wardens? They'd be in charge of a group of shelters; that might help. I'm also thinking of a compulsory fire-watching order; every decent-sized business would have to appoint fire watchers who would be on site around the clock.'

Pat felt confident enough to mention something else that was bothering her: 'There's talk of German reconnaissance planes flying over the city.'

'Yes, they fly very high and most people don't know they're overhead, but lately the frequency of the flights has increased.'

'Then we need to tell everyone that. Can the ministry put out statements, maybe through the *Belfast Telegraph*, telling people the Germans are taking a real interest in the city?'

'Yes, that's a good idea. Make them think about it every day, and the need to observe the blackout. It's time we started fining people like they do in England.'

'What about more anti-aircraft guns? There don't seem to be very many – should they not be on the hills around the city?'

'Yes, they should. In fact I'm part of a delegation going to Westminster to put Belfast's case for anti-aircraft defence equipment. I leave immediately after Christmas.'

Pat and the rest of the staff filed into the meeting room in sombre mood. William was standing at the front, a little nervous, she thought, as he stood to address them. His suit was immaculate, his shirt pristine white, his tie maroon with a thin stripe. He cleared his throat and the room fell silent.

'We have a duty to the citizens of Belfast to keep every one of them safe. Their lives will depend on the actions of this ministry. Since this conflict began, people have been prepared to dream until the bombs awake them. The population has not yet had the educative experience of being attacked, but when it happens it will be sudden and terrifying. It is time therefore to wake the people early from their dreaming so that, when that dreadful night comes, they are well practised in how to save their lives. I will now outline the strategic plan to raise citizen awareness.'

At the end of the meeting, William caught up with Pat as she was leaving. 'Miss Goulding, may I have a word with you?'

In the empty meeting room, he took her hand in both of his and brought it once again to his lips. 'Pat, it meant a lot to me to hear your views and suggestions.' Then he moved quickly back to his briefcase. 'I have a small gift for you, a Christmas present, I suppose, but really it's for … well … for being you.' He held out a small square box.

'William, you didn't need to …'

'I didn't need to, but I very much wanted to. Open it.'

The box was lined with green satin and inside was a bracelet of coral with a silver clasp.

'William, it's beautiful.'

Peggy collected her wages at five from Goldstein and rushed out of the shop calling 'Merry Christmas!' over her shoulder. She ran all the way to Robb's and was delighted to see the lights still on, but when she got to the door it was shut in her face by a man in a suit, presumably the manager, and through the glass he mouthed, 'We're closed.'

'You can't be,' shouted Peggy. 'There's still customers in there!'

He shook his head, content in his authority. Just then Peggy noticed a familiar figure inside the store. Grace McCracken!

She waited for the manager to move away then she knocked on the door and waved frantically. Grace's face lit up in recognition.

'Hello, Peggy, what are you doing here?'

'Hello, Grace, I'd like to buy something.' It was all Peggy could do to keep the sarcastic tone out of her voice.

'But the shop's shut.'

'Yes, but there are still a few customers inside, you could let me in, couldn't you?'

'I don't know … the manager …' Grace looked right and left, then undid the bolts on the door.

'What is it you want to buy?'

'The dress in the window, the red one with the black belt and lace collar,' said Peggy quickly. 'I need it for a dinner dance tonight.'

'Wait here.' Grace went to the window and returned with the dress draped between her outstretched arms. 'I don't think there'll be time to try it on, Peggy.'

'It doesn't matter, it looks the right size.'

'But what if it doesn't fit?'

'I'll bring it back. How much is it?'

Grace read the label. 'Three pounds.'

Peggy checked her wage packet to see how much bonus Goldstein had given her – two pounds. 'Can you get me any discount, Grace?'

'Sorry, Peggy, we only get discount on things we buy for ourselves.' Grace, a God-fearing woman, had no idea what it was like to go to a dinner dance, but she recognised disappointment when she saw it.

'Look, why don't you wait for me on the corner there and I'll see what I can do?'

Fifteen minutes later Grace hurried along Castle Place to where Peggy was waiting and handed her a Robb's bag. 'There you are, Peggy, two pounds ten shillings, a good discount.'

'Thank you so much, Grace. Did you tell them you were buying it for your niece?'

'No,' said Grace. 'I told them it was for me. Sometimes it's good to surprise people.'

On Christmas morning Martha was up at six and downstairs, washed and dressed with the fire started and a cup of hot strong tea in her hand, by half past. She gave thanks again to Anna for her gift of a smoked ham large enough for several Christmas dinners and plates of sandwiches. There was also a beautiful iced Christmas cake from Harry Ferguson, which he'd brought when he came to take Peggy to the dinner dance. She wasn't altogether sure how she felt about the two of them going out again, but he looked prosperous enough and he had a good trade. She was less sure about Sandy. Irene was excited about meeting him on New Year's Eve, but Martha could see no future in such a relationship in wartime and, besides, he was a Scotsman.

All five of them went to morning service, although Peggy was so tired she almost fell asleep during the sermon. They returned to eat a good dinner. Then all afternoon the sisters played games from a compendium Martha had bought them – ludo, snakes and ladders and draughts, games remembered from childhood – but with such a competitive attitude that Martha frequently had to intervene to warn them to play fairly or else she'd take the compendium away.

On Boxing Day they had invited the McCrackens to come for their tea. John arrived in his full warden's uniform because he was going on duty at nine. He and Pat discussed his duties at length, until Irene, to everyone's relief, suggested a game of charades.

Grace and Aggie threw themselves into it and Martha was glad to see them enjoying themselves and John resisting the temptation to criticise them for it. The following morning Irene, Pat and Peggy were back at work and Martha and Sheila cleaned the house from top to bottom, ready for the new year.

Chapter 23

Wen Irene arrived home from work on New Year's Eve, she was surprised to find an envelope behind the clock. It looked like it had been damaged in the post. Inside was a crumpled Christmas card and underneath the printed greeting was one line in Sean's handwriting: 'Coming home New Year's Eve.'

Irene caught her breath. Where had the card been? Delayed in the post? She had to warn Theresa, but it might already be too late. She ran downstairs and into the kitchen. 'Mammy, change of plan, I have to go out early. I don't want any tea!' She was out the back door and away before Martha could say a word.

It was over a year since Irene had last been to Northumberland Street and that night she had ended up in hospital fighting for her life. In the gathering darkness, very little of the main road looked familiar. Fortunately, she found the only landmark she could remember, the sweet shop that sold yellow man. She turned the corner and followed the noise to the bar. Inside it was packed with men, and cigarette smoke hung like a winter fog over their heads. They stood three and four deep at the bar and, although she was the only woman in the room, none of them made way for her.

'Excuse me, please, I need to speak to Mr O'Hara.'

'You and me both, darlin',' said the man next to her, 'and when you see him tell him mine's a pint of porter!'

She waited five minutes hoping she could move to the front as others were served, but they remained standing at the bar to drink. She was beginning to despair when a young man spoke to her. 'What is it you want, miss? You're surely not here to buy drink?'

Irene was close to tears, feeling the time slipping by. 'No, I'm not. I need to talk to Mr O'Hara. I've a message for him.'

'Come on now, lads. Can you not see there's a lady here? Let her through for pity's sake.' He elbowed his way through the crowd, pulling Irene behind him.

She recognised O'Hara immediately and the physical memory of the pain and disorientation she experienced last time she faced him returned in a rush. She spoke quickly. 'Theresa told me to find you if I received a message from a certain person. She said you would see she got it.'

He looked at Irene as though she was mad. 'I'm not here to pass on messages. I've a bar to run!'

'You don't understand, this is a message from someone very important for Theresa ...'

'Look, missus, it's New Year's Eve. I don't care if it's a matter of life or death, I'm not leaving my bar to play the message boy.'

O'Hara was already walking away when she shouted, 'If you won't pass the message on, at least tell me where I can find Theresa and I'll tell her myself.'

O'Hara raised his arm and pointed. 'Down there, turn left, number twenty-six.'

At the far end of Theresa's street, a house blazed lights in defiance of the blackout and by its light Irene found number twenty-six. She knocked and moments later Theresa's voice called out.

'Who is it?'

'It's me, Irene. I've a message for you.'

The door opened a crack and Theresa peered through the gap.

'What are you doing here?'

'Let me in, Theresa, it's about Sean.'

The door opened and she slipped inside. 'Down the hall, the kitchen's at the end,' said Theresa, locking the door behind her. The room was tiny and smelt of mince and onions. A table covered with a lace tablecloth filled the middle of the room and against one wall was an ancient cast iron gas cooker on top of which was a blackened teapot over a low flame.

Theresa pulled out one of the chairs at the table and motioned Irene to sit down. She remained standing.

'I got a Christmas card from Sean today.' Irene spoke quickly. 'I don't know when he posted it, but it said he was coming back tonight.'

'What? He can't come here. It isn't safe!'

'What can we do?'

'I don't know. What exactly did it say?'

'Just "coming home on New Year's Eve", that's all.'

Theresa looked distraught. 'If I'd known sooner I could have written to him and told him it was too dangerous. The police know Mammy's really ill, the prison authorities told them. We tried to get Daddy home, but they wouldn't have any of it. They'll be waitin' for Sean to do something stupid. Think, Irene, could anyone have seen the card?'

'No, I only got it today and as soon as I read it I hid it in my room and came straight here.'

'Why has it only come today?'

'Delayed in the ...' Irene's hand went to her mouth.

'What? What is it?'

'The envelope was damaged.'

'Oh God! Somebody read it, somebody ...' Theresa stopped abruptly and tilted her head, listening for a sound above their heads. 'It's Mammy, she's woken up. I'll be back in a minute.'

Irene tried to picture the envelope. How had it been damaged? Had it been ripped a little or enough for the card to be removed and read? She thought not. Then with a start she realised it hadn't been torn, it had been opened carefully, but resealed carelessly. Someone had steamed open her mail.

Mammy!

Theresa came back carrying a tray. 'She's awake, wants a drink of tea. She's talking about Sean again. Part of me hopes he'll come and she'll get to see him before ...' Her voice trailed off.

'Listen, Theresa, I think I know who opened the card. My mother's always asking who's writing to me. I think she was just being nosey.'

'Are you sure? I don't trust the police. I'm telling you, they read our letters.'

'Yes, but they wouldn't read mine ...' Irene hesitated and Theresa finished her sentence.

'Because you're a Protestant and I'm a Catholic.'

'I don't think ...'

'Shut up!' hissed Theresa. She quickly turned off the light and Irene sensed her move to the door. There was a rush of cold air and someone entered the room. The door closed, the light came on and there stood Sean O'Hara, unmistakable despite the turned-up collar and scarf covering half his face.

He hugged Theresa. 'How is she? I'm not too late, am I?'

'No, no, you're not, she's been a bit better these last two days, but she's been asking for you all the time. Sean, you shouldn't have come. The police are still looking for you.'

'Sure it's New Year's Eve, the police are too busy dealing with drunks to mount an ambush for the likes of me.' He turned to Irene, and if he was surprised to see her he didn't show it.

Instead, he kissed her quickly on the cheek.

'Well, you're a sight for sore eyes, Irene. I never imagined you'd be here to welcome me.' And he gave that slow smile that made her heart leap.

'Take your coat off and sit yourself down,' said Theresa. 'I'm just going to make Mammy some tea and I'll get you something to eat as well.'

'Where's the rest of them?' he asked.

'They've gone to Aunty Mary's to see the New Year in. They weren't going to go, but Mammy was a wee bit brighter and she says to them, "You go on and have a good time. I'll still be here when you get back." Right enough, Marie was so excited about being allowed to stay up so late, it would have been a shame for her to miss it. I said I'd stay with Mammy.'

'So you didn't know I was coming?'

'No, I only found out a while ago when Irene arrived. She didn't get your card until today.'

'That's a bit strange, isn't it?'

'Sean, you don't think somebody intercepted it, do you?' asked Theresa.

'No, I don't think so. Why would they connect me with Irene? Anyway, I don't really care. I'm here now. I'll take that tea you're makin' up to Mammy and stay with her for a while. Then I'll fade away into the night and nobody will be any the wiser.'

When he left the room Theresa explained, 'Everyday she prays for him and lately she's been asking the Virgin Mary to intercede and allow her to say a proper goodbye to him.' They sat a while in silence, each trying to imagine the conversation going on above them. Then Theresa seemed to brighten up.

'I'm glad you're here, Irene. Tell me how you've been. Still singing with your sisters?' Irene told her about the concert for the military. 'And what about that Scottish airman you were keen on? What was his name again?'

'Sandy.' Irene froze. 'Oh God, what time is it?'

Theresa looked over Irene's shoulder at the dresser, 'Just after nine. Why?'

'I was supposed to be meeting Sandy at eight o'clock! He got a pass. He's been waiting for me outside the City Hall for over an hour! I'll have to go.' She grabbed her coat and frantically looked around for her bag.

'Irene, I think you'll have missed him. It'll probably take you half an hour to get there.'

'Maybe he's waited for me.'

At that moment there was a shout from upstairs. 'Theresa, come quickly!'

She was out of the door and up the stairs with Irene at her heels. In the bedroom Sean was standing over his mother shouting, 'Mammy, Mammy!' and from her throat came a noise the like of which they had never heard. Her face was grey and her eyes had rolled back into her head with only the whites showing. Theresa rushed to her while Sean backed away, almost into Irene.

'She's still breathing,' said Theresa, her head pressed to her mother's chest. 'We need to get the doctor and a priest.' Sean pushed past Irene and was taking the stairs two at a time when Theresa screamed at him. 'Stop, you can't go! You stay. I'll get them.'

Irene followed her downstairs and closed the door after her.

Then she took Sean's arm and said softly, 'You need to go back upstairs and sit with your mother until Theresa comes back.'

He put his foot on the first step and stopped. 'I can't. I can't,' he whispered.

'It's all right, I'll go with you.'

He sat on the bed, held his mother's hand and spoke only one word over and over, 'Mammy', and the sound in her throat quietened and each line of her face seemed to soften. From where she stood at the foot of the bed, Irene was astonished to see a silver wisp, like steam from a cooling kettle, rise from the body of Sean's mother and float upwards towards the picture of the Virgin Mary.

At the same moment the street outside exploded with noise: crashing bin lids; shouting men; heavy boots on cobbles. Sean was on his feet and out to the landing, where he jumped on the banister and punched out a flimsy cover in the ceiling to pull himself up into the loft. Once inside, he lowered his arm back down and shouted, 'Irene!' Without hesitation she took his hand and felt herself lifted into the darkness.

Outside was pandemonium. The street was a blaze of light as people poured out of their homes to add to the confusion.

The police were exposed in their clandestine mission to arrest a fugitive and had no alternative but to storm the house, breaking the door down and ransacking the rooms. Theresa rushed in after them screaming and grabbing at their uniforms. A priest followed her. There was the sound of splintering wood as a policeman rushed at the bedroom door with his shoulder and fell into the room. Theresa ran past him and positioned herself between him and the bed.

'Get out! Get out, you bastard!' she screamed. The priest took one look at the dead woman and stepped forward, his arms outstretched. 'You are abusing the sanctity of the dead. Leave us in peace, I've work to do here.'

'That's all very well, Father, but we're after a man wanted for murder. We have to search everywhere. He could be hiding in here.'

'Well he isn't,' said the priest. 'So take your anger and disrespect elsewhere and leave this woman with some dignity.'

The policeman looked around as if weighing up the possibilities and backed out of the door. Theresa closed it behind him and the priest turned to give Mrs O'Hara the last rites.

Once Irene was in the loft, Sean carefully replaced the board in the ceiling. It took a few moments for her eyes to adjust to the darkness.

'Keep your head down, there isn't much room.' Sean held her arm. 'You're standing on a joist, just put one foot in front of the other.' The smell of neglect and the dust of decades surrounded them and the unrelenting clamour from the street far below seemed muted and irrelevant. She followed him gingerly across the roof space until they reached the far wall where an old door lay on its side. Sean lifted it and they crawled through a hole into the adjoining house, then he reached back and carefully replaced the door. Again and again they repeated the process until finally they crawled into the fifth house, the end of the terrace, where the loft floor had been boarded and Sean and Irene were able to sit and lean against the wall. 'We'll wait here until someone comes to tell us the coast is clear,' he said.

They sat in silence and Irene thought about the sequence of events that had brought her to this dusty loft on New Year's Eve with Sean, when she should have been safe in the city at a bar or a dance hall with Sandy. But somehow she knew she was meant to be here. She reached out in the darkness to touch his face and felt the tears. She had no idea what to do, had never considered that a man might cry. Instinct made her put her arms around him and he rested his head on her shoulder. Time passed and the sounds from the street faded a little. He raised his head.

'Mammy said she'd waited to see me before … she could let go. I'm glad I came back. Even if they catch me, I'm glad I was there with her.'

'You knew they'd try to arrest you, didn't you?' said Irene. 'Did you plan this escape route just in case?'

'Not really, but I knew that after the last internments the men in the street had decided to give themselves a fighting chance if the police came for them again.'

'You didn't need to take me with you, you know, the police would have let me go.'

'I'm sure they would, but your name would end up on a list somewhere and one day just knowing me could go against you.'

She felt his arm around her shoulder. 'There's another reason why I pulled you into the loft. I've thought of you so often since I left Belfast. There were nights away from home when I tried to picture you, your eyes, your hair, the way your body felt when we danced that night at John Dossor's. Do you remember? And when I saw you again tonight I wanted you with me. Will you come with me, Irene?'

'Come with you to Donegal?'

'No, to America, that's where I have to go. There's nothing left for me here.' He pulled her close to him. 'Will you come with me?'

'You want me to go to America?'

'Yes, tonight!' Sean's voice was suddenly excited. 'We'll go back over the border; there are people there who'll help me. There's many a man I know who's gone the same way. Come with me, Irene.'

In the time it took to draw breath, hold it and breathe out, Irene saw the possibilities. She felt so alive with Sean; he made her understand what it was to be attracted to a man, and he was offering the drama of escape from Belfast and the prospect of a new life in America. She had only to nod her head or whisper 'yes', but her head didn't move, no word escaped her lips. She thought of her mother and knew she wasn't ready to leave her or her sisters. Knew also that she wanted to sing in concerts and work in the aircraft factory. Maybe a few years from now, asked the same question, she might say yes, but not now. She wasn't done with Belfast yet.

'I can't,' she whispered.

There was a sudden noise, a crack of light and a head peered up through a hole in the floor. 'Sean, are ye there?'

'Aye, I am.'

'The police have been in and out of every house in the street. There's half a dozen in your house and outside, but we can get ye out of here and away to the Shankill. They won't look for ye there.'

He turned to Irene. 'You won't come with me?'

She shook her head.

'Wait five minutes, then come down. Walk straight across the street and on past my house to the main road. You'll find your way home from there. Goodbye, Irene.' He kissed her and was gone.

When she emerged from the house the street was quiet. She put her head down and walked quickly. As she passed Sean's house she saw a policeman at the door and hurried on. She had just turned into Northumberland Street when someone gripped her arm and pulled her into the shadows.

'Well, well, Miss Goulding, I knew we'd find ye here somewhere. We missed your Fenian boyfriend this time, but he won't get far. There's half the force out lookin' for him.'

'It was you, wasn't it? You read the card Sean sent me, you brought the police here! So what are you going to do now? Arrest me?'

'No, I don't think so. I wouldn't want to upset Martha like that. No, I'll just keep me eye on ye, check your post that sort of thing. If ye know what's good for ye, ye'll have nothing more to do with that murderin' ...'

In the dark, the slap across his face took Ted Grimes completely by surprise and he staggered backwards, loosening his grip just enough for Irene to pull her arm free and run and run until her breath was spent.

Chapter 24

'Go on then,' said Myrtle. 'Tell us where ye were and it had better be good, 'cause ye ruined my New Year's Eve!'

Irene sighed. 'I'm really sorry, Myrtle. It couldn't be helped. I went round to see Theresa and her mother was really bad. I couldn't leave her – the poor woman was dying. Theresa had to go for the priest while I sat with her and while I was with her she died.'

'Oh God, that's terrible!'

'It was awful, Myrtle. I can't bear to think about it.' She felt herself close to tears yet again.

Irene had decided to stick to the truth about what happened on New Year's Eve, but leave out any mention of Sean. She was still shaken up by the whole thing, especially the threatening encounter with Ted Grimes and, truth be told, she was half-expecting the RUC to appear at any time. As for Sean wanting her to go to America with him, she had been over his words so many times in her head that she was glad to get to work to force herself to think of something else.

'What did Sandy say when I didn't turn up?'

'Not a great deal. He doesn't say much, does he? And what he did say was hard to make out. I couldn't understand him half the time.'

'Did you wait long for me?'

'God Irene, we were foundered, the temperature was below freezin'. I'd only a wee cotton dress on under me coat, thinkin' I was goin' te be in a bar or the Plaza all night.'

'Myrtle! Will you tell me what happened?'

'All right, keep your hair on! We waited 'til nine, then me and Robert went for a drink, hot whiskey and lemon to warm us up. Sandy said he would wait a wee bit longer. Well it was all right for him, sure he had his big RAF overcoat on him.'

'Is that it? Did he say anything about me?'

'Not much. Then when we were goin', I says te him do ye want me te ask Irene te write to you? I told him, something's happened, Irene wouldn't just not turn up. "No", says he. And I'm thinking is that no, he doesn't want you to write, or is he agreeing with me that you're not the sort of girl who leaves a man who's come a long way to see her on New Year's Eve standing like an eejit outside the City Hall.'

Myrtle paused to draw breath.

'So does he want me to write to him or not?'

'God knows. I says te Robert come on then, let's get a drink inside us before it's 1941 and we're still sober.'

'Myrtle!' screamed Irene.

'Ach, sure why don't you write te him anyway. He can ignore it if he wants.'

When Irene arrived home after work that evening she was horrified to see Ted Grimes in the kitchen drinking tea with her mother. They immediately stopped talking when she walked in.

She ignored them both and went through into the front room, intending to go to her bedroom, but at the foot of the stairs she stopped and quietly retraced her steps.

'I'm telling ye, Martha, you've got to get a grip on those girls of yours. There's no father to keep them in line. It's you that's got to impose some discipline.'

'Do you think I don't know that? I do my best with them, but they're growing up. They're young women now. I can't lock them up in the house, even though many's the time I wish I could.'

'Bad company, Martha, that's what I'm talking about. It's the undoing of many a girl, believe you me!'

Martha stifled a cry and Irene could stand it no longer. She opened the door and went straight to Ted Grimes. 'How dare you come in here telling tales and upsetting Mammy. It was bad enough that you tried to frighten me. You won't get away with doing it to her as well!'

He pushed back his chair and drew himself up to his full intimidating height. 'Now listen here, young madam, you're a disgrace that's what ye are and if ye were mine I'd give ye a good hidin'!'

Suddenly Martha was on her feet. 'Ted, no one speaks to my daughter like that. You're a grown man, an RUC officer, what are you doing frightening women? You come in here standing in moral judgement on us: how I bring up my children, how they conduct themselves. I won't have it in my house. Now you get your belongings and leave.'

Ted took his time placing the cap on his head, pulling down the peak.

'Goodnight to you, Martha,' he said and without another word went out the door.

The two women breathed hard controlling their tempers.

Each struggled to find appropriate words to begin to unravel what had just happened. In the end they both spoke at once.

'What have you …'

'I didn't do …'

'Irene, so help me, if you've been doing anything to let me down …'

'I haven't, Mammy, honest I haven't.'

'I'll take my hand to you, don't think I won't! Now you'd better tell me what this is all about.'

Irene wanted to tell her Ted Grimes had been reading her letters, to somehow put the blame on him, but then she'd have to explain about Sean and that would connect her with someone wanted by

305

the police and suddenly Ted would look like a caring friend. No, she'd been secretive and underhand and her mother would surely blame her for that. But she'd done nothing bad, had she? She'd helped Theresa, her friend, how could that be wrong? Sean hadn't killed the policeman – of that she was certain – and so she'd helped an innocent man evade capture. Her conscience was clear.

'Mammy, I'm not going to explain everything that happened: it would mean betraying someone who's a good person even if Mr Grimes says they aren't. You've always taught us right from wrong and I'm telling you I haven't done anything wrong. Please trust me, Mammy, and believe me that it's really important.'

'Is this to do with you and the airman?'

'No, it isn't.'

'Have I your word that you'll never do anything like this again?'

'You have.'

'And what about Ted Grimes?'

'He's a bully and he frightens me and I'll never speak to him again.'

Martha looked at her eldest daughter and knew full well her capacity for kindness and common sense. She nodded.

'Then neither will I.'

'Here we are. This is it, Peggy, what do you think?' Harry pulled up outside a boarded-up shop just past the Crumlin Road jail.

'It's not very big is it?' said Peggy, her face showing a distinct lack of interest.

'No, but it's deceptive, so it is. It goes right back, plenty of room for ovens and everything we'll need. Come on, I'll show you.' He was out of the car in a moment and round her side opening the door and helping her out. He jangled a bunch of keys and made for the shop. Peggy hung back looking up at the building, then she looked to left and right, taking in the decrepit surroundings.

'Right, Peggy, do you want lifting over the threshold?' he joked. She gave him a withering look and stepped inside. It was filthy and stale-smelling. It had been a bakery: there was a counter, display cases and wooden shelves just the right size for loaves. On the walls were faded posters for Rank flour and Tate & Lyle sugar.

'Do you see the possibilities, Peggy, do you?'

She looked at the cobwebs spanning the ceiling corners and shuddered to think what made the floor gritty underfoot, but still she said nothing.

'Come on through here to the bakery. You'll be amazed at the size of it.'

There was a row of ancient ovens along one wall and racks of shelving. A large work table stood in the middle of the room; some stairs led to a second floor.

'We won't go up, they're a wee bit rickety. Now I think we could fit this out with modern equipment and do it all up so it's nice and fresh looking. Same out the front of the shop and get a nice sign up above: 'Ferguson Family Bakers, established 1941'.

What do you think, Peggy, eh?' She wandered around the back room then into the shop again with Harry chatting all the while.

'I think for three hundred pounds we could buy this and turn it into a wee goldmine. There's no other bakery around here and there's plenty of houses down all these streets, hundreds of families wanting bread every day. We can't go wrong. Eh, Peggy, what do you think? You remember Dessie we met at the dinner dance on Christmas Eve? Well, he'd be interested in lending us the money to set up here.'

'Dessie? I thought you said he was a chancer.' Peggy had moved to the open door and stood looking into the road. 'And I suppose that's his car you've borrowed.'

'Ach, he's all right. He's plenty of money. I've done many a job for him, never let him down. He'd trust me to pay him back. Mind you we'd have to work hard. I'd be up from four in the morning baking the bread and then I could do a few cakes, provided I could get the sugar, maybe some gravy rings, Paris buns, wee Victoria sponges. Things like that would sell well round here. Then you'd open up at eight, we'd close at six.'

'What did you say?'

'Aye, we'll close at six, try and catch people needing bread for their tea.'

'You said I'd open up at eight.'

'Well, I'll still be busy in the back for a few hours.'

'You want me to serve in this shop?'

'That's what we agreed, didn't we? Sure you've the experience.'

Peggy looked at him as if he had taken leave of his senses. 'If you think I'm going from working in a music shop on Royal Avenue to a pokey wee bakery on the Crumlin Road you've got another think coming. I wouldn't work here if you and Dessie paid me ten pounds a week and all the Paris buns I could eat!'

They drove back to Joanmount Gardens in silence. Harry stopped the car outside the house and turned to her. 'I'll tell you what, Peggy, how about I employ a wee girl to work in the shop, someone from the Crumlin? I wouldn't need to pay her much and you could carry on at Goldstein's for the time being.'

Aye, for as long as I like, she thought, and kissed him on the cheek. He drove off in search of Dessie, delighted that Peggy had agreed to something, but he couldn't shake off the feeling of having been wrapped around a finger.

Peggy pushed open the back door to find Martha draining the potatoes, engulfed in a cloud of steam, Pat setting the table, Sheila stirring gravy and Irene wetting the tea.

'I'm thinking about marrying Harry,' she announced.

Chapter 25

They approached the Royal Air Force base at Aldergrove just as the light was fading, throwing the rows of Nissen huts into sharp relief against the horizon. Their passes were checked at the gate and the driver was directed to follow the road to the large hangar. They saw it loom out of the darkness, impressive enough, but nothing compared to the rows of Hurricane bombers lined up beyond it.

'Look at all those fighter planes!'

'What are they all doing here?'

'They're waiting for the Luftwaffe,' said Goldstein.

In the hangar there was an impressive stage at one end and, at the other, an elaborate gantry from which hung rows of lights.

'This looks very professional,' whispered Myrtle, as a bright spotlight lit up the empty stage then narrowed to focus on the single microphone in the centre.

Goldstein disappeared and returned with three small RAF uniforms for the Golden Sisters. It had been such a success at their first concert for the armed forces that they'd continued to use this change of costume, but this was the first time they would wear air force blue.

'Now Irene,' said Goldstein, 'I am told there is a corporal who is a really good dancer. He will be standing down to your right, a tall man with dark hair. Get him up on the stage and the Lindy Hop routine will be a sensation.'

The sisters changed into their new polka dot blouses and black pencil skirts for their first-half appearance and Pat suggested a run-through on stage before the audience arrived. Peggy was delighted to find the piano was a baby grand and didn't argue.

She played the first few bars of 'I'll Take Romance', but just before Pat and Irene's cue, she stopped and went back to the beginning. She played it again, then the introduction to the second song. Pat had had enough.

'Peggy, what are you doing? You need to give us a chance to sing the opening line at least.'

'This piano's no use. I'm not playing it.'

'What's the matter with it?' asked Irene.

'Can you not hear? Pat, you can hear it, can't you?'

Pat knew it wasn't pitch perfect. 'Ach, it'll do rightly.'

'No, it won't. I'm not playing an out of tune piano!'

'You and I will be the only ones who notice, Peggy, and I'm prepared to put up with it.'

'Well I'm not.'

'You'll have to, we can't perform without accompaniment.'

'I'm not playing it!' Peggy shouted and left the stage.

'I'll find Goldstein,' said Irene, 'maybe he can talk to her.'

He was in the officers' mess talking to a well-decorated officer. 'Can I have a quick word with you, Mr Goldstein?'

She explained the problem and he nodded. 'I'll come with you and listen to the piano myself.'

He sat at the baby grand and ran through the scales, his head cocked to one side. Then he played the few bars of 'I'll Take Romance' that had so offended Peggy's musical sensibilities. He tutted and walked purposefully towards the dressing room. Within a few minutes Peggy returned, all smiles, and played the songs without a word of complaint.

'Well, I don't know what he said to her,' said Pat, 'but I'm going to find out for the next time she tries to give us a heart attack.'

Over the preceding months Sammy had learned to tailor his material to suit each audience and this time he had lots of jokes about RAF types and much ridiculing of the Luftwaffe, at which the audience roared its approval. The conjuror known as the Great Horrendo had almost perfected his disappearing and reappearing doves routine especially for the night, until one of them flew into the rafters of the hangar and some wag in the audience offered to make the bird an honorary tail-end Charlie.

The girls' first appearance was greeted with whistles and their lively routine brought clapping and cheers. Pat had been asked to sing 'The Wings of a Dove' which drew warm applause. No one seemed to notice the very slightly out-of-tune piano.

They changed at the interval. 'I prefer this uniform to the others we've worn. It has much more shape and style,' said Peggy. 'I'm going to keep it on when we come off stage.' Irene and Pat exchanged puzzled looks. Usually Peggy couldn't wait to change. The appearance of the girls in uniform had the audience on their feet and they took several bows, turning round as though modelling, before Peggy made her way to the piano and their military medley began. When it came to the moment when Irene was to dance with one of the men, she took the microphone off the stand and moved downstage, remembering her instructions from Goldstein.

'For this next song I'm going to need someone to help me.'

There followed shouts and catcalls as dozens of men volunteered. 'You don't know what you'll be asked to do yet!'

Irene smiled wickedly. 'Are any of you good dancers?' Still they shouted. She moved to the right where a tall dark-haired airman was waving at her.

'Me! Me!' he shouted.

She moved closer to him, put her hand up to shield her eyes from the glare of the spotlight. 'Don't I know you?' she said.

There were more whistles. 'What's your name?'

'Tommy!'

'It is you, Tommy! I'd know you anywhere!' The audience were enjoying the joke. 'Stranraer beach, 12 July 1939.'

Uproar!

Irene came down the steps at the side of the stage and returned holding Tommy's hand. 'Now then, last time we met you had your friend Sandy with you. Am I right?' Tommy nodded. 'And where is he now?' She thrust the microphone towards him.

'He's up there!' shouted Tommy and pointed up to the lights' gantry.

'He's not!'

'Oh yes he is!'

Irene's heart was thumping. Sandy was here watching the show! She forced herself to concentrate, and moved to the front of the stage and shielded her eyes.

'Hello, Sandy! Good to … not quite see you again.' Then she signalled to Peggy and the music started. Pat stood beside the piano singing and Irene and Tommy, who was, as promised, an excellent dancer, gave a near-perfect demonstration of the Lindy Hop.

As Tommy left the stage to uproarious applause, Irene blew him a kiss and another in Sandy's direction high above her in the darkness. Then she returned to the microphone.

'This is our last song, 'I'll Take Romance', and it's dedicated to Sandy.' As the last note died away, they left the stage to loud applause and cheering and Irene waved again to the gantry.

'What was all that about?' asked Pat as they changed out of the uniforms.

'The airman who sent me the sari, you remember? I think he was operating the lights.'

It was soon time for the finale. 'Peggy you haven't changed, hurry up!' said Pat.

'I told you I'm keeping the uniform on.'

'You're not supposed to.'

'I don't care.'

The finale was a huge success and went on for much longer than it should have done. It seemed that neither the audience nor the performers wanted the evening to end, but eventually the Squadron Leader stepped on to the stage and asked for the house lights to go up.

'Ladies and gentlemen of the Barnstormers, that was truly a barnstorming performance. We are immensely grateful for your wonderful talent and dedication. But the evening is not quite over.'

He paused as though for dramatic effect. 'Let me introduce you to our special guest this evening who flew here secretly from London this afternoon. Please welcome our illustrious prime minister, Mr Churchill.'

All eyes turned to the back of the hangar from where the instantly recognisable figure emerged. The audience were on their feet straining for a view of him as he walked down the aisle drawing gasps, then applause and cheers. Leaning heavily on his cane he climbed the stairs to where Goldstein was waiting to introduce the performers. The sisters were towards the middle of the line.

'May I introduce the Golden Sisters, Irene, Pat and Peggy,' said Goldstein and the prime minister shook each hand in turn.

'I thoroughly enjoyed the dancing. Great fun!'

'Aah, "Wings of a Dove", a favourite of mine, beautifully sung if I may say so.'

'And you must be Peggy. You were quite right, my dear.' He held on to her hand, patting it. 'The piano was slightly out of tune, but you coped with it admirably and very few would have noticed. May I also say, I have never seen an RAF uniform look so –' he searched for a suitable word, '– impressive.'

So that's how Goldstein got her to play, thought Pat. He told her Churchill would be watching the show.

The Barnstormers were invited back to the mess for a nightcap before the long journey back to Belfast, but at the door of the hangar Irene excused herself saying she had left her scarf backstage. As she suspected, a shadowy figure was still moving about overhead. She thought of calling out, but then noticed a series of ladders leading up to the gantry high above her. She slipped off her shoes and began to climb, silent as a cat. He was sitting on the edge of the platform, his legs swinging. He heard movement behind him and called out, 'You're a bit late, Brian. I've sorted everything up here.'

'It isn't Brian, it's Irene and I don't think we've sorted anything yet.'

'How did you get up here?'

'Like you did, I climbed.' She sat down next to him and swung her legs in time with his.

Surprisingly, he was the first to speak. 'I thought you were very good tonight. I didn't know you sang ... and danced,' he added.

'There's a lot about me you don't know.'

'I know you've a head for heights.' She could hear the smile in his voice.

'Sssh!' she hissed and pointed below. Two figures wandered on to the stage hand in hand. The woman was unmistakably Myrtle, but who was the man? As they watched, he took her in his arms and kissed her. Irene felt uneasy watching this intimacy with Sandy and she thought to call out to let them know they were being watched. Suddenly, Sandy leaned away from her, there was a click, the lights blazed from the gantry and Irene found herself looking at Sammy's surprised face, before Myrtle grabbed his hand and they ran laughing from the stage. Sandy flicked the switch and they were in darkness again. She felt him turn towards her, his hand touched the side of her face and a second later his lips were on hers. She closed her eyes and felt a lightness in her head as it tilted backwards. Then his arms were strong and steadying around her, high above the world and completely safe. The kiss that lasted and lasted was all she needed to know about him. Later, they came down the ladder and wandered out under the midnight sky to stare at the sickle moon. From the mess came the sounds of ordinary people and their meaningless chatter. Instinctively, they walked towards the Hurricanes and under the fuselage he kissed her again as if to reassure her that the excitement was not fleeting, but could be created anew each time he held her.

'I never stopped thinking about you from the moment we met,' he said. 'I could stand here with you forever.'

She could have told him about New Year's Eve, could have asked him if he received her letter apologising, but all of that was irrelevant. She lifted her head to be kissed again.

Pat's voice echoing in the hangar reached them. 'Irene, Irene where are you? We're going now!'

He held her even tighter. 'I know we haven't spent a lot of time with each other, but does it matter? Irene, I want you to think about something ...' He paused and she held her breath.

'Will you think about whether you would like to be my wife?'

314

Irene looked up at him, her eyes wide.

'No, don't answer now. Think about it. I'll get a pass for next weekend. I'll come to your house on Saturday afternoon.'

Pat's voice came again, louder and more insistent. Irene nodded and ran to meet her sister.

'You're a bit of a dark horse, aren't you?' said Irene.

'What do you mean?'

It was the first chance Irene had to talk to Myrtle about what she'd seen on the stage at Aldergrove.

Irene looked around the canteen to make sure no one was listening then whispered, 'You and Sammy!' Myrtle feigned surprise. 'Come on, I saw you on the stage kissing.'

'You didn't!'

'I did, right in the spotlight you were.'

'Where were you?'

Irene pointed skywards.

'Up in the lights?' Myrtle looked confused. 'What were you doing up there?'

'I was with Sandy!'

'Were you, now? You're a bit of a dark horse yourself.'

'Me? What about you! Here's me thinking you and Robert McVey must be about to post the banns and there you are with ...'

'Sssh!' Myrtle looked quickly around her, but everyone was busy chatting. 'You know how it is.'

'No, I don't. Have you finished with Robert?'

Myrtle raised an eyebrow at Irene's naivety. 'Anyway, never mind about me. What were you and Sandy up to?'

'You know.' Irene blushed. 'He's very nice and ...'

'And what, Irene?'

'He asked me to marry him.'

'What?' screamed Myrtle. People at the tables nearby turned to look at them.

Irene lowered her voice 'He asked me to marry him and ...'

'And what?'

'... and he's coming to my house on Saturday.'

'You think he's expecting you to give him an answer?'

'Probably. Oh Myrtle, he is so nice.'

'But you don't know him.'

'I do – a bit.'

'But you've only spent a few hours with him.'

'And there's the letters he sent me from India.'

'Look, take my advice, see how you feel on Saturday in the cold light of day. Don't rush into anything.'

'I could give you the same advice about Sammy!'

It was Friday night before Irene plucked up the courage to tell everyone that Sandy would be coming to visit the following day.

They were sitting around the table and the chatter fell silent when Martha placed the bowl of potatoes in their skins on the table. Irene cleared her throat and said quietly, 'There's someone coming to see me tomorrow.' Something in her tone caused them simultaneously to stop peeling and look at her. 'It's Sandy, you know the one who …'

'Wrote to you from India,' said Sheila.

'Took you up the Cave Hill,' said Peggy.

'Worked the lights at Aldergrove,' said Pat.

'What's he coming here for?' asked Martha.

'He's probably going to take me out somewhere, but I thought you'd like to meet him?'

'Will he be here for his tea?'

'Maybe … probably … oh I don't know!'

Every night since she and Sandy had stood under the wings of the Hurricane, Irene had been awake into the early hours searching for an answer. Sometimes she would see how ridiculous it was to marry someone she hardly knew and that of course she must say no. Then the alternative answer would present itself with as much force and she would remember how he kissed her. Now it was Saturday and soon Sandy would be on his way. She panicked and thought of going back to bed, pulling the covers over her head and telling her mother to say there was no one called Irene Goulding living here.

She was watching from the front bedroom when she heard the faint roar coming up the Oldpark Road. Louder and louder, then a softer purring into Joanmount Gardens and finally a whine as it slowed outside the window. She was out the front door before he had climbed off the bike. She saw at once two things: how nervous he was and how handsome.

Martha was out the back hanging out the washing. There was a stiff breeze, good drying weather. She was just using the clothes prop to hoist the underwear of five women into the air when Irene came into the garden on the arm of a handsome airman.

'Mammy, this is Sandy, remember I told you he was coming today?'

Martha wiped her damp hands on her apron and shook his outstretched hand. 'Pleased to meet you,' she said. She had never seen the RAF uniform up close before and it instantly marked him out as different. 'Was that a motorbike I heard?'

Sandy nodded.

'Why don't you bring it round the back before it's covered in wee boys?'

As Sandy left to get the bike, Irene heard a suppressed giggle and looked up to see her sisters hanging out of the bedroom window. 'Why don't you come down and meet him properly?' she shouted.

From the saddlebag of his bike Sandy produced some lemonade and they went inside. As he was introduced to each sister he gave a little smile and shook her hand, repeating her name as if committing it and her face to memory. Sheila fetched some glasses and Sandy poured them all a drink.

'Did you enjoy the concert?' asked Pat.

'Yes, I did … you were very good.'

'And you did the lighting?' said Peggy.

'Brian and me, aye yes.'

They sipped the lemonade.

'Where are you from, Sandy? You've a bit of an accent, so you have,' said Martha. Irene shifted in her seat. Her mother was trying to find out 'what manner of man he was', as she would put it.

'I'm from the north east of Scotland, a wee fishing town on the coast.'

'Near Edinburgh?'

'Och, no it's a long way from there, closer to Aberdeen.'

'You've family there then?'

'Aye I have, most of them trawlermen; fishing, you ken, in the North Sea.'

'So why aren't you in the Navy then?' interrupted Sheila.

He laughed. 'Because I get seasick, always have since I was a boy.'

'So you took to the air instead,' said Pat.

'Aye, then they sent me to India on a boat. I was at sea for six months.'

'And you got over your seasickness?'

'No!' He laughed again. 'I was ill the whole time and all the way back too.'

Later Irene took him for a walk up Buttermilk Loney and as they left the house he took her hand. 'I like your family,' he said.

'They like you too.'

'Can you tell?'

'Oh yes, they wouldn't have invited you to stay for your tea if they didn't.'

There were primroses pale as churned butter on the hedgerows and somewhere on the hill above them a cuckoo called. They walked a while in silence. The question hung between them. The lane steepened and narrowed until they came to a five-bar gate. They leant against it looking across the rough pasture towards Napoleon's nose.

'Irene ...'

'Yes.'

'What I asked you the other night ...'

'Yes.'

'Have you thought about it?'

'Yes.'

'Have you decided?'

'Yes.'

Sandy stood in front of her and rearranged a strand of hair that had blown across her face. 'Well?'

'Yes.'

'Does that mean …'

'Yes … yes I will marry you!'

He took a small velvet drawstring bag from his pocket, undid it and shook its contents into his hand. It was a gold ring with a milky grey stone. He took her hand and placed it on her finger. 'It's a moonstone from India. I chose it for you the day I bought the sari.'

She looked into his eyes and saw such an expression of love.

'But we'd only met the once in Stranraer for a couple of hours.'

'It was long enough,' he said.

Martha was not altogether surprised when the two of them returned to the house for tea and Sandy asked shyly if he could have a word with her in the front room. She'd seen the way Irene looked at him, a softness around her eyes, and her voice too was different when she spoke to him. She'd been younger than Irene herself when Robert had proposed. What would she have done if someone had stood in their way? Sometimes you have to trust your instincts, she told herself, and instinctively she knew that Sandy was an honest and decent young man.

Even so, she was shocked when they told her they wanted to be married as soon as possible. Sandy knew his work would not be completed at Aldergrove until the end of April, but after that he could be sent to any RAF base in the country. He had already asked about a two-day pass, hoping Irene would accept his proposal. They had less than a month to arrange an Easter wedding.

Chapter 26

W illiam Kennedy was incandescent with rage. He stormed out of the stinking bomb shelter in Donegall Place leaving the rest of the delegation from the ministry of public security inside. He had marched nearly a hundred yards down Chichester Street before he had calmed down sufficiently to return to his staff. Pat had seen it coming, knew how angry he would be, how he would rage against the apathy.

They had driven down to the city centre in two cars, intending to see for themselves 'the state of preparedness' as it was termed. 'The bombs will fall,' he'd said time and again and recently he'd taken to adding, 'but how many can we save?'

Judging by what they'd seen so far, very few.

He had been full of determination and hope when he returned from London in January. 'They said they'd help us,' he told Pat. 'I gave them a list: searchlights, anti-aircraft guns, barrage balloons, money for shelters. God knows they're stretched themselves. The bombing in London was terrifying to experience, but you felt that the authorities were ... well sort of looking after you. I went into a shelter in the Old Kent Road. It was packed, people had brought bedding and food and they even had a singsong. Can you believe it, Pat, as the bombs fell and shook them to their core, they were singing.'

They returned to Stormont in silence, discouraged beyond belief. As they drove up the long drive towards the grandeur of the shining Portland stone building, William ordered the driver to stop. He got out and stared at the building in horror. 'Good God,' he said. 'Even the seat of government will gleam like a beacon in the moonlight to guide the enemy to our heart.'

Later, as Pat left the office to go home, William was waiting for her. 'Sorry about that little display earlier,' he said.

'Don't apologise. You were absolutely right to be angry after all you've tried to do.'

'It's not just me, Pat. It's everyone at the ministry and you especially.' He paused as though considering something. 'Pat, I'd like you to meet someone.'

He drove towards the university and pulled up outside a three-storey Edwardian terrace close to the Botanical Gardens.

They had just got out of the car when the front door flew open and a little girl of four or five rushed up the garden path and into William's open arms. He swung her above his head then carried her to the door, where there stood an elegantly dressed woman with blond hair piled neatly on top of her head. William kissed her quickly on the cheek and turned to Pat.

'Pat, this is my sister Helen and my niece Rosemary. They live with me.'

Pat found herself looking into eyes identical to William's.

'Hello, Pat, lovely to meet you at last, William has told me so much about you. Would you like some tea?'

Later, as William drove her home, he explained that Helen's husband was stationed permanently at the war office in London and she and Rosemary had been living with him since the start of the war.

'So you see, Pat, the reports of my marriage were greatly exaggerated.'

'William, I understand what you are telling me, but it really is none of my business.'

'But it is, Pat.'

'I never presumed ...'

'I know you didn't, but I want to make it clear that my intentions are honourable.'

The concert at the Palace Barracks in Holywood had gone well. The Barnstormers had done several encores and by the time they boarded the bus for the drive back to Belfast, it was nearly half past eleven. Pat and Peggy were chatting quietly when Pat stopped mid-sentence. 'Listen,' she said, 'can you hear that?'

Peggy sat up, surprised by the urgency in Pat's voice. 'Is there something wrong with the bus?'

One or two others had also noticed it, an intermittent drone, behind them, above them. The bus slowed, the driver cut the engine and the noise became louder and louder.

'Oh God!' breathed Pat. 'Enemy aircraft – the Germans are over our heads. I'm going to have a look!'

'Don't leave the bus, Pat, they might see you and shoot!'

'They won't see us; their eyes are fixed on the city, the docks probably.'

In seconds, each person on the bus was alert. Suddenly everyone was screaming and shouting and pushing towards the door, desperate to get out. Outside there was a half moon, enough to make out the black shapes of planes following the line of the coast, some with their navigation lights on. The performers, many still in their stage costumes and make-up, lined the pavement – some crying, some cursing, all stunned.

'Where's the bloody air-raid siren?' shouted Sammy. 'They're not warnin' people. They'll be in their beds, for God's sake!'

As if in reply, there was an almighty crack and the anti-aircraft guns began to roar. The noise was deafening and their fire left tracers across the sky.

'That'll be the guns at Victoria Park,' said Pat.

'But that's no good,' shouted Sammy. 'They're already over the gantries!' and he pointed to where dozens of cranes, bathed in moonlight, stood as markers for the target. Then, at last, came the distinctive sound of the air-raid siren.

They watched as thousands of pinpricks of light, like iridescent snow, fell from the sky. 'Magnesium flares,' said Pat. Another wave of bombers followed the first. Someone counted them and there were eight in total. 'They'll drop the incendiary devices,' said Pat.

'How do you know so much about German bombers?' asked Sammy.

'Because she works for the ministry of public security,' said Peggy, 'and they've been expecting this for months.'

With the incendiaries came the beginnings of fires in the docks and the streets surrounding them. The Barnstormers huddled together watching the flames turn from a glow to a conflagration until the sky was ablaze.

'It's like the burning of Atlanta,' whispered Peggy.

The following waves of bombers, guided by the flames, brought high explosives and parachute bombs. One group came in from the south, right over their heads and under the barrage balloons. The Barnstormers covered their ears and watched the bombers race above the road then veer towards the docks, but it seemed one pilot had been over eager and released his bombs too soon. There was a piercing scream and Myrtle broke away from the group and began running. By the time Sammy caught her she was hysterical. 'Them's my streets!' She kept shouting. 'Them's my streets!' That the Newtownards Road had been hit was obvious, probably Templemore Avenue too, but Sammy held her fast, shushing her. 'I know, I know but you've got to stay here. It's not safe.' They returned to the bus to wait in sombre mood.

Shortly before three thirty, there was a heavy assault of high explosives on the docks area so severe they felt the ground shake and rumble beneath their feet. Then, mission accomplished, the bombers dipped and rolled and disappeared over the Black Mountain, leaving behind a city wide awake to the dawn and the realities of war.

The Barnstormers waited a while, subdued by what they'd witnessed, then at four o'clock the all-clear sounded.

'Come on, let's get home,' said Sammy. 'And I'll tell ye what, youse uns should never complain again about doin' encores; that extra wee bit of singing might well have kept us from bein' in the middle of all that.'

Across the city, Martha as usual had found it hard to sleep with the girls still out. Around midnight she too became aware of the droning and knew instantly what it was.

She thought about going under the stairs, but the siren hadn't sounded. The intermittent drone grew louder. Suddenly there was a deafening noise and flashes of light.

'Sheila!' she screamed. 'Wake up! We're being bombed.'

They followed the drill Pat had taught them and within minutes were huddled under the stairs with all the small comforts they would need to spend the night.

'Mammy, where do you think they are?'

'Somewhere safe, I'm sure, maybe in a shelter. Why don't you say a wee prayer to keep them safe?'

'God, you know where Irene, Pat and Peggy Goulding are and that there are bombs falling on Belfast. Please will you keep them safe and me and Mammy too. Amen.'

And in her head Martha repeated over and over. 'Please God let them be somewhere safe.' It was at times like these she wished she had some rosary beads.

The bus made good progress towards the city, but as they drove along the Newtownards Road they began to see evidence of the destruction. A church was blazing fiercely – they could feel the heat through the bus windows – but there was no sign of the fire brigade. Further on, the bus started to fill with choking black smoke from a burning timber yard and they had to make a detour. Soon they began to see the severe damage caused by high explosive bombing. The streets were strewn with slates and rubble and glass. At the end of one terrace a gable wall was bulging and in imminent danger of collapse and everywhere was bathed in the orange light of many fires. Near Templemore Avenue, Myrtle left the bus and Sammy went with her.

'I'll see her home,' he said. 'These streets aren't safe and God knows what she'll find when she gets there.'

The bus crossed the river just before five in the artificial dawn of burning fires and the sight from the bridge was so striking that the driver stopped the bus and one by one they filed out in silence to stand and stare at the blazing docks.

Martha and Sheila were drinking tea in the kitchen when the girls came in. Everyone was talking at once.

'Thank God you're safe.' Martha kissed each daughter.

'We saw the whole thing!' said Peggy.

'You two went in under the stairs, I hope,' said Pat.

'Aye, don't worry, we followed the drill exactly. It was cold, but quiet. I'd guess there were no bombs dropped up this end.'

'It's all round the docks, a bit along the Newtownards Road.'

'I'm starving, so I am,' said Irene. 'I'll make us all some breakfast before I go to work?'

'Mercy me!' Martha threw her hands in the air. 'Work is it? There'll be no work for you girls today after the night you've had!'

'Mammy, it's because of the night we've had that we have to be there.' Pat was adamant.

'But there might be no buses running.'

'It doesn't matter. I'll walk all the way if I have to.'

'And so will I,' said Irene.

'Me too,' said Peggy, 'if I can find any flat shoes.'

Irene crossed the Queen's Bridge, walking slowly, taking in the scene along the river. There were remnants of fires still burning and the air was clogged with so many smells: wood smoke from smouldering timber, melting roof felt from factory buildings and, pervading everything, the stink of cordite. She rounded the corner and her heart leapt. There it was, still standing, with workers crowding through the doors. She saw a woman they sometimes sat with in the canteen and shouted to her. 'I can't believe it's not damaged. I thought it had taken a direct hit.'

'We all did, they missed it by a whisker, but there was a parachute oil bomb. It just skimmed Shorts and floated across into the Harland & Wolff factory. The whole place burned like firewood. There were fifty Stirling fuselages in there, all gone.'

'That's terrible! They were to replace the planes they've lost in England.'

'Worst of it is, a few men on the night shift saw the bomb coming towards them and thought it was a parachute with a German hanging from it and there's them runnin' after it to catch him, when the whole lot exploded. Kilt them stone dead!'

Inside the aircraft factory there was some incendiary damage that had been quickly dealt with by the fire watchers and in some of the offices glass skylights had blown in. Irene clocked in and went in search of Myrtle, but found instead Robert McVey.

'When the all clear sounded I went to check on Myrtle's family. Her father, brother and sister were in a shelter safe and sound, but her Grannie refused to leave the house. Found out later the house was bombed, but she survived. Myrtle's trying to find some cousins to take them in.'

By early afternoon Pat had read enough reports to give William information on how the public had responded to the raid. 'The shelters weren't used much; they're still in a bad state and some were locked.'

'And how did people behave?' asked William.

'Where there was a lot of damage, people were frightened, but in some places they went on to the streets just to watch the bombs.'

'When will these people realise the horrors of an air raid? They're acting like front seat spectators at a gigantic Brocks' firework display!'

'Any word on the number of casualties?' asked Pat.

'Much lower than expected, thank God. We've been lucky, but next time they'll come back stronger, with twice as many bombs and a wider range of targets.'

'When do you think they'll be back?'

'Before we know it,' said William.

When Irene arrived home that evening she was surprised to see Thomas Wilson's car parked outside the house. He and Anna were in the kitchen drinking tea with Martha.

'Anna and Thomas took a wee run over to see if we were all safe after last night. Wasn't that good of them?'

'We've been meaning to come over since we received your wedding invitation. So I said to Thomas, never mind RSVP, let's just take a wee run over to Joanmount and hear all about it. Your mammy has been telling us about Sandy and the wedding arrangements.'

'Oh it's going to be a very simple wedding,' said Irene, 'just the family, yourselves, the McCrackens and a couple of friends from work and a few from the Barnstormers – Sandy's family live too far away to come. Pat's going to sing. Then we'll all come back here for some sandwiches and Peggy's friend Harry is going to make the wedding cake.'

'Well, that sounds very nice and I hear you're getting married at Donegall Square Methodist.'

'Yes, we are. They couldn't fit us in at Oldpark Presbyterian, but Donegall Square always makes room for those in uniform.'

Anna beamed. 'Do you know the Imperial Hotel just nearby?'

Without waiting for an answer she went on. 'Thomas and I go there quite a lot when we're in town and we ...' She nodded towards Thomas. 'We would like to pay for you to have your reception there. What do you think?'

Irene looked at her mother in amazement. Martha raised an eyebrow very slightly, which could have meant anything. 'That's very kind of you Aunt Anna, but we couldn't.'

'Nonsense,' said Anna. 'Martha and you girls were very supportive when Thomas and I were ... you know, after the mail boat sank ...' Her voice seemed to lose its strength. 'Anyway, we'd really like to do this for you. What do you say?'

'I say it's very kind of you and thank you very much,' said Irene and she kissed first Anna then Thomas, the first time she'd ever done so. 'And Uncle Thomas,' she added, 'will you give me away?'

Since the visit to William's house when she had been introduced to his sister and niece, Pat had found him waiting for her after work on a few occasions. 'I'll drop you off in town,' he'd said the first time and she'd protested that it was out of his way.

'Not at all, it's no more than a few minutes' detour and it'll save you time only having to catch one bus home instead of two.' Today as he drove he vented his fury at the final draft of the report made to the prime minister, John Andrews, about what was now being called the 'Dockside Raid'. 'I tell you it's a whitewash; a piece of propaganda full of all that positive language that makes people feel self-satisfied instead of the blunt words that tell them they're living in a fool's paradise! There was one other piece of news today. You remember when I went to England they said they'd send us what they could by way of anti-aircraft protection?'

Pat nodded.

'Well, I had word that a shipment arrived in Larne yesterday.'

'That's great news.'

'Not that great, Pat, they sent us one searchlight and one anti-aircraft gun. It's not going to make much difference; we need ten times that number at least.'

'My mother listens to the wireless a lot for war news and she heard Lord Haw-Haw warn of 'Easter eggs for Belfast'. Do you think it's possible they'll attack again over Easter?'

'That's coming close to the full moon, ideal bombing conditions. I wouldn't be surprised by them coming up the lough any time soon.'

'Oh, I hope not. We've got a big ENSA concert at Balmoral Camp on Easter Tuesday and Irene's getting married the day after. Goldstein has been hinting that a star is coming over from England for the show, but he can't say who it is, of course.'

'I wish I was still a member of the Barnstormers. I really miss it.'

'You could come along if you like.'

'I'm sorry, I couldn't do that.'

'Don't apologise,' said Pat, her voice noticeably cooler.

'No, I'd really like to, but I've been doing tours, spot checks, each night, checking on the precautions: fire watchers, shelters, guns. I was out during the dockside raid. It's the only way I can get a feel for what's happening on the ground each night.'

Pat saw the tiredness in his face and understood why his frustration was so intense. 'It's fine.' Her voice was softer now. 'I understand.'

'When all this is over, Pat, we'll sing again won't we, a duet from *Figaro* or *La Bohème*, maybe?'

'I'd like that,' she smiled. 'I'm singing something from *Figaro* at Irene's wedding, Cherubino's aria.'

'I'd love to hear you sing that.'

'Well, if you're not doing anything at noon on Easter Wednesday, come along.'

William's eyes lit up, all tiredness gone. 'Maybe we could sing the Suzanna and Figaro duet like we did in the concerts.'

Then suddenly his enthusiasm evaporated. 'But maybe Irene wouldn't want that.'

'Not want it? She'd love it!'

'Did you find anywhere to stay, Myrtle?' asked Irene as they sat in the canteen.

'Aye, thank God. Me da's cousin lives in Thorndyke Street. We're stayin' there for the time bein' and Grannie's gone te her sisters up the Castlereagh Road.'

'You look really tired.'

'Tired? I'm exhausted, so I am, but at least we've got a wee bit of a holiday over Easter. And you'll never guess where I'm goin'.'

'Where?'

'To a wedding and the reception's at the Imperial Hotel, no less!'

'I'm surprised you mix in those sort of circles.'

'Well, sometimes you've got to spend a bit of time with the lower classes, just to see how the other half lives!'

There was a loud rapping on a table at the far end of the canteen and they looked up to see the production manager on his feet.

'This morning, I am delighted to make a small presentation to one of our workers. Some of you may know that Irene Goulding will be getting married on Wednesday.' He paused to consult the piece of paper in his hand, '... to a member of the RAF who is, I understand, currently stationed at Aldergrove. So I'd like to ask Irene to come up and receive her gift.' There was a round of applause and some cheering as Irene was presented with a canteen of cutlery.

'Them knives is all blunt ye know,' shouted someone at the back, 'but ye can sharpen them after yer married!'

Irene leaned over to Myrtle and said with a laugh, 'Worth getting married just for the knives and forks. It'll be your turn soon.'

'What d'ye mean, my turn soon?'

Irene was surprised by her sharp tone. 'Nothing really,' said Irene. 'I just thought you and Robert ...'

'Well, you thought wrong!' shouted Myrtle, pushing her chair back with a loud scraping noise and marching out of the canteen.

Irene caught up with her in the corridor outside. 'Myrtle, what's the matter? I'm sorry, I didn't mean anything ...'

'It's not you. It's between me and Robert.'

'What is? What's going on?'

'We're finished, it's over.'

'It can't be. Sure he dotes on you.'

'Not anymore he doesn't.'

'Why, what's happened?'

'Nothin', I can't tell you.'

'This is about Sammy isn't it? Has Robert found out?'

Myrtle nodded and wiped her eyes.

'But sure Robert's a good man. Tell him it didn't mean anything with Sammy.'

'He'll never forgive me, never.'

'Of course he will. Do you want me to speak to him?'

'No, there's nothing you can say.'

'Let me try ...'

'Irene!' she cried. 'Will you shut up? Nobody can do anything. If you must know, I'm pregnant and Robert knows for certain it's not his!'

On Easter Sunday morning the Goulding family returned from church to find Harry Ferguson leaning on his borrowed car waiting for them. 'A wee bird told me you're all going out for the day. Where's it to be then? Bellevue Zoo? Bangor and back for a bob?'

'We're going to the Waterworks for a picnic,' said Sheila. 'It's a family tradition.'

'Well, I've just called round to let you know that the cake is ready. I finished icing it this morning, the first wedding cake to be baked in Ferguson Family Bakers. I was going to take it down to the hotel later.'

'So the bakery is open then?' said Martha.

'Not quite. Everything is finished and ready. The grand opening's on Saturday.'

'Why don't you come on the picnic first,' suggested Peggy. 'Then you and I can collect the cake from the shop and take it to the hotel?'

'Ach no, sure it's a family tradition. I'd be in the way.'

'No, you wouldn't,' said Peggy. Harry had been so elusive lately. They'd hardly been out anywhere. He was always working on getting the shop ready.

'You're very welcome to join us, Harry,' said Martha. 'We've plenty of sandwiches, but I'm afraid we don't have an egg for you to roll.'

'That's very kind, Mrs Goulding. I've some shortbread in the car I'll bring along.'

'Oh shortbread,' said Sheila, her mouth watering. 'We haven't had shortbread since before the war.'

'Ah, it's the sugar, you see, not a lot of that to be had.'

'Then how did you get it?'

'Ask no questions, be told no lies,' said Harry, tapping the side of his nose. Peggy shot him a withering look.

There were several families already at the Waterworks, but they found a quiet spot near some trees and laid out the blanket.

Martha poured them all some lemonade in the old cups she'd brought. 'I think we need a toast,' said Harry. 'Here's to Irene, the first Goulding girl to tie the knot. I wonder who'll be next.'

There was a moment in which they all paused in the raising of their glasses. Martha caught the look that passed across Peggy's face and immediately filled the silence.

'Here's to Irene and Sandy,' she said. 'I'm sure Wednesday will be a day to remember.'

The afternoon passed in idle chatter, silly jokes and the sharing of memories. No one spoke of the bombing less than a week before, even though the scars of it were visible not far from where they sat drinking lemonade and eating shortbread.

Around three o'clock, Peggy and Harry left and drove to the Crumlin Road. The closer they got to the shop, the more sullen Peggy became. 'What's the matter with you? Cat got your tongue?' – Harry's usual tease when Peggy was in a mood.

Her answer was a sideways glare. He took his eyes off the road long enough to catch it.

'Wait 'til you see the shop, Peggy. You'll love it.'

The sun had faded to a watery glow by the time they pulled up outside. Peggy looked at the newly painted lemon and white shop front and had to admit that it did look quite pretty.

'Inside's even better!' Harry was bursting with excitement.

The interior was painted white and the late afternoon light reflected off the walls making them shine. The counter and display cabinets were all new and, instead of brown curling posters on the walls, there were stencilled shapes of cakes straight out of a child's picture book with cherries on the top and thick jam and cream; biscuits sprinkled with hundreds and thousands; and the brownest crustiest loaves imaginable.

'What do you think, Peggy?'

She looked all around, and even went to look closely at the stencils on the walls, nodding as she took it all in.

'Come through into the back; that's the best bit of all.'

Everywhere gleamed: the counters, the ovens, the sinks, the mixers, the utensils hanging on the wall. Pristine. Expensive.

'Isn't this great, Peggy?'

Finally she spoke. 'How much did all this cost?'

'Oh it wasn't cheap, but you get what you pay for.'

'All three hundred pounds?'

'Ask no questions, be told no lies. Now don't you be worrying. I'll pay it all back within a few months.' He crossed the shop and wrapped his arms around her. 'Tell me, do you love our wee shop?'

In spite of herself Peggy smiled. 'I do,' she said simply.

He drew her closer. 'And tell me, do you love me?'

She nodded.

'Say it.'
'I do.'
'Say all of it.'
'I do love you.'
He bent to kiss her, then stopped. 'And?'
'And our wee shop,' she added.

Chapter 27

'I'm telling you, playmates, it's Arthur Askey,' said Sammy.

'How do you know that?' asked Peggy.

'Because he's always touring the country entertaining the troops, I read it in the paper.'

'When did you last read a paper?'

'Could be Vera Lynn?' suggested Irene.

'It could be anyone,' said Pat.

The mess door opened and a familiar-looking pair came in and Captain Ayres, again in charge of proceedings at Balmoral Camp, went to greet them. After much handshaking, he turned to address the room. 'Ladies and gentlemen, may I welcome on your behalf our special guests for the evening. I'm sure they need no introduction: Flanagan and Allen.'

There was a spontaneous round of applause and Bud Flanagan stepped forward. 'Thanks everybody. We're really pleased to be in Belfast. Now, I need to report to Mr Goldstein – I'm told he's the impresario in charge.'

Goldstein made his way forward beaming with delight amid the cheers from his company.

'Flanagan and Allen,' whispered Irene. 'Mammy loves listening to them on the wireless. Just wait 'til she hears we've been on the bill with them.'

Peggy moved behind Irene and put her hand on her shoulder and together they strolled a few paces singing 'Underneath the Arches'. Then they realised Bud was watching them and quickly stopped, their voices dissolving into embarrassed giggles.

There were so many things to do the day before the wedding that Martha had made a list as soon as she woke up and pinned it to the back door. She'd crossed off several things, but added others, so by the time it got to eight in the evening she was already exhausted and expected to stay up until at least midnight to get everything done.

Mrs McKee had made the final alterations to Irene's dress and brought it round mid-morning. It was hanging now over the back of the door in Irene's room, a soft blue crêpe with ruffles on the bodice. She'd made Sheila's bridesmaid dress herself from a good-sized remnant she'd had since before the war and saved for something special, and Irene's wedding was certainly that. They'd only decided on the final hem length in the afternoon with Sheila standing on a chair while Martha worked in a circle round her, constantly checking it was even before pinning it up. By four it was neatly hemmed, pressed and also hanging behind the bedroom door. All their shoes had been polished and lined up in the hall. Sheila had her bath and washed her hair, rinsing it with vinegar to make it shine. Then Martha trimmed it neatly, before curling it in rags.

'Your hair's grown back thicker than ever since you cut it short.'

'I looked like a boy then, didn't I?'

'No, it looked lovely, showed off the shape of your face.'

'Maybe I should cut it again then.'

'Maybe not,' laughed Martha.

'You know the earrings you bought me that Christmas because my hair was so short?'

'Yes.'

'I've lent them to Irene to wear tomorrow. You know, something borrowed?'

'That's kind of you and she's got something blue already – her dress.'

'What about something old? That should be easy; we've plenty of old things!'

'I've got that little silver evening bag that was my mother's. You know the one I mean?'

'Yes, that'd be really good. Do you think she'd like it?'

'I'll root it out and we'll see what she says, eh?'

'She needs something new too, doesn't she? Can her dress count for two things blue and new?'

'I don't really know. Maybe it'll have to.'

'I can't believe Irene's getting married tomorrow,' said Sheila wistfully. 'Do you think she'll be different when she's married?'

Martha gave a little laugh. 'I don't think so, why should she be?'

'I mean, it won't be just us anymore. She'll have Sandy and maybe she'll move away. She could even go and live with his family and then we won't see her so often. She won't make us laugh when we're sad. She won't stop Pat and Peggy arguing.'

Sheila's voice had risen a little with each thought of loss that came to her. Martha let the hair in her hand fall away and moved round to face her daughter. There were tears heavy in Sheila's eyes. She blinked and they fell.

'Aah, shush, shush now.' Martha hugged her. 'Sure it'll be all right. Irene's not going anywhere for a while, she's staying with us while Sandy's at Aldergrove, isn't she? Who knows what'll happen after that. Anyway, we'll always be her family, won't we? She'll always love us, won't she?' Martha fought back her own tears as she answered the questions for Sheila that she'd been asking herself all day.

Irene, Pat and Peggy had just changed into their black and white polka dot blouses and black skirts and hung up the soldier uniforms ready for their change in the second half, when there was a knock on the dressing room door and Horowitz called, 'Golden Sisters to see Mr Goldstein right away!'

Horowitz ushered them into a small room backstage which looked like someone's office, but had been converted into a dressing room for the stars of the show. Five minutes later they emerged, all smiles, having had a conversation with Flanagan and Allen themselves.

'Curtain up, five minutes!' shouted the stage manager.

Sammy began with the monologue 'The Ballad of William Bloat' which told the story of a man who, tired of being nagged by his wife, slits her throat. Full of contrition, he then takes his own life – not realising that she has survived the attack.

The audience cheered at the final line: 'The razor blade was German made, but the sheet was Belfast linen!' The acts came and went until it was time for the top of the bill. Irene, Pat and Peggy waited anxiously in the wings. Sammy gave the big build-up and finished with, 'And now all the way from London, please welcome Flanagan and Allen!'

The soldiers were taken completely by surprise; there had been no advance warning, not even a whisper that they were coming. The lights dimmed and the famous moth-eaten fur coat and squashed hat appeared from the wings. But there was something odd about it. The lights came up and the audience roared with laughter when they realised it was Bud Flanagan's coat and hat, but he wasn't wearing it. Instead they saw all three Golden Sisters inside the coat – Pat with her arm down one sleeve, Peggy with hers down another and Irene in the middle wearing the hat. They went into the famous Flanagan and Allen routine. 'Underneath the Arches', they sang and swayed as they walked in a line one behind the other inside the coat across the stage. The audience laughed and clapped. Suddenly, there was a loud shout from the wings, 'Oi you lot! What you fink you're doin', pinching our act?' On to the stage ran the real Flanagan and Allen and amid loud whoops and cheers from the audience they chased the sisters off the stage.

'We're very glad to be in Belfast,' Flanagan began, 'home of Britain's secret weapon.'

'What's that then, the Stirling bomber?' asked Allen.

'No the linen bedsheet!'

'Did you know that Belfast has come up with a way of hiding its entire docks area?'

'No what's that then?'

'It's a giant smoke screen.'

'You mean they have a machine to create smoke on a vast scale?'

'Well no, at the moment it's twenty dockers and a packet of Woodbine, but you get the idea.' He waited for the laughter to die down. 'Time for a song I think, Mr Allen.'

'Of course, Mr Flanagan.'

The two were coming to the end of their act and the whole company were ready in the wings for the finale when the air-raid siren sounded. It was exactly ten thirty.

Bud Flanagan stopped and announced, 'I'm told that over here in Belfast you do things differently. The alert comes after the sound of planes overhead and after the sound of the ack-ack guns.' Howls of laughter from the audience. 'So, either we are already under attack, and I can't hear any planes, can you? Or it's another of those false alarms you're very fond of. In which case, I say we carry on with the finale. What do you think?' The audience made their views quite clear.

Captain Ayres was apoplectic. 'Goldstein,' he shouted. 'The artists are your responsibility. You need to stop this. We need to get everyone into the shelter; that's the required procedure!'

When the siren sounded Martha was using the leftover material from Sheila's dress to make a matching headband. She had also put a pair of white lace gloves to soak in a little bleach to brighten them. Sheila was in her nightdress eating supper of bread and milk.

'Are we going under the stairs, Mammy?'

'Not just yet, I need to finish this. We'll wait a wee while and see what happens.'

'Do you think it might be a false alarm?'

'Who knows?' She was trying to thread a needle by holding it up to the light at arm's length and narrowing her eyes. 'I thought they might have attacked over Easter, but they didn't and the full moon is still a week away, so it could be a false alarm.'

Sheila finished her supper and kissed her mother goodnight. 'I'm so excited, I'll not sleep, so come and get me if you think we should go under the stairs.'

At eleven thirty Martha thought she heard a noise somewhere in the distance. She went upstairs to her bedroom, opened the window to the sounds of the night and stood in the light of a three-quarters moon looking east. There was the noise again quite clearly, still distant, but a little louder than before.

She stood there listening for five minutes, until the sound became unmistakable.

'God save us,' she whispered.

Sheila woke up as soon as Martha touched her. 'Get up quick as you can, there's a good girl, warm clothes, hat on your head.'

'Is it a raid?'

'Yes, yes. Quickly, quickly.'

Martha ran downstairs and grabbed the blanket and torch from under the stairs. When Sheila appeared she led her quickly out the back door.

'Why are we not going under the stairs?'

'I've seen them coming. There's so many we'll need to get well away. We'll go up past Carr's Glen school as far as the fields, then higher towards the Cave Hill. They won't drop bombs on an empty hillside.'

Close to midnight they were at the top of the Oldpark Road when Sheila slowed down. 'We've got to keep going,' urged Martha.

But something had caught Sheila's eye. Martha followed her line of vision. Out over the lough towards Whiteabbey was the strangest sight, surreal and breathtakingly beautiful. Glowing magnesium flares hung in the air, colouring the world a ghostly silver grey. More and more of them appeared at different levels, hurried along by the light breeze towards Belfast, which lay clear as a stage in the limelight ready for the show to begin.

Minutes later, another wave of planes flew over just above the barrage balloons and the flares multiplied. Still there was no sound of the anti-aircraft guns. Martha took Sheila's hand. 'Come on – we need to get even higher.'

The finale was over by eleven, the Barnstormers' bus was in the city centre before midnight and Goldstein dropped the girls at the bottom of the Cliftonville Road half an hour later. Within minutes they heard the enemy planes and witnessed the first of the magnesium flares in the sky.

'It's just like last time,' said Irene. 'Next we'll see the incendiaries. Then they'll drop the bombs.'

'I don't think we'll make it home in time,' said Pat. 'We need to get into a shelter quickly. There's one on Atlantic Avenue. It isn't far.'

As they approached the shelter, the sound of singing and laughter could be heard. Inside it was cold as a tomb. From the light of a few candles and glowing ends of cigarettes, they could just make out the huddled shapes of people lying, sitting and leaning.

'Not much room is there,' said Irene.

The man next to her agreed. 'All right 'til ten minutes ago, then this crowd were put off the tram comin' from the dance at the Floral Hall – the driver said he was goin' no closer to the centre.'

Irene stepped into the street again, watched in awe the beauty of the flares and knew for certain she wasn't going back into the shelter. Of course she wanted to be at home with all her family the night before her wedding, but it was more than that …

'Pat, Peggy, we can't stay here!' she said, and she reached in and pulled them out.

'Irene, the worst place to be during a raid is out on the streets,' shouted Pat.

'Maybe, but we can get home before the bombs fall if we run.' Pat and Peggy looked at each other, unable to decide what to do, but by then Irene was twenty yards away. 'Come on!' she screamed. Then they too were running for home.

Just past Cliftonville football ground the first incendiaries began to fall with crackling sounds like sparks from tramlines followed by bursts of flame. Little fires were breaking out all around them and still they ran. Roofs of houses were ablaze.

They passed a public house burning fiercely, the heat so intense they had to take a detour down a side street where incendiaries were burning harmlessly in the road. An ARP warden shouted at them to get indoors immediately, but still they ran. In the distance they could hear the anti-aircraft guns, but dominating every sound was the ceaseless droning of the Heinkels overhead.

By the time they came to Joanmount Gardens their eyes were streaming from the acrid smoke of the thousand fires they'd passed, but they were home at last. They ran round the back of the house. Irene was first into the kitchen.

'Mammy! Mammy! We're home, are you all right?' She pulled open the door beneath the stairs, but the space beyond was in darkness.

'How many times do I have to tell them to go in the shelter!' shouted Pat. Peggy and Irene listened to the sound of her feet on the stairs, heard her scream, 'They're not here! They're not here!'

'She's taken the blanket and the torch,' said Irene.

'And their coats are missing,' said Pat.

'What are we going to do?' Irene was frantic. As if in answer, there was an enormous roar followed by a heavy thud as the doors and windows shook and the sky turned red.

'Get in here quickly!' shouted Pat and the three of them crawled on hands and knees into the only shelter they had.

Martha and Sheila were not alone in the lanes beyond the city. Whole families were climbing the hills, some pushing prams containing not only children, but possessions they wanted to save from the bombs. A few had little billycans and were making tea and passing round sandwiches.

Martha spread out the blanket and they sat together hunched up, nursing their knees. The main roads running north out of the city could be seen clearly, all of them on fire. The sky was blood red. Shortly after one o'clock, the heaviest bombing began and the sounds reverberated around the cauldron of the city.

Time and again the waves of planes passed over, dropping high explosives, and it became clear that the targets were homes and families, not industry.

'God help us, where are those wee girls of mine, out in all this?'

'They'll be all right, Mammy, they're probably in a shelter somewhere, at the camp maybe.'

'And us with the wedding tomorrow.'

Martha awoke with a start, feeling a stiffness in her neck that she quickly realised was in every joint of her body. Sheila was still asleep and leaning heavily against her. She shook her gently.

'Wake up, there's a good girl. It's time to go home.'

The sky was suffused with soft pink and below them hung a heavy pall of smoke. Fires were still burning across the city and a thousand spirals of smoke meandered upwards.

They saw the first bomb damage at Carr's Glen school, where incendiaries had crashed through the roof and destroyed the upper storey. Further down the hill, broken windows and slates littered the road. They instinctively reached for each others' hands as they turned into Joanmount, praying the house was still standing.

It was there! Martha let go of Sheila's hand and ran. 'Please, please. Let them be ...'

Irene's face was at the kitchen window. The door opened – one, two, three girls all there, all smiling.

'Praise be to God!' laughed Martha and hugged them all.

She was happy to take the scolding she received, not just from Pat, but from Irene and Peggy too. 'Whatever possessed you, Mammy, to go away up there?'

'Sure you were just as bad, running up the Cliftonville, when you could have been in a shelter!'

'Never mind all that now,' said Peggy. 'Haven't we a wedding to go to?'

Chapter 28

Martha would have been hard pressed to say who was the most beautiful of her daughters. It would depend on what was meant by beautiful. One by one they came downstairs and each in turn took her breath away. She imagined Robert next to her, sharing each moment and knew that her thoughts were his thoughts.

Pat with her rich auburn hair and fair skin, enhanced by her emerald dress, had a voice to make the heart soar.

Peggy so slim and elegant in her navy costume, skirt fashionably short, had the darkest hair, olive skin, brown eyes and a sharp ear for melody and rhythm.

Sheila, all softness of looks, of voice, of nature, dressed in primrose yellow.

Finally Irene, eyes full of laughter, a talker, a listener, a peacemaker, in her wedding dress the colour of flax flowers.

Harry arrived at ten in a large grey Rover, looking tired and drawn. 'It's not so bad down the town, but up this end there's terrible damage. We'd better get going, but I'm warning you, it's bad out there.'

Martha, Pat and Peggy were to go with him, leaving Irene and Sheila to travel with Thomas and Anna a little later in their car. Martha took Irene's hands in hers and stepped back. 'You look lovely, so you do.' Then she kissed her cheek and whispered, 'Daddy would be so proud.'

Half a mile from Joanmount Gardens they began to see the damage, a row of shops black and smouldering, and the further they drove, the thicker the air became with smoke and the stench of burning. People on the streets seemed wide-eyed and dazed. Near the Antrim Road the walking wounded appeared, many bandaged or bleeding, all with blackened faces. Then the worst of it. Houses with every window blown out gave way to those that were roofless or without gable walls. A piano stood in the middle of the road undamaged. Further on there were crumpled terraces. Looking up the side streets they saw only ruins, rubble, dust and people like worker ants, crawling and clawing over the mounds. There were people in uniforms too, civil defence and military, better equipped, but just as desperate.

Here, they saw the first shapes on the ground covered in coats or blankets and one small shape under a checked tablecloth. They fell silent then.

A fire tender raced past them, bell ringing. 'Look at that,' said Harry, 'the Drogheda Fire Brigade. I heard de Valera gave the order for them to cross the border early this morning. They've probably just got here. God knows, we could've done with them last night when incendiaries were burning people's homes and businesses to the ground.' The fire tender braked suddenly and shot down a side street. 'It'll be on its way to the Victoria Barracks – or what's left of it after the bombers destroyed the searchlight.'

'What did you say?' Pat leaned forward in her seat.

'They had a new searchlight, arrived last week.'

'Yes, I know, but what happened to the Victoria Barracks?'

'A direct hit.'

She couldn't think straight. The words 'direct hit' lodged in her brain. There was no room for any other thought. She tried to regain some reason; instead she saw his face, heard his last words to her. 'Of course I'll be at the church by twelve. I'm planning to call in

344

at Victoria Barracks to see how effective the searchlight is, maybe check some shelters. I'll have time for a couple of hours sleep before coming to the church. Don't worry. I wouldn't miss an opportunity to sing that duet.'

Around Carlisle Circus the footpaths were fringed with ruins, but from there down into the centre, the damage lessened again. Buildings were still standing and men were boarding up windows. On down Royal Avenue they drove, took a detour for a crater in the middle of the road, and on into Donegall Square East and the church. It was unscathed.

In Joanmount Gardens, Thomas and Anna arrived to find Irene and Sheila agitated.

'I thought you weren't coming,' said Irene. 'I was trying to think how to get to the church without you.'

Thomas kept his voice light. 'Well, there's quite a bit of damage you know, especially around the Newtownards Road. Filthy black smoke by the docks slowed us down too, but we're here now. Are you ready to go?'

Irene nodded, but didn't move. Thomas in full morning dress stood with his hands across his waistcoat and twisted the gold ring on his little finger. Anna adjusted the fox fur around her shoulders and surreptitiously consulted the tiny marcasite watch on her wrist. After a few minutes Sheila whispered, 'We need to go now, Irene.'

'I know I know, but ... what if Sandy isn't there? If something's happened to him and ...' her voice trailed off.

Thomas was businesslike. 'If he's been delayed at the base, I'm sure he'll try to let you know, but you must understand that there may be some people missing ...'

Anna saw the shock in Irene's face and interrupted. 'Because of the delays and disruption, but if you and Sandy are there, then the wedding'll go ahead.'

Still Irene didn't move. She needed finally to quell the doubts that had grown every day since she had accepted Sandy's proposal. She thought she loved him, but maybe it was the whole romantic notion of being married that she loved?

Sheila touched her hand. 'Sandy'll be there, you'll see.'

'Sandy…' Irene closed her eyes and tried to bring his face to mind. She couldn't see him as he was at Stranraer the first time they met, or at the castle, or in the moonlight under the Hurricane bomber when he held her. But slowly a memory took shape, her mother and sisters around the kitchen table and in their midst Sandy in his Air Force uniform. She saw him at last … his kind eyes … and gentle smile.

She took a deep breath and turned her bouquet so that the trailing gypsophilia fell at the front and the sprigs of white heather were clearly visible among the flax flowers. Thomas offered her his arm and together they went out into the street where the women and children were waiting to see her off with handshakes, shouts of 'good luck' and even some clapping.

Within ten minutes of leaving the house, Thomas was forced to make a detour. A soldier waved them down. 'Had to shut the road, mate, ruptured gas main, dangerous with all these fires still burning. Tell you what, go back up a couple of streets; you'll see some army vehicles where they've cleared the road. Along there, make a right and it'll take you straight on to the Antrim Road.'

It was no longer a street, but a series of mounds interspersed with blackened house fronts. The road was strewn with glass and slates that crunched under the car wheels. Thomas, fearful of puncturing the tyres, drove slowly and his passengers had time to take in the terrible damage. In places there was so much splintered wood piled on rubble at crazy angles that it looked like a bonfire waiting to be lit. Soldiers were shifting the debris hand to hand. Suddenly, there was a shout further down the street and a soldier with a little boy hanging in his arms slithered down a slope. They watched as he laid the child gently on the ground and within seconds a medical orderly rushed past them. Through the rear window, Irene watched anxiously until she saw the boy raise his blackened head to drink water from a canteen.

Towards the end of the road an army lorry was parked facing them and, when they paused at the junction, Irene found herself puzzling at the misshapen load it carried until a blackened arm fell out from under the tarpaulin.

They joined the main road and almost immediately slowed to a crawl.

'My God!' whispered Thomas. 'It's a shelter. Must have taken a direct hit.'

'Where are we?' asked Irene, knowing the answer.

'Corner of Atlantic Avenue, I think.'

They were already lining up the bodies on the pavement.

The City Hall stood defiantly in the middle of the square with as many buses, cars and people on the streets around it as there would have been on any Wednesday. A small crowd, on hearing a wedding was about to take place, had gathered on the pavement outside the church in the hope of seeing the bride. The guests were beginning to congregate under the colonnade. Each new arrival was greeted with warmth and relief that they had come safely through the night, but there was anger too.

John McCracken voiced his opinion. 'They attacked us without hindrance. There was no proper barrage. There wasn't a single enemy plane hit, let alone brought down! The people in charge of the defence of this city should hang their heads in shame this morning.'

Pat, who was anxiously scanning the square in hope of seeing William, couldn't let that pass. 'John, that's not fair. There are people at Stormont who have tried so hard to find the money and resources needed.'

'That's as maybe, Pat, but it's no comfort to those finding themselves homeless or bereaved today.'

She could take no more and hurried into the cool interior.

Keep calm, she told herself. He might still come. But he was always punctual, hated letting people down and the feeling that he was lost threatened to overwhelm her.

'Excuse me? Aren't you one of the singers?'

'Sorry?'

'I'm the minister. Bad news, I'm afraid, the pianist hasn't arrived. There'll be no accompaniment for the hymns or the singing.'

347

'My sister could do it,' said Pat. 'Would that be allowed?'

'I don't see why not. I'll just fetch you an order of service.'

Meanwhile, Peggy was deep in conversation with Harry.

'What's the matter with you, today?' said Peggy.

'That's a stupid question to ask.'

'Don't call me stupid!'

'I didn't. I said it was a stupid question and it is considering the night we've all had and what we've just driven through.'

'I feel that too, we all do. But it's something else isn't it.'

'Peggy, this is a wedding. Can we get through it without an argument, do you think?'

'Oh suit yourself!' she snapped and stormed off into the church. Harry stayed outside, lit a cigarette with trembling hands and inhaled deeply.

Pat was on her way outside when Peggy marched in. 'There's no pianist. You'll have to play.'

'Me? I don't think so.'

'Peggy you have to. We can't have a wedding without music!'

The guests were filing into the pews, but there was no groom or best man at the altar, there would be no music and Pat knew for certain that there would be no William either. She bowed her head and wept. Peggy watched her a moment then, without a word, walked up the aisle and sat at the piano.

In the distance a clock began to strike the hour. Outside Harry was just finishing his cigarette when a car pulled up and he glimpsed Irene in the back. He ran over and opened the driver's door.

'There's been a bit of a hold up, we're waiting for a few more guests to arrive. Do you think you could drive round for five minutes?'

Moments later a powerful motorbike roared into the square and screeched to a halt outside the church. Sandy jumped off, removed his goggles and helmet and shouted to Harry, 'Sorry I'm late, is everyone inside?'

'All except you and Irene and she's on her way.'

'I've no best man. All leave has been cancelled, but they let me go when they were sure there'd be no follow-up daylight raid.'

'Well ...' said Harry, 'I'm far from a best man, but as you're desperate, I'm your man!' The two of them shook hands, Sandy gave him the ring and they went quickly into the church.

The service was simple and beautiful and included, at Irene's request, prayers for all those who had suffered as a result of the bombing: the dead and injured; the homeless and bereaved. When the bridal party left to sign the register in the vestry, silence fell like confetti from the vaulted ceiling. Peggy placed her hands ready on the keys. The seconds slipped by, but Pat remained seated. Then, after what seemed like an age, she stood and walked slowly to the nave. Something in her expression caused Peggy to hesitate, uncertain whether to begin the introduction. Pat fixed her eyes on the triptych window high on the wall in front of her, took a full breath and began to sing. It was not what they had rehearsed; Peggy struggled to recognise it. One bar ... two bars ... suddenly she had it. Gently she laid her hands on the keys and played the accompaniment. The song told of a love lost. Pat sang in Italian, her pitch and pronunciation perfect and towards the back of the church, Kathleen closed her eyes and silently sang it with her. Only when the final notes had floated upwards, like little motes of sadness into the air, did Pat open her eyes.

He stood framed in the doorway in morning dress, a glint of silver on his tie. He came up the aisle and took her hand just as they had rehearsed. This time Pat smiled and nodded at Peggy, who began the introduction to the opening aria of *The Marriage of Figaro*.

When Irene and Sandy walked down the aisle and out into the sunshine of the April afternoon it seemed the mood had altered perceptibly, as though the city had absorbed the terrible night and counterbalanced it with the joy of two young people on their wedding day.

Pat and William also emerged together talking quietly.

'I didn't hold that last note quite long enough,' said Pat.

'It was fine, don't worry. Sorry I was late, things happening, you know.'

'Yes, I know. It didn't matter, you came.'

Pat noticed Sammy watching Irene as she posed for a photograph and was shocked by his appearance. She excused herself and went to speak to him. 'Hello Sammy, I didn't see you inside.'

'No, I arrived late, just sat at the back.' He was clearly agitated.

'What's the matter? Has something happened?'

'I'm not staying for the reception,' he said in a rush. 'I wasn't going to come at all, but I thought you'd want to know, Irene would want to know.' He was close to tears.

'Know what, Sammy? What is it?'

'It's Myrtle. We were going to come to the wedding together.'

He struggled to find the words.

Pat waited.

'I went to collect her this morning from Thorndyke Street. I knew the area had been badly hit, but I hoped … I was sure she'd …'

'What happened, Sammy?' asked Pat softly.

'The street was in ruins … I was there when they brought out the bodies.'

Pat reached out to touch him, but he pulled back, his face angry.

'Leave me be,' he shouted and turned away from her, pushing his way through the guests. She saw him moments later running across the road towards the City Hall.

Irene was chatting to the McCrackens, laughing with Grace and Aggie. I can't tell her now, thought Pat, there'll be time enough for mourning later.

Inside the lobby of the Imperial Hotel the wedding guests stood around in small groups chatting and sipping sweet sherry.

Peggy and Harry were alone at the bar.

'Harry, I know something's the matter. Tell me.'

'It's nothing, everything's all right. Don't worry.'

'You've got yourself into something again, haven't you?'

At that moment the head waiter announced, 'Ladies and

gentlemen, the bride and groom invite you to join them for lunch in the dining room.'

'Now isn't the time, Peggy.'

Irene and Sandy appeared arm in arm, happy and excited, and took their seats at the top table. The room was splendid with red velvet curtains, white linen tablecloths, silver cutlery, crystal glasses and posies of white and blue flowers. In the centre of the table there stood an impressive three-tier wedding cake, iced with intricate lace patterns and finished with little clusters of forget-me-nots.

The minister said grace and gave thanks, not just for the meal, but for the safe deliverance of everyone there from the terrible danger they had come through. After the speeches and toasts, the bride and groom cut the cake.

'Peggy, I'm going out to get some fresh air,' said Harry. 'Do you want to come with me?'

He took her hand as they left the hotel and they crossed the road into the grounds of the City Hall. He stopped at a bench and they sat down.

'I was sitting here the first time I saw you,' he said.

Peggy looked around. 'And I was sitting over there on the grass.'

'You looked like the girl I'd imagined I would meet some day, so I followed you ...'

'To Goldstein's shop.'

'And later, we danced.'

They sat in silence a while, remembering.

'Harry what is it, please tell me?'

'I wanted us to have the bakery,' he began. 'It was a way to start a life together.'

She wasn't clear what he was saying. Did he think she didn't want to be part of it? 'I love our shop,' she said. 'You know that.'

He shielded his eyes with his hand. 'I know ... but it's gone.'

'Gone? What do you mean gone?'

'Last night ... an incendiary ... there's nothing left. I went there early this morning. It's just a blackened shell. Only the ovens are standing like twisted biscuit tins.'

Peggy thought of the lemon and white shop, its counter and display cabinets burned out, like the buildings they had passed on the road this morning. 'But you can get new premises, new ovens can't you. We'll start again. I'll leave the music shop and help you.'

He shook his head. 'You don't understand, Peggy. It's gone! I can't rebuild it.' He shook his head. 'All that money and effort for what? A wedding cake and a tray of shortbread, the only things I baked there.'

'But isn't there insurance or something to help you?'

His laugh was humourless. 'There was no money for insurance. I borrowed from Dessie and when that wasn't enough, I borrowed some more.'

'More than the three hundred pounds?' Peggy was shocked. 'Who did you borrow that from?'

'Someone I used to do some work for and he's expecting it paid back every week from the shop takings, except there won't be any takings. There isn't any shop. And Dessie'll want his money too.'

'What are we going to do?'

'I know what I'm going to do. I'm going to get out of Belfast – fast.'

'It can't be that bad. We'll go and speak to them. The shop was bombed. It's not your fault!' Peggy's voice had risen and passers-by were staring.

'You don't know these people, Peggy. There's no reasoning with them. I owe them a lot of money. I have to go.'

She saw the desperation in his eyes, guessed at the fear he felt.

'Where will you go?'

'To England.'

'When?'

'Tonight on the Liverpool boat.'

She stood up. 'I'm coming with you.'

'No you're not, Peggy. I'm going to join the army. It's the only thing that makes any sense now. I can't take you with me.'

He reached for her and held her tight until she stopped crying. Then they went across the road and slipped back into the hotel just as Goldstein rose to speak.

'My dear friend Martha and her family have asked me to say a few words about the circumstances in which we find ourselves today. Here we are celebrating the marriage of Irene and Sandy and trying to be positive about their future, when our city has suffered and is suffering extreme hardship and despair.

'This war is not of our making, but we are determined to stand against tyranny. We thought we might escape what had befallen others in Poland, across Belgium and France into England, but last night we felt the full force of evil. So today, should we cower in fear? Should we hide in the ruins and say our lives have changed and we can no longer plan for our future? No. Today of all days we must celebrate the spirit of Belfast. Our young people will have a future. We have borne witness to that today with the marriage of Sandy and Irene. So I ask you to raise your glasses to toast the people of Belfast.'

Around the room the guests stood. 'To the people of Belfast!'

'And now,' said Goldstein, 'I think I noticed a piano in the corner of the room and we have three … no, on this special day … four Golden Sisters to entertain us.'

Peggy lifted the lid on the piano and tried a scale.

'Is it in tune, Peggy?' shouted Irene.

'Of course not,' she laughed, 'but who cares!'

Irene, Pat and Sheila joined her. They had no trouble identifying the introduction and all came in on cue.

'I'll Take Romance' they sang in close harmony.

At the end of the song, the four sisters stepped forward and took a bow. Peggy raised her head and saw Harry in the doorway.

He smiled just for her, raised his hat and put it on. She bowed again and he was gone.

'Let's do one more,' said Irene. 'What will it be?'

'It's your wedding, you choose,' said Peggy.

'Let's have "Whispering Hope".'

Goldstein turned to Martha. 'You must be so proud of them.'

'Aye, they're good girls, right enough.'

'Indeed they are, Martha, indeed they are.'

Acknowledgements

Over the many years it has taken to write this book, my husband Jeff and sons Adam and Dan have supported and encouraged me in so many ways and always believed it would be finished.

To my sister Heather, I owe a huge debt of gratitude. She was alongside me – despite being 3,000 miles away – reading each chapter as it came into being and commenting, enthusing, encouraging. This is her book as much as mine. Thanks also to Dennis, my brother, for advice on all things Belfast and cousins Bernice and Noreen who added to our collective knowledge of the Goulding family. I am grateful to the Manchester Irish Writers, an immensely talented group of individuals, for their advice and the craic.

In writing an historical novel, it is essential to have access to comprehensive research that encompasses the social, historical and cultural climate of the period. I found all of this and much more in Brian Barton's book *The Blitz – Belfast in the war years*. Heartfelt thanks to him. Last, but by no means least, I am grateful to Blackstaff Press for their belief in the book and to Helen Wright, in particular, for her sensitive editing.

It is thanks to all these people that the story has at last been told.